S.S. BAZINET

TAINTED BLOOD

BOOK FIVE

The Vampire Reclamation Project

Renata Press
Albuquerque, New Mexico

This book is a work of fiction. Names, characters, places, businesses, organizations and events are either the product of the author's imagination or are used fictitiously. Any resemblance to actual persons, living or dead, events or locales is entirely coincidental.

Published by Renata Press
Albuquerque, New Mexico
www.renatapress.com

Visit the author's website:
www.ssbazinet.com

ISBN-13: 978-1-937279-23-3

For all those who enjoy a
journey into the light!

One

PEGGY WALKED UP to her brother and put her hands on her hips. "Kevin! Isn't there a line in that old vampire movie that says that you should never invite a vampire into your house?"

Kevin retreated a couple of steps, putting some distance between his six-foot-four inch body and Peggy's fiery temper. "Yeah, I guess so, but what does a vampire have to do with anything?"

"Oh please, you were here all evening! Didn't you notice that we've been entertaining one? Elise is a blood sucking—"

A tap on her shoulder made Peggy pause in mid-sentence and swivel round. Her husband, Tim, was staring down at her.

"Peg, sweetheart? Can I talk to you?" Tim asked.

Peggy let her hands fall to her sides, but a scowl remained on her face. "Tim, please, can't you see how important this is?"

"I know you're angry, but you don't need to yell at Kevin."

Peggy stood up straighter, trying to reinforce her position with more height, but she was still more than a foot shorter than Tim. He was almost as tall as her brother. "This isn't about me yelling. It's about that horrible woman, Elise."

"Don't worry, sis. I feel the same way about her," Kevin said.

Peggy returned a weak smile. "Thanks, Kevin."

Tim reached out for Peggy's hand and pulled her closer. "We all feel the same way. I just don't like seeing you upset."

Peggy took a deep breath, trying to rein in her emotions. Her anger had been building all evening. It had been almost impossible to keep from screaming out in frustration. On the other hand, she needed more self-control. She had baby Sara to think about. She didn't want her child growing up with a hot-tempered mother as her role model.

Tim tugged on her hand and led her over to the sofa. "Let's sit down and talk about it."

"Fine." The word was sort of heaved out as Peggy did her best to listen to reason. After she sat down, she retrieved a tissue from her pocket and glanced at Kevin. "Sorry if I shouted, Kev, but I've run out of patience."

Kevin nodded. "We're all feeling the strain."

Peggy swiped at her nose. "I'm just mad at myself. I should have never invited that awful woman and Arel over for a visit. I knew better. Still, I wanted to give them one last chance. But Elise is a shrew, a snake in the grass, a real—" She stopped herself, afraid to let herself get started again.

Carol, Peggy's closest friend, sat on the sofa too. She gave Peggy an understanding look. "Kevin and I have been talking about this situation. We agree that it's not getting any better."

When Peggy responded, she knew her face was stuck in a grimace. "I'm sorry for making a scene, everybody. I guess the bottom line is that I don't care anymore. I love Arel dearly, but this is a classic 'evil sorceress bewitches the handsome bachelor' syndrome. I'm just happy that Arel is single and that there aren't children involved. Elise would have them on the black market as soon as he turned his back."

Tim put an arm around Peggy's shoulders. "She can be very rude."

Peggy looked down and adjusted her blouse. "She wouldn't even talk to our little girl. When Sara tried to give her a cookie, she gave our baby a dirty look. Of course, Arel was out of the room when she did it."

Tim sighed. "You're right. We can't have someone like that around Sara."

Carol turned to Kevin. Her green eyes were filled with concern. "We're going to have to let Arel know that he's welcome in our home, but Elise isn't."

"Absolutely," Kevin said.

Peggy sniffled into her tissue again. "The worst part is that I know it's what she wants. She wants to isolate Arel from us. Then she can suck him dry."

"Maybe she also wants his money," Carol said. "I think he's very comfortable in that department."

Peggy let out a heated laugh. "She wants everything. She's probably the type that gets off on power and domination. And she's smart. It wasn't an accident that she let me see the look she gave Sara. She enjoys being bad-mannered."

"It's a shame we have to have this conversation," Carol said. "Besides William, we're the only family that Arel has. And with William in London, we're the only ones who are around to support him."

Kevin reached out to Carol. "Honey, he does have Michael and Carey."

Carol took his hand. "Yes, but they're too passive and nice to tell him that he's making a terrible mistake."

Peggy shrugged. "I don't think it would matter what anyone said. We've all tried, and Arel doesn't seem to get it."

A strained silence followed the remark, but a moment later, there was a knock at the door. It was followed by the sound of someone letting themselves into the foyer. Everyone looked up, but nobody said anything. As soon as they identified the unexpected visitor, they lowered their eyes.

Without hesitation, Arel stepped forward, let out a sigh and walked into the living room.

* * *

Arel's shoulders were slumped and his heart pounded as he prepared to face the people he thought of as family. Years earlier, when he was in a very bad way, they'd taken him into their lives and hearts. They'd helped him climb his way out of a very dark pit of depression. And how had he recently returned the favor? He'd let them down.

Once inside Peggy and Tim's house, he peeked into the living room, knowing that his face was red with embarrassment. After he'd left earlier, he walked Elise back home. He didn't have far to go. He lived next door to Peggy and Tim, and Elise had rented the house next to his.

On the way to Elise's, he'd confronted her, asking her about her behavior and why she insisted on being so discourteous. Instead of showing any sign of remorse, Elise had been aloof, even insulted. When they got to her house, she quickly climbed the stairs to the porch, unlocked her front door and slammed it in his face.

Arel was relieved to be shut out. Spending time with Elise wasn't fun or even pleasant. He'd tried his best to be understanding, and Elise didn't seem to appreciate his efforts. It was just the opposite. She became even more hostile and spiteful.

As Arel returned to Peggy and Tim's house, he'd made a decision. It was time to tell Elise exactly how he felt. But first he had to make amends. He wanted his friends to know how sorry he was for allowing Elise to act so inappropriately.

Standing in Peggy and Tim's living room, he tried to verbalize how he felt. "I came back to apologize about tonight. I know that Elise was very unpleasant, and I'm very sorry about what happened."

An awkward pause followed his admission of guilt. Peggy avoided his eyes while Carol blinked back with confusion. Kevin and Tim's faces were blank and non-committal. The uncomfortable moment finally ended when Peggy wiped her eyes with a tissue and gestured him to a chair.

"Please sit down, Arel," she instructed without looking up at him.

Arel noted that her words were delivered in a voice that was too soft for someone like Peggy. But he didn't dare comment. He walked over to a chair and sat down.

Peggy's eyes finally shifted in his direction. "I'm glad you're here. We need to talk."

Arel had always hated the words, "We need to talk." When Michael, his angelic friend, used those words, they always implied something serious and unwanted was probably coming. But when Peggy used the phrase, he knew there was no way to avoid hearing her out.

He tried not to fidget as he waited for the inevitable dressing down. Elise had been offending people for months, and he'd allowed it. Now, it was time for those punishing moments that he'd known were coming. However, he realized he did have something to say after all.

Taking a deep breath, he tried to explain his position. "Just one more thing, everyone, even if you think that I haven't been listening to your advice about my relationship with Elise, I have. But I didn't know what to do. I really hoped I could help Elise change." As he spoke he glanced up and saw Kevin look away. His buddy was letting Arel know that he'd expected more from a friend.

Arel continued on anyway. "The bottom line is that I didn't think Elise would behave so inexcusably around the children. That should have never happened." He paused, remembering what he'd observed earlier in the evening. Elise didn't know it, but he'd seen how callous Elise had been when she interacted with Peggy and Tim's beautiful little Sara. It was a decisive moment. "I wanted you to know you'll never see Elise in my company again. I've decided to stop dating her after what happened here tonight."

Peggy glanced up with a pained look. "I have to ask you something. Why did you date her in the first place? You're a wonderful person, you're handsome, and you have so much to offer. And there are so many women out there who would love to be with you. Why Elise?"

Arel stared down at his clasped hands letting his mind return to his first impression of the woman in question. Elise was very attractive, but it was more than her physical looks that reached out to him. It was as if he could see who she was on a deeper level. He sensed that she had hidden virtues. Months later, he felt like he'd misread the woman.

He sat up straighter. "When we first talked, I almost felt like I knew Elise. She kind of reminded me of myself when I was lost. Unfortunately, the longer we dated, the more hostile she became."

Peggy's eyes softened. "Sweetie, you're new at this, aren't you? I mean, I get the feeling that you haven't had too much experience—"

Arel tried to lighten the moment with a smile. "With dating? No, you're right. It's been a long time since—" He hesitated as his mind flashed back to a time when he was a very young man. He'd fallen in love with a beautiful woman named Justina. She was very young too, but she was Elise's opposite. She was completely giving and sweet. Unfortunately, their relationship had ended very badly. He'd never attempted another one until he met Elise.

He stood up, wanting to forget both entanglements. "Never mind. I won't bore you with my troubles any longer. It's been quite an evening. I better go."

* * *

When Elise got back to her house, her heart was pounding. In a burst of anger, she'd slammed the door on Arel. After that, she yelled out her frustration as she stormed through the house and into the kitchen. "Why won't he just let go? How much more obnoxious do I have to be?"

With a trembling hand, she opened the refrigerator and grabbed a beer. For weeks, she'd been trying her best to free her heart from the man she'd started to really care about. But her heart was like Arel. It was stubborn too. It kept urging her to take a chance on another relationship, but she knew better. "Relationships are hell!"

As her anger and her self-pity joined forces, she slammed the refrigerator door shut. Bottles of ketchup and mayonnaise rattled, but she held on to the hope that a beer would help calm her nerves. She pried up the cap on the bottle, tossed it in the trash and grabbed an unwashed ice tea glass from the sink. As she poured the beer, she studied the white foam and amber liquid that filled the glass. But she knew from experience that nothing could fill the emptiness she felt inside. She'd once thought that a relationship could help, but she'd been wrong on a number of occasions. She was making the same mistake again.

She sniffled as she walked back to the living room. She used her free hand to pull out the pins in her blond hair and shook her head to loosen the bun she was wearing. After she sat down, she swallowed back some of the beer and leaned into the sofa with a sigh.

She'd sworn off relationships years earlier and resisted dating. Then she met Arel. The first time she saw her neighbor, she knew she was in trouble. It was a moonlit night, and she was letting herself into the house she'd just rented. Arel was out staring at the stars and happened to glance her way. She'd only gotten a glimpse of him, but it was enough. There was something extremely appealing about him from the start, an enticing energy that radiated from his person. Later, when they'd both been out getting their mail, they ended up talking. It only took a few minutes for Elise to know she was smitten.

Arel was gorgeous. From the top of his thick, dark hair down to his soft leather, Italian loafers, he was physically everything she'd ever loved in a man. Then there were his dark lashes and his amazing eyes. His eyes could turn to liquid gold when he smiled. If he stared at her long enough, her defenses were useless. That was one reason she didn't make eye contact very often.

12

Arel seemed almost perfect. He could be as kind and understanding as the best of friends. He had flawless manners, and he always dressed impeccably. His English accent added a nice touch of class. All in all, she'd been unable to stop herself from surrendering to him emotionally. It was that feeling of surrender that made all the flags go up. As soon as she realized she was falling for another guy, she started her campaign to drive Arel away.

Now, sitting alone on the sofa, she needed to convince herself that she was doing the right thing. Was she really sure about her decision? She took another sip of beer, and let her mind wander back into her past. When she thought about what she'd been through, her whole body went rigid. "Men are bastards!"

Her verbal outburst and the anger that triggered it made her sit up too quickly. When she did, she tipped her glass. Beer doused her shirt and the couch. She moaned as she got up and ran back to the kitchen. After she retrieved a roll of paper towels, she dabbed at the sofa arm. She'd just purchased the couch and appreciated her foresight in getting the fabric treatment option. Hopefully, it would protect the piece from her clumsiness.

All in all, she enjoyed living in a house, even if it was rented. She'd moved out of her apartment because she'd needed privacy and quiet. The people in the apartment above her had sounded like they lifted weights morning and evening, not to mention the loud music. Now, she had the peace she needed to keep her nerves from fraying.

Thinking about the privacy part, she went over to the window and closed her curtains. She didn't want Arel seeing her drinking herself into oblivion. Of course, that couldn't happen. She always fell asleep before she ever got drunk. Once she'd fallen asleep on Arel's shoulder after only a couple of glasses of wine. He'd been too polite to move and take a chance on waking her. After a half hour, she woke up feeling totally embarrassed. She'd drooled on Arel's shirt. Again, Arel was the nicest of people, trying to assure her that everything was fine.

Maybe that was the problem. Arel's amiability made her realize how vile she'd become. She'd been so rude around his friends and their children. That evening was the first time Arel had called her on her behavior. In response, she got even meaner and shut him out.

"Really great, Elise," she said as she took the damp paper towel to the kitchen trash. "You're taking your crap out on babies and the sweetest guy around."

13

She folded her arms with fresh resolve. She couldn't keep doing what she'd been doing. It wasn't right. She was starting to hate herself, and she sure as heck wasn't being fair to Arel. It was best for both of them if she broke off their relationship.

She sat down again, confident that she was making the right choice. She'd met seemingly perfect guys like Arel before. They were wonderful at first. But as soon as she let herself trust them, things changed. In the end, she always felt betrayed and hurt. Truly gracious, caring guys were just part of fairy tales. And she should know all about fairy tales in her line of business. She was a successful, romance writer.

Two

AREL SAT OUT on the patio in a light jacket, staring at the yard. The late autumn weather was getting colder, but there hadn't been a hard frost yet. The garden still had some roses in bloom. Michael, the garden's caretaker, sat in a chair next to him.

Sometimes, it still surprised Arel to think that his friend was an incarnate angel. But Michael looked the part. Tall, with blond hair and an ideal, masculine body, he reminded Arel of a Nordic seaman. However, Michael's true nature differed drastically from that of a human.

Michael was compassionate, but he never entertained emotional moods swings. His mind never strayed from positive possibilities. He was definitely powerful, but his power came out in subtle ways. He treated Arel like he treated his garden, with a kind, nurturing hand.

Arel sometimes forgot to acknowledge how much Michael had helped him. As his gaze swept over the scene in front of him, he smiled. "You've transformed a once weedy patch of ground into something incredibly beautiful, Michael. Your flowers were a feast for the eyes all summer."

Michael returned Arel's smile. "Yes, gardening has become quite a passion."

"I'm sorry I haven't been able to share your enthusiasm. I guess I don't have your green thumb."

"We're all different."

Arel agreed about being different than Michael. His attention could easily be diverted into unhappy scenarios. The most recent was his disastrous situation with Elise.

Michael returned a knowing glance. "I'm sorry about things not working out with Elise."

Arel gave the neighboring yard a fast once-over, making sure that the woman in question wasn't around. "Unfortunately, at this point, I'm relieved that it's almost over. Poor Peggy looked so upset last night. So did everyone else. I should have never accepted her invitation knowing that Elise was invited too. It was a nightmare. The way Elise treated little Sara was shocking. She literally pushed the child away with a hateful scowl. And little Sara just stood there, not knowing what she'd done wrong. Can you imagine what a horror Elise would be as a mother?"

"Sounds like a very stressful situation."

"I should have been more careful, but I kept thinking that maybe Elise would change. Now I know she's going to be more difficult as time goes by. I have no choice but to stop dating her." Arel stood up. "Anyway, let's go into the house. Maybe you can help me figure out what to say to her."

* * *

Elise was down on her hands and knees in her back yard, ready to tackle the flower beds. She'd neglected them during the past couple of months. With the weather getting colder, she wanted to clear the weeds and leaves before winter set in. The yard wasn't technically hers, but she felt an obligation to keep the house and grounds in the same carefully-tended condition she found them in when she rented the place.

When she heard a door open and close, she paused. Someone had come out of Arel's house. Whoever it was couldn't know that Elise was listening. A five foot, wooden fence separated the properties. That didn't stop Elise from being nosy. She peeked through a crack in one of the wooden slats. It was wide enough to see Arel sit down in a patio chair. Michael sat next to him.

At first, she'd been tempted to get up and go back into the house. The moment passed as soon as she caught a scent of the captivating fragrance that Arel was wearing. It had a woodsy element, yet it was also exotic and laced with spice. Arel told her that he special ordered it from a shop in Paris.

She inhaled deeply and hated herself for still being attracted to him. She hated that her heart started pounding when she caught of glimpse of his eyes. Their golden color was fluid and alluring, two open invitations to dream about how amazing it would feel to be in Arel's arms.

Without wanting to, she pressed her face closer to the fence and sighed. Fortunately, her little moan of wanton lust was overridden by Michael's deep, soothing voice. He and Arel were chatting about the garden, but then Elise's name came up. She knew it was wrong to eavesdrop, but she couldn't help herself.

A short time later, after hearing Arel's remarks, she wished she hadn't been so curious. Was he accurate when he discussed her fitness as a mother? Would she be a terrible parent? Her mind raced back to the night with Arel's friends. After her awful interaction with Peggy and Carol's babies, she had to admit that Arel was probably correct. But correct or not, that still didn't give him the right to judge her.

When the sound of voices died away, she took another quick peek through the fence. The chairs on the patio were empty. Arel and Michael had gone back inside. Sitting back on her heels, her cheeks went hot with hurt and anger. Arel was ready to break up with her, but she wouldn't give him the chance.

She quickly stood up and brushed the dirt off her pants. She had to set her neighbor straight. Tossing her gardening gloves on the ground, she turned and marched into the house. She paused in the foyer long enough to check her hair. It was just long enough to realize that she shouldn't care about how she looked. Arel sounded like he never wanted to see her again. So what difference did her appearance make?

She should have been happy with his decision. It's what she wanted too, or at least some part of her did. But that other part of her, the one that still clung to their relationship was stubborn. It was the part that wanted to cry.

Instead of giving in to her emotions, she threw her shoulders back and forced herself to remember that she was doing what was best. She would not let herself be hurt by a man again.

With resolve, she headed for the door and let herself out. As she hurried over to Arel's adjoining front yard and walked up his sidewalk, she was determined not to chicken out. When she got to his front porch, she gave the doorbell a quick couple of taps.

She was surprised when the door opened almost immediately, and Arel stared back at her. But she wouldn't let his open, handsome face distract her. She wouldn't pay attention to her heart as it struggled to stop her from doing something she might regret. She blurted out what she'd planned to say. "I don't want to see you anymore. Is that clear, Arel?"

She didn't wait for him to respond. She turned and quickly walked back to her house. Once safely inside, she knew she'd closed the door on any future she might have with the man of her dreams.

* * *

After watching Elise return home, Arel shut the door and wandered into the living room. As he took a seat on the sofa, his mind was reeling with relief. Elise had severed their ties in a way that left no doubt that they were finished. Before he had a chance to fully enjoy the moment, Michael came in and sat down too. Arel looked up at him. "I'm sure you heard what Elise just told me."

"Are you okay?" Michael asked.

"I suppose I should be doing cart wheels. Elise has made things very easy. I don't have to sit around for hours trying to find the right words for a break-up speech. I have to admire her approach. It was short and to the point."

"Yes, for a writer, she didn't waste any words."

"She barely looked at me when she made her announcement." Arel paused and rubbed the sofa arm in a slow deliberate motion. "You know that I've been trying not to use any of my powers when I've been around her. I really want to be like Kevin and Tim, as normal as possible. But a person would have to be dead for three days not to feel Elise's anger."

Michael smiled. "Everyone reacts to energy. People call it different names, like vibes or feelings, but it's the same thing. It's the way people know what's best for them."

"Then my relief is a good thing, right?"

"A person isn't supposed to feel unhappy when they're in a relationship."

Arel's hand stilled, but he continued to study the white linen sofa fabric. "I understand that, but at times, I think I cheated. I looked deeper into Elise's makeup. She does have a big heart as I'm sure you know. It's just that she's so wounded and miserable. I thought I could help her like you helped me."

"Do you think I saw you as wounded?"

18

Arel laughed. "How else could you see me? I was some kind of long-suffering wretch when you came along."

Michael relaxed back into his recliner. "What I saw was an amazing human being. I saw a person who was capable of great things in his life, happy things."

"I wish I could see that for Elise, but I'm afraid her bitterness will keep her very isolated and hateful."

"Perhaps."

Arel looked up. "Maybe you or Carey could do something for her. What do you think?"

When Michael didn't respond, Arel ignored the angel and let a happy smile replace his concern. "Anyway, now that this thing with Elise is over, I might go back to London and even Paris for a while."

Michael nodded. "Seeing William and Rolphe might be a good idea. Both of them have been very busy these past few months."

"Yes, when I got that call from William, asking me to be his best man, I think it was one of the happiest days of my life. The wedding was simple and very private, but it was also beautiful. Annabel was like something out of a dream. And William has never been more handsome. When he put that ring on Annabel's finger, he looked like he was visiting heaven again. They make a perfect couple. But I didn't have time to visit Rolphe."

"I think Rolphe wants you to meet his lady friend, Myra."

"Yes, she sounds very nice too. So while I'm checking on the two couples, maybe I can get some advice about relationships. I'm obviously doing something wrong to end up dating someone like Elise."

"May I offer a thought?" Michael asked.

"Of course."

"If you want to experience heaven, you have to leave hell behind."

Three

AS LONDON'S FALL temperatures grew steadily colder, William knew his life was still changing on all fronts. Besides being a recently married man, he was still learning how to handle the angelic blood that flowed through his veins. In a more mundane area of life, he'd completed the first stage of remodeling the lower level of his home. It was a good project to keep his mind busy and his emotions steady and balanced.

When he looked around the new entertainment room, he couldn't help but admire his planning and handiwork. He was pleased that the area was finished in time for Arel's visit. If there was anyone who would appreciate what he'd done, it was his expected guest. Arel didn't have the know-how to drive a nail into a block of wood, but he did value beauty when he saw it.

Of course, Arel didn't have to know about handling carpenter tools. The man could create a world. It wasn't a world that existed in a normal sense. A person had to travel to Arel's creation in their astral body. However, that didn't make Arel's world less tangible to the person visiting. William could have died on Arel's world. When Arel's emotions took him down a path of insanity, Arel had turned his creation into a war zone, and he insisted on fighting William. The battle that took place was very real indeed.

William would always have a reminder of that day. It hung on his wall. Rolphe had sent him a large painting as a present. Rolphe's note explained that it was a tribute to William's courage and dedication. Rolphe felt that William had acted as a protector of all that was good and holy when he fought Arel.

William admired the painting. He even enjoyed Rolphe's thoughtful sentiments, but he still had his moments when it came to Rolphe himself. The man was six foot, five inches tall with a powerfully-built, intimidating body. When he stared at William with his piercing, green eyes, he could still send a chill down William's spine.

But there was another reason for being cautious when he thought about Rolphe. Rolphe had been a very dangerous enemy when he was still a vampire. He repeatedly tried to kill William and nearly succeeded. However, after Rolphe's change of heart, the man had tried to atone for what he'd done. Hopefully, the painting was an example of Rolphe's true spirit.

William leaned in to examine the piece of art more closely. Rolphe could rival the masters when it came to skill. His rendering of William in battle was magnificent. It was so magnificent that William's heart began to pound with exhilaration. He remembered how he'd commanded an army of angels. The thrill of such a glorious experience made him smile, but his thoughts were interrupted. Annabel called out to him from the upper level.

"William? Arel is here!" Annabel announced.

William took a deep breath and backed away from the painting. "Coming," he said as he quickly walked to the stairs. The scenes of battle were replaced by the reality of the moment. He and Arel were finally at peace with each other. They enjoyed each other's company. When Arel had come to London for William and Annabel's wedding ceremony, he appeared healthy and content.

William climbed the newly-carpeted stairs to the upper level, hoping that he looked just as content. As soon as he had the thought, his eye twitched. The incident made him hesitate. That type of thing hadn't happened in a long time.

* * *

Arel was still smiling at Annabel and how happy she looked when William came walking into the living room. The man whom Arel considered a brother looked his usual tall, serious self. "Will! It's good to see you again," Arel said as he extended his hand.

William grasped it firmly. "You continue to look like you've been surfing."

Arel shrugged as they all got seated. "Not surfing, but I still play a lot of tennis with Carey when the weather permits. He loves the game and can't get enough of it. I have to admit, I'm getting pretty good myself. He only beats me half the time." He sat back on the sofa. "But enough about me. I want to hear about the two of you."

21

Annabel reached out for William's hand. "We haven't been playing in the sun, but we are as happy as can be." She paused and glanced at William. "Right?"

William's distracted, blue eyes had strayed in a preoccupied sort of way, but he smiled as soon as Annabel nudged him. "Right."

Arel tried not to think about the feeling he was getting when he studied William's overall manner. He'd given himself a number of strict orders after his last emotional foray into insanity. No reading other people's minds. No interfering in other people's lives. If Michael could view everyone as capable of handling themselves, so could he. Yet, he noticed that William's eye twitched when he responded to Annabel's question. The little spasm was probably nothing, but Arel felt his chest tighten anyway.

Annabel seemed oblivious to anything but her own exuberant mood. "Arel, you won't believe how William has transformed the lower level. It's beautiful."

Arel sat up attentively. "When I was here the last time, it was still in the hammer and nails stage."

"Then you're in for a treat," Annabel said as she gave William's hand another squeeze. She stood up and looked down at him. "I have to clean up my sculpting station. So why don't you show Arel what you've been doing downstairs."

William remained in his seat. "Are you sure that you don't want to show him around too?"

Annabel laughed. "I'm sure. Besides, I bet you two could use some 'man' time. Anyway, that's what Peggy and Carol call it."

Arel got to his feet. "I can't wait to see what you've done, Will. I've been curious."

William stood up too and started out of the room. "It's just a bit of remodeling, nothing too exciting."

Annabel called back to them as she headed down the hall in the opposite direction. "When you're finished, come back to my studio. I have a little present for Arel."

Arel stared back. "For me? A present?"

Annabel turned and put her hands on her hips. "Yes, I know you didn't care for my knitting, but maybe you'll like the clay figures I've made."

Arel cleared his throat. "I'm sorry if you got that impression about your knitting being—"

22

"Never mind," Annabel laughed. "Now go with William and look at what a beautiful job he's done."

Arel did as he was told, remembering the first time he had followed William down the stairs to the lower level of the house. He'd come to London, hoping to help William. The man was going through a rough transition after Arel had passed on Michael's blood. Unfortunately, things didn't go the way he'd planned. In fact, he'd nearly killed William a couple of times with his well-intentioned blunders. But he had to remind himself that those unfortunate incidents were all in the past. He'd learned a lot since then.

He skipped down the carpeted stairs, determined to stay focused on the present. Luckily, when he was ushered into the new living area, he felt his energy shift. He knew William had excellent taste, but the newly remodeled lower level was a surprise. He let out a low whistle of admiration. "Great job, Will, you've outdone yourself."

Turning around in a slow circle, he noted some of the details of the carefully planned space. Elegant, narrow-wood paneling made for a contemporary but cozy atmosphere. It also made the walls an excellent backdrop for the large pieces of modern and traditional artwork. The well-chosen paintings exhibited the best when it came to expressing color and form. But there was even more to admire. When he looked down, he was standing on plush, light-colored tan carpeting. It transformed a floor that had once been covered by gray tile.

The furniture was tastefully chosen too. Twin sofas sat at ninety degree angles in the center of the room. They were liberally overstuffed for comfort and covered in a pleasing, pale green and yellow plaid fabric. A circular glass-topped coffee table with a wrought iron base added to the elegance. It sat on a large, exotic, tiger print area rug.

Arel approached a sofa and ran his hand over the back of the couch, enjoying the feel of the soft chenille. "What a wonderful place to relax."

William walked to one end of the room and pressed a button over a self-contained fireplace. A panel over its mantel responded. It disappeared into the built-out wall, revealing a very large, flat screen television.

When Arel returned a broad grin, William smiled too. "I might have gone a little overboard with the entertainment center, but what the heck, Annabel loves it all."

"I'm sure she does." Arel said. "What you've done is incredible. You turned this space into a showcase for one of those interior design magazines."

Arel continued his inspection, going over to one of the pieces of art. "Rolphe did a great job with this painting, but he couldn't capture your true splendor on that battlefield, Will. I'll never forget seeing you on that big, angelic mare. Your soul was shining through, and your face was as radiant as any angel's."

William joined him and stood silently staring at himself. After a moment, he sighed. "Yes, but those days are over. I'm not commanding Michael's legions anymore. I'm ordering speakers and the latest in sound equipment."

Arel hesitated when he heard the heaviness in William's tone. "Will, is everything okay?"

"Of course, look around. I live in luxurious surroundings. I have an ex-angel for a wife. My life is great." William waved to Arel and started for a sofa. "And now you're here. So let's sit down and talk about what you've been up to. You've talked about dating a writer, correct?"

Arel had to fight back an urge to question William further. Instead, he took a seat and concentrated on William's inquiry. "Yes, I went out with Elise. She writes romance books."

"Romance? Then she probably enjoys the sensual aspects of life."

"I wouldn't know. Elise is a bitter woman who guarded her body like a holy relic. I barely got to kiss her cheek."

"Count your blessings."

"What do you mean?"

"You're lucky you didn't get a taste of her. She probably has tainted blood."

Arel returned a look of surprise. "Tainted blood?"

"Yes, during my early 'vampire' days, I was still young and inexperienced. I knew a couple of women who were like the person you dated. Their bitterness spoiled them. When I got a taste of their blood, I spat it out immediately. It was vile stuff."

"I don't know about tainted blood, but Elise is a difficult person to say the least." He glanced over at the painting of William. "But like you said, the past is past. I'm ready for a new chapter in my life. That's one reason I'm here. I need some guidance when it comes to relationships."

William grimaced as he twisted at the band on his finger. "Just make sure to get a ring that fits if you tie the knot."

"I saw Annabel put that band on your finger when you were married. It seemed to fit just fine."

William continued to tug on his wedding ring. "Maybe, but it's not fine now. It's cutting off the circulation in my finger."

Arel got up and went over to where William was sitting. "If that's true, don't keep agitating it." He paused and gave William's hand a closer look. "I think your finger is swollen. That's the problem."

William let his hand drop to his side. "It's the blood thing. You know what I mean. When the stuff gets stirred up inside, the heat that's generated can affect the body."

Arel did know about such matters. He'd often experienced high fevers and other physical problems when his negative emotions got out of control. He grabbed William's hand and examined it. "William, your finger doesn't look too good. You have to get this ring off."

"That's what I was trying to do," William said as he pulled his hand out of Arel's grasp. He started twisting the ring again.

Arel stared back with curiosity. William was usually adept and calm. So why would he get so agitated over such a simple problem? "Do you have any cooking oil?"

"Annabel uses olive oil on her salads."

Arel headed for the stairs. "Great, let's go get it and use it on your finger. We'll have that ring off in a snap."

A few minutes later, William found some oil in a kitchen cupboard and handed it to Arel. "Thanks for helping."

Arel smiled. "Put your hand over the sink, and I'll douse your finger with the oil."

William's eyes brightened. "Very practical idea. I should have thought of it myself."

Arel poured a generous amount of the lubricant on William's finger. "There you go. Try taking off the ring again, but this time, don't tug on it. Twist it slowly."

William did as he was told, but the ring still resisted his efforts. "It's not working. The blasted thing won't budge."

Arel reached for William's hand. "This is ridiculous. I can use my powers to help."

William tried to pull back. "Something always seems to go wrong when you try to help."

25

Arel held on to William's hand and laughed. "That was before. I'm much more competent. In fact, look at this." He held up William's ring triumphantly.

William frowned. "How did you do that?"

"I don't know. Maybe you relaxed," Arel said as he flipped the ring in William's direction.

William's hand went up to catch it, but his fingers were so oily and slick that the ring ended up bouncing off and landing in the sink. After a couple of spins, the ring slipped down the drain.

Arel's eyes went wide with panic. "Oh no! Your wedding band!"

William studied the sink with furrowed brows, but his tone was composed. "It's okay. That's the side with the garbage disposal."

Arel let out a gasp of relief and started to reach a hand down the drain. "I'll get it."

William immediately pushed Arel back from the sink. "Are you crazy? Do you want to lose some fingers? With your powers, what if you set off the disposal?"

Arel glanced at his hands. "I never thought about that. Do you think I could affect an electrical appliance?"

"With your powers, anything is possible."

"No, that's taking it too far. I'll be fine. Just let me retrieve your ring."

"At least let me unplug the disposal," William said in an insistent voice.

"Stand back," Arel said as he opened the lower cabinet door and crouched down. "I'll do it. Your hand is all greasy."

"Fine, the plug is to the left, but just be careful."

Arel peered under the sink and soon discovered an electric cord connected to the disposal. He began to smile as he thought about the situation he was in. He was visiting his best friend, a friend who was still trying to look out for him. It had always been that way in their relationship. William was truly a brother who was always there, trying to keep him safe.

The thought made his chest respond with an expansive feeling of gratitude. As he reached for the electric cord, the feeling expanded even more, filling his entire body with a sudden surge of happy energy. He'd been keeping his powers contained for months. It was a relief to let his powers have a joyful outlet. But the unexpected happened. As soon as he grabbed hold of the plug, the disposal came alive. A terrible grinding noise followed. It stopped when he'd pulled the plug out of the socket, but he knew it was too late.

Four

ANNABEL STOOD IN front of William and Arel, looking at one, then the other. Both men were seated at the counter in the kitchen. A short time before, when she heard a loud, disagreeable sound coming from the kitchen, she'd rushed in to find Arel half-hidden under the sink. William stood over him with his eyes wide and his face pale and bloodless. After explanations were made and both men were free of greasy hands, they both went speechless. Annabel didn't know what to say to either of them. However, she did feel the need to clarify a few things.

"William, why didn't you tell me your ring was too tight? We could have gone to the jeweler and had it adjusted."

"I didn't want to upset you."

"Why would I be upset?"

"You place a lot of importance on what our wedding bands signify. I didn't want you to get the wrong idea."

Annabel smiled. "A ring is simply a symbol. The only thing that's really important is the love that we have for each other."

Arel's hand shot up. "As for the ring, I promise to have a duplicate made ASAP."

Annabel walked over to where Arel sat and kissed his cheek. "Arel, you were trying to help William. I'm just happy that you thought of using oil to get the ring off."

Arel's eyes had been mostly downcast since the unfortunate incident with the disposal. He glanced up and eyed Annabel anxiously. "I'm truly sorry about the disposal turning on. Nothing like that has ever happened before."

"Then maybe it's fortunate that you found out about your ability in a way that wasn't dangerous."

"That's a good point," Arel said. "Thank you for being so understanding." He gave Annabel another grateful smile. "William is a

28

lucky guy. You are such a treasure. After dating a very unpleasant woman back in Chicago, I can only hope to find someone half as nice as you."

"What a sweet thing to say," Annabel said as she moved to the doorway. She gestured for Arel to follow her. "Would you like to see what I made for you?"

Arel quickly vacated his seat. "Of course."

"Then come back to my studio." She looked at William next. "You too, sweetheart."

With both men joining her in her studio, Annabel went to a cupboard and took out two gift boxes. She handed one to Arel and one to William. "Actually, I have a surprise for each of you, but Arel's our guest, so he can open his first."

Arel accepted her present and quickly lifted off the top of the box. "Isn't this exciting? I'm going to be the proud owner of a piece of an artist's early work."

Annabel corrected him. "Actually, it's my second piece! William's is my first."

Arel stiffened. "Oh, Annabel, are you sure you don't want to hold on to your second piece? It must be very special to you."

Annabel gave him a reassuring smile. "I know how much you value art, so I know you'll appreciate it as much as I do."

Arel's face drifted into a sort of awkward smile as he removed a small object from the box. "Thank you, this is quite an honor."

Annabel clapped her hands. "What do you think?"

Arel held up the six inch figure and studied it carefully. "It's very unique. It's a little . . . mouse, right?"

Annabel shook a finger in his direction. "Oh no, it's not a mouse. Guess again. I know you'll get it."

Arel tugged at his collar with his free hand and glanced at William. "Will, my mind is so scattered today, especially after the incident with your ring. Take a look at Annabel's amazing piece of art and tell me what you see."

William let out a heavy breath. "It's a rat. Can't you tell? Look at the long nose."

Arel turned the small figure around and smiled. "You're right. I missed that detail."

Annabel gave William a squinty-eyed scowl. "It is not a rat or mouse. They have long tails. I made Arel a bear."

Arel's eyes widened as he continued to stare at the small figure. "Oh, yes, it is a bear. How could I have thought otherwise?"

Annabel let her frown soften. "You seemed to love buying stuffed bears for Carol and Peggy's children. I thought you might like a keepsake one for yourself."

Arel's head bobbed up and down a number of times. "I love it. It'll have a place of honor in my home."

Annabel's shoulders relaxed as she turned to William. "Now, open your gift, William."

William sucked in a breath. "I can't wait," he said. After he retrieved a small clay sculpture from its box, he held it up and smiled. "Annabel, thank you. It was sweet of you to make me a fox."

"A fox?" Annabel asked.

Arel stepped forward and laughed. "William, look at those long legs. That's a deer."

Really, a deer?" William asked.

Annabel snatched it out of his hand. "You're both wrong. It's a horse. It's Boda, the horse in Rolphe's painting!"

William paused. "I guess my brain is as addled as Arel's after what happened to my wedding band. Can you forgive me?"

Annabel laughed. "Of course. And don't worry. If you want a fox, I'll make that my next project." She looked at Arel. "And I'll make you a mouse."

Annabel realized what great fun she was having. She knew that her skills were still at the beginner's stage, but William and Arel were trying very hard to appreciate her efforts. She experienced a wonderful feeling of support until she caught a glimpse of William's face. When he thought she wasn't looking, he gave Arel a quick, furtive look. It was the kind of look a desperate animal has when it's caught in a trap.

It was also the look William often had when she surprised him with her presence. He covered it up by pretending to be figuring out some problem with his remodeling project. Annabel had gone along with the ruse. She hadn't wanted to think that his unhappiness had anything to do with their relationship. And even if there was trouble in paradise, she figured it would work itself out eventually.

As she allowed herself to see the truth, she knew she was in denial. William was slipping away from her. Just the thought sent a chill through her body. On the other hand, she also felt determined to do something about the situation. And perhaps, she had an ally. Arel was standing a few feet away. More than anyone in the world, he understood William. She had to reach out to him. She needed to talk to him privately and get his advice.

As Arel was putting his small bear back in the gift box, she gave him her most earnest smile. "Arel, you had some time with William. Now, I'd like you to accompany me to the pet store. I need some supplies for the mice."

William spoke up at once. "What supplies? I went to the shop a couple of days ago."

Arel frowned. "Where are the mice? I didn't see them downstairs."

Annabel smiled. "The neighbor boy has them. He watches them for us when we're gone. He's grown to love them so much that he sometimes asks to keep them at his house for a couple of days."

"Exactly, Annabel," William said. "So you don't need to visit the pet store."

Annabel gave him a dismissive wave and took hold of Arel's arm. "Whatever, William, Arel needs some fresh air, and so do I."

* * *

Arel felt uneasy the moment Annabel insisted that he take a walk with her. His instincts told him that she wanted something. The ex-angel had changed a lot after she gave up her wings. If her fears took over, she could be very intense, even demanding.

Once they were on their way, Arel gave her a questioning glance. "Annabel, is something wrong?"

"Yes, I think there is. You have to tell me why William is so upset. And don't spare my feelings if you think I'm at fault."

Arel avoided Annabel's intimidating eyes. "Please, if William has something he wants to talk to me about, he'll tell me. Otherwise, it's not my business. As you know, I've interfered too many times in the past. I refuse to interfere again."

"I'm not asking you to interfere. I just want to know what's going on. Today, seeing you two together, I realized that I've had blinders on."

"What kind of blinders?"

"After that episode in Paris when you and William were battling it out in that alternate world, I was so happy to come back home to London. It was such a relief to think that William and I were finally going to have time to be a normal couple. But I don't think William felt the same way."

"But he married you. That says something about his feelings."

Annabel stopped abruptly and batted her long, dark lashes at him. "Maybe so, but William's problem with his wedding band was an obvious indication of how he feels now. He couldn't stand having it on his finger."

Arel smiled. "That's ridiculous. There's a much simpler explanation. His body is still adjusting to all the changes that come with having angelic blood in his veins."

Annabel stared back with a look that was anything but appeased. "You don't really believe that, do you?"

"Why shouldn't I?"

"Stop trying to ignore the truth. You and William are very close. You could feel that something wasn't right as soon as you got here, couldn't you?"

Arel thought about William's twitching eye and the way he gritted his teeth when he was trying to remove his ring. "Look, Annabel, as I just explained, I can't interfere. If you think William has a problem, talk to him. After all, you're man and wife."

"And you think that makes it easy to understand one another?"

Arel blinked back. His mind was getting more muddled by the moment. "I guess I do. When people are in love—"

"Being in love doesn't solve anything!"

"Annabel, please, why are you dismissing everything I say?"

"Because I think you're lying."

"Lying?"

Annabel crossed her arms defiantly. "Yes, for some reason you're evading the truth."

"I'm sorry. I don't know what to tell you."

Annabel hesitated for a long moment. When she stepped closer, her beautiful, emerald eyes were softer. She put a hand on Arel's arm and gave it a gentle squeeze. "I'm sorry for being so emotional. I know it's wrong of me to pressure you. It's just that you're the only one who understands what William is going through. So I need your help. You know how reserved he can be. He pretends everything is fine when I talk to him."

Arel could feel Annabel pulling him in with her earnest tone and explanation. He almost let himself yield to her plea for help. But as he opened his mouth to reply, his past mistakes resurrected themselves. He remembered how many times he'd tried to fix a problem and only made it worse. This time, he had to make a stand. Instead of surrendering, he tried to offer Annabel the only advice that seemed appropriate. "Annabel, remember when you were an angel? Remember how you believed in people and their ability to help themselves? You have to do that now."

Annabel reacted instantly. "Right! And how did that work out for you? You didn't have a clue about helping yourself. You spent all those years alone and in misery. Now you won't help William when he's lost. What kind of friend does that?"

Before Arel could reply, Annabel turned and ran back up the street. When she reached her home, she ran up the steps, threw open the door, and ran inside.

Arel followed her back, but he didn't rush. When he arrived at the property, he took the steps to the porch in a slow, deliberate manner, hoping to understand how things had escalated so quickly with Annabel. When he opened the door to William's house, William was standing in the foyer, glaring at him.

"What did you say to Annabel?" William asked in a brusque voice. "She looks very upset."

Arel paused, meeting William's angry stare with a blank expression. "I don't know. I don't have an explanation. All that I can say is that I'm going to have to give the idea of a relationship a lot more thought."

"What are you talking about?"

"Annabel questioned me about the subject, but I don't think I had the answers she wanted. That seemed to upset her."

William's eyes immediately changed from angry to sympathetic. "Annabel's take on things can be different, even confrontational."

"Maybe you need to talk to her. I think she's still struggling with a lot of fear."

"And what do you suggest I say that's going to change that?"

Arel scratched his head, but nothing came to mind. "But you love each other, right?"

"Of course."

"Then what's going on, Will? I came here hoping to understand how two people can happily spend their life together, but so far, the whole idea is more puzzling than ever."

William returned an annoyed look. "When you find the answer to that one, fill me in."

Five

PEGGY LAY IN bed, thankful that she couldn't think of anything to worry about. Her family was thriving, and her friends were all in good places in their lives. Even Arel, who had had numerous ups and downs, was doing very well. After his fiasco dating Elise, he'd decided to visit Annabel and William, to enjoy time away with people who were happy with their relationship.

"At least I hope they're happy," she whispered to herself. She hadn't talked to Annabel for a couple of weeks. However, earlier in the month, all seemed fine when they chatted. Annabel was busy trying out some new hobbies, and William was finishing up a remodeling project.

Peggy reached over and put a hand on Tim's slumbering body. He was sleeping so soundly he didn't even notice. Peggy wished that she could fall asleep too. She was tired after a busy day, but she was still restless.

Carefully throwing back the cover, she slipped out of bed and went to the window. When she looked next door at Arel's rancher, there were no lights in the house. Michael and Carey had announced that they'd be away for the weekend. Carey mentioned something about a hiking trip and sleeping outdoors in a tent. The thought of him getting up at dawn and traipsing through the woods all day was fun to ponder, but not something she would relish. Where did the young man get so much energy? When he wasn't working on his motorcycle, he was calling up Tim and Kevin, inviting them to play an impromptu game of basketball. Michael was the older, calmer type. He loved gardening. Then again, if Carey urged him on, he'd play ball or go hiking too.

Peggy pressed her forehead to the pane of glass. She just wanted to sleep. Their baby, Sara, was an early riser, and she could be very fussy. If Peggy didn't get her eight hours, she wouldn't have the energy she needed to keep up with the baby's demands.

She was about to turn away and go back to bed when she noticed a movement in the yard next to Arel's. On closer inspection, Peggy's sleep-deprived eyes instantly went wide with irritation. Elise was standing out on her sidewalk, puffing away on a cigarette. It was a bit of a surprise. Peggy didn't remember Arel mentioning that Elise smoked.

With a censuring shake of her head, Peggy closed the blinds. As she returned to bed, she offered a prayer of thanks that the horrible woman was no longer a part of Arel's life. Her sense of relief was enough to make her shoulders relax as she got back under the cover. As she began to feel the first hints of sleepiness take over, she also sent out a heart-felt request into the ethers. "Listen up all you helper angels. Please assist Arel in finding a wonderful woman, one who'll make his heart sing."

* * *

Elise threw the cigarette down on the sidewalk and used her foot to rub out its seductive life. When she was especially unhappy, cigarettes called to her with promises they never kept. At least her smoking sprees didn't last long, usually a couple of weeks. They were long enough for her to get a grip on whatever emotional turmoil upset her life. The current upset revolved around Arel. She hadn't seen him for days in spite of the fact that her side window was a great observation portal. She told herself that the chair she'd placed there caught the light she needed to go over her current manuscript. Her self-deception didn't go very far, but it was better than admitting that she was spying on him.

When she went back inside, she stopped in front of the foyer mirror. A hardened, bitter woman with sad eyes stared back at her. "What's happened to me?" she groaned.

She hadn't always looked so pathetic. Recently, she'd gone through some old photos. The ones from her first year in college pictured a sweet, pretty girl who had lots of blond hair and bright, blue eyes. Her hopes and dreams were shining through. "I was such an optimist, even after a crappy childhood."

She turned away from the mirror and quickly walked to the kitchen. Besides cigarettes, food could be comforting. She'd had emotional lows after break-ups before, but this one was the worst. Something told her that she'd driven away the best guy she'd ever meet. "But I didn't have a choice," she insisted.

She went directly to the cupboards and scoured the shelves. Her staples were gone. Earlier in the evening, she'd finished the last of the chips. The oatmeal raisin cookies were reduced to a few crumbs, and the container of assorted nuts was empty. The situation was borderline critical. Her loneliness was peaking, and she needed something to make it go away.

The feeling was there before she'd met Arel, but she'd had ways of dealing with it besides food. She wrote books. By filling page after page with scenes of fictional romance, she could forget reality. She lived in a make-believe world where she was in charge and love triumphed in ways that she arranged.

Everything had changed when she moved next door to Arel. The charming man was a perfect example of the sexy, romantic hero she described in her books. Suddenly, all her imaginary men paled in comparison to a flesh and blood version of a partner she'd once longed for.

When Arel asked her out, she should have refused to see him. Experience told her that dreams could turn into nightmares. But she couldn't stop the way her body felt when he was near. All of her deep yearnings surfaced. After years of denying her needs, they wanted gratification in the worst kind of way.

She'd been weak and gone out with Arel, but in the end, she did what was best. "I just have to get through this break-up period, and then I'll be fine."

She was paying the price for letting her heart get involved again. That part was persistent. It was still hanging on to the idea of a relationship. She prayed that the refrigerator would offer something to subdue her longings. She bent over, desperately searching its shelves. There was nothing there. As usual, she hadn't wanted to go shopping. Now all her food supplies were gone. Almost shaky with anxiety, she remembered the cheese drawer. "Please, there's got to be something I can eat." Nothing.

As she was about to close the door, she saw an item she'd missed on its lowest shelf. "No! I will not drink syrup. That's going too far."

Even as she made the announcement she was reaching for the bottle. An image came to mind. She was like some wino in a dark alley, a broken person who had no self-respect, only a need to blot out their life. The picture was so horrible that she put the syrup back and closed the door.

As she pushed herself away from the appliance, she thought about going to an all-night grocery. She'd stock up on some healthy foods and make herself adopt a stricter diet. She was about to change out of her robe and pajamas when she saw a manuscript sitting on the counter.

The black binder held a work in progress that would never be seen by the public. It was Elise's own story. She'd wanted to explore the events and people who had shaped her life. Maybe it would help her to understand herself, and how she'd lost faith in just about everything. Clutching the binder to her chest, she returned to the living room.

Once she was seated on the sofa, she slowly paged through the chapters. None of them were complete, but at least she'd made a start. Her finger stilled when she reached the last one that she'd been working on. She read the chapter heading aloud, "Jack."

As soon as she said the name, she winced, as if the man she'd once loved could still hurt her. She could see his face etched in anger, ready to discipline her for stepping out of line. After a couple of breaths, she came back to the moment and threw the manuscript on the coffee table. Another smoke break was in order. She snatched up her pack of cigarettes and headed for the front door. A person didn't face years of misery without some kind of crutch.

She almost made it to the door when the empty feeling hit again. Her life was meaningless. The few friends who remained barely communicated. She was lucky to get a half dozen Christmas cards. She never talked to her parents or her sister. There was no one she could confide in. She hated to admit it, but she was truly alone in the world. "Oh hell, I need that syrup after all."

A few minutes later, after swallowing several ounces of liquid sucrose, she was standing outside, lighting up a cigarette. The first puff was helpful. As she exhaled, she felt calmer. With the cigarette held close, like her only friend, she began to think about working on the manuscript again. She'd already written about her childhood and what a disappointment she was to her father. She'd also started to explore her teen and college years. She couldn't believe how easily she'd given away her body along with her self-respect. It was a reckless time in her life, completely lacking in good judgment.

She took a long drag on her cigarette. The next part of her life was even more painful. It involved her relationship with Jack. Her friends took one look at him and told her he was a keeper. She'd felt the same way. She worshiped the handsome man, and he knew it. He took advantage of her devotion. The guys in college might have taken liberties with her body, but Jack knew how to undermine her heart, the core of who she was.

"Why? Why did I let him do what he did?" Her stomach tightened as she remembered times when a disapproving look could make her feel so small that she couldn't speak. She didn't dare tell her friends about the side of Jack that got off on abuse. Besides, she didn't have many friends after a while. Jack made sure to keep her to himself. After her relationship with Jack ended, others took his place.

"They were all like you, Dad," she whispered.

Maybe that was the clue. When she finished her smoke and went back inside, she'd study the facts about her childhood again. She'd try to understand why she still carried so much emotional baggage over events that happened years before. "I should be writing mysteries, not romances," she hissed as she flicked the long ash off her cigarette. That's what her life felt like, a depressing mystery she couldn't solve.

She was about to extinguish her cigarette when a clap of thunder and another bout of queasiness hit at the same time. She held a hand to her stomach and checked the sky. A storm was moving in fast. A sudden gust of cold wind tore at her robe and her hair. Her nausea seemed to be escalating just as quickly. Holding on to her robe, she remembered her father's face when she'd come home for a visit. He'd had no compassion for what she'd gone through. His words still played out loud and clear in her mind. "Men aren't your problem, Elise. You're the problem."

His condemnation was like the storm. She couldn't change her father's opinion any more than she could control the weather. She couldn't stop the onset of a pounding headache either. Her emotions and her body were ganging up on her as heavy drops of rain quickly turned into a downpour.

Before she had a chance to run into the house, she knew she was going to be sick. For an instant, she welcomed the idea of throwing up. She needed to empty herself of everything she hated about herself.

She threw her cigarette aside and tried to get the hair out of her eyes as her stomach lurched.

Her father had once questioned her common sense. "How can I be proud of a daughter who doesn't know how to come in out of the rain?" She didn't have an answer. The stormed raged around her as she fell to her knees and threw up on the grass.

* * *

Peggy woke up to the sound of thunder. Rain was pelting the window. She couldn't believe that Tim could sleep through the storm. For a second time that night, she got up, opened the blinds and stared out. Her gaze traveled across Arel's property and beyond. "That's strange," she whispered. The street light was giving off enough illumination for her to see someone on Elise's lawn. "Oh my, Elise is out in the rain."

Peggy hesitated for only a brief moment. Then she turned back to the bed. "Tim, honey, wake up!"

Tim groaned. "What? What's happening? Is it Sara?"

"No, it's Elise. I think she needs help."

"What's wrong with her?"

"I don't know. She's out on her lawn on her hands and knees."

"She's what?" Tim got out of bed and shuffled over to the window. "Why is Elise out in the rain?"

"I think she's in trouble. And this rain is coming down hard."

"I'll go check on her," Tim said with a yawn.

Peggy shook her head. "No, normally I'd agree, but something tells me that she needs a woman to help her."

"Is that your intuition talking?"

Peggy frowned. "Unfortunately, it is. I better get my raincoat and umbrella."

* * *

Elise couldn't remember when she'd felt so sick. But she shouldn't have been surprised. She'd eaten tons of junk food and washed it down with beer and syrup. A pounding headache added to her woes. So did the rain. It was coming down in driving sheets. She tried to get up, but she couldn't stop dry heaving long enough to get to her feet. Fortunately, she wasn't alone for long.

She lifted her eyes enough to see feet running towards her. She glanced up and saw Arel's neighbor, Peggy. The woman stopped and held an umbrella over her. Then there were two more feet stopping at her other side. Then there were voices.

"Tim, what are you doing here?" Peggy yelled out.

Tim shouted out his answer. "I want to help, too!"

Elise was mortified. Both of her neighbors, people she'd insulted, had come to her aid. She didn't know how to respond. Before she could say anything, Tim leaned down and told her that everything was going to be okay. Not only that, but he picked her up. It was such an unexpected kindness that she started crying. She found herself clinging to his jacket and bawling away as he rushed her inside the house.

Once they were in the foyer, Tim and Peggy became a team. Peggy got some towels and quickly lined the sofa. When Tim put Elise down on the couch, he did it carefully, letting her know she was in good hands. Elise collected herself enough to start apologizing. "Sorry you had to come out—"

Tim and Peggy were both dripping from the rain, but they ignored their own discomfort. They put aside their own needs to tend to her, the horrible person who lived two doors down. In her fragile emotional state, their unselfishness was overwhelming, something she didn't deserve. She'd been at her worst when she'd seen them last. The thought of all her ugliness sickened her, like the bile in her throat. Without any warning, she began to vomit again, retching so violently she thought she'd pass out.

Peggy grabbed a nearby trash can for her to use. She also tried to hold back Elise's hair. Luckily, Elise didn't have much left inside. After the bout was over, she laid back again. "Thank you," she whispered. Her head continued to feel like it was splitting in two. She closed her eyes, hoping the pain would let up before too long.

* * *

After getting Elise settled, Peggy quickly sent Tim home in case little Sara woke up. Elise fell asleep shortly after he left. Peggy decided to stick around for a while. Elise had acted so out-of-character that Peggy was worried about her. What could have happened to make the stiff, unemotional woman fall apart like she had?

When Peggy inspected Elise's home for signs of some physical disturbance, the house seemed neat and orderly. The living room décor was pleasant. Traditional furniture dominated the room. Muted browns and pale greens in the upholstery and throw pillows softened the look. Only the coffee table sported clutter. There were a couple of unwashed cups and a glass. Peggy automatically walked over to take them to the kitchen. As she leaned down, she noticed what looked like part of a manuscript. It was opened to Chapter Five.

Peggy stared at the spiral notebook for a few moments, wondering if she dare read any of it. It was probably nothing too interesting. Elise was probably working on a new romance. Peggy snickered at the irony. A woman who was incapable of common decency was in the business of selling stories about intimacy and love. "So I wonder what kind of make-believe rubbish is going to be in her next book."

Peggy picked up the binder and read the first few sentences. "Jack and I met when I was barely twenty. By the time I was twenty five, there wasn't much left of the person known as Elise. The only thing that remained was a hard, outer shell."

Peggy gasped. "Oh no, this must be Elise's journal."

She quickly replaced the notebook on the coffee table and hoped that she could forget what she'd read. It was easier to think that Elise was a terrible person than to reflect on events that made her so bitter. Besides, Peggy was tired. She didn't have the energy to be burdened by Elise's problems.

Unfortunately, that burden got heavier when Elise woke up. For an instant, she stared at Peggy with clear, unguarded eyes. It was just long enough for Peggy to see more of what made the woman tick. The information came in a flash of clarity and imagery. Someone had taken a young, fragile girl and crushed her spirit under the heel of cruelty and abuse. Peggy also gleaned something even worse. She could gauge Elise's bleak future. The woman was a tormented soul who didn't trust anything or anybody. With her attitude and bitterness, it would take a miracle to turn her life around.

Six

THE MOONLESS NIGHT was a pleasing complement to the evening. Its deep cover of darkness made the sparkle of the city lights of Paris even more beautiful. But Rolphe's thoughts of beauty were also sparked by Myra. The lovely redhead stood next to him, gazing out her window, enjoying the view with a contented smile. Theirs had been an ongoing affair that spanned a number of years. It had never been too serious until recently. Now, they were not only good friends and lovers, they were establishing a more meaningful bond.

But there was more than having Myra in his life that made Rolphe the most fortunate of men. His good fortune revolved around his friend and savior, Arel. Just the thought of Arel's upcoming visit made Rolphe's chest swell with gratitude. He had to swipe a tear from his face when the feeling overwhelmed his emotional nature.

Myra noticed his fluid eyes and reached out for his hand. "What are you thinking about, my great giant of a man?"

What could Rolphe tell her? Could he explain that he'd once been a vampire, a monster who existed on the blood of his fellow humans? Could he share the details of his deliverance from his heinous ways? No, Myra had never known that part of him, and she never would. It would serve no purpose. He wasn't that monster anymore. He was now a "child of God." That term might seem outmoded to some, but it was the basis for his new life.

His answer to Myra was simple. "I'm thinking about Arel, the man I told you about, remember?"

Myra nodded attentively. "Of course I remember. He sounds wonderful."

"He's more than that. He's the person I'll always be indebted to. When I went through what you call my 'change of life' crisis, he saved my life."

"I wish I could have been there for you."

Rolphe's heavy brows furrowed. "But you were there for me."

Myra laughed. "How? We never saw each other during those months."

"Whenever I phoned you, you were understanding and kind. You never needed explanations. You gave me the time I needed to come back to myself."

"I'm glad I could help in some small way."

Rolphe's face brightened even more. "You were there for my kitten, Dantela, too."

"I loved having her around. You know that. But I have something else to discuss with you. Come with me. I want to show you something."

Myra led the way through her dining area to a small lamp table in the hallway. She rummaged around the contents of its drawer and triumphantly withdrew a photo. She gave it to Rolphe. "You mentioned that Arel wants to find someone. I think my American friend's daughter might be perfect for him. Her mother sent me Claire's picture in a Christmas card."

Rolphe sucked in his breath. "Mon Dieu!" With the eye of an artist, he studied the gorgeous woman in the picture. Her dark hair, pale olive skin and nearly black eyes were only part of what made her exquisite. Her features were fine, with high cheekbones, and just enough pouty fullness to her rosy lips. Her body was sleek, but had curves in all the right places. "You're right about her. But why hasn't she been snatched up already?"

"My friend, Eddie, says her daughter has been studying at a school here in Paris. In fact, she just finished her doctorate in archaeology."

"That's an impressive accomplishment."

Myra sighed. "I've only met Claire once, but she seemed very dedicated. Can you believe she does charity work when she has time off? But now, her mother said she's considering the possibility of a relationship. When I remembered what Eddie said, I thought about your friend."

"You're right. They should definitely meet."

"I called Eddie, and she said that Claire has some time off. She's free tomorrow night. Would that work?"

"Yes, Arel, Annabel and William are arriving in the afternoon." Rolphe stared at the photo again with a satisfied smile.

Myra stood back and frowned. "If you keep looking at her like that I'm going to be jealous."

Rolphe's eyes narrowed, and he put the photo aside. The woman in the picture was stunning, but she couldn't distract him from the blessing that stood next to him. "Myra, never say such a thing. You're the most beautiful woman in the world to me."

Myra's brows arched with concern. "Are you sure? I'm not as young as I used to be."

Rolphe pulled her into a close embrace. "In my eyes, you're more beautiful every day."

Myra laughed. "Flatterer."

* * *

Arel walked around Rolphe's apartment and noted that it hadn't changed at all. Rolphe had been diligent in keeping it vacuumed, dusted and tidy. Even the windows and balcony doors were spotless and shiny. In other words, it was just the way Arel liked it. A well-groomed home helped him experience a sense of calm and serenity.

But he wasn't thinking about housekeeping as he wandered around aimlessly. Every muscle in his body seemed to be readying itself for what was coming. Rolphe's girlfriend, Myra, was arriving soon, and she was bringing along a friend. The friend was supposedly someone very attractive and a possible match for Arel.

The whole idea scared him on such a visceral level that he couldn't stop pacing. He traveled a path that went from balcony to the foyer to the living room. But his nervousness was well founded. After his failure with dating Elise, he'd come to London full of hope and expectation. Surely, Annabel and William would be the model couple to observe. Sadly, the couple didn't seem to be getting along as well as he'd hoped. In fact, his visit seemed to spark a kind of discontent on both their parts. They sat on one of Rolphe's sofas, looking civil, but barely talking to one another.

Rolphe seemed out-of-sorts too. He sat on the sofa opposite Annabel and William, barely offering any conversation. Every couple of minutes he checked his watch and made a similar announcement. "I'm sure Myra and Claire will be here shortly."

Annabel finally spoke up. "Please stop fretting, Rolphe. They're only ten minutes late."

William seemed compelled to speak up too. "Arel, stop pacing and sit down. I feel like I'm watching some caged animal in a zoo."

Arel had to agree with William's assessment. He felt trapped. The situation he was facing could turn out very poorly. What if Myra's friend was hostile like Elise? Or what if she wasn't his type, and he was stuck with going out with her?

He stopped next to the piano and noted the bouquet of pink roses sitting astride the beautiful instrument. One flower was decidedly angled in the wrong direction. It was only a small annoyance, but one that Arel intended to rectify. He was familiar with the proper way to arrange flowers. When his heart was failing years before, he'd learned the art because he didn't have the stamina to do much else. He couldn't tolerate a second rate job. He reached out for the offending stem just as the doorbell rang. Startled by the sound and what it portended, he grabbed hold of a thorny section. His finger suffered from his lack of attention. When he retrieved it, it was bleeding freely. Small droplets of blood were spoiling the piano's newly polished surface.

William had obviously been watching him and hurried to the rescue. "Here, take my handkerchief."

Arel tried to obey, but he didn't think he could move. When the bell rang a second time, panic seized hold. "William, this is a terrible mistake. I know it. I can feel it in every bone in my body."

Instead of replying, William wrapped Arel's finger with the kerchief.

"William, are you listening to me?" Arel gasped. He was sure his lungs had stopped working too.

William gave him a look of irritation and moved away, issuing whispered orders. "Stop imagining things. Just relax and enjoy the evening."

Before Arel could obey, Rolphe was escorting two women into the room. He paused a few feet away from where Arel was standing. With a broad smile, the tall, robust man stepped aside and gestured to his guests. "Arel, I'd like to introduce you to Myra and Claire."

Arel's eyes flickered their way over to where the two women were standing. He nodded to the first woman, a pretty redhead, and let his gaze continue on. As soon as he saw the second, younger woman, he stepped forward. He heard himself uttering a polite, but husky-voiced, "Nice to meet you," greeting as he stuck out his injured hand. William's make-shift bandage fell away, but he didn't notice. He was mesmerized by the gorgeous woman who was staring back at him.

As soon as the woman saw Arel's bleeding finger, she came forward. "What happened to you?" she asked as she took his hand in hers.

"A thorn," Arel muttered back. He knew he should say something more meaningful, but he couldn't make himself do anything but admire the woman named Claire. He was sure the term, love at first sight, applied.

* * *

William watched the interaction between Arel and Claire with a scowl. Arel was right about his fears. William had the same reaction as soon as he saw Claire. It wasn't that the woman wasn't a ravishing beauty. Rarely had William seen a more stunning example of the feminine. Almost as tall as Arel, the enchantress had thick, silky, nearly black hair. It was pulled back to expose her elegant neck and flawless, Mediterranean complexion. When she entered the room, her body was fluid and graceful, like that of a model, ready for the runway. But none of her physical qualities could override the feeling of apprehension that had hold of William.

Annabel reached over and took his arm, pulling him towards her. "Why are you making that face, William?"

William replied in a whisper. "Don't you feel what's happening?"

"What's happening?"

"The making of a disaster."

"I don't understand."

"I don't either, not yet."

As William was speaking, Rolphe approached the couch with Claire in tow. He smiled as he made the introductions.

"Annabel, William, let me introduce you to Myra's talented friend, Claire."

William stood up at once. He tried his best to be courteous, but having Claire so close boosted his anxiety. When she extended her hand to him, he found it difficult to move his arm. He finally managed a polite shake.

Claire seemed unaffected by William's uncomfortable state. She nodded back and then began to talk to Annabel. Soon, both women were discussing something that Claire had said. William excused himself and quickly joined Arel on the other side of the room. Arel looked animated and happy as he chatted to Myra.

William cut in with a forced smile. "Sorry to interrupt, Myra, but Arel has a call waiting for him in the other room."

Arel hesitated. "What call? I didn't hear a phone."

"It's one you need to take," William insisted. He latched on to Arel's arm, guided him towards a back bedroom and closed the door.

Arel turned to face William with a curious smile. "What's this all about?"

"You were right about this woman, Arel. She's bad news."

Arel laughed. "Elise was bad news. Claire is the person I've been dreaming about."

"You're letting yourself be seduced by her beauty."

Arel's face lit up with a faraway kind of glow. "She's like some kind of resourceful goddess." He held up the finger that had been damaged by the thorn. "Do you know she had a bandage in her purse?"

"Arel, you're not hearing what—"

Arel gave William a curious look. "You're really worried about me."

"This isn't about me worrying. This is about that feeling you had in your bones—"

Arel reached out and gave William a gentle shake. "That was just my nerves. Everything's fine."

William was about to reply when Arel's eyes locked on to his. They were bright, penetrating pools of focus that shut down William's mind in an instant. Caught in a time warp, he floated in space where control seemed beyond his grasp. He knew his only recourse was to pull himself out of Arel's grip and look away. As he came back to himself, his jaw tightened with a hint of resentment. His own powers were lacking in many ways. He wondered if they'd ever match Arel's.

Arel seemed to understand. He studied the rug with downcast eyes, clearly wanting to demonstrate his desire to look out for

William's welfare too. "We're both still learning. But your wisdom is never lost on me. I'll remember what you said to me earlier."

William hesitated, still struggling to clear his muddled thoughts. "What did I say?"

Arel's gaze turned boyish and sincere. "You told me that we need to relax and enjoy the evening."

William rubbed at the throbbing pain that shot through his brow. "Yes, I guess I did give you that piece of advice."

"But I'll go a step further. Let's both forget about everything but the prospect of a new adventure, one that centers around a lasting relationship with a partner. What do you say?"

William suddenly felt tired, too tired to argue. "If you think that's what will make you happy, I won't stand in your way."

Arel turned to leave and offered a final look of appreciation. "Thank you, William. I'm lucky to have a brother like you."

After they returned to the gathering in the living room, William began noticing things about himself. He was slumped in his seat. If he had his notepad, he'd add other details. His physical vessel felt sluggish and worn. Observing himself was a practical tool he'd used ever since Arel had passed on Michael's blood. At first, his observations were meant to help him cope with the drastic changes he went through. Presently, an examination of his physical and emotional state felt useless. What good did it do him to note his downward spiral when he couldn't reverse it?

For months, he'd been working to keep his mind busy and hopefully balanced. It was a moment by moment struggle. He tried not to think about the past, a glorious past. When he'd been in the world that Arel had created, he'd never felt more challenged. On the other hand, he'd never felt more alive and fulfilled. Now, everything exciting was behind him. He was living Annabel's ideal life. He was slipping into that fatal existence that people called normal. It was such a suffocating thought that he knew he needed to go out on the balcony and get some air.

* * *

Rolphe threw back his broad shoulders as a wave of happiness took hold. Mission accomplished. Arel and Claire appeared to be totally at ease, even blissful with one another. The match was definitely a good one, and it was all Myra's doing.

When he looked around the room and saw his redheaded sweetheart talking to Annabel, he was doubly grateful. They seemed to be enjoying each other's company too. That left only one person to check on. Where was William? Rolphe did another quick sweep of the room and frowned. Then he noticed someone standing on the balcony. That someone was leaned forward on the rail with his head down.

Rolphe let out a groan. "I was afraid of this."

Ever since the episode involving Arel's alternate world and its dramatic conclusion, William didn't seem as happy as Rolphe thought he should be. Interacting with William the past couple of hours confirmed his fear. Instead of celebrating his amazing triumph in the face of a terrible challenge, William displayed little enthusiasm about anything. His eyes sometimes went vacant, with none of the spark that he'd had when he was happy.

When Rolphe tuned into William's energy, he was more concerned than ever. William wasn't coming back to his powerful self. Quite the opposite was happening. He was drifting into the dangerous waters of despondency.

Rolphe knew he had to act quickly. Minds like William's and Arel's were too powerful to be allowed to stay in negative states for very long. The tricky part would be gaining William's trust. Rolphe's track record with the man was a rocky one. They had cooperated when Arel's life was at stake, but that was an extreme circumstance.

As Rolphe approached the balcony, he hoped he could strengthen their bond. For starters, he paused after he quietly opened the door. He didn't want to startle the man with his presence. "William?" he called out in barely a whisper.

William jerked around and returned a scowl. "Dammit, Rolphe, Arel is right. You're always sneaking up on people."

Rolphe didn't think he'd acted inappropriately, but he held his tongue. William had good reason to still be angry with him. Before Rolphe's transformation back to his benevolent self, he'd tried to kill William, not once, but twice.

He adopted a penitent attitude as he approached the railing. Avoiding William's censuring gaze, he stared out at the cityscape. "It's nice to have you here again."

"Annabel and I are leaving in the morning."

"I'm sorry to hear that. I hoped you'd stay for a few days."

"Definitely not. You can deal with Arel yourself this time."

Rolphe stole a quick glance in William's direction. He hadn't expected William to bring Arel into the conversation. "What do you mean? He and Claire seem to be—"

"Don't be a fool. Look a little deeper, Rolphe. This match you've arranged is going to backfire."

Rolphe almost let William's warning derail him from his purpose. He quickly realized that William's outlook was probably compromised by his negativity. "I appreciate your concern, but before we talk about Arel, I have something to show you. I want your opinion on a canvas I've been working on."

William gave him a more forgiving look. "By the way, if I haven't thanked you properly, I want you to know that I appreciate the painting that you sent me. It must have taken you quite some time to complete."

Rolphe gave him a dismissive wave and started inside. "Good, I hoped you'd like it. Come with me and inspect my latest endeavor."

When he got to his studio, Rolphe flipped on the light and went directly to one of his easels. It was a heavy duty unit, made for large canvases. The one that it held was covered. He looked at William who stood in the doorway. "Would you help me take the cover off?"

William approached the easel with an expectant look. "That canvas must be one of your largest."

Rolphe took hold of a upper corner of cloth and began to lift it. "Yes, I usually work on smaller pieces, but this one is about seventy inches wide."

William grabbed the opposite corner and helped Rolphe put the cloth aside. When he turned back to the canvas, he let out a small gasp of surprise.

Rolphe watched with anticipation as William inspected the painting. An army of angelic warriors was displayed on a battlefield. Their golden radiance overpowered the darkness that surrounded them. "What do you think?"

William didn't reply, but Rolphe smiled anyway. For the first time that evening, William's energy had shifted. His face had brightened. "I wanted to capture what took place on that field. The painting I gave you depicted a smaller portion of the battle. This piece is a bigger, more detailed version."

William stepped back and continued to stare at the canvas. "You've done a remarkable job."

Rolphe pointed to one of the most impressive angels. "And look at you on your great, white horse. You're so gallant and brave. You're as bright or brighter than any angel on the field."

William's face turned dark again. "Arel said the same thing, but I'm not one of . . . them."

Rolphe frowned. "That's not true. When I caught a glimpse of you that day, you glowed with light. I was afraid I'd be blinded when I gazed at you."

William laughed. "That's because you were viewing a world that Arel created. But none of it was real, not in terms of the reality I live in now."

"Please, don't say that. Arel's world or not, you are that brilliant angel. I'm sure of it."

William's jaw tightened as he turned away. "You're delusional, Rolphe. That's your problem."

As William started for the door, Rolphe trailed after him. "But what about everything you've witnessed, all the miracles?"

William swiveled round, glaring back. "So what have those miracles done for me in the long run? I'm married to an ex-angel who tells me life should be quiet and uneventful. I'm supposed to be planting posies and watching movies on a big screen television."

Rolphe paused, silenced by the bitterness in William's voice. For a long moment, he studied his hands. He'd tried to get all the paint off, but there were still bits of it around his nails. "William, I'm sorry if I've offended you."

William started for the door again. "Paint whatever you like, Rolphe. But here's a piece of advice. Don't make the mistake of thinking any of your visions are going to free you."

"Free me from what?"

"From the worst and cruelest of fates, from the chains that bind you to an ordinary life."

Rolphe hurried after him. "Wait, please. You said something about Arel earlier. Is there something I should know?"

William continued down the hallway. "Other than being headed for another disaster, Arel is fine."

Seven

PEGGY BROUGHT OVER a tea pot and poured a generous amount of liquid in Carol's cup. "Hope you like this jasmine tea. The tea shop was out of the kind I usually buy."

Carol took a sip and smiled. "It's wonderful."

Peggy held out a bakery box of scones. "It's also wonderful having our guys take the babies to swim class every Saturday."

"Yes, I love little Ariel like crazy, but sometimes I feel like I need a break."

"Speaking of breaks, can you believe Arel has met someone who sounds like she's exactly what he's looking for?"

"And beautiful too." Carol frowned. "Kevin's eyes were glued to her photo."

"Tim's too. I've never heard him use the word, stunning, until he saw this Claire person."

"I'm thrilled for Arel, especially after the rough time he had with Elise."

Peggy grimaced. "Don't get me started with Elise."

Carol giggled. "So you've been seeing quite a lot of her?"

"Ever since Tim and I helped her out that rainy night, she's tried to be nice. First, she brought over flowers as a thank you. Then she stopped by with a present for Sara. I also ran into her at the mall, and she insisted on buying me coffee and a dessert."

Carol took a pastry and placed it on her plate. "It sounds like she's changed completely."

"I thought it was bad when she acted like a shrew. It's even worse when she forces herself to be sweet."

"So you think it's just an act?"

Peggy broke off a piece of her scone and chewed it thoughtfully. "I suppose she tries, but I don't think she's capable of being a truly, nice person. She has too much pent up anger."

"What's strange is that she writes romance novels. I've read a couple of them. They're good. You'd never suspect that a person like Elise wrote them."

"People like that live in an imaginary world when they write. They never deal with their real life."

"That's kind of sad."

Peggy's brows narrowed. "Tell me about it. While we were having coffee, she opened up, and I got a glimpse of her background. She was with a jerk named Jack for quite a while."

"What did he do to her?"

"I guess he was very manipulative, and Elise was the perfect patsy. Like a lot of unwary women, she wanted someone to love her. She did whatever it took to get that love. She even quit college so that this guy could pursue an acting career. By the time their relationship ended, she was working two jobs and supporting both of them."

"How long were they together?"

"Five years. Then she found out he'd been cheating on her most of the time they were together."

"No wonder she's bitter, but like you said, why hasn't she moved on?"

"She did admit that she's a slow learner. After Jack, she let other men take advantage of her."

Carol leaned back and smoothed out her napkin. "What I don't understand is why she treated Arel like she did? I know he tried his best to be understanding and kind when he was with her."

"Unconsciously, she might have been comparing him to the jerk she'd been with. Seems Jack was very handsome too, and at first, he was nice."

"Wow, Peggy, you really do know a lot about it all."

"I know too much."

Carol laughed. "You have a very nurturing side. It makes people feel safe to tell you stuff."

"I'm just happy that she's moving soon."

"Oh, you're right. I saw the 'For Lease' sign on her lawn today."

"Yep, once she's gone, I won't have to worry about going to the mailbox and running into her."

* * *

Elise snuck out of the front door, looked towards Peggy's house, and sprinted down her driveway. Her mission was to collect her mail. She prayed that she wouldn't see her neighbor. Every time they met, Elise felt like a total idiot. It started when she'd tried to make amends. Peggy and Tim were so thoughtful when she was ill. Afterwards, she felt a debt of gratitude. None of her attempts to express that gratitude went well.

Whenever she was around Peggy, she became a bundle of nerves. She said ridiculous stuff and embarrassed herself. On one occasion, she had dominated their conversation with her bleak story of Jack, trying in some way to justify why she was what she was. She babbled on and on, sounding like the most pathetic loser ever. She only stopped when Peggy's eyes lost focus. Taking stock of their exchanges, she realized how unable she was to interact with people. She'd become an eccentric writer who had hidden herself away for too long.

Between the Arel fiasco and the awkward times with Peggy, Elise decided to move, to slip away quietly and start over. But for the moment, the best she could do was avoid neighborly contact. Her tight shoulders relaxed a little when she got to her mailbox without being seen. Her relief was somewhat diluted by the state of her mail. Circulars, junk mail and bills filled the box to capacity. As she tried to remove some of the excess, several pieces dropped to the ground. She was bending over to pick them up when someone jogged up to her.

"Hi, Elise!"

Her hand tightened on a utility bill. She recognized the male voice. It belonged to the young man who lived with Arel. She pasted on a smile and stood up. Trying to be pleasant was her penance for being so horrible to everyone when she was dating Arel. "Oh, hi Carey."

"Let me help you with that," he said as he crouched down. "By the way, one of your pieces of mail got mixed up with Arel's. I tried to return it to you yesterday, but you didn't answer the door."

Elise's brows automatically tightened into a scowl. Of course she didn't answer her door. She didn't want to see anyone. "Sometimes I have the music blasting when I'm working, and I don't hear the bell."

Hurriedly, she snatched more of her mail from the box, and more pieces fell to the ground. Carey picked up those letters too.

"Hand stuff to me," he suggested as she continued with her task.

She glanced at him and noticed how his eyes glowed. In fact, she'd never seen anyone who could look so enthusiastic. In spite of trying to stay in her usual serious mode, she laughed. "How'd you get so cheerful?"

Carey shrugged. "I have a great life. Arel has been really nice. He took me in when I was kind of homeless."

Elise winced. She'd stopped spying on Arel's house, but she still thought about him more than she wanted. "I haven't seen him around."

"He went to London. Now, he's in Paris."

Elise's chest took a hit. A sinking feeling grabbed hold, making it difficult to get air. But she'd started down a road called "I'm going to be nice no matter what." She couldn't turn back now. "I hope he's having a good time."

"He's having a great time. He even met a beautiful woman who—" Carey hesitated. "I'm sorry, I didn't mean to say—"

Elise spoke up at once in spite of a lump in her throat. "Carey, please, it's okay. Arel and I have nothing to do with each other. If he's met someone—"

Carey didn't answer. Instead, he quietly turned away and began to take the remainder of the mail from Elise's mailbox.

As Elise watched Carey diligently completing his task, she thought about his take on Arel. Carey thought of Arel as a very kind person, not at all like the scoundrel, Jack.

The information made Elise swallow hard. She'd made a terrible mistake and pushed away someone who was genuine. But she still had feelings for Arel. They were the kind that made her heart speed up when she let herself think about being with him. It didn't matter. Carey's slip of the tongue made it clear that it was too late for regret.

On the other hand, Elise had to find out more about what was going on. When Carey tried to hand her the mail, she didn't take it. She started for the house and glanced back at him. "Would you please bring that in for me? And by the way, I just bought a chocolate cake. Maybe you'd like a slice."

Carey quickened his pace and caught up with her. "Chocolate cake? How can I refuse?"

Once Elise had the young man seated at her kitchen table, she quickly served him a generous slice of cake and a large glass of iced tea. Strangely enough, her ravenous hunger, a hunger that had added five unwanted pounds, was absent. How could she think of food when there were important questions to be asked. She sat down opposite Carey and smiled. "So tell me more about Paris and Arel. How long is he planning on staying?"

Carey had just forked in a large bite of cake and blinked back. "Don't know," he sputtered. He took a swallow of tea and used his napkin to swipe his mouth. "Sorry, but this cake is delicious."

Elise didn't need a critique of the cake. She needed more facts about Arel. She forced herself to smile patiently. "So you said that Arel met someone."

Carey took another bite of cake and nodded.

"Did you know that I write books about people falling in love? I'm always curious about what it is that attracts one person to another."

Carey swallowed his second bite and smiled. "That one's easy in Arel's case." He took his phone out of his pocket and did a quick search. He handed the phone to Elise. "Take a look at the two of them. Don't they look great together?"

Elise tried to maintain a pleasant expression as she gripped the phone. Arel's handsome face stared back at her, but she was more interested in the woman he was with. Everything about her was gorgeous. Her features, her amazing hair, her thin, sexy body. She was something out of a glamour magazine. With Arel next to her, they looked like a movie star couple.

Elise handed the phone back to Carey as he was getting up from his seat. That's when she noticed he'd finished his cake. He was folding his napkin, ready to leave. She panicked. She still had questions, and she needed answers. "Let me get you another piece."

Carey rubbed his stomach. "Thanks, but I better not. I have to get back. I'm cleaning up the garage. I try to keep the place the way Arel likes it."

When they were dating, Elise had noticed that Arel was very tidy. Maybe he was also a bully when it came to house guests. "So, is he some kind of tyrant? Does he have you doing all the chores?"

Carey laughed. "No, it's more like me being a slob. He's always cleaning up after me."

Elise felt her temper getting ready to unload. She didn't want to see pictures of Arel with some Parisian goddess. She didn't want to hear about how tolerant he was. But she clenched her jaw and kept herself in check. She couldn't afford to alienate Carey. He seemed to be a great source of information that she wanted and needed. "Thank you again for helping me with my mail."

Carey smiled and started out of the kitchen. "Thanks for the cake." He stopped short before he got to the door and pointed to the laundry room. "Elise, there's some water on the floor—"

Elise pushed Carey aside. "Oh no, I'm storing some boxes in the laundry room! Quick, help me move them!"

Carey rushed forward and threw open the door. The source of the problem was immediately evident. The washing machine was overflowing. Carey grabbed his phone, tapped the screen a number of times and gave it to Elise. "Tell Michael to come over as fast as he can! He knows a lot more than I do about these things. In the meantime, I'll move the boxes."

* * *

Elise sat back on the living room sofa and looked at the piles of books and papers sitting on the rug. Some of the books had towels under them. They were the ones that got slightly water damaged in the laundry mishap. Her gaze traveled over to the two men who had saved them from a worse fate.

Michael and Carey were seated across from her. She sat up and broke the silence that had settled over the room. "Thanks for all your help. I don't have much experience with washing machines going haywire. Because of your fast rescue, my papers and books survived without much damage."

Michael returned a friendly smile. "If you ever need anything else, please don't hesitate to ask."

Michael had declined Elise's offer of an award in the form of dessert, but Carey was finishing off his piece of cake. He looked up as he was taking a bite and nodded. "Like Michael said, we like helping out."

Their offers made Elise sit up attentively. At the end of the month, when she packed up and moved away, she wanted to know how she'd gone so wrong in her interaction with Arel. Michael and Carey were his friends. Perhaps they could shed some light on the subject.

There was something else that made her want to see the pair again. When they were helping her, taking care of her run-away washer and cleaning up the aftermath, she'd never felt safer around anyone. That was something very new for her. Looking at Michael's kind eyes and feeling Carey's boyish enthusiasm, she felt a deep down sense of security. This pair was different. They weren't there to get something from her.

Now, they were offering their services again. As she pondered their thoughtfulness, an interesting idea surfaced. "Michael, Carey, do you think you could help me with a book I'm writing? I need a new perspective, a man's take on romance."

Eight

AREL TURNED AND put a hand under his head, propping it up at just the right angle to admire the woman lying next to him in bed. He'd heard about people dying and going to heaven. They were thought to be the lucky ones. But he was even luckier. He'd found heaven on earth.

Claire was probably the most beautiful woman he'd ever seen, with the exception of his first love, Justina. But there was so much more to Claire than outer beauty. She was strong and steadfast. She approached everything with an unswerving attitude. She was dedicated to her work and was selfless in her devotion to helping others. As he watched Claire sleeping, he knew he was experiencing a bit of paradise. If he never left their bed's soft confines, he'd be the happiest man alive.

When Claire finally stirred, she stared back at him with sleepy eyes. "You look very content. What are you thinking?"

Arel caressed her face, sure that he was touching his soul mate. As soon as the idea slipped in, he was confused. Soul mate? Was there such a person? He'd thought of Justina as his soul mate, but in a vision she'd indicated otherwise. It was a very puzzling topic.

Claire pressed for an answer. "Stop holding out, Arel, and tell me your thoughts."

He brought himself back to the moment and made a decision. It didn't matter if Claire was a soul mate or not. "I'm thinking that I'm happy just being with you. I want us to always wake up to each other."

Claire's brow creased. "I had a terrible nightmare last night. We were working together in a poor village, but you disappeared. I couldn't find you."

"I know all about bad dreams. I also know they don't mean anything unless you hold on to them. So let's forget everything but this moment, and what we can make of it."

60

Claire returned a playful look. "I'm open to suggestions."

Arel reached out and pulled her closer, kissing her softly and then more fervently. As love and desire surged through his body, he wanted it to invade Claire's body too, like a warm, sensual wave of devotion. Because that's what he intended his relationship with her to be. He'd failed Justina. He wouldn't make that mistake again. His connection to Claire would be lasting and true. He wanted to dedicate himself to her, to let her know that she could always count on him no matter what.

Claire responded with a giggle, then became more serious, as if she could read his thoughts. "I didn't know you existed until a few days ago. Now, look at us. We fit together very nicely."

Her statement was spoken in a light, playful tone, but Arel knew it was true as he ran his hand slowly up and down Claire's back. His touch was light and teasing as he began to kiss her neck.

Claire trembled with delight and returned a mischievous glance.

Arel paused just long enough to study her eyes. They were dark with mystery and the unknown. But he was determined to explore that unknown part of the woman who seemed like perfection itself. "When I touch you, I feel more alive than I've felt in a very long time," he whispered.

Claire buried her face in his chest and breathed deeply. "You remind me of Christmas and those wonderful spice cookies I love. You make me hungry, very hungry."

Arel smiled, tipped up her chin, and kissed her again.

Claire responded by letting out a breathless moan.

Arel immediately pulled her so close that he could feel both of their hearts beating, pounding with excitement. The vessels seemed to be waiting anxiously for that moment when they joined and gave themselves to each other with abandon. When he'd lost Justina, he didn't think he'd ever find someone who could share his passion so completely again. But he was sure Claire's eyes were as bright with want and need as his own.

* * *

Annabel stood at the entrance to the living room and stared at William. He was sitting on the sofa, studying a journal. As she noted his uneven brow, it was easy to feel his discontent. She'd ignored it until now, but she had to be honest with herself. The man she'd married wasn't happy. She let out a sigh of frustration. She needed to do something to stop whatever was causing his restlessness. But she didn't know what that something was.

William sighed. "Oh please, Annabel, stop always giving into your worries."

Annabel frowned back. William had spoken to her without even looking up from his magazine. She came forward and stopped a few feet in front of him. "Are you reading my mind?"

"Your mind is like a radio with the sound turned up. It's impossible not to know what you're thinking."

Annabel took a seat in a chair opposite the sofa. "Maybe that's just as well. I hate having to always explain myself."

William finally put his magazine aside. "What's there to explain? We both know what you want."

"I want us to love each other."

William held up his hand. A new wedding band was prominently displayed on his finger. "We're married, like you wanted. Isn't that enough?"

"William! Why are you being so cold?"

"You think I'm being cold, but I think I'm being candid about our situation." William sighed again. "Are you happy, Annabel? I don't think so. But you've convinced yourself that it's my fault."

Annabel looked away. William had a point, but it was a point that made her hold herself in a tight hug. "I don't know what I'm supposed to do. Can't you see that? When I still had my wings, I wasn't personally involved in people's lives."

"And if I had to evaluate the job you performed when you were an angel, I'd say you did it very well. Unfortunately, you seemed to forget everything as soon as you took off your wings. And that's why you're so miserable."

"I wasn't miserable until recently. I was happy." She gulped in some air. "Then you tossed your ring down the disposal."

"You were happy because you were living in a dream world, pretending that we were just another normal couple."

"And what's wrong with that?"

"It doesn't have anything to do with being truly alive."

"I don't understand."

"When you were an angel, what did you do?"

"I enjoyed helping people. It could be very challenging, but it also felt wonderful when people found ways to be happier."

"I've been thinking about angels a lot ever since Rolphe said I looked like one."

Annabel smiled. "Rolphe said that?"

"I thought he was crazy at first, but maybe I was wrong. When I was in Arel's world, with all your ex-friends around me, and they all looked to me for leadership—"

Annabel jumped up. "That's the problem. Your ego got inflated after that experience. Now, you want thrills instead of love and commitment."

William laughed. "I had those thoughts too, but it's not how I see any of it now. After recalling the time I spent on that battlefield, I understand that it wasn't my personality running the show. I had to forget about my supposed *big* ego to do what I did. I had to focus on the real me, the person who faces his fears and does what he thinks is best in spite of them. I still want that."

"So how does a normal life get in the way of you being who you are?"

"I'm still thinking that through."

"And how long will it take for you to come up with an answer?"

William twisted the gold band on his finger again. "What difference does it make to you? You're free to work on your sculpting or do whatever you like."

"I don't feel free!"

William picked up his journal. "That makes two of us," he said in a barely, audible tone.

Nine

ELISE SAT AT her desk, staring at a blank screen on the computer monitor. She thought she'd had the story outline for her next book worked out. She managed to finish the first chapters, but she was stuck. Events weren't going as planned. She couldn't get her main characters to fall in love. Her protagonist, Linda, was the principal problem. She was pretty but independent. When it came to her interactions with an attractive man named Mason, Linda became aloof. She adopted a hard as nails attitude to Mason's advances.

"My Linda character has hijacked my personality, the witch!" Elise rubbed her temples. The story's plot had begun to parallel her life. She hadn't intended it to happen. But recently, Linda and Mason made all the decisions about how the story line was proceeding. They wouldn't let Elise change their personalities or their reactions to each other.

As a writer, Elise was familiar with characters taking on a life of their own, but she had never had a female heroine who acted so completely in line with Elise's negative emotions. However, her stubborn protagonist wouldn't budge or allow Elise to move her in a more romantic direction. "This is a totally unacceptable situation! I have no time for a fictional character side-tracking my story!"

She'd battled the keyboard for hours that morning, trying to find words to put in the male character's mouth. She needed Mason to solve the problem. "But he's a complete idiot who doesn't know anything about handling a difficult woman!"

As soon as Elise spat out the statement, she knew she wasn't being fair. Her male character was simply too nice, and Linda the witch wouldn't listen or allow his sweetness to influence her.

Elise got up and scowled at the monitor. Her patience was long gone, and her anger was taking over. When it peaked, she didn't think, she acted. With a well-aimed thrust of her foot, she sent a nearby trash can flying. It slammed into the lower shelf of a bookcase. The sound of something breaking made Elise come back to herself. She rushed over to the bookcase and pushed the can aside.

"Oh no!" she screeched as she picked up the remains of a fragile statue. The little ballerina had been a gift from a friend in high school. The thoughtful girl knew Elise had always wanted to dance. The idea made Elise's mother laugh, but her friend tried to encourage her. The statue had remained a small reminder that at least somebody believed in her. Now, the figurine was missing its head and one arm.

As she sat on the floor and examined the damage, the doorbell rang. She was immediately irritated again. She didn't have time for interruptions. Then she remembered that she'd invited Michael and Carey to come over. As she got to her feet, she almost smiled. The two men had great timing. They'd arrived during another small crisis.

After she placed the broken ballerina on her desk, she visited the wall mirror by the office door. Her brows furrowed when she noted the numerous strands of blond hair sticking out at odd angles. They had escaped the little barrettes that were supposed to keep them under control.

She'd gone to a salon at the mall to have her hair trimmed. The woman at the reception counter had recommended a girl named Sissy, and Elise had taken a chance on the young woman. She was paying for her mistake. Her hair was much too short and totally unmanageable. "Dammit! It's going to take forever to grow out!"

When the doorbell rang again, Elise decided she needn't worry about her hair. Michael and Carey were just neighbors. Besides, she'd soon move away and never see them again.

She felt more at ease when she welcomed in her visitors. She even made small talk about the weather as she took Michael and Carey back to her office. But once she got them seated on the couch, she quickly got down to business. "You both got my text, right? You understand why I asked you here."

Carey gave Michael a nod and looked back at her. "Yes, we've been going over some possibilities for your story."

Elise leaned back in her office chair. "Good, because I have a deadline to meet. I don't have time to waste, especially since I'm moving soon. So tell me how my male character, Mason, can make some headway into Linda's closed-off heart."

Michael raised his hand. "We were thinking about a puppy."

"A puppy? That's ridiculous," Elise yelped. "What does a puppy have to do with a romance novel?"

Michael returned a curious look and stood up. "I'm sorry, Elise, I don't want to upset you. Maybe I better leave."

Carey stood up too. "He's right. Neither of us has a clue about writing."

Elise jumped up and held on to her temples. A steady throbbing had taken hold. "Just wait a minute, both of you. The first thing you need to learn is that you can't get jumpy every time I raise my voice. It's just the way I sometimes communicate."

Carey and Michael exchanged glances and sat down again. Both stared at Elise as if waiting for further instructions.

Elise returned to her seat. It was obvious that she had a couple of very sensitive guys on her hands. She'd have to try to appease them. "Alright, let's say I indulge you, Michael. Why a puppy?" She had wanted to say, "worthless puppy," but she'd stopped herself when she remembered that her father had thought in those terms. His statement still rang out loud and clear in her mind. "Dogs are a worthless waste of time and money."

Michael gave her a hopeful smile. "Sometimes animals can help when people don't know how to go forward. Maybe your character, Mason, thinks that the puppy will help Linda to be more open."

Elise blinked several times. "But I can't write about something like that. I never had a pet. My sister did, but I didn't. I wanted a dog like most kids, but my parents refused to get one for me."

Carey frowned. "So how did your sister get a pet?"

"My sister is the baby. She whined a lot, and my parents gave in to her." Elise paused and swallowed back the resentment that she still felt for her sibling. "I hated her dog, and it hated me. It bit me twice."

Carey's eyes brightened. "But a puppy might be the ideal gift for your heroine, Linda."

"Even so, how can I write about a subject I don't know anything about?" Elise asked.

Carey moved to the edge of his seat and offered Elise another smile. "You could do some research by getting a puppy. Then you could write about what it's like to have one."

For a moment, Elise flashed back to a time when she would have done anything to have a dog of her own. As an adult, she'd started to see her father's point. "Even if I went for your idea, I don't want the responsibility of a pet."

Michael spoke up. "You wouldn't have to keep the puppy. After you learned what you needed, you could find it a proper home."

Elise felt her mood lift a little. She had a book deadline, and she needed something to advance her story. Michael's suggestion was the only one she had to work with. Practically, the addition of a puppy in her story could have added benefits. People loved books with animals in them. Maybe a dog for Linda would sell more copies.

She stood up and began to pace. "If I got a dog, it would have to be a small one. I don't see myself using a king-sized pooper scooper. And it can't shed. I detest dog hair. Probably a Bichon Frise would do. They don't need a lot of exercise, just a daily walk. They do need to be groomed, but I wouldn't have it that long, would I!"

Carey gave her a curious look. "What kind of dog is a Bichon Frise?"

Elise smirked. "It's the kind I wanted when I was a kid. They're white and fluffy, sort of like a puff of fur."

"I thought you didn't know much about dogs."

Elise avoided Carey's eyes. She didn't want to admit that she'd read every dog book that she could get her hands on when she was a child. She'd even forgotten that fact herself. "Yes, well, I said I never had one, but I do know a little about breeds and stuff like that."

"You might be able to get one at an animal shelter," Michael said.

"No, I think I'll go to a breeder. I want a dog with a pedigree. It'll probably cost a considerable amount, but that's okay. It'll be easier to find it a home afterwards."

Elise went to her desk and got her car keys from a drawer. "Carey, could you do me a favor and get me a local paper so I can check the ads? You can use my car."

"Yes, ma'am," Carey said as he stood up and retrieved the keys.

Elise smiled at Michael as Carey rushed out the door. "Thanks for the idea. It's sort of brilliant. I never would have thought of it."

"You're welcome. Now, I better get back to some chores in my garden, but call me if you need anything else."

"Don't worry. You're at the top of the list if I get stuck again."

* * *

Elise hadn't thought that she'd have to call on Michael so quickly. But after Carey came back with a paper and the puppy ads, everything spun out of control. A breeder Elise called said she had one puppy left. Some interested party was going to look at the dog the next day. Elise had to act fast to get to the breeder's house first. But she didn't want to go alone. She needed all the support she could get. Since the dog was Michael's idea, it was only fair that he come along with her and Carey.

Afterwards, when the three of them returned to Elise's house, she was still in a state of shock. Strangely enough, she also felt rather content. She'd never dared to imagine that her childhood wish would come true. But it had come true. She marched through her front door with a small, white, curly-haired puppy cradled in her arms.

Carey followed with a dog crate and dog bed. Michael brought up the rear with dog food, food bowls, and bags of dog treats.

"One call to a breeder, and I'm stuck with this little mutt," Elise complained as she walked over to the sofa and sat down. She was trying very hard to maintain her usual stiff attitude around her neighbors. But it wasn't easy. The puppy was snuggled close, with slits for eyes as he dozed. Elise figured he'd worn himself out with excitement earlier.

"Where do you want this stuff?" Carey asked.

"Put it anywhere," she said as she held up her purchase for inspection. "But it is cute, isn't it?" She was talking more to herself than to Carey and Michael. They were busy putting away her purchases.

"I left the food and bowls in the kitchen," Michael said as he came over to inspect the puppy.

Elise looked up and frowned. "I didn't get much for my money. Plus, I wanted a female, but this little runt was the only one left." She let out a hiss. "Can you believe that woman's story? She claimed she was thinking about keeping the puppy for herself. Likely tale to drive up the price."

Michael stroked the puppy's head. "On the plus side, since he's a little older, she said he was almost housebroken."

Elise put the puppy down on the rug and watched it waddle forward a few steps. Then it ran back to Elise and began to scratch her shoe.

Carey smiled. "I think he wants to be picked up again."

Elise exhaled heavily as she gave in to the pup's demands. "How am I going to write if I have to hold it all the time?" Then she gave Carey a worried look. "I just hope it's not hard to find it a suitable home when I'm done with this silly experiment. I don't want my money back. I'll just want to find some good people who'll take proper care of the little thing."

Michael walked towards the door. "I'm sure it'll work out."

Elise felt her breath catch. "Michael, where are you going? You're not leaving me alone with this animal, are you?"

Michael laughed. "I think you two will do just fine."

Carey turned to leave too, but he paused long enough to give Elise a few words of advice. "Remember to let him out every couple of hours. That's what the breeder told me."

Elise's shoulders slumped. After ridding herself of Jack and the other men she'd dated, she hadn't thought about caring for anyone besides herself. Now, a small, helpless puppy was depending on her. She hurried after Michael and Carey as they were letting themselves out the door. "I can count on you guys if I need you, can't I?" she called after them.

Ten

PEGGY PUT HER phone on the table with wide, staring eyes. She was in such a state of surprise that she hardly noticed Tim when he walked into the kitchen. She was still processing some extraordinary information.

Tim came over and looked at her with concern. "Is everything alright?"

Peggy nodded and finally found her voice. "That was Arel on the phone. He called to tell me—" She paused and took a deep breath.

"Is he okay?"

Peggy nodded again. "He sounded so happy."

"About what?"

"Arel's getting married."

"You're kidding! Who's he marrying?"

"That woman he met a couple of weeks ago in Paris. Arel said she was wonderful, a woman with high ideals. I guess they liked each other right off."

Tim's face lit up with a broad grin. "So, Arel is tying the knot. Somehow I never thought it would happen."

Peggy pulled out a kitchen chair and sat down. "I hope he's not jumping into marriage too quickly. How can he be sure that this woman, Claire, is the right person for him?"

"Please, Peg, don't start. You've been hoping that Arel would find someone."

"Of course I want that. And thank goodness he found someone he thinks is perfect. When he was dating Elise, I cringed every time I saw them together."

"Have they set a date?"

"I didn't get any details. Arel said they were still in the planning stage."

Tim raised his brows and sighed. "She is very attractive."

Peggy scowled. "Oh please, Tim."

Tim laughed. "I'm just saying that Arel knows a good thing, that's all."

"Just because Claire is gorgeous, I'm going to reserve judgment. After I meet her, I'll decide if she's right for Arel."

"Peggy, it's none of our business."

Peggy stared at her phone with pursed lips. "You're right. And no matter what, the woman has to be better than Elise."

* * *

Annabel was a little apprehensive when Claire and Arel arrived. She didn't have much experience with entertaining guests. Happily, the evening started off nicely. Once everyone was seated in the newly finished, lower level, there was a general feeling of ease and coziness. Claire and Arel sat close, holding hands as they kept staring at each other. They seemed almost oblivious to their surroundings.

Earlier that afternoon, the couple had returned to London. After they checked into a hotel, they had stopped by for just a brief visit. When Annabel first saw Arel's face, she smiled. The man was clearly smitten with his fiancé. Claire's face was serene when she looked at Arel. Together, they projected a vision of dreamy commitment as if they were already joined together on some ethereal plane of happiness.

When they returned in the evening, they were still blissful. Annabel was happy for them, but she wondered if William felt the same way. He sat in his recliner, gazing out with eyes that were direct, focused and noncommittal. But whenever he glanced at Annabel, she felt uncomfortable.

Ever since their discussion, Annabel had been thinking about what William had said to her. She knew he had a point about how she'd been arranging her life. She pursued activities that were safe, but contained no passion. She'd contented herself with making little clay figurines. When she sat in her studio, she liked the idea of everything being secure and stable. She liked thinking of William always remaining close, working on projects around the home.

But William clearly stated that he needed more. It wasn't an unreasonable request. If Annabel still had her wings, she would have agreed with him. When the Creator started fashioning worlds, the souls who inhabited those worlds were supposed to let their

71

imaginations soar and expand. They were supposed to challenge boundaries and go beyond the known.

An angel could appreciate the idea of risks and possible danger, especially if a soul wanted to be free of restrictions. But Annabel didn't have an angelic perspective anymore. She was filled with the stuff of normal humans. That stuff often took the form of fear. She'd seen what could happen when William wanted to soar. He'd almost ended up dead.

Arel seemed to share Annabel's approach. He looked content to sit next to Claire and do nothing but admire her. For Annabel, it was the scenario that she'd fantasized about. If only William felt like Arel, their life would be heavenly.

She was just relaxing back into the idea of the idyllic romance when Claire began to talk about her life. Annabel sat up with anticipation, eager to learn more about the wistful states of love between a man and a woman. She wanted to feel validated by another woman's desire for a peaceful, harmonious co-habitation.

Annabel's dreams were crushed almost immediately. As soon as Claire engaged in laying out her views of the world, her eyes morphed. The softness was replaced by a fierce determination. Arel's pretty fiancé didn't dream about settling down and having a normal life. Quite the opposite.

* * *

William sat quietly, trying to remain objective. He had no desire to challenge Arel's choice of a partner. He and Arel were finally getting along, and he liked it that way. He'd even decided that his earlier feelings of a doomed relationship might be ill-founded. After all, Arel was extremely sensitive. He rooted out danger like a pig going after truffles. So if Arel looked totally at ease with the woman he'd asked to marry him, maybe William needed to do the same.

When William questioned Claire, his intention was to learn more about her, to access some practical facts. He deliberately kept his voice as neutral-sounding as possible. "Claire, tell us about yourself."

Claire sat up, looking delighted by the question. "I like solving mysteries. I guess that's one reason I decided on archaeology. How can we understand the cultures of today if we don't know about the people who came before us?"

Arel squeezed Claire's hand. "Claire's not only curious about the past, she's very involved in helping with the plight of the people of today. In her spare time, she volunteers to go to places like Africa to help the less fortunate." His eyes glowed with admiration. "She inspires me to be a better person."

Claire smiled. "Thank you, Arel. I'm pleased that you understand where I'm coming from."

Arel nodded adoringly. "I'm looking forward to knowing everything about you."

Claire gave him a dismissive smile. "I'm sure we'll definitely explore more as time goes on. However, I wanted to comment on Annabel and William's home." Her dark eyes did a quick sweep of her surroundings. "I feel like I'm in a model house."

Arel laughed. "That's exactly what I said!" He looked at Annabel, then William. "Can you two believe how much Claire and I think alike?"

Annabel shrugged, as if she hadn't heard Arel's comment. "William did most of the remodeling. I'm content to sit back and enjoy his handiwork. When he started, it had tile flooring and wallboard. That's about it."

"This room makes me think about redoing my lower level," Arel said. "I like the lighter look William has achieved."

"Your place is gorgeous, Arel," Annabel protested. "Claire, wait until you see his home. Everything is perfect."

Claire looked at Arel with a frown. "I hope it's not too perfect. I'm not the neatest person when it comes to housekeeping."

William raised his brows. "Don't worry. Arel will whip you into shape."

Arel frowned. "I'll do no such thing. Whatever Claire does is fine with me."

Claire laughed. "My last roommate said I was the worst housekeeper that she'd ever seen. However, I do have a split personality. When I'm working on a dig, I'm extremely neat."

Arel sat up proudly. "Claire's been asked on a very important project. Tell them about your new adventure, my love."

"I'd already committed to going to Africa before I met Arel. Our wedding plans will have to be put on hold for a little while."

Arel's face lost some of its glow. "We're going to be apart for about six weeks, but after that, Claire is joining me in Chicago. We'll plan the wedding together, no expense spared."

Claire nudged him. "You are the biggest romantic on the planet, but I'd prefer something small and informal."

Arel smiled back. "Whatever you want is what I want."

William could see that Arel meant every word. The man who had argued with William from day one was the opposite around Claire. Totally compromising, he looked like an ill-treated, hungry animal that had been adopted and was thankful for every scrap of kindness that came its way. William had no problem with gratitude, but he did question Arel's self-image. On the other hand, Claire looked completely content with herself. Her eyes were clear and focused on what she wanted.

* * *

After the visit with Annabel and William, Arel was still floating on clouds as he and Claire taxied back to their hotel. His euphoric state was becoming the norm. During his weeks in Paris with Claire, he wanted to shake himself to make sure the woman he loved was real.

When he opened the door to their room and turned on the light, he did have a moment of hesitation. Claire had insisted that room service be dismissed. She didn't believe that sheets should be changed every day or that other people should work on her behalf. Resources needed to be respected, not squandered on petty human desires. It had taken quite a bit of effort on Arel's part to get her to stay at an upscale hotel. She only conceded when he told her it was a very special occasion. They were celebrating their engagement.

The room was classy, but he did have to be careful as he walked to the bedroom closet. Claire's habits were different than his. Her clothes were casually thrown to the floor as she undressed. An assortment of garments littered the floor like leaves in fall, littering the lawn. When they were in Paris, staying at Claire's apartment, he'd been tempted to pick up after Claire. He stopped himself in time to remember how unimportant it was to maintain his sense of tidiness. He had been given a precious gift, a woman who made his heart sing. Everything else was trivial in comparison.

His reasoning was reinforced when he and Claire went to bed that night. They were in each other's arms immediately, enjoying the warmth and hunger of each other's bodies. They made love in a timeless place of joy. It was a place that made Arel's personal habits and idiosyncrasies seem ridiculous.

Eleven

WHILE ANNABEL AND Claire went shopping together, William had a chance to talk to Arel in private. They sat in the upstairs living room. Arel had taken a seat on the sofa, looking slightly dazed. William shifted in his chair, determined to remain as impartial as possible. He made sure that his opening statement was purposefully dispassionate. "I hope Annabel and Claire enjoy their outing."

Arel sighed. "Yes, our two gorgeous women are together. I love that."

William nodded. "It gives us a chance to catch up."

Arel leaned forward and straightened the magazines on the coffee table. "With everything that's happened, I haven't had a chance to talk to anyone. I did give everybody back home a quick call to tell them the news about getting married. I think they were all surprised."

William forced a smile. "Yes, but as long as you're happy, that's what counts."

Arel's gaze shifted to William for only an instant before he looked away. He stared down at the arm of the couch. With narrowed brows, he studied the upholstery. It seemed to draw him in. After a moment, he touched it with flighty fingers. They danced over the fabric, as if his mind was still searching and unsure. But after a moment, he began to rub the slightly uneven weave in earnest. When he finally spoke up, his voice was cautious, but direct. "So what do you think? Have I found the perfect person?"

William hesitated, distracted by Arel's preoccupation with his sofa. Arel had a habit of interacting with his surroundings. Sometimes that interaction resulted in unintentional harm to whatever he was focused on. "Arel, please, would you stop messing with the furniture. Remember the last time?"

"What?" Arel looked up and smiled sheepishly. "Oh, you're right. Sorry about the time I pulled on that nub of thread." He inspected the sofa arm with a discerning eye. "Don't worry, at least the glue seems to be holding. But you're right. I need to concentrate." He stood up and reseated himself in the middle of the couch.

William sighed. "I'm sorry too. I didn't mean to sidetrack you. You were asking about Claire."

"Yes, she's a saint in a perfect woman's body."

"She's very beautiful."

"She's the person I've always wanted in my life, someone I can love." He paused and clasped his hands together in a tight grip. "And more importantly, she's someone who can love me."

"You make it sound like loving you is a chore."

Arel scowled back. "Isn't it? Caring about me has been a nightmare for you."

"That's because you made it almost impossible to care. Remember when we met? You went around acting like you were worthless. When I tried to point out how gifted you were, you never listened."

Arel returned a weak smile. "But that's all changed, hasn't it?"

"Yes, I suppose it has. Still, bringing someone into your life is a big step. Do you think you have enough of yourself to take that step?"

"Look, I made a terrible mistake with the first woman I loved. Justina was a gift, and I turned my back on it. But I've learned from that mistake."

"What did you learn?"

Arel's face went suddenly pale. "Justina and I were both very young. I wanted to break off the relationship because I didn't feel I could live up to her expectations. Like you just explained, I was very depressed. I didn't think I had anything of value to give in a relationship. When I tried to express myself, Justina took everything I said the wrong way. She felt totally rejected and went into a fit of anger and outrage. Before I could stop her, she killed herself."

"Arel, you tried your best. And the bottom line is that you can't save anyone. Look at what happened when I tried to save you? You hated me for it. All you could think about was getting revenge."

Arel sat up in his seat and gave William a contrite smile. "For the record, no matter how I reacted, I'm thankful for what you did. And I'm very sorry for the way I behaved."

"But the point is that I didn't save you. I might have passed on a virus that extended your life span, but in the end, you had to save yourself."

77

"Fine, but we're getting off the subject. I've found someone to be with, and I refuse to do anything that might ruin what I have."

William saw that their conversation was doing the opposite of what he'd intended. Instead of considering his relationship from an unbiased point of view, Arel was digging in his heels. "Arel, believe me when I say that I just want the best for you."

Arel's shoulders relaxed a little. "Thank you."

William tried to find a more detached subject. "By the way, I'm still curious about that woman Elise that you dated back in Chicago."

Arel crossed his arms. "I can't believe I wasted my time. Elise was horrible. And in the end, she broke off the relationship."

"Why did you go out with her? You never explained that part."

"She was really rather pathetic, so angry and hostile all the time. I guess I wanted to show her some kindness."

"As far as a lasting relationship, it sounds like you already felt she was unsuitable—"

"Absolutely unsuitable, but we do have Michael's blood. I guess I wanted to go beyond normal duty and—"

"And what? Be a sacrificial lamb on some dragon lady's altar of bitterness."

Arel smiled. "Of course not. Like I said, I've been trying to be more like Michael."

"I don't think that's the way angels work. Take Annabel. When she had her wings, she never gave an inch. She challenged me constantly."

Arel fidgeted again, drumming his fingers on the sofa cushion. "I hate challenges."

"So, did you finally tell this Elise person how you felt?"

"No, what good would that do?"

"Maybe the woman would have had a chance to defend herself."

"Defend herself against me?"

"Of course. You set yourself up as judge and jury. She didn't have any place to go."

"Will, are you getting upset with me?"

William looked upwards and frowned, studying a small crack in the plaster ceiling. He was the one who was getting off base emotionally. "You're right. I'm probably upset with myself, and I'm taking it out on you."

"What's bothering you?"

"Where do I start?" The words slipped out before William could stop himself. But he needed to share some of his feelings with Arel. The man was bent on a relationship without thinking about their complexities. "I love Annabel, but she still has so many fears about life. If she had her way, I think she'd wrap me up like one of her clay figurines and keep me on a shelf, safe and secure from any danger."

Arel's face flushed a deep red. "I'm the one responsible for most of her fear. If I hadn't gone half-mad—"

"Stop it, Arel. If you want to be some continual, contrite sinner, that's your business, but each of us is responsible for our life."

"Sorry, I guess I still get confused about it all."

"Don't you realize that sometimes craziness is part of something bigger and better?"

"What do you mean?"

"Going up against you on that battlefield was one of the best experiences of my life. It should have been one of your best too. Talk about challenges, we both had something extremely difficult to face, and we faced it. Afterwards, we both knew we not only survived, we were stronger and better for the experience."

Arel looked down, but a smile slowly spread across his face. "I'll never forget what you told me when the battle was over. You said I wasn't broken, that I'd never been broken. Michael used to tell me stuff like that, but when you said it, I heard it. It sunk in."

"It sunk in because you finally realized it was true."

"Yes, it was one of the most enlightening moments of my life."

"And we can have more enlightening moments if we allow ourselves to keep going after what we want."

"I don't know about that, but—"

"What is it?"

Arel's smile slipped away. "Tell me what I should have done with Elise? From what you just said, I feel like I failed her in some way."

"If you really cared about her well-being, you should have never dated her and led her on."

"Led her on?"

"Yes, you're a very charismatic man. The poor thing probably had a crush on you."

"But she was so distant."

"People know when they're being judged and don't have a chance. But she probably liked you and didn't want to get hurt."

"A couple of times, I nearly let my temper get the best of me. I wanted to tell her what a hateful person she was."

"At least you would have been honest."

"Should I apologize to her?"

"Let it go. Learn from it. Start being truthful instead of acting like some saint."

"I'm honest with Claire. I tell her what I feel, that she's incredible."

"If you say so."

"What are you getting at?"

"You've decided that she's perfect, right?"

"Yes."

"That's another judgment. It's how you've decided to see her."

"I can't help it. When I look at her—"

"You're in love with love," William said. "But you need to see past your ideas of perfection and look at Claire, the person. Are the two of you truly compatible? Do you share enough views on life to co-exist in harmony?"

Arel laughed off his question. "She's smart and dedicated. And if she sees things differently, I'll adjust."

William almost commented, but he held his tongue. He was struggling with his own relationship. Why should he think that he had any answers? Still, when he studied Arel's bright, expectant eyes and boyish expression, his protective side couldn't be silenced. "I wish you the best, I really do. But please, be careful."

* * *

The small café was one of Annabel's favorite places for lunch. She sat across from Claire at a table located by a window. Lacey curtains filtered the light and added to the coziness. The eatery had a nice assortment of sandwiches and amazing desserts, including their specialty, Sticky Toffee Pudding. Thinking about its thick, rich, warm toffee sauce helped Annabel forget the morning she'd had with Claire. "I hope you like this place as much as I do."

Claire tossed back her dark hair and glanced around. "I rarely eat out. It seems like a waste of money when so many people in the world are starving."

Annabel's breath caught as she picked up her menu. The thought of starving people made her stomach tighten. How was she supposed to enjoy pudding when others in the world had nothing? The guilt she'd felt during her shopping trip with Claire returned immediately.

Arel's fiancé seemed to have very definite ideas about Annabel's conduct. When they were browsing in a small boutique earlier, Annabel had found a dress she liked. Its pretty, blue floral-print would have gone perfectly with a pair of shoes she'd recently bought. As she was taking it to the counter to pay for it, she noticed Claire's reproachful look. It was so stern and disapproving that Annabel wondered if something was wrong.

When she asked for Claire's opinion, Claire questioned her. Did Annabel need another dress? Of course, the answer was no. She and William had gone shopping on numerous occasions. William had made sure that Annabel's closet was filled with an assortment of garments for all occasions. Question number two. Did Annabel understand how the money spent on another dress could help the needy? When Annabel returned a look of confusion, Claire lectured her on personal responsibility.

After Claire finished her lecture, Annabel abandoned the dress and quickly left the shop. She'd hoped that lunch would help both of them relax. They could talk about topics that didn't involve anything too serious. With starving people topping the conversation, Annabel started to panic.

Claire frowned. "Are you okay? You look a bit wilted."

Annabel smoothed out the napkin in her lap. "I don't feel very hungry after all."

"I thought you said you were famished."

Before Annabel could answer, the waitress approached their table. "Annabel, so nice to see you again."

"Hi Dorothy," Annabel said. "I'm here with my friend, Claire."

The waitress smiled politely. "What can I get you two today?"

Annabel looked at Claire. "What would you like, Claire?"

Claire snapped the menu shut and handed it to the waitress. "I'll have a cup of chicken soup and a glass of water, please."

Annabel hesitated, then handed in her menu too. "I'll have the same."

The waitress frowned back. "Really, Annabel? You usually have your favorite, a tuna sandwich, curly fries and coleslaw."

Annabel kept her eyes averted. "Thanks, but I'll just have the soup."

"Annabel, get whatever you usually get," Claire said in an insistent tone.

Annabel stood up and put a hand to her stomach. It felt very queasy. "Claire, you're right. I don't feel well. Would you mind if we leave? I think I need to lie down."

Dorothy offered a kindly smile. "I'm sorry, dearie. Hope you're feeling better soon."

Claire stood up too. "I'm afraid you'd never survive the digs I go on, Annabel. And when I think about some of the remote places I've seen, let's just say you'd fold after the first day."

Annabel started for the door. "I guess you're right."

Once they were outside, Annabel hurried down the sidewalk, but she didn't get very far before Claire took hold of her arm.

Claire had more advice to impart. "Do you know what I do when I'm not feeling well?"

"No, what's that?"

"Stand up straight and breathe, Annabel. You have to take in some oxygen and get your blood circulating. You have to take command of your body and let it know what you want."

As Claire continued with her instructions, Annabel tried to comply obediently. She took a number of deep breaths and stood at attention. But in the back of her mind, she was also counting the minutes until she was back in her own home and out of Claire's clutches.

* * *

William waved farewell as he watched Arel and Claire climb into a taxi. Since the couple would be parting company the next morning, they seemed anxious to spend the rest of the day alone. After his conversation with Arel, he'd returned to a more impartial position. After all, he'd told Arel that people were responsible for themselves. He had to adopt that viewpoint when he thought about Arel and Claire.

He had barely closed the front door when Annabel came tiptoeing in from the hall. When she'd returned from her shopping trip with Claire, she'd complained of feeling sick and having to go to bed. Now, her face was bright and her cheeks were rosy again. "You look like you're feeling better."

Annabel paused long enough to give the room a quick once over. "Are they gone?"

"Yes, they just left. I didn't know you wanted to say goodbye. You looked so ill earlier and—"

"Oh, William, my darling, sweet William!" Annabel sang out as she ran over to him.

Before William had a chance to respond, Annabel flung her arms around him so enthusiastically that he had to brace himself to keep from stumbling backwards. "What's going on?" he asked with a curious grin.

Annabel hugged him even tighter. "Do you know how wonderful you are?"

William put his arms around her and smiled. "Yes, actually I do, but I didn't think you'd noticed."

Annabel closed her eyes and continued to hold on to him. "After spending some time with a very harsh person, I've come to my senses."

"Are you talking about Claire? What happened?"

"Oh, William, how could I have complained about you? You're gentle and sweet. You have your ideas about life, but you're not a bully. You're always taking me out to eat and wanting me to enjoy life. You're always encouraging me to have faith in myself. You're the best man in the world."

"That's nice to know."

Annabel pulled back a little. "Claire talked about mysteries the other night. Well, now we have one that needs solving."

William studied Annabel's narrowed brows. "What mystery?"

"Maybe it's me, but I can't understand how Arel can possibly be in love with that woman. How can he want to spend the rest of his life with someone who nearly drove me crazy after only a few hours?"

Twelve

AREL KNEW THAT he was dreaming, but he was so angry, he couldn't wake himself up. The argument he was having with Elise was the worst ever. His dream body had never felt so volatile, like it had been wired up to a bomb and the timer was ready to go off at any moment. His speech was explosive too. "You're a bloody witch! Except for my spiteful mother, you're the most, intolerable woman I've ever met!"

Elise stood in front of him with her hands on her hips. When she replied, her caustic voice was deafening. "Your mother? She must have been a female viper to give birth to the likes of you!"

"Why can't you speak in a civil tongue instead of yelling like a banshee?"

"What choice do I have? I'm dealing with a pompous, conceited, arrogant phony!"

"You're insane! I treated you like a queen in spite of your toxic outlook!"

"That's a laugh! I thought I had it bad before, but at least the other men I dated showed their colors. But you pretend to be lily white, you lying scum!"

"Have you seen yourself? You belong in a cage, like all the other vicious animals!"

With her face livid with rage, Elise gestured back with her finger.

Arel didn't think his anger could escalate, but he felt his blood getting so hot, he was afraid it would begin to boil. Luckily, before that happened, someone shook him. He opened his eyes and squinted. As he came awake, he sighed with relief. "Claire?"

"Arel, wake up!"

Arel looked around and realized that he was in their hotel room. "What a nightmare I had," he gasped.

"I can only imagine from the shouting that you were doing. I was in the bathroom, brushing my teeth, and I heard all this cursing."

84

"I'm so sorry," he whispered. "I was dreaming about that woman I told you about."

Claire gave him a sterner look. "Elise?"

Arel tried to slow the pounding in his chest. "Yes, dating her wasn't one of my smartest moves. I guess I felt sorry for her."

"So why would you dream about her?"

"It's William's fault. He told me I should have confronted her. I think his suggestion got buried in my subconscious."

"Oh, William, I see. Instead of remodeling rooms and advising you, maybe he should invest his energy in something more productive."

Arel pulled her close. "Forget William, we have planes to catch later. Let's make the most of the time we have."

Claire leaned in close and kissed him. "I agree," she said as she ran her hand over his chest. "I'm going to miss you."

"Are you sure? When you talk about that project you're involved in, your eyes light up."

"They light up because I love my work. You'd understand that feeling if you were involved in something you were passionate about too."

Arel blinked back awkwardly. His life didn't measure up to much when he compared it to Claire's. "When we're married, maybe you can help me find something worthwhile to do too."

Claire laughed. "Of course I will."

* * *

Elise hurried to her bedroom, slightly panicked. Her new puppy, Freddie Poo, was protesting his confinement in no uncertain terms. She hated to put the puppy in his doggie crate, but at times, she had no choice. If her writing stalled or her frustration levels soared, she had to vent. She didn't want the puppy around during those emotional tirades. She was ashamed to have him present when she inflicted more punishment on the trash can. On the plus side, she was getting better at staying calm for longer periods.

What she couldn't tolerate was hearing Freddie Poo's cries of distress. The sounds not only grated on her nerves, they made her feel a sense of urgency she'd never felt before. "Fine, I'm here!" she called out as she stopped in front of the puppy's crate. When she leaned down to look in, two black, round eyes stared back at her. A small paw scratched at the grate. When she hesitated for just a moment, the puppy yowled again.

"You little bugger," she cooed as she undid the latch. "You know how to get your way, don't you?"

Once she swung open the door, Freddie Poo bolted forward, tripped over a bit of towel padding and tumbled out. Once he recovered his footing, he immediately came over and pawed at her slipper. She tried to be disgusted, but she could only manage a state of amusement as she scooped him up and held him close. She knew she was getting attached to the little dog, but she couldn't help it. He was the most adorable creature she'd ever seen.

The doorbell rang as she carried him into the living room. "Coming," she said in a subdued tone. She was very aware of the puppy's sensitive ears, especially when he was nestled in his usual spot under her chin.

Life had become more complicated having the puppy around. Feeding him, taking him out, and playing with him took up more of her day than she wanted. She was trying to write a book for goodness sake. However, having Freddie Poo around did have its plus side. She didn't think about Arel as much. Arel's friends were a different story.

It was strange, but she liked having Carey and Michael come over for visits. When she opened the door and saw them waiting on the porch, she even gave them a sincere smile. "Thanks for coming," she said as she gestured them in. "I need to pick your brains again."

Once the three of them convened in her office, Elise put Freddie down on the floor. As he ran off to explore, Elise explained the cluttered condition of the room. The rug was completely covered with blankets and towels. "Looks like a mess, but Freddie Poo didn't get his name for nothing. I got wrapped up in the writing yesterday and forgot to take him out."

"Do you want me to take him out now?" Carey asked as the puppy sniffed at the blankets and pawed enthusiastically.

Elise shook her head. "It's okay. I took him out fifteen minutes ago. He's looking for this." She picked up a chew snack from the desk. "I was saving it. While you're here, it'll keep him occupied."

She crouched down and waved the treat in front of the puppy. "Come here, Freddie."

Hearing his name, Freddie's head jerked up, and he looked at Elise. When he saw what she was holding, his short legs were instantly put into forward drive. He ran over, but paused before he went for the treat. When he retrieved it from her hand, he was very careful.

Elise smiled her approval. "See that? He's so smart. At first he grabbed it like a rude, little scoundrel, but he's learning manners."

She stood up and sighed. "Now, for the bad news. I'm not blaming anyone, but—" She paused and looked at Michael.

Michael came to attention. "Bad news?"

"Sorry, Michael, but the puppy idea didn't work. My heroine fell in love with the dog, but she still wouldn't give Mason the time of day. Which brings me to another problem. Mason isn't as well adjusted as I'd hoped he'd be. His father wanted a boy and got a boy, but it didn't end there. The jerk wants to tell his son how to live his life. Mason is getting sidetracked."

"What's your ultimate goal with the situation?" Carey asked.

"I want Mason and Linda to let go of their problems and be happy! Is that too much to ask?"

Michael spoke up. "How realistic do you want your novel to be?"

"It's a romance, but it's supposed to be believable."

"You could rewrite the part about the father."

"But I don't want a two dimensional character. Mason has to have a life, some background."

"Write about him in a way that says he came from a happy home," Carey suggested.

Elise paused. "Is there such a thing? Really? Does anybody get a break in this world?"

"Look at Carol and Kevin's little boy. I think he'll grow up just fine."

"And he'll automatically be happy?" Elise asked. "If my parents had been sweet, I'd be sweet too?"

Carey frowned back, but didn't comment.

Elise rubbed her forehead. "Anyway, there has to be conflict for a story to be interesting to the readers. And I'm good at that, but I wanted this story to be special. So I'm making the characters more complex. What I need from you two is some answers. If Mason has a villain for a father, how do I fix his situation? He needs to be free. That way he can be the noble prince charming and save Linda from herself."

Carey and Michael exchanged glances and remained silent.

Elise sighed. "So you don't have a clue either. I was afraid of that." She pushed herself out of her chair. "Okay, you can go home. Sorry that I bothered you."

Carey held up a hand. "I have a thought, but you probably won't like it."

"I'm listening," Elise said.

"Mason decides that he's had enough. He tells his father that he's going to do what he wants to do."

Elise remembered wanting to voice her feelings with her father, but he'd always been too domineering. However, Mason was a man. He'd probably have the guts to stick up for himself. "Yes, that's a possibility. Mason could tell his father to go to hell, right?"

Carey grinned. "Maybe, but if he wanted to maintain the relationship, he might go easy on the hell part."

Elise waved him off. "Whatever, let's move on to Linda. How does Mason break through her harsh personality?" She glanced at Michael. "And please, no more pets. I don't want Linda to end up with her own zoo."

"He could back off and stop pursuing her," Carey offered.

Carey's suggestion took Elise by surprise. "Right, like Arel wanted to do with me!" The words spewed out in spite of her attempt to remain passive. "I bet you two agreed with him."

"Is that what you think?" Carey asked.

When Elise saw Carey's boyish expression fade, she sat back in her chair. "Sorry, don't mind my paranoia. I got off the topic."

Carey's eyes brightened. "What I meant is that Linda might feel overwhelmed by someone pursuing her directly. If Mason gives her some space, she might be more secure when they meet again."

"Why does she need to feel secure? She's hard as nails."

"How did she get like that?" Michael asked.

Elise laughed. "As a young woman, she was knocked around. She learned to be hard or suffer the consequences."

"Does she believe that there's such a thing as a good man?"

"How can she? They've all been brutes."

Michael sat back. "That's a difficult situation."

"Yes, it is," Elise said in a firm tone. "In Linda's mind, it's more than difficult. It feels hopeless."

"Hopeless? How?" Carey asked.

Elise sighed. "I think it started in Linda's childhood. Like Mason, Linda had an overbearing father."

As Elise explained her character's back story, her own story resurrected itself. Michael mentioned good men, but all she could think about were people like Jack. Day in and day out, she'd listened to men telling her how life was supposed to be. They were the important people in the world, and she, a lowly woman, had only one function, to serve them. She gradually got to a point where she stopped trying to please. She walked out of her last relationship with a suitcase in her hand and a few dollars in a secret, bank account. Living on her own was scary at first, but it was better than being with a guy. Unfortunately, she'd lost her zest for life along the way.

Just thinking about her depressing state made her head pound. She hoped it didn't turn into a migraine. She glanced at Carey and Michael. "Thanks, you've given me lots of ideas to work on. Maybe I can get some chapters written. We can start fresh tomorrow."

"Any time," Michael said as he stood up.

Carey stood up too and turned to follow Michael out of the office. As Elise watched them leave, her loneliness came back more powerfully than ever. She was stuck like her character, Linda. Neither of them could move on. In Elise's case, she'd become one of those old, cranky spinsters who lived alone forever.

"Oh lord, it's straight downhill from here," she mumbled to herself. Her wave of self-pity cut so deep that her eyes welled up. As she swiped at her wet cheeks, Carey looked back from the doorway.

"Are you okay?" he asked.

Carey's face was a mixture of concern and youthful promise. Why hadn't she met a man like him instead of Jack? So many years of her life had been wasted on cheats and liars. She grabbed a tissue and tried to speak, but she knew she'd sound pathetic. Instead, she shrugged.

Michael returned a moment later. He looked over Carey's shoulder with bright, sky-blue eyes. "Would you like us to stay for a little while?"

Elise sat down on the couch. "I don't know. I'm having a ridiculous, pity party. It sometimes happens when I get writer's block."

Michael moved Carey aside and walked over. "I just had a thought about your heroine."

Elise wiped her nose again. "Go on."

Michael sat down next to her. "You said you didn't want a two dimensional character, but I think that's how you've portrayed Linda. We know she's had a tough background, but you've kept her stuck there. What about this? People can change. They can mature into well-rounded persons."

Carey sat down on Elise's other side. "Michael's right. You should have seen me when I first met Arel. He said I was hot-headed and impulsive. He claimed I had a chip on my shoulder."

Elise sat up and stared at him. "Really? You seem so even tempered and happy."

"I guess I am. The more I was around Arel and Michael, the more they insisted that I was okay. Before that, I guess I did act like a person who had a lot of hang-ups."

Michael laughed. "Remember that dinner party when you started to storm out of Arel's house?"

Carey nodded. "When a person feels worthless, they do a lot of crazy things."

Elise blinked back the last of her tears as she thought about her character, Linda, and writing again. Michael's ideas and Carey's contribution were possibilities that might turn the story around. "Okay, let's bounce around a couple of ideas."

Carey's hand shot up. "I've got it! What if Linda has had time to get some perspective on her past? She's learned enough to trust her judgment about men. She knew she wouldn't let herself be fooled anymore."

Elise rubbed her brow. "I guess that could happen."

Michael nodded his agreement. "And when it came time to choose a partner, she'd be careful and pick a man who had integrity."

Elise surprised herself and smiled. "She'd pick a man like—" She stopped herself when she almost said the name, Arel. "She'd pick a man like Mason."

"And Mason can be a person who's grown too," Carey said.

Elise felt a small glint of hope trickle in. Even if her own life was hopeless, at least her characters could have a chance at something better. "How would Mason change?"

Carey grinned back. "If he stood up to his father, I think he'd have the confidence to approach Linda, don't you?"

As Elise saw her book coming into focus, she was about to get up to jot down some notes. Instead, she felt Freddie trying to get her attention by scratching her foot.

Carey bent down, retrieved the small puppy and handed him to Elise. "I think Freddie wants his mom."

Elise held Freddie close. "Mom? I never thought of myself that way."

Carey laughed. "I think Freddie does."

Elise held Freddie up and looked at his black, shiny eyes and his tiny, pink tongue. He was giving the air puppy licks. "Thank goodness I only have a dog to worry about. The little guy is enough of a burden. I'm sure I'd be terrible with a kid."

Carey gave her a troubled look. "Please, don't say that. You've been very kind to me, Elise."

Elise laughed at how serious Carey suddenly sounded. "Fine, I'll try to be more positive if it will make you happy."

Carey sat back contentedly. "Thanks, I'd appreciate that."

Thirteen

WHILE TIM WAS getting ready for work, Peggy stared out the front window with her morning coffee in hand. Two doors down, Elise was out in her yard with her new puppy. It was bouncing around in the grass like a tiny, white bunny. Peggy smiled. Animals were her weak spot. As a child, she was always excited when a stray dog or cat wandered by.

Carol had already met Elise's puppy. She'd gone by Elise's house while taking little Ariel out in the stroller. Elise had been very friendly. She even brought the puppy over so that little Ariel could pet him. It seemed out of character for Elise.

Peggy turned to Tim when he joined her at the window. "Do you think I've been too harsh? I've said some very unkind things about our neighbor."

"What neighbor?" Tim asked.

"Elise, of course. Carol seems to think she's not as bad as I first thought."

"She did seem grateful that night we helped her out."

Peggy handed Tim her mug. "Yes, and she's tried to be nice ever since, but I thought it might be an act."

Tim took a sip of Peggy's coffee and smiled. "You've got great instincts. You have to trust them."

"I do, but I'm starting to feel better about Elise. Maybe Carey and Michael are having an influence on her."

"What do they have to do with Elise?"

Peggy frowned. "I don't know. But I've seen them going over to her house on a couple of occasions."

"Sounds like you've been a one-woman neighborhood watch."

"I'm curious."

Tim's smile broadened. "I better get going. I've got an early morning meeting to attend."

Peggy started for the kitchen and went directly to the refrigerator. "Don't forget your lunch. I knew you were going to have a busy day, so I packed you a tuna fish sandwich, fruit, and some oatmeal cookies."

Tim had followed her into the kitchen and took the lunch bag. "Thank you. It'll make things easier if I don't have to go out for lunch."

"Don't get too stressed, Tim."

Tim kissed her cheek. "I'll be fine, but I do have a suggestion for you."

"What's that?"

Tim gave her a teasing glance. "Invite Elise over and tell her to bring her puppy."

Peggy blushed. "I would love to see the little guy close up. Carol said his name is Freddie."

"So tell Elise to bring Freddie when she visits."

Peggy followed Tim into the hall. "Maybe you're right. I'll get to meet the puppy and also see if Elise's attitude is improving. I might even find out how Michael and Carey are involved."

* * *

Elise stood at Peggy's front door with Freddie in one hand and a box of pastries in the other. She'd already rung the bell and was waiting for Peggy to answer the door. She kept repeating a mantra to herself. "I'm not going to get nervous this time."

When the door opened, and she saw Peggy, the words stuck in her throat. All that she could manage to do was hold out the pastry box to Peggy. "Uh, hope you like filled doughnuts."

Before Peggy could reply, Freddie started to squirm. He'd spied a potential pack member and was eager to introduce himself. He was struggling so hard, Elise panicked. She was afraid she was going to drop him.

Peggy came to the rescue. With a big smile, she took the puppy from Elise and held him close. "My goodness, aren't you the cutest and friendliest little guy."

Elise felt her nerves relax a little. "He loves people, but sometimes he gets so excited."

Peggy waved her inside. "That's normal for a puppy. He'll probably calm down as he gets older."

Elise followed Peggy into the kitchen. "Having Freddie is so new for me. I hope I'm doing the right things."

Peggy put Freddie down on the tile floor and laughed again. "He looks very happy."

"Oh, maybe he's too happy," Elise said as Freddie took off running. His feet lost traction for only a moment, slipping on the smooth floor. Once he got his footing, he took off. He ran out of the kitchen with Elise trailing after him. "Freddie, come back here!"

Peggy followed too. "It's okay. He just wants to explore. He'll come back once he gets the lay of the land."

Elise stood in the living room, watching Freddie run from one corner of the room to the other, sniffing as he went. She glanced back at Peggy. "He just pottied outside so I think he's safe."

"I think you're a worrier, Elise."

Elise blushed. "I am now. I hardly get any work done with Freddie around. He's my first puppy, and I wouldn't have him except for your neighbor, Michael."

"What's Michael got to do with it?"

"Michael and Carey are advising me on my novel. Michael thought Freddie would help me identify with my heroine."

"That's interesting."

"It didn't help me to solve her problems, but now I'm stuck with Freddie."

Peggy frowned. "Don't you want to keep him?"

"Of course, I do," Elise said. She stooped down as Freddie ran back to her. She scooped him up, smiling. "I love the little scamp. It's just that I didn't expect him to make such an impact on my life."

"Wait until you have kids," Peggy laughed. "Now, come back to the kitchen. I want to try some of those doughnuts."

Once they were settled at the table and the refreshments were served, Elise watched Freddie doze in Peggy's lap. "You really have a way with animals."

"Someday, when Sara is older, I want to get a family pet."

Elise looked around. "Where is Sara? Is she napping?"

"No, she's at Carol's house. We take turns watching each other's kids a couple of times a week. The children get time together, and we can go to the hair salon or whatever."

Elise ran a hand through her short hair. "Speaking of hair, the woman who cut mine did a butcher job. I'd ask for a recommendation for someone I could trust, but I'm moving soon."

Peggy had been examining Freddie's soft ears and looked up. "Have you already set a date to move?"

"I was going to leave at the end of the month, but with a deadline pending for my novel and the house still unrented, I'm staying longer than I expected."

"Do you like writing books?"

"Sometimes, I do, but this one has been a challenge. That's why I got Michael and Carey involved. I thought they could bring a male perspective into the mix. But sometimes—"

Peggy stared back. "But sometimes what?"

"I don't know. Those two are so different than any men I've known. But I guess that's just me."

"Different how?"

"Take Michael, he's so together all the time. He never looks ruffled or upset. As for Carey, he's just a sweetheart. He claims that he was once a difficult type, but that's hard to believe."

"I understand, especially when it comes to Michael. After observing him for some time, he reminds me of one of those guru types. He's always kind and understanding. Carey's nice but he has a bottomless pit for a stomach."

"You're right there. He loves sweets. The bakery where I got these donuts is going to miss me when I move."

Peggy got up and handed Freddie to Elise. "I'll get us some more coffee," she said as she went to the coffee maker and grabbed the carafe. She returned to the table and began to refill Elise's cup.

Elise hesitated. She was having such an easy time talking to Peggy, yet she felt there was unfinished business in their past. "Can I ask you something?"

Peggy backed up a little. "Sure, what is it?"

"Can we start over? I know I was very difficult when I was dating Arel. Now, when I think of moving away, I hope you can remember me as someone who's not so terrible. I don't expect you to think of me as a friend, but maybe you could forgive me for whatever I said or did."

Peggy put the carafe back and sat down. "I guess I still don't know why you behaved that way. Arel is wonderful—"

"I know that now, but when we were dating, I didn't trust him."

"If you felt that way, why did you go out with him?"

"Peggy, please, he's adorable! Some part of me couldn't resist him. I know that sounds stupid, but it's the truth. If I had it to do over, I'd have simply said no the first time he asked me out. I wasn't ready to date anyone."

"I hear you, but let's face it, you did say yes and after that, you were pretty mean at times."

Elise swallowed the lump in her throat. "I know, and I'm sorry you and your friends got in the middle of it all." She stood up. "Anyway, I've embarrassed myself again. I better go."

Peggy stood up too. "No, it was very brave of you to come clean like you did."

Elise held Freddie under her chin, and sniffled. "Thank you. It's nice to hear you say that." She paused. "Can I ask one more question before I go? Do you believe that people can change? Michael and Carey insist that they can. Of course, they were making suggestions for a character in my book. Now, I want your opinion because I respect you, Peggy."

Peggy laughed. "Of course, people can change. I've changed, so has my brother and Carol. Tim, my sweet husband, has always been a saint, but Arel has changed big time."

"How has Arel changed?"

"He was very reclusive when we met. It took a long time for him to come out of his shell. Now, look at him. He's engaged to a lovely woman and is happy as a clam."

"I guess he'll be coming home soon."

"He's already home, but I think he's been busy catching up on things."

Elise started out of the kitchen. "I hope I don't run into him. I might have enough courage to come clean with you, but I'd be mortified to see Arel again."

Peggy paused. "Elise?"

Elise turned to look at her. "Yes, what is it?"

Peggy smiled. "Elise, try to go a little easier on yourself from now on. Like you said, maybe it's time to start over. The past is past."

Fourteen

WILLIAM HELD ANNABEL'S hand as they strolled through a park within walking distance of their home. After some heavy fog, the gardens were still misty and damp. It was early morning, and the grounds were quiet. Annabel was quiet too. When William glanced down at her, she seemed far away, as if she'd rejoined her angelic friends instead of being there with him. "I don't understand why Claire had such an effect on you, Annabel."

Annabel hesitated. "Hmm?"

"I asked you about Claire. You haven't been the same since you spent time with her."

"Oh, yes, Claire. I did find her challenging. In fact, she really scared me at first."

"Of course, she did. Claire is a go-getter, a woman on a mission. You want a quiet life."

"That's what I thought too. When the four of us got together that first evening, Claire made me feel small and unimportant. However, after I had time to think about everything, I have a different opinion."

"What do you mean?"

"When we went shopping together, I got a better idea of how Claire views the world. You might say my old angelic senses kicked in enough to see that her life is founded on fear. Instead of trusting life, Claire's at war with everything. Even our luncheon turned into a battle. In the end, she could only order soup and water."

"Maybe she wasn't hungry."

"No, it was more than that."

"I think Arel would disagree with you. He thinks she's perfect."

"That's Arel's business, but I'm happy that I met Claire."

William frowned. "You just said she scared you."

"It was more of a shock. Her energy was so intense that I got physically sick. Then I realized that she was reminding me of how much of the time I've been living in fear."

97

"That's not anything new. We've discussed your fears many times."

"That's true, but seeing myself mirrored in someone else was sort of an epiphany. I realized how I must look to you." Annabel paused, gazing up with wide, emerald eyes. "William, I don't want you to see me as some pitiful person who's afraid of everything.

"I never said you were pitiful."

"Maybe not, but I know the truth."

William came to an abrupt stop. "Hold on, Annabel. Are you saying that Claire is the opposite of how she appears?"

"Yes, she fools people by acting very confident. She's like one of those lionesses in a nature film. It's the most ferocious when it's protecting its cubs against any kind of danger. For Claire, the whole world is in danger. That's why she's so dedicated to causes. But underneath, I don't think she has much faith in anything or anyone."

"Annabel, if you're right, where's that leave Arel? He's going to marry her."

"I know, but I don't think you should interfere. He's made up his mind about Claire. He loves her. And who knows, maybe they'll find a way to work things out."

* * *

Arel walked through his living room, inspecting the tidiness of the space. His suburban rancher had been well cared for while he was away. His only wish was that Claire could have returned with him. After spending two weeks with her, it felt strange to be by himself again. Of course, he wasn't actually alone. Michael and Carey were around. At the moment, Michael was out in the backyard, taking care of fall clean-up duties, and Carey was in the garage, working on his bike.

Arel was staying busy too. While Claire was away, he'd decided to start his own project. With cold weather just around the corner, he wanted to winterize the house. That meant getting the furnace serviced and possibly getting more insulation for the attic. Soon, he'd have a wife and maybe even a family to think about. He wanted their home to be in the best shape possible. As an added bonus, Claire would commend his efforts to minimize heating costs.

As he checked out each room, ideas came to mind. Perhaps, he could replace some of the windows. A number of them were drafty during cold weather. A side window in the living room was particularly bad at letting in a steady current of chill air. He was checking its condition when an outside movement caught his eye. A white dog was wandering around in his neighbor Elise's yard. As he noticed how small it was, he remembered that Carey had mentioned something about Elise getting a puppy. His response had been immediate. "No living creature should be subjected to a woman like Elise." Carey just laughed at his remark. He said Elise loved her little pup and treated it very well.

Arel wasn't convinced. After all, he'd dated Elise. He'd felt her quick temper and need to lash out. "Poor animal," he mumbled as he pulled back from the window. He prayed that Elise hadn't seen him. Fortunately, she was on the other side of her yard. When he took another quick peek, he saw Elise pick up the puppy and go back into her house.

Seeing Elise again made him even more grateful for Claire. His beautiful bride-to-be was tall and lithe. Elise could be pretty, but she didn't have a model's body. She was probably only a little over five feet. Instead of Claire's dark, silky locks, Elise had short, blond hair. The short part was new. When they were dating, her hair was longer. He liked the way it had softened her overall look.

He frowned and let out a sigh. "I wonder why she got it cut."

As soon as he had the thought, he caught himself. Elise had no significance in his life. She could do whatever she wanted. That fact should have been the end of the matter, but he couldn't stop thinking about her. As he continued inspecting windows, flashes of his blond neighbor kept bugging him. Not only was her hair too short, but she wore kiddy barrettes in it. They did nothing to make her more attractive.

It was an annoying image. He hated when people made bad decisions. And from what he knew about Elise, she'd been making them all her life. Now, she'd chopped off her hair and was running around looking like an orphan.

* * *

Elise chased after Freddie as he ran to the front door. The puppy had already learned that the sound of the doorbell meant there were visitors calling. As Freddie stood waiting for Elise to catch up, his whole body trembled with excitement. Elise laughed as she picked him up. "Okay, I know you love everyone, but please mind your manners."

She had invited Peggy, Carol and their children over for a "get acquainted with the puppy" party. She thought that it would be a nice way to start over with Sara and Ariel. She opened the door with a smile and a friendly greeting, grateful for the opportunity to make amends with the youngsters, too.

Once everyone was in the living room, Elise presented Freddie to the children. Ariel was the first to get to pet him. Carol's little boy took after his father, Kevin. Even though Carol said he wouldn't be two years old until the spring, he seemed older. He was tall and had a generous amount of brown hair. He was also very gentle with Freddie. When it was Sara's turn, the tiny, golden-haired tot knew exactly what she wanted. She was quite animated at first, but with Peggy's help, she soon learned how to pet Freddie properly.

"I also have some toys for the kids in that basket," Elise announced. "Some blocks and stuffed animals I found when I was shopping. Now, excuse me while I get lunch on the table."

Carol followed her into the kitchen. "Can I help?"

"Thanks, I made pasta and a salad for us gals. And I put together an assortment of foods for the kids." She took out a large serving tray from the refrigerator. "Does it look okay? There are cheese and tuna chunks, miniature meat balls, bite size pieces of vegetables and fruits, several kinds of crackers, and kids yogurt cups."

Carol smiled. "You've been busy."

Elise blushed. "Michael and Carey gave me a hand after our morning book meeting."

"They're great guys, but are they helpful when it comes to a romance novel?"

"They've been absolute knights in shining armor. I got stuck a couple of times with difficult chapters and almost shelved the project. With their suggestions, the book is taking shape very quickly. If I really work diligently, I should have the first draft done before I move."

"Where are you going?"

"I don't know yet. Maybe I'll just throw a dart at a map and let fate decide."

Carol stared back wide-eyed. "Really?"

Elise laughed. "If I didn't have a streak of chicken in me I would. I also thought about going out-of-state."

"There are nice towns in the general area."

"Maybe I'll check some out."

"Have you thought about staying here?"

"No, I can't. The rental agency thinks they may have found some people who want the place. I'll be gone in a few weeks."

"Oh, oh, oh!" Little Ariel called out from the living room.

When Elise and Carol hurried in to check out what was happening, Freddie was circling the room on frenzied feet, acting like he'd had too much sugar.

Elise laughed. "Freddie must love the kids. He has these puppy crazies when he's happy and excited."

Peggy sat on the floor with the children. "I think you got the perfect puppy. He was very sweet with both of the children."

Carol sighed. "At least when you move, you'll have Freddie."

Elise agreed. "Yes, the little rascal is my faithful, male companion."

Peggy gave her a quick glance. "But he might not always be the only one. Maybe you'll meet someone soon. What do you think?"

Elise shrugged. "Who knows, after spending time with Michael and Carey, I feel better about the idea of dating again."

Fifteen

ELISE STEPPED OUT of the house and yawned. It was six-thirty in the morning, and Freddie had to go out. She should have been grateful that he didn't have an accident in the house. Instead, she frowned at the idea of leaving her warm bed. It was too early to be up. Besides, there had been a heavy frost, and she started shivering immediately.

She wasn't prepared for the fall drop in temperatures. She was still wearing her summer pajamas. Her exposed legs were quickly covered in goose bumps. She didn't have her slippers on either. They were missing. She suspected Freddie of being the culprit. He had a shoe fetish. If she didn't keep an eye on him, he often carried off a sneaker to chew on.

"Okay, make it fast," she said as she put the puppy down on the porch. He immediately started for the steps. Yawning again, she closed the front door. When she heard it click, her sleepy lids flew open. She twisted and turned the door knob, but it didn't help. "You have got to be kidding!"

"Elise? Is something wrong?"

As soon as she recognized Arel's voice, she glanced over her shoulder and saw the man she'd recently been pining over. She remembered that Arel often got out early for a run. She cringed, turned back to her door and clasped the knob anxiously as if she could use her willpower to open it. "Uh . . . Arel?"

"Yes?"

"I think I'm locked out."

"Do you want to come over to my place?"

"No, I gave Carey a spare key. Could you go home and get it for me?"

"What about your dog?"

Elise turned around enough to see Freddie. He was out on the sidewalk with Arel, jumping up on Arel's leg and pawing his sweats. "Uh . . . could you bring him here."

102

"No problem, but give me a minute to get hold of him. He's pretty frisky."

Elise let out a barely audible moan. She hadn't even combed her hair. After the restless night she'd had, it was probably sticking out in all directions. She wasn't wearing makeup, and if that wasn't enough, she was wearing her faded, Minnie Mouse pajamas. Even if they were her favorites, they should have been replaced years ago.

None of it should have mattered. Arel's opinion shouldn't have mattered, but the lump in her throat was a clear sign that it did matter. "Dammit, I still have a crush on the handsome bugger."

Until recently, she'd also had a lot of fantasies. They were the delicious kind, where she played the gorgeous heroine, and Arel played the suitor who couldn't keep his hands off of her. Even after they broke up, she indulged in her daydreams with the same fervor that Freddie displayed when he enjoyed a fresh bone from the butcher.

She realized how silly she'd been when she found out that Arel had asked someone else to marry him. It was a devastating change of events. Elise still had reveries about the man, but they involved a lot cursing and phrases like "I hate you, you rotten scoundrel!" and "How dare you think I'm not good enough for you!"

But seeing Arel in the flesh was different than any of her fantasies. As she watched him pick up Freddie and walk towards the porch, her emotions were all over the place. She cared about what he thought of her, but at the same time everything about the man irritated her. As he climbed the stairs, a whiff of his cologne, his Christmassy pine and spices cologne, made her frown. Her face morphed into a mask of disgust when he ran a hand through his thick, dark hair.

As he closed the distance between them, and he glanced at her with his amazing, golden eyes, Elise's thoughts were filled with an unspoken plea for mercy.

Please, Arel, those beauties need to be hidden behind sunglasses.

As Arel came up to her, Elise heard herself let out a little gasp of longing. That's when she grabbed Freddie out of his hands and thanked him with a grimace.

Arel stepped back quickly. "It's cold this morning. Do you want my jacket?"

The simple question was the most irritating element of all. She shook her head. No, she didn't want Arel's jacket. In that moment, she wanted Arel, all of him, right down to the last whisker in his beautifully groomed, facial hair. "No, I'm fine," she said too forcefully.

Arel looked confused, but a moment later, he gave her a hasty wave and was off.

She watched him skip down the steps like a school boy bolting from the school yard. They had barely exchanged any words, and she'd alienated him. Instead of feeling good about her attitude, she felt a wave of regret. Why couldn't she be nice? If she was honest, like she was with Carey and Michael, she knew Arel had never done anything wrong. She'd made up all the fantasies about him, both the good and the bad ones, like she made up stories for her books. She wasn't proud of herself. In fact, as she considered how unfair she'd been, she knew she wanted to make amends like she did with Carol and Peggy.

She was thinking about how to apologize when Freddie squirmed and twisted. It was such a quick, forceful action that she lost her hold on him. He half-fell to the porch, but he recovered immediately. After that he didn't hesitate. He clearly had an objective in mind. After navigating the stairs in record time, he took off after Arel.

As Elise watched him bouncing across the frosted grass, her mind began to race ahead. Freddie still had a full bladder. If he followed Arel into the house, the warmth would hit him. He'd find a spot to take care of his needs. Arel's beautiful white, wool carpeting would be the perfect place for Freddie to relieve himself.

"Oh, no, don't do it, Freddie!" she shrieked as she hurried down the porch steps too. She'd been around Arel enough to know how particular he was with his house and furnishings. He'd seemed especially concerned about his pristine rug. He picked up every crumb that might blemish its fibers. Since she'd just decided to make amends, having her puppy soil something that he valued was the last thing she wanted. She had to act fast.

The thought spurred her on. Her bare feet sprinted across the lawn in an almost effortless motion. Glancing ahead, she saw Freddie approaching Arel's house, and she started shouting. "Freddie! Come back here! Freddie!"

The thought of what the puppy would do when he got inside made her pick up her pace. She ran faster than she'd ever run before.

* * *

Arel hurriedly unlocked his front door, cracked it open and took a deep breath. He'd been holding it after spending a few minutes with his neighbor, Elise. She had that effect on him. It was like she resented men who dared to breathe freely around her. Now, he had one goal in mind. Get her key, return it to her and try to forget he'd run into the sour-faced woman. And later, when he saw Michael and Carey, he'd let them know how wrong they were. The truth was plain and simple. Elise hadn't changed at all.

Just the thought of what he'd endured when he dated her made his temples throb. But that was behind him. He was engaged to Elise's opposite, a perfect woman in a perfect woman's body. Claire made him smile. He remembered how lovely she'd been when they said goodbye in London. The memory was quickly dispelled by the grating sounds of someone shouting behind him. His morning wasn't going well.

He took another deep breath, determined to stay in a better place. After all, Michael kept harping on how Arel's thoughts and feelings determined how the world responded. And he knew it was true. When he decided not to give in to all his negativity, he was happier. He was back home with his friends, enjoying life. He'd even found someone he loved and who loved him. He had to keep those facts in mind.

He turned to see who kept calling out and froze. Something about the environment had radically changed. The cold morning air had turned foggy. His front lawn was suddenly shrouded in a heavy mist. Was there something wrong with his eyes? He blinked several times, but the scene remained constant.

A pixie-like being was running towards him out of the fog. The pixie was stuck in midair, as if the frames of time weren't moving. He let out a gasp as he realized that time itself seemed to be stuck. In fact, it had stopped. But something about the pixie had him spellbound.

He'd read about fairy-like beings. These magical creatures fascinated him as a child. He'd sometimes dreamed of seeing one. But he'd never expected to have one leaping about in his yard. This one had a bare leg stretched out in front of her. She was the size of a small woman, but he couldn't make out the details of her face. Her hair definitely had pixie qualities. It was short, blond and spiky.

He blinked a couple of times and noticed details about her clothes. She wore a loose-fitting shirt and short pants. If he concentrated, he could make out the image of a mouse on her shirt. That was nice. He loved the tiny creatures.

Still, it made him curious. Why a mouse? As the image of the mouse began to clear, he recognized it. It was a Disney character named Minnie. He let out another gasp. "Elise was wearing an identical shirt!"

Just the thought of the woman made him shut his eyes and groan. Why did he have to run into Elise that morning? Recalling the unpleasant encounter, he was jolted by another shout of distress. When he opened his eyes, things were back to normal. There was no pixie. Whatever he'd just experienced was quickly forgotten as he watched Elise running towards him. Then he felt something brush his pant leg and run into the house. It was Elise's dog. That's when things began to click. Elise was trying to catch her puppy.

He held up a hand. "It's okay. I'll get him for you."

His offer went unnoticed. Still running and yelling for her pet, Elise tripped on a raised edge of the sidewalk. With her momentum propelling her forward, she threw out her hands and came down hard on the cement.

Arel's throat caught. He wasn't fond of Elise, but he didn't want to see her get hurt. He was about to rush over to help her, but she was on her feet so fast that he didn't get the chance. Never hesitating for even a moment, she rushed forward again, like a soldier in battle who doesn't let a bullet wound slow them down. When she reached the porch stairs, she was panting, but she took the steps two at a time. When she got to the door, she gave him a panicked look and ran into the house.

Arel took a moment to calm himself. "She must really love that dog!"

As he hurried after her, he heard Elise's voice raised in prayer. Her request was short. "Lord, give me strength!" It was followed by a much louder request. "Michael! Carey! Get in here!" Her shouts reminded Arel of a drill sergeant who was gathering his men for roll call.

He was about to volunteer for duty when Michael and Carey came running down the hall towards him. That's when Elise's puppy came running out of the living room. It skidded on the tile floor of the foyer and kept going.

Elise was shouting again. "Michael, fast! Get the paper towels. Carey! Hurry! Get the key to my house! Bring me the rug cleaner for stains! It's in the laundry room!"

Without responding verbally, both Michael and Carey were in motion. They each took off in different directions. Arel didn't know why, but Elise's energy had his heart pounding as he ran into the living room. He hesitated when he saw Elise kneeling on the rug. Her voice was much quieter than before, a mere whisper of repeated words. "No, no, no!"

A moment later, Michael ran past him and crouched down next to Elise. She didn't acknowledge him. Instead, she grabbed the paper towels out of his hands, unrolled a few feet and began to press down on the carpet. Her actions and the focused look on her face reminded Arel of a medic tending to an accident victim. When he got a closer look, he realized that the accident victim was an inanimate object. His rug had suffered from animal abuse.

Michael looked up and sighed. "Sorry, Freddie had a little mishap."

Michael's soft-spoken explanation, made Elise's head jerk up. "It's under control. Don't worry about a thing."

Arel stepped closer. "Elise, please, get up. I'll take care of—"

Elise's tone turned insistent. "No! It's my fault! I'll handle it."

Arel frowned, but his instincts told him to give Elise space. "Do you want me to check on your puppy? I think he ran into one of the bedrooms."

When Elise looked up this time, her eyes were wide pools of fear. "The bedroom? Where you keep your shoes?" She didn't wait for an answer. She glared at Michael. "Quick, go look for Freddie. He's been chewing on everything lately. I've had to put all my shoes on a closet shelf."

Michael, like a faithful soldier, was up and on his feet at once. After he left the room, Arel knelt down in his place. "Elise, what's all that red stuff on the paper towels."

Elise had been throwing used towels to the side without looking at them. Arel's question made her pause, then shriek again. "Oh no!" When she held out her hands, both were scraped and bleeding.

It was Arel's cue to take action. Taking hold of Elise's arm, he started to help her up. "Let's take care of—"

His offer was interrupted by another of Elise's outbursts.

"I can't believe it! My knees must be bleeding too!"

When Arel looked at where Elise had been kneeling, there were two dark, red stains spoiling the white carpet.

Michael returned to the living room a moment later. He was carrying Freddie in one hand and a shoe in the other. "Arel, I think Freddie likes your slipper. It might have a few blemishes."

His statement seemed to push Elise over the edge. She let out a short, shrieking curse and burst into tears. Next, she jerked her arm out of Arel's grasp, hurried over to Michael and grabbed Freddie. She also grabbed Arel's slipper, cursed again and ran out of the house.

Arel didn't know how to respond. Should he go after Elise and make sure she was okay? When he looked to Michael for advice, the angel remained quiet.

Arel's instincts told him to save himself, to let Elise do what she insisted on doing. It was plain she wanted to take care of everything herself. It was a relief until he looked at his carpet. He had a job he needed to tend to.

Sixteen

PEGGY WAS SURPRISED when Arel called and said he'd like to stop over. He mentioned something about needing a woman's advice. She told him that she was having coffee with Carol. If he wanted, he could have the advice of two women. When Arel arrived, he looked confused. Since he didn't say much, Peggy decided to start off the conversation. She put down her mug and smiled. "Arel, did I hear shouting coming from your place this morning?"

Arel slumped in his chair. "You heard Elise. Her puppy got away from her, and she was chasing him, screaming like a banshee."

Carol sat in the chair next to Arel's. "Is the puppy okay?"

Peggy leaned in, waiting for Arel's answer. She was already attached to Elise's pet. "He's not hurt, is he?"

Arel's brows narrowed even more. "The only things that suffered are my rug and my slipper. Elise's dog managed to damage both of them. Not to mention the blood stains Elise left behind."

"Blood?" Carol gasped.

Peggy sat wide-eyed as Arel related his tale of woe. When he finished, she was eager for more information. "How's Elise now? I hope her hands and knees aren't too bad."

Arel gave her an annoyed glance. "I tried to call her, but she wouldn't answer. Finally, Carey came back from her place and told me she'd be fine. I guess she's banged up and sore, but she'll recover in a day or two."

"Why was Carey at her house?" Carol asked.

"Elise sent him there to find some cleaning solution for my rug. When she ran back home, he was still there. And you know Carey. He's always everyone's friend. He helped to take care of her scrapes."

Peggy smiled. "Carey is wonderful."

Arel shifted in his seat. "That's not the point. I want to know if I should do anything more. Elise acted like she'd lost it. The way she was down on her knees, going at my rug with that crazy look in her eye, she was scary."

Carol laughed. "Oh my, I bet she knew how important it is that your house stays immaculate."

Arel winced. "How can I keep my house immaculate with Carey around? He's always dropping stuff and—"

Peggy grinned too. "And you're always cleaning up after him. I wonder how many miles you've put on your vacuum."

Arel studied his clasped hands. "I was raised to be very neat."

Carol reached over and patted his shoulder. "And there's not a thing in the world wrong with that. Kevin and I loved staying at your place. It was like being in some fancy resort."

Peggy nodded. "Your artwork and your beautiful bronzes could be in a gallery."

Arel let his frown ease a little. "Thank you, having pleasant surroundings has always been important to me."

"Someday I'd like to make some changes," Carol said. "But for now, toys and baby accessories are everywhere. A couple of days ago, Kevin was going to the kitchen for a late night snack and tripped over little Ariel's play workbench. I'm just happy little Ariel slept through his father's noisy expletives."

"Elise let out a few expletives, too," Arel said.

"I'm sure she was upset," Peggy offered.

"Fine, but why act like it's a life or death situation when her dog had an accident?"

Peggy looked at Carol and let her face ease into a broad smile.

Arel noticed their silent communication. "What's so funny?"

Peggy studied her coffee mug and ran a finger around its edge. "Poor Elise."

"Yes, I feel sorry for her," Carol said.

Arel looked at each of them and sat up straighter. "Why would either of you feel sorry for a woman who treated you so badly? Like you told me, she's horrible."

Carol bit her lip. "Not always. She has her good side."

Peggy sighed. "Carol's right. Elise can be nicer than I thought."

"But what does that have to do with me?" Arel asked. "I just want to get on with my life with Claire."

Peggy sat up too. "Arel, you don't have a clue, do you?"

"No! That's why I'm here. I want to know what's going on."

Carol smoothed out her napkin. "I think Elise is in love with you, Arel."

Peggy grabbed Arel's arm. "Or at the least, from the way she's acting, she must have a terrible crush on you."

Arel blinked back like they'd announced that the moon really was made out of cheese. "You two are as nutty as Elise. She hates me!"

"Oh boy, she really does have it bad," Carol said quietly.

Arel stood up. "I better go talk to her."

"No!" Both Peggy and Carol yelled out the word at the same time.

Arel hesitated. "Why not? This latest episode with her was ridiculous and exhausting."

Peggy stood up too. "Arel, you came here for advice. So please, you don't want to have that kind of conversation with Elise."

Carol was nodding her head. "Listen to Peggy."

* * *

Arel had paid Peggy and Carol a visit with one objective in mind. He needed advice about his unpleasant, early morning experience with Elise. He walked back home feeling completely dissatisfied. Instead of helping him, the two women went on and on about how incapable he was in understanding anything. They even used the word, clueless. No matter how he tried to explain himself, they seemed determined to take Elise's side. What was wrong with them? Couldn't they see that he was the injured party? He was the one who suffered repeatedly when he was around the woman.

And as for their explanation about Elise having a crush on him, that didn't excuse the woman's foul attitude. Carol even said something about love.

"Over my dead body!" he mumbled through clenched teeth. The whole idea of Elise liking him was completely unacceptable. He didn't want to be associated with his neighbor. To be the object of her romantic intentions made his entire body go rigid with resentment. After how she'd treated him when he was dating her, he didn't want to hear about her starry-eyed, lovesick feelings.

As he was about to turn into his driveway, he paused for only a moment and then kept going. If Peggy and Carol didn't care about his feelings, he didn't have to care about their advice. He had to put an end to any connection he had with Elise. He had to confront her, face on, and set the woman straight. Her feelings about him were not appreciated. He'd also establish some boundaries. The next time she locked herself out of her house, she wasn't to bother him. She could go to someone else for assistance.

As he approached Elise's front door, he'd never felt so at ease about voicing his feelings. If Elise could blurt out whatever she wanted, so could he. William had even questioned Arel's lack of expression. But that was the old Arel. The new one was one hundred percent ready to communicate with ease.

After a couple of short rings on the doorbell, he heard Elise call out from inside. As usual, she had plenty of volume when she yelled, "Coming." He cleared his throat, ready to turn up his own volume.

* * *

With Freddie tucked under an arm, Elise hurried along as quickly as she could to answer the door. In her present condition, the term, quickly, meant that she sort of shuffled to the foyer, trying not to overdo her stiff knees. But in spite of her body's woes, she felt like a new woman. She'd had a startling breakthrough that morning.

After the disastrous events that involved Arel and his belongings, she'd come back to her house almost traumatized. But it wasn't the events themselves that scared her, it was the way she'd acted. She'd allowed her emotions to take over to such an extent that she'd acted like a maniac. The embarrassment she felt afterwards was overwhelming. She didn't want to ever repeat that kind of behavior.

When she calmed down, she remembered what Michael and Carey had said to her. They were advising her on how to develop her heroine Linda's character, but she felt their words affect her on a much deeper level. When she was still very young and inexperienced, she'd made decisions that had terrible consequences. But she wasn't that young, naïve girl anymore. She had matured. She was strong and very competent.

The thoughts had been taking shape in her book and in her psyche, but it hadn't been until that morning that she had a lightbulb moment. As Carey helped her with her scrapes and told her that he was sure everything would work out. She began to believe him. No, it was more than that. She realized she could believe in herself.

After Carey left, she had a couple of hours to just sit calmly in the living room with Freddie asleep on her lap. She used that time to take stock of her life. Some parts were perfect. She loved writing, and her novels were successful enough to give her financial freedom. She was physically healthy, and if she improved her eating habits and did a little more exercising, she'd be in the best shape of her life. Then there was the idea of a relationship. She didn't know if she was ready for one, but if a man did come into her life, she'd approach the idea of dating with more confidence this time. Which brought her to her final consideration, Arel.

She'd made quite the mess when they dated. Her current performance left her blushing every time she thought about it. However, Carey had made another good point. He'd said that sometimes extreme situations were a wake-up call, a signal to move on to something better in life. When that concept sunk in, she suddenly felt free of Arel. Her handsome neighbor had served a purpose. He'd helped her to know that there were good men in the world. Now, Arel was engaged to someone, and she was ready to move on.

When she had the thought, she could breathe easier. Some of the tension in her body drained away. At first, she didn't know why she felt better, but one of Michael's explanations about life made sense. He'd said, "Children often learn to seek love on the outside instead of valuing themselves."

That was it. Mystery solved. She'd been taught not to love herself. Her father had a list of reasons for denying her worth, but as Elise went over the list, none of the reasons made sense. Even if she didn't know enough to come in out of the rain, that didn't mean she wasn't lovable. Maybe she was just too preoccupied with other thoughts to run into the house. Maybe she liked the rain. Whatever the reason, she didn't have to believe in her father's opinions. She could have her own. And if she wanted to stand in the rain, that was okay.

Freddie seemed to second the motion. When he woke up, he stretched, turned around on her lap and then jumped up on her chest. His black eyes were bright and happy as he tried to give her doggy kisses. That was when the doorbell rang, and she realized that she wanted to see whoever was there, especially since it might be Carey coming back to check on her. She was feeling so much better about herself that she smiled and shouted out the word, "Coming!"

She was pleasantly surprised to see Arel standing on her porch. Words came out on their own. "Great to see you again! I was going to visit you later and return your slipper. Please, come in. I have so much to tell you."

Arel hesitated, but she reached out carefully and took hold of his arm with a bandaged hand. With a broad smile, she pulled him inside, handed him Freddie, and shut the door. "Wait here, I'll go get your shoe." She glanced back at him as she went to her office. "I'm happy to report that there are a couple of little tooth marks in the leather, but nothing serious. If that bothers you, I'll be happy to pay for a new pair." She paused. "But I must say, that would be expensive, wouldn't it. They look custom made. I'm guessing Italian."

* * *

Arel couldn't understand what had happened to the woman who answered the door. She looked like Elise, but he'd never seen this version. This version had a face that was unlined and glowed with, dare he think it, sweetness. As he tried to fathom what was going on, Elise's puppy kept trying to lick his face. He struggled to avoid the puppy's long tongue as Elise returned with his shoe in her hand.

"I know," she said, still smiling. "I'm trying to teach Freddie not to do that, but he's such a lovable, little guy. Please, just put him down." Elise laughed. "I don't know why I handed him to you in the first place. But giving him to people is beginning to be a habit. Peggy and Carol and their kids love the little rascal."

Arel set the puppy down and started to stand up when Elise paused in front of him. When their eyes met, Elise's eyes were glossed over.

"Do you know you're a godsend?" she asked. "You're an angel, straight from heaven. And I want to thank you for turning my life around."

Arel glanced over his shoulder. He had to be in the wrong house. "I don't understand."

Elise held out his slipper. "Please, give me a chance to tell you what I've been thinking. Since this morning, I've been going over everything. I went back to when I first saw you. I was in such a bad place. I didn't trust what my heart was telling me. I wanted to put you in the same category I'd put all the men I dated. But you were generous and very kind in spite of all my bitterness and ugly ways. Now, I want to apologize for the way I behaved."

Elise stood up straighter and took a deep breath. "I can finally move on to a new chapter in my life. And I promise you, when I meet the next guy, I'll think of what you've given me, a new perspective. I can't say I'll trust the next guy entirely, but at least I won't be the evil witch that I was with you." She paused again. "Anyway, there it is, my revelation and apology. Now, I won't detain you any longer with my tales." She bent down, scooped up Freddie and went to the door. "Thank you again and congratulations on your engagement. Your fiancé is a lucky woman. I wish you both the best."

Arel managed to nod and offer a little wave as he left the house, but he was too dumbfounded to speak. He walked back home in a kind of daze. When he got inside his house, he went straight to his bed. He needed a good nap. Hopefully it would clear his head. He felt like it was spinning in a wobbly orbit after Elise's complete turn-around.

In the back of his mind, he was entertaining two words, multiple personality. When he had more clarity, perhaps he'd call Rolphe. They still weren't that close, but Rolphe was very psychic. He might be able to shed some light on Arel's perplexing neighbor. Unlike William, who had opinions about everything, Rolphe could be counted on to remain objective, especially when it came to subjects like Arel's feelings and uncertainties.

Seventeen

ROLPHE PUT HIS phone on the coffee table and sat back on the sofa. He tried to collect his thoughts after talking to Arel. Arel's call had been filled with questions. They were pushy, insistent queries. The man seemed to think that it was Rolphe's duty to come up with answers. However, none of Rolphe's thoughts or possible explanations seemed to appease Arel's agitated state.

Rolphe tried to relax his shoulders. Arel's manner had been intense when he related his complaints, and his energy had a disturbing effect. Rolphe had had a nice evening planned. When Myra arrived, he'd looked forward to a leisurely time together. After talking to Arel, the room felt too warm and his body was almost as agitated as Arel sounded.

Myra came out of the kitchen with her glass of wine. "Is everything alright with Arel? You have that look again."

Rolphe hesitated. "I didn't know what to say to him. Whenever he gets into one of his moods, I always end up feeling like I've failed him in some way."

"Maybe it's the other way around. I overheard some of what Arel was saying, and he can be very brusque with you."

Rolphe knew she was right. Arel's manners were often lacking when they spoke. But after what he'd put Arel through in the past, he had no room to complain about ill treatment. "He's troubled, that's all. He's concerned about the woman he was dating before he met Claire."

Myra sat down next to him and caressed her wine glass. "Why is he involved with another woman's business when he has Claire?"

"I'm not sure. But Arel is very sensitive to other people's energy."

Myra laughed. "Like you. You always seem to know when I'm the least bit upset."

"When it comes to Arel's sensitivity, multiply mine by a hundred. On the other hand, if he gets into a negative space, he can imagine the worst. I think that's what happened after some interactions with his neighbor. He thinks she's unbalanced."

"I thought he disliked her. Why would he be concerned?"

"Arel tends to get involved when he's worried." Rolphe leaned down and picked up Dantela. The cat had come over to where they sat and started rubbing his leg. The black feline was small for her age, but Rolphe loved her and considered her a very dear friend. As he stroked her back, she kneaded his lap with tiny feet. Her toes were special. They looked like they'd been dipped in white paint. Rolphe let out another sigh as he continued to pet the cat.

Myra put her glass on the coffee table and slipped her arm around Rolphe's. "From what you told me, Claire and Arel were together constantly after they met. Now, Arel is back in Chicago wanting to see her again. I bet this Elise woman is a distraction for him."

Rolphe turned his attention to the beautiful woman who sat next to him. "Even if you were away, I wouldn't think about another woman."

"That's where you and Arel are different, thank goodness."

Rolphe noticed how Myra's eyes lit up when she glanced at him. "Carey once told me to try to concentrate on my life instead of worrying about either Arel or William. Maybe he's right."

Myra caressed Rolphe's cheek. "Yes, perhaps it's time to think about you and me," she said in a teasing voice.

Rolphe smiled, gathered up Dantela and got to his feet. "It's also time for Dantella to try out her new bed."

Myra returned a curious glance as Rolphe carried the cat over to a recently, purchased wicker basket. "My darling, do you know how many beds your Dantela has? I've never seen so many for just one kitty."

"She didn't need another one, but I couldn't resist it when I saw it at the pet shop," Rolphe said as he placed Dantela on a thick, fluffy cushion. He smiled at Myra as he returned to where she was sitting. He reached out for her hand. "I can't resist thinking about you either."

"Good, I'm very happy to hear that," Myra said.

Rolphe noted her sparkling, brown eyes. They were reminders of how lucky he was to have such a wonderful woman in his life. As for Arel, Rolphe had to trust that his friend would figure out things for himself. But it wasn't an easy task. It was hard to put aside his concerns. He often thought about Arel like a son.

William sat on the new, downstairs sofa, drumming his fingers on the padded arm. He glanced at Annabel. She sat on the other end of the couch, knitting. "Look at us, Annabel. We're like a couple of old people, frittering away our lives."

Annabel put her knitting down. "William, you know I want to support whatever you want to do."

He gave her a forlorn smile. "I know. I realize now that I was blaming you for my boredom when all the time it's been my problem."

"But you had lots of interests before. You collected artwork. You traveled." Annabel's face lit up. "Maybe we could plan a trip to a place you haven't seen before."

William settled deeper into the confines of the sofa. "Fine, if you want, make the arrangements."

"What's wrong? You've always had so many questions about life and new adventures. You wanted to delve into unknown mysteries."

William closed his eyes. "I'm ruined, Annabel. All of Arel's carrying on, his astral travel and his alternate worlds, have ruined my life."

Annabel laughed. "You're too magnificent to be ruined. Just look at that painting Rolphe did of you. You're still that person."

"What good is any of it if I don't have a place for that magnificence? I'm like one of those knights who come home after all the wars are over. They have nothing to do but sit in front of a fire and get old."

Annabel frowned. "Maybe you'd like to create your own world."

"No, Arel's done that. In the end, there was nothing left but problems."

"You could be creative, like Rolphe. His artwork is amazing."

"Please, my mind is a wasteland. I have no desire to paint or sculpt or write a book."

"You love nature. What about photography? You could travel to exotic places and—"

"Sorry, I know you're trying to help, but there's nothing I want to do." William let out a heavy sigh. "Nothing."

Annabel got up and stood in front of him. "What about us, William? You're still interested in us, aren't you?"

He reached out for her hand. "I want to be interested. You're everything I could want in a woman, in a wife, but it's like all feeling has left my body." He let her hand go. "Can't you understand what I'm saying? I'm an empty shell, and I don't know how to change that fact."

Annabel went back to her seat and picked up her knitting. "Have you heard from Arel?"

William straightened his shoulders. "Let's not get into all of that."

"All of what?"

"From what I can tell, he's caught up in more drama."

Annabel's busy fingers stilled. "Is he having problems with Claire?"

"No, he's all worked up about his ex-girlfriend, Elise."

"So he called you?"

"I think he called Rolphe first, but he didn't get any resolution. I guess he thought I could help."

"So what's going on?"

"Arel decided to let Elise know how he felt about the poor treatment he got when they dated."

"Maybe that's a step forward. It might help him to get in touch with deeper feelings. We both think he's in denial with Claire."

"He never got a chance to tell the blasted woman anything. She switched gears and started being nice. She even apologized for her bad-mannered behavior."

"People can have a change of heart. As an angel, I've witnessed it many times."

"Arel sees it differently. He thinks she's mentally unbalanced."

Annabel laughed. "Arel amazes me. He has Michael's blood, plus Carey and Michael are always there to help him, yet he still seems very distrusting in situations like this."

"I don't know. What if he's right? He says that Elise changed in the space of a few hours. That seems a bit strange."

"So how is he handling the situation?"

"He's going to see if he can join Elise's book group. Carey and Michael have been offering advice for weeks. It might be the perfect place for Arel to observe Elise."

"How is that going to help?"

"I think it's an interesting idea. When I considered myself a scientific type, observation was a critical part of every process."

"Yes, but I've been reading articles in your science magazines. Some researchers believe that the observer can affect the outcome of an experiment."

William glanced up and smiled. "Really, you've been reading my magazines? It's refreshing to know you're interested in science."

"Of course I am. In fact, I've been thinking about learning more about my abilities. I sometimes wonder about what powers I possess as a human being."

"Would you be interested in exploring that idea a little more?"

"Do you think you could come up with some experiments?"

William sat forward in his seat. "Why not? I'm not doing anything useful with my life."

"Remember that time we challenged each other with the marigold experiment."

"You cheated. You still had your wings."

"Well, I don't have them anymore. So maybe we can try another challenge."

"Please, Annabel, I wouldn't want to take advantage of you."

"Don't worry about me. I might not have my wings, but I'm very aware of the potential power every human possesses. I might surprise you."

William stood up and stretched. "Don't say I didn't warn you if your human potential falls flat."

Eighteen

ELISE SAT AT HER desk waiting for a question to surface. Arel and Michael sat on the couch opposite. Carey couldn't make it to the meeting, and Arel had volunteered to take his place. "It's strange, but I can't think of anything to ask either of you."

"Perhaps you don't need our input anymore," Michael said.

Arel gave Michael a sidelong glance. "Great, as soon as I join this little group, I find out I'm not needed."

Elise smiled. "It's great having you here, Arel. If you have anything you want to ask about writing or my novel, I'm all ears."

"Since I'm a newcomer, would you give me a brief synopsis of what you've covered so far?"

Elise's smile deepened when she looked at Michael. "Your friends came in when I was stuck in the middle of the story. I guess you could say that my heroine was stuck. Now, she's over a lot of her problems and is falling in love with the male character, Mason. With Michael and Carey's help, the story is close to a successful conclusion."

Arel's brows narrowed as he began to pick up some crumbs off the sofa cushion. "Great, I'm happy it all worked out.'"

Elise got up and walked over to where he was sitting. "Freddie's dog biscuit," she explained. "I'm trying to get him to eat them in his bed, but he prefers the sofa."

Arel dusted off pieces of biscuit into Elise's out-stretched hand. "I suppose he'll learn more manners as he gets older."

"I hope so," Elise laughed. She went back to her desk and deposited the crumbs in the trash can next to it. When she turned back to Arel, she tried to keep the tone of her voice cheerful. "But getting back to the business of romance, I want to congratulate you again on your recent engagement."

Arel's demeanor changed immediately, going from careful and discerning to wistful. "Thank you. Claire is the best thing that's ever happened to me." His face reddened when he looked up at Elise. "I mean . . . she—"

Elise cut in, trying her best to keep her voice steady. "I understand what you mean. Unlike me, she's probably very nice."

Arel sucked in a breath. "You're nice too . . . now."

Elise sat down at her desk, straightening the desk blotter and some mail. Twinges of her old feelings for Arel were worming their way back, but she knew better than entertain more fantasies. She looked up with a weak smile. "You helped me more than you can know, Arel. Claire is a fortunate woman to have you." She turned to her other guest. "You helped too, Michael. The two of you were perfect examples of how wonderful men can be. Someday, perhaps you both will be congratulating me when I find my match."

Michael smiled. "That day may come sooner than you think."

Elise felt her breath catch and went back to stacking some papers. "Anyway, before you go, Arel, I'd like to ask you a few questions. Since I'm a romance writer, I'd like to get your take on what makes the perfect woman."

Michael looked at Arel. "That's a good question, don't you think?"

Arel leaned back on the couch and sighed dreamily. "The perfect woman is . . . I mean, she's—" He sat up and blinked a couple of times. "I'm sorry, but it's hard to describe the feeling."

Elise agreed. "Being a writer, I understand your problem."

Arel stood up and straightened his shoulders. "I'll think about the question and get back to you."

Michael stood up too. "Don't try too hard, Arel. Sometimes it's best to let the answer come in on its own."

"Michael's right," Elise said. "My best writing is inspired. I'll be taking a walk or washing the dishes and the ideas flow in unannounced." She got up and started for the front door. "Anyway, thanks for everything."

"But I didn't do anything," Arel complained as he trailed behind her.

Elise paused and turned to face him. Deep in the best part of herself, she knew that she needed to give Arel her blessing. He was a good man with a good heart. "I'm happy for you, Arel." Without thinking, she reached up and kissed his cheek. "You deserve a perfect woman."

Arel stepped back and issued a quick, "Thank you."

Elise felt embarrassed by her impromptu expression of affection. But it felt good to do something nice for a change.

* * *

After Arel came back from the meeting with Elise, he knew that he needed to stay focused on his current projects. The furnace was now in tip-top condition, and people were scheduled to come and add insulation to the attic. He'd also accomplished an unrelated task earlier that week. He'd had the closet in the lower level bedroom enlarged. It was now a walk-in closet. When Claire moved in, there would be room for her things.

He grabbed his notepad. He'd decided to definitely replace several windows in the house, and he needed to call some contractors for estimates. He wandered over to the side window in the living room, the one that gave him access to his neighbor's house. It didn't make any sense, but he often found himself standing in front of it and thinking about the one person he wanted to forget.

He turned away quickly and looked at Michael. As usual, the angel was reading a book on gardening.

"How can I help you," Michael asked.

"I can't figure out what's going on with Elise. I attended the book discussion to find out more about her sudden transformation, but I'm more confused than ever. She's still being too nice, and I don't know why."

"Elise is great," Carey said as he walked into the room carrying a plate of cookies. "She's always buying goodies at this wonderful bakery she found."

Arel frowned and pointed to the sofa. "Please take a seat, Carey. Maybe you can help too."

Carey bit off half of a large oatmeal cookie, chewed a little and waved his plate in Arel's direction. "How did your meeting go? Did you help Elise with her book?"

Arel watched a small spray of cookie crumbs scatter, but he held his tongue. He was practicing tolerance since he'd been with Claire. "It seems that Elise doesn't need any more help. But that's not the point. She's too nice."

Carey leaned in and smiled at Michael. "We made a good team when it came to getting her over the rough spots."

Michael smiled back. "Yes, but Elise was eager to make some changes once she realized that she had options."

Carey took another bite of cookie. "All in all, she's an angel's dream-come-true. It was pretty easy to help her turn her life around."

Arel grabbed hold of the back of a recliner. "She's an angel's dream because she got all of her anger out when she was dating me."

Carey put his plate on the coffee table and sat back. "Sorry, I'm sure it wasn't a pleasant experience."

Arel stiffened. "Not pleasant? She was a shrew around my friends. I was afraid they'd have nothing to do with me afterwards."

Carey brushed off his shirt. "Yes, but that's all behind you."

Michael gave Carey a brief look of censure. "Carey, I think you're forgetting yourself."

"What is it?" Carey asked.

Michael pointed to the carpet. "You know that Arel is concerned about crumbs."

"Oh, that's right," Carey said as he leaned down and began to pick up oatmeal morsels that were scattered around his feet.

Arel crossed his arms. "Never mind that."

Carey glanced up. "What do you mean?"

"After being with Claire, I realize I have to get my priorities straight. After all, what's more important, a happy Claire or some carpeting that I can replace?"

Carey looked at the cookie remains in his hand and then at Arel. "Are you sure?"

Arel squinted, but he was determined to improve his level of tolerance. "I'm sure."

Carey opened his hand and let the crumbs scatter again. "What about the vacuuming schedule? Do you want me to continue going over the rugs on Wednesdays and Saturdays?"

Arel crossed his arms. "I don't want to talk about vacuuming. I need your advice. Elise asked me a question, and I want to come up with the right answer."

"What question?" Carey asked.

"I'm supposed to tell her what makes a woman perfect."

Carey laughed. "Arel, nobody's perfect."

"Maybe, but Claire comes close. At least she's everything that I could want in a woman. It's just that I can't explain my feelings in words. And I don't want to spend a lot of time thinking about it."

Carey stood up and grabbed his empty plate. "Then forget that Elise asked you for your opinion. It was probably just something she threw out on the spur of the moment."

"You're right. I don't owe her anything, but still, I wonder—"

Carey headed for the kitchen. "I'm sure Elise has already forgotten that she asked you the question."

Arel adjusted his posture. "Yes, but just in case you're wrong, I better make sure."

Carey stopped and gave him a curious look. "Make sure of what?"

"I'll go over to her house and tell her that I don't have time for her inquiries."

"Or you could just drop the whole thing," Michael offered.

Arel started for the front door. "No, I think Elise is the type of woman who expects answers. I'll do her the courtesy of putting the issue to rest."

"That's very considerate," Carey said.

Arel glanced back it him, noting Carey's blameless face. Angels always had a way of making him feel like their comments were useless. Maybe that was the point. He had to learn to make his own decisions.

In this case, he knew he had to clear the slate with Elise. When they broke off their relationship, they'd parted without totally making peace with each other. More importantly, Elise had recently planted a kiss on his cheek. He needed to make sure she knew it didn't mean anything to him. They could be friends, but nothing more.

When he arrived at her front door, he knocked instead of ringing the bell. It felt like a friendlier gesture. As he was adjusting his posture, Elise answered the door. Before she had a chance to greet him, Arel blurted out the speech he'd prepared.

"I know you're interested in subjects that pertain to your writing, but I won't be able to contribute anything new. I've tried, but I can't put words to the feelings I have about my relationship with Claire. I'm sorry."

"Oh, that's okay," Elise said as she tried to hold on to the excited puppy in her arms. Freddie was struggling to free himself, clearly excited about Arel's visit. "Would you like to come in and chat about anything else?"

Arel took a step back. "Thank you, but I better go home. I have a million things to do."

Elise moved closer and peered up at him with concern. "What happened to your cheek? It looks very red."

Arel rubbed his face and winced. "That's strange. It hurts."

Elise's blue eyes narrowed even more. "My goodness. It definitely looks blistered."

"Really?"

"Come in for a moment. I have an excellent medication. It helped a lot when I had a bad sunburn. Oh, and close the door, please. So I can put Freddie down."

Arel stepped into the house, closed the door and waited as Elise scurried off. Freddie took the opportunity to jump up repeatedly on his pants leg. Arel hardly noticed. Elise was right about his cheek. It was painful to the touch, but he didn't remember injuring it.

When Elise returned, she was clutching a small tube. Before she gave it to Arel, she moved in very close and fingered his cheek. "Yep, you definitely have tiny blisters. But if you follow the directions on this medication, I think it will help."

Arel instinctively grabbed her hand, trying to smile as he moved it away from his face. "I'm sure it's nothing—"

Elise frowned. "Your hand is very warm. Do you have a fever?"

Arel immediately let go of her. "It's nothing. Fevers come and go with me. It's a condition I've lived with for a long time." In part, his statement was true. When he got very upset or emotional, his temperature could soar. However, he didn't think he was upset when he rang Elise's door bell.

Elise sighed. "And I thought my headaches were bad." She leaned down and picked up Freddie. "Maybe you better go home and rest."

Arel paused. "Before I go, I have a quick question."

"Go on."

"What's your take on a perfect relationship?"

Elise laughed. "That's easy. If I loved a man, and we could put up with each other's shortcomings and be willing to work out ways of getting along, I think he'd be perfect."

Arel took in a breath as he toiled over her answer. Elise had no difficulty expressing herself. "You're very good with putting feelings into words. I'll have to check out some of your books."

Elise cuddled Freddie a little closer. "Go home and take care of yourself."

Arel nodded and turned to leave. As he walked back to his house and thought about his cheek, he was sure the injured area was the place where Elise had kissed him. But how could a kiss cause blisters? As he climbed his porch stairs, he smiled as an explanation came to mind. He was extremely sensitive and probably allergic to Elise's lipstick.

Nineteen

WILLIAM STOOD IN his laboratory, fingering the smooth surface of his work table. For years, he'd spent much of his time there, working on mysteries that fascinated him. Recently, he'd had plans to tear out the lab and make it part of the living space. However, after his conversation with Annabel, he'd put his plans on hold.

He and Annabel had agreed to try some new experiments. When they discussed the idea, William had felt a momentary excitement. After being stuck in a miserable, boring mood for months, contemplating something new and challenging was a welcome change from putting in walls and flooring.

The problem came later when he tried to devise an experiment that motivated him. Pitting his abilities against Annabel might have been exciting when he knew very little about such matters, but things had changed. Even if Annabel proved that she had powers too, what difference did it make? Abilities were of no consequence if a person had no use for them. It was like having the ability to see color when you lived in a world that was all gray.

"You haven't been in your lab for a while," a voice called out.

William looked up and saw Raphael. His angelic friend stood in the doorway. "And you haven't been around for quite some time."

Raphael's face lit up with a smile. "You haven't wanted to see me."

"Why bother?" William asked. He walked towards the doorway, past Raphael, and into the new entertainment room. He sat down on the sofa, staring straight ahead, ignoring Raphael when the angel took a seat in William's new recliner.

"You were making progress with controlling your abilities," Raphael said. "Are you ready to continue?"

"I don't see the point in having special abilities. Why would I want to work on them?"

"You seem depressed. Are you unhappy with Annabel? I'm sure that being married might take some adjustment after being a bachelor for so long."

"I don't think it has anything to do with her. In fact, she's probably the only thing that keeps me on this earth."

"William, are you saying you don't enjoy being in this amazing world?"

William narrowed his eyes in Raphael's direction. "After seeing and feeling what paradise is like and knowing what we humans have settled for here in these bodies, why would I think that this is an amazing world?"

"I don't understand."

"Of course you don't. You're an angel, Raphael. You live in a state of bliss. You never come down from your high."

"But you can have bliss, too. Human beings can experience unbounded joy."

"Perhaps, but when I contemplate the future, I have zero desire to seek out that joy. Nothing interests me. Even my feelings for Annabel have changed. I love her, but the flame of passion is waning more and more each day."

"William, you need to change your perspective. If you don't, your physical vessel will suffer."

Raphael was right. William could feel his body's life force declining. "With a little luck, I'll soon be free of the physical. And this time, Arel won't have the power to stop me from crossing over."

"What about Annabel?"

"I've been observing her. She's not nearly as afraid as she once was. It will take some adjustment, but I have faith that she'll be fine. In fact, I think she'll find someone else to love. She can have that family that she talks about."

"What about you? Don't you want children?"

William glared back. "Haven't you been listening? I have no wants or desires. And I'm tired of being like this. I've never been a complainer or whined about ill fortune. I despise myself for sounding this way, but I don't want to change either. I'm done with this life."

"What about Arel? The two of you came into this lifetime vowing to help each other."

William smiled. "Arel is fine. In fact, he's my opposite. He's more involved with life than ever. When I check in on his mindset, he's like some happy child exploring every feeling and experience he stumbles across. Everything in his environment gets his attention. Even some small problem, a few crumbs on his rug, is a cause for concern, a reason to hold on to life and restore the balance of order. Soon he'll be married and totally caught up in even more drama. I have no desire to stick around for that."

"You act like you don't really matter to him or anyone else."

"That's not the problem. The problem is that I don't matter to myself."

"Do you still resent Arel for passing on angelic blood?"

William laughed. "What good would that do? What's done is done. And there's no way to go back to that time when I loved life from a limited perspective. Besides, I've had a very good run. I've had many years of loving who I am. Maybe it's time to move on."

Raphael got up and stared down at William. "What if you move on and find out that you made a mistake? What if the other side isn't as interesting as you think?"

William sighed. "Then I'll have a challenge again, won't I? And maybe that's what I lack here, something that tests my mettle."

* * *

Arel stood by the kitchen door. His phone was pressed to his ear. Annabel was on the other end, calling from London. As soon as he said hello to her, she started sharing her fears. She'd overheard a conversation that William had with Raphael. Her first reaction was to panic. Her second thought was to contact Arel and find out what to do.

Arel knew he needed to reassure her, but how? He was almost as scared as Annabel. When she announced that William had lost his will to live, Arel's heart nearly stopped. His jaw seized up, and every muscle, from head to toe, went rigid. He had to take a deep breath to steady himself before he replied. "William isn't going anywhere." His tone was insistent even if his inner thoughts were lining up with Annabel's panic.

"How can you know that?" Annabel asked. Her weak, pitiful voice turned angry as she continued. "I don't think you care anymore,

Arel! Since you've discovered someone new in your life, you've ignored William and me completely."

Arel put his hand to his face. It had taken a couple of days, but his cheek had finally healed. Now, as he stressed out over William, it was instantly on fire again. But pain was the least of his worries. He had to clear his mind and concentrate on what Annabel was telling him. Was she right? Had he fallen into his former, self-indulgent pattern again? He began to backtrack at once. "If that's true, Annabel, I'm sorry. I promise to do whatever it takes to help you and William."

"What are you going to do?" Annabel yelled. She paused after her question. There was a long moment before she whispered her next words. "I hear William in the foyer. He's back from his walk. I have to go."

"I won't let you down," Arel blurted out. It was too late. The line was dead before he could deliver his promise. "Dammit!" he protested.

He walked out of the kitchen, calling out as he approached the living room. "Michael, we have a problem." When he looked up, Michael wasn't in his usual chair by the window. Before the phone call, the angel was serenely staring out. Currently, Carey was sitting in Michael's chair, studying a motorcycle magazine.

"Where's Michael?" Arel asked.

Carey looked up. "He stepped out for a while."

"Stepped out where?"

Carey put his reading aside. "Can I help?"

Arel knew he should be patient, no matter how urgently he needed to talk to Michael. He also knew that the young man who sat in front of him was a powerful angel in his own right. But it was hard to think that Carey was as wise and capable as Michael.

Carey's boyish face broke out in a smile. "I'm sorry if I don't inspire as much confidence."

Arel sat down on the sofa. "I'm sorry, too. It's just hard to think of you in the same way as I think of Michael. Maybe it's just me, but the two of you seem very different."

"We are different, but that doesn't mean I can't be a friend when you need one."

"Then I won't sugarcoat my feelings, Carey."

Carey's smile turned into a grin. "I don't think you've done that since you found out my true identity."

131

Arel ignored the remark. "Please, I have a very serious problem."

"Are you referring to the situation with William?"

Arel touched his cheek and winced. The blister he'd had after Elise kissed him was nothing compared to what he was experiencing now. His skin felt like it had been seared with a branding iron. When he allowed himself to tap into the source of the pain, he remembered his initial reunion with William in New York. After many years of not seeing each other, their meeting was extremely upsetting to Arel. In his mind, William had betrayed him by making him a vampire.

The hatred in Arel's heart was so all consuming that he'd sought revenge. He'd taunted William until William bit his cheek and swallowed a bit of Arel's blood. That tiny taste passed on angelic blood to William, and it altered William's life.

Elise had kissed Arel's cheek in the very same place. With a heavy sigh, he rubbed the spot in spite of the pain. "Every time I think of how strong and self-assured William was before my need for—"

"Payback?"

"Yes, but in spite of all the hell that William went through as a result, I never felt the satisfaction I thought I'd feel. It's been the opposite. It's like I have two lives to worry about now, my own and William's."

"So you're blaming yourself for William's current condition?"

Arel put his head back on the sofa. "When I was in London, I noticed that William was having a hard time, but I thought he'd handle it in his own way. I guess I was hoping he'd returned to his old, confident self."

"I'm sure that William appreciates that you still believe in him."

"Oh please, William doesn't care about what I think. Give me some sage advice about what to do, something that will work."

Before Carey could answer, Arel heard Michael in the foyer. "Finally, the prodigal angel returns."

"I saw Elise walking Freddie," Michael explained. "I wanted to ask her how she was doing."

"I'll let you two talk," Carey said as he excused himself.

Arel stood up and crossed his arms. "And where do you think you're going, Carey? I thought you said you wanted to help."

Carey hesitated at the garage door. "Michael's back. Besides, I got new brake pads for my bike."

Arel studied Carey's face and frowned. The angelic wisdom was gone, replaced by a youthful mischief. "Angel or not, are you being careful when you take that aging machine out on the highway?"

Carey tossed back a quick nod. "Absolutely."

Arel knew that angels didn't lie, but he wondered if Carey didn't stretch the truth at times. He turned to Michael with a frown. "I worry about him."

"Why?" Michael asked.

"I think he sometimes forgets that he's an angel."

Michael walked into the living room. "Elise asked about you. She hopes you're feeling well."

"I don't want to hear about her well-wishes. She nearly finished me off with her lethal lips. But that's not important. I want to discuss William. He's entertaining a death wish."

"Yes, I know."

"Why didn't you say something to me?"

"I try not to interfere, you know that."

"I'd think you'd make an exception when it comes to life and death."

"Are you planning on talking to him?"

Arel held his cheek again. "I have to be careful. William doesn't know that Annabel's been spying on him. But I promised to help. And you have to advise me on what to do."

"I'll do whatever I can," Michael said.

"Annabel says William talked about needing a challenge."

"Do you think that's going to solve anything?"

"No, but it might buy some time. William is going through a phase, just like I did with the good and evil business. Once he gets past this part of the process, he'll bounce back."

"Bounce back? To where?"

"I don't know! That's why I'm talking to you."

Michael hesitated. "My advice never seems to satisfy you."

"Because it's usually airy-fairy, and I'm dealing with hard facts. William is sitting in London trying to bow out."

"Arel, I agreed to give you my blood. I don't think there was anything airy-fairy about that."

"You're wrong. Your blood is the most airy-fairy element of all. It's about connecting to the invisible, to the intangible. I've been able to make adjustments and learn how to use it, but William can't do that."

"What do you mean?"

"After I talked to Annabel, I tapped into William's thoughts. It only took a moment to see the problem. William never wanted your blood, and he still can't live with its effects."

"But he's proven otherwise. He's very capable. He's demonstrated that over and over when he's helped you."

"Yes, but that's not enough. After all those experiences with angelic armies on my crazy, alternate world, he's turning towards your kind, Michael. Your blood is ruining his chances of finding happiness on the earth."

"Or perhaps something else is bothering him. Remember that my blood is about helping a person reclaim who they are, all parts of who they are."

"The only thing I know is that William seemed fine before I gave him your blood. Now, he seems lost."

"Arel, before you gave him angelic blood, he lived a very controlled, solitary life. Now, he has a wife, and he's facing the possibility of having a family. To fully embrace those things, he needs to recover the parts of himself that he left behind."

"How can I help him to do that?"

"You might need to let William understand himself a little better before you take action."

Arel let out a laugh that was tinged with bitterness. "I'm sure you're right. If I did anything to help, he'd probably be resentful and think I was butting in on his business again. On the other hand, I promised Annabel that I'd do something."

"Yes, you did, but—"

"Annabel doesn't want to hear any buts, Michael."

"I understand."

Arel glared back. "I understand, too."

"What's that?"

"From now on, I'm going to be more like you. You don't go around making promises. You keep your angelic nose clean and your mouth shut."

Twenty

ELISE CLOSED THE front door and hung up Freddie's leash in the closet. She'd just come back from their second walk of the day, and Freddie was tired. Elise smiled as she watched him getting ready for a nap. When he jumped into his dog bed, he dug furiously at the cushion. He circled round and round a number of times. Finally, he settled in and closed his eyes. The puppy was enthusiastic and deliberate, no matter what he did.

When Elise glanced around the living room, she realized how different the house felt since she'd adopted the puppy. Freddie's presence was everywhere she looked. Toys were scattered about, along with some remnants of things he liked to chew. Michael was right about dogs. They were good at helping their owners forget their problems.

Still, Elise felt that something was missing in her life. A partner. Someone who loved her. Someone she loved. She instantly thought about Arel. It had been a few days since he stood in her foyer and talked about having fevers. She believed him. His hand was hot to the touch. In fact, the heat that radiated off his person seemed to set off a fire inside of her. It ignited her heart and made it pound. Her blood felt too hot as it traveled through her body. It was a frightening, yet wonderful feeling that lingered long after he left the house.

As she remembered Arel's last visit, she had a moment of irritation. She was disappointed with herself. In spite of being more content with who she was and finding peace in her own doings, Arel still intruded on her thoughts more than she wanted. "Of course he does, Elise," she mumbled aloud. "You're a romance writer. You have love on the brain."

She frowned. Was her occupation the reason that her judgment was clouded, or would she think about Arel if she was an accountant? Would she tap out numbers and still imagine kissing him again?

She sighed. Her kiss didn't do Arel's cheek any good. Her lips left marks, tiny blisters on his skin. When she talked to Michael about it, he told her that Arel was convinced that he was allergic to her lipstick. Elise didn't bother to tell Michael the truth, but she hadn't been wearing lipstick when she kissed Arel.

She walked over to Freddie and crouched down to pet him. "Bad news, Freddie. Maybe our handsome neighbor is allergic to me. If that's the case, it's good that we never got too involved."

Freddie's eyes opened a little. He licked the air a couple of times, as if to console her. But his caring response didn't help. Elise knew the marks on Arel's cheek were there to keep her from prolonging any attachment. The universe or fate or some force of nature was telling her to move on.

She went over to the corner and grabbed a packing box. But any enthusiasm for leaving her home and getting a fresh start was lacking. Even if she put Arel out of her mind, she was going to miss Carey and Michael. In her darkest moments, they were like beacons in the storm, always dependable and helpful. She'd never met anyone who came close to being so understanding and insightful. Who would she turn to if she needed help again? Happily, they both gave her their phone numbers.

Just as she was letting a familiar feeling of depression take over, the phone rang. When she took the call and heard Peggy's voice, it lightened her mood. "A pizza party tonight?" she asked.

"I know it's short notice, Elise," Peggy replied, "but Carol and Kevin are coming over, and we thought you might want to join us. Arel is busy, but Carey and Michael will be here too."

Elise looked over at Freddie. He was sleeping so soundly that he was snoring. "Can I bring Freddie?"

As soon as Elise got off the phone, she rallied. A spark of hope was pushing out her feeling of loneliness. Perhaps, when she saw Michael that evening, she'd ask him about how to handle the move she'd be making in the near future.

* * *

Peggy walked into the kitchen carrying a stack of empty plates. Carol and Elise trailed behind her with other serving dishes. The three of them had abandoned the four men in the living room. With the guys talking sports and motorcycles, Peggy wanted to take a time out for a conversation with her friends. After she put the plates on the counter, she let out an uncomfortable sigh. "I shouldn't have eaten that last piece of pepperoni pizza."

Carol put down a serving tray and laughed. "I have to say that I'm very proud of myself. I stopped after two pieces."

Elise edged a couple of glasses onto the crowded counter. "It's strange, I'm usually ravenous when it comes to pizza, but I wasn't hungry."

Peggy turned and studied Elise's face. "Are you feeling okay?"

"I'm fine, but my mind's on things other than food. I'm busy with moving details, trying to find a house to rent when I'm not sure where I want to live."

Carol crossed her arms. "You could stay where you are."

Elise blushed. "No, that doesn't feel right."

Peggy pulled Elise into the corner of the room. "Is it Arel?" she asked in a whisper. "You still have feelings for him, don't you?"

Elise looked down and studied the floor. "It would have never worked, even if I hadn't acted, you know, so horrible."

Carol gave her a puzzled look. "But why? He seemed to like you."

"First of all, I don't know that Arel really liked me," Elise said quietly. "I think he's just a nice guy who didn't know how to break it off. Secondly, he's allergic to me."

Peggy pulled back. "Allergic to you? I didn't know that was possible."

Elise blinked back. "I haven't investigated the subject, but the proof was on Arel's cheek. I gave him the smallest, little kiss goodbye, and his cheek blistered. And it wasn't my lipstick because I wasn't wearing any."

"Wow, you did that?" Carol asked. "I thought he'd hurt himself again."

Elise shook her head. "No, it was me. In the past, I know I've had a sharp tongue, but I didn't know my lips were caustic."

Peggy smiled. "How do you know it was all you? Arel is a very different kind of guy. He's always surprising us with something new, especially when it comes to his body."

Elise's eyes brightened. "Really?"

Carol nodded. "Yes, he's a bit of a mystery."

Elise walked over to the counter and started scraping the plates. "All I know is that he and I don't seem to do well together. I thought we could at least be friends, but now I feel like we can't even have that kind of relationship, not if he breaks out in blisters if I touch him."

Peggy went over to Elise and tapped her shoulder. "Thank you for helping, but your feelings are more important than cleaning up. Do you want to talk about what's going on?"

Just as Elise turned around to answer, Freddie came running into the kitchen. He was followed by baby Sara and Carol's little boy, Ariel. Both toddlers were laughing as they tried to reach out to the puppy. Freddie didn't give them a chance to catch him. He skidded on the tile, swiveled and headed back out of the room.

Elise crossed her arms and laughed. "Did you see the expression on his little, puppy face? He's having a ball with your kids. Back home, with me writing all the time, I think he gets bored."

The sound of someone knocking on the back door interrupted Peggy's response. She was about to tell Elise that she was an exemplary dog owner. Instead, she went to the door to see who could possibly be visiting. After pulling the curtain aside, she promptly opened the door. "Arel, what are you doing here? I thought you were busy."

Arel started to answer, but he paused as soon as he saw Elise.

Elise practically jumped when their eyes met. "Excuse me, Peggy," she said as she started out of the kitchen. "I have to leave. I think I left something on the stove!"

Peggy understood Elise's nervous response. Elise was trying very hard to forget Arel, but it was easy to see that she still had a crush on him. She also seemed to be upset about injuring Arel's cheek.

Peggy felt sorry for the poor woman and excused herself. "I better go and see if I can help," she explained as she hurried to the living room. Once there, she paused. The room was a hub of activity. Elise was frantically trying to retrieve Freddie. The puppy had other ideas. He raced around the room even faster, delighted that someone else had joined in his "you can't catch me" game.

When the puppy ran towards the kitchen again, Elise stopped abruptly. She stared at Peggy with imploring eyes. "Please, Peggy, will you get Freddie for me? I can't go near Arel."

Elise's statement got the attention of the men who were seated around the coffee table. Kevin, Tim, Michael and Carey all looked at Elise with confusion.

"Is there a problem?" Tim asked.

Kevin joined in. "Yeah, what's going on? Can I help?"

Peggy held up her hand and signaled for quiet. When she looked at Elise, she smiled in a reassuring way. "Don't worry, I'll get Freddie. In the meantime, please, try to relax."

"Relax? With Arel around, I feel like some kind of Typhoid Mary," Elise protested.

"Everything's fine. I've got the puppy," Arel announced as he walked into the living room. He was carrying Freddie. "The little bugger was trying to eat my shoe."

Carol trailed in after Arel. "Yes, Freddie stopped running and became engrossed in Arel's footwear."

Elise began to back away. "Thank you for catching him, Arel, but keep your distance."

Kevin stood up and stared at Elise. "What's this about you being a Typhoid Mary?"

Peggy walked over to Arel and patted Freddie's soft, furry head. "Elise is convinced that Arel is very allergic to her."

Arel cleared his throat. "Actually, it's just her lipstick."

Peggy leaned in and thoughtlessly let Elise's secret slip out. "Arel, Elise told me that she wasn't wearing lipstick."

Arel immediately eyed Elise and frowned. "No lipstick?"

"I'm sorry," Elise whispered, flushing a deep pink and backing away. "But don't worry, I'm leaving," she said as she turned and made a dash for the door. As she was about to step outside, she paused long enough to issue orders to Carey. "Carey, please get Freddie and bring him over to my house."

Carey stood up and was about to comply when Freddie started struggling in Arel's arms. His efforts were so spirited that Arel wasn't able to hold on to him. The puppy slipped out of his grasp and onto the floor. Without hesitation, the little dog ran after Elise. He took advantage of the partially open door and disappeared outside.

Arel only hesitated for a moment before he too became part of the chase. He grumbled loudly as he rushed for the door too. "What is that woman's problem? She's so excitable!"

Peggy stood in the middle of the living room, not knowing what to say as Carey hurried past her and followed in Elise and Arel's tracks.

Kevin walked over, looking confused. "Is Arel kidding? He's complaining about Elise when he's the most excitable person I know."

Peggy agreed. "Those two are both very high strung."

Kevin crossed his arms. "It's a good thing they didn't fall for each other. Can you imagine what they'd be like if they lived together? It would be constant mayhem."

Peggy sighed. "We don't have to worry about that. Arel will be married soon, and I'm hoping his fiancé is the easy-going type."

* * *

Arel's sharp eyes followed the flash of white fur known as Freddie as it moved swiftly through the grass. There was enough moonlight to make his tracking task an easy one. The dog was headed for home. Arel also noticed Elise. As she sprinted towards her residence, she reminded him of the time when he'd thought she was some kind of other worldly sprite. In the moonlight, she looked almost like that fairy again. There was a glow to her energy that was quite interesting.

Unable to help himself, he tuned into her thoughts. He wanted to know what it was about her that could upset his equilibrium. He didn't get any quick answers. Even though her aura was quite pretty overall, Elise's mind was a jumble of erratic thoughts. She was definitely embarrassed. She was also mad at herself for being unable to control her feelings. She wanted to let go of the infatuation that she'd had for Arel, but there were obstacles she didn't know how to overcome. The thought of him being with another woman added a fiery element to her body's response. Elise was fighting it, but she was having a very difficult time managing something that was new for her.

Arel paused, sorry that he'd violated his neighbor's privacy. He severed his connection to her thoughts, but now he knew more than he wanted. He frowned as he watched Elise pick up her puppy and go inside her house. A moment later the porch light was turned off.

Carey joined him and smiled. "I see that Elise has her little dog."

"Yes, Freddie is safe."

"What's wrong, Arel? You sound upset."

"I did something I shouldn't have. I tapped into Elise's thoughts."

"I thought you swore off that kind of thing."

"Yes, but Elise is such an unpredictable kind of person that I needed to know more about her, what makes her tick."

"But you have Claire now. Why are you concerned about Elise?"

Arel wanted to offer an answer, but he couldn't stop thinking about the passionate fire in Elise's core. It almost matched his own. Happily, he'd learned some control. "I think Elise needs more help, Carey. Otherwise, she could suffer the way I suffered. And I wouldn't wish that on anyone."

"Michael and I are working on it."

"Work harder," Arel barked back. "With that kind of energy next door all the time, I'm distracted. And I don't have time for such distractions. I have a wedding to plan, and more importantly, I have to figure out how to help William."

Carey stepped back with a look of surprise. "What do you mean? With your powerful shields, how can Elise be a problem?"

Arel averted his eyes. Carey had an excellent point. There was no reason why he couldn't shut Elise and her energy out. He offered the angel a sly smile. "You're right. Maybe Elise isn't the problem. I might be a bit overwhelmed by my current situation with Claire."

"You still want to get married, don't you?"

"Of course, I just mean that falling in love happened so quickly, so unexpectedly. We were so close when we spent time together in Paris, but now, when we talk, Claire is different."

"How is she different?"

"She's very excited about her work, but we don't talk very much about our relationship."

"Are you concerned about the bond that you share?"

Arel shook his head, reminding himself of how wonderful it was to hold Claire in his arms. "No, Claire just loves what she's doing. I'm sure we'll be very close again once she's back here with me."

Carey smiled. "Good. And don't worry about Elise. Michael and I will make sure that she knows we are always there if she needs us."

Arel took a last glance at Elise's empty porch. "Listen, Carey, an angel doesn't have the same problems as a human. So please be careful in how you help Elise. If she doesn't manage her feelings properly, she could end up very bitter again."

"Your concern is admirable, but from what I've experienced, Elise learns and integrates the things we've helped her with very quickly. With a little more assistance, I think she'll get through this stage quite nicely."

Arel grunted out his complaint. "What you're really saying is that she's a lot faster at learning than I am."

"No, of course not. You've done an amazing job at changing your life, and you've done it in a very short time."

"Really?"

"Arel, you've cleared many emotional roadblocks. Be proud of yourself."

"Thank you, but I do have a question about a different matter. Why did you call me on my phone earlier?"

"Is that why you showed up at Peggy's house this evening?"

"Yes, I got a call from you, but then I couldn't call you back. I didn't know if it was something important, so I stopped over to investigate."

"Sorry about that. I must have pocket-dialed you. I hope I didn't interrupt your evening."

"No, thankfully your call came in just after I said my goodbyes to Claire."

"How is she?"

"Busy. In fact, our conversations are usually short. A lot of the time she doesn't have cell phone coverage or access to the internet. I'll be happy when she's finished with this project she's on."

"And the wedding plans?"

"Initially, I had a lot of ideas, but when I described them to Claire, she asked me to hold off on anything concrete until she gets back. I guess we have very different thoughts when it concerns the ceremony and celebration."

"Are you okay with that?"

"Of course."

"And what about William? Have you decided how you want to help him?"

"Unlike you, Michael gave me sound advice about giving William space to figure things out for himself."

Carey returned a look of surprise. "I guess I thought I said something similar."

"You say a lot of things, Carey. I can't remember it all. Anyway, I know that I have to stop trying to control everything. Like tonight, what business do I have to make a judgment about my neighbor or her life? Elise is someone I dated for a little while. But I never really got to know her."

"So you've decided to stay out of William's current situation?"

Arel looked at his hand and examined the scar on his palm. It was the result of his blood brother ceremony with William. "William is his own man, a most thoughtful one at that. He's always been much more responsible too. So what right do I have to think I know what's best for him?"

"And what about Annabel?"

"I have to put some things straight with both of them, and I want your support, Carey. I want you to come to London with me."

"You're going to London?"

"Yes, what I want to tell Annabel and William is something that has to be said face to face."

Twenty-One

WILLIAM WATCHED AREL as the man leaned forward in his seat. Arel's eyes were focused on the books scattered about on the coffee table. He was stacking them. As he did, he carefully edged each one into conformity. Carey, his angelic companion, sat in a chair next to Arel, looking on with fascination. It was as if the young man was purposefully blanking out everything but Arel's actions.

William found himself chuckling silently. Arel had always been a fascinating subject to study. His interactions with the world were carried out in a cautious, controlled and detailed manner. Yet, Arel could change in an instant. His care and concern could be swept away by an emotional outburst that was anything but ordered. Those eruptions were frequently chaotic. However, at the moment, everything Arel did was carried out with a calm, boring attitude.

The silence was broken by the clinking of tea cups on a tray that Annabel ferried into the room. Carey jumped up to help her set it on the coffee table. His young face brightened as he checked out the sweets on the tray.

"Annabel, wow, those Napoleons look amazing," Carey said with eagerness.

Annabel reached up and caressed his cheek. "I knew they were one of your favorites."

Arel sat back and gave Carey a cautious frown. "Remember, don't overindulge, Carey. Moderation is a virtue."

Carey sat down quickly and put his hands together. "Maybe I'll just have something to drink, maybe some water."

Arel rubbed his brow. "Sorry, I shouldn't have said anything. You're quite able to make your own decisions. It's just an old habit I'm going to break." He looked at William and then at Annabel. "In fact, while I'm apologizing, I want to say something to both of you."

William's muscles instantly. His physical body knew to be wary. When Arel made announcements that had an edge, it was time to

144

brace oneself. It was clear that Annabel felt the same. She quickly sat down next to him and reached out for his hand.

"Why did you come here with so little notice, Arel?" she asked. "Is there something wrong? Troubles with Claire?"

Arel smiled. "No, everything is fine." Still smiling, he got up and put two pastries on a plate and handed them to Carey. "Here you go. Enjoy yourself." When he looked at William, his face was all smiles, but his eyes were still and almost vacant.

William's hand tightened on Annabel's so quickly she winced. He loosened his grip at once, but he could feel the atmosphere in the room changing. There was still sunlight streaming through a window, but there was no warmth to it. "So why are you here, Arel? And don't tell me that everything is fine. You have an agenda."

Arel averted his eyes, staring at his palm. "An agenda? Is that what you think?"

Carey took a large bite of his pastry, his eyes riveted on Arel again. "Arel, I wish you liked sweets. These Napoleons are fantastic."

Arel's hooded lids suddenly opened wide, meeting Carey's bright gaze with one of wonder and curiosity. "Maybe I should," he said. "I'm going to be married to Claire soon. I need to act more like a normal person."

Carey laughed. "All that I know is that I love food."

Annabel smiled. "Me too," she said with a bit of mischief in her voice. "Especially when I get nervous."

Arel nodded pensively as his eyes wandered over the tray of food and drink. "Yes, I have a lot of bad habits that I'm determined to leave behind."

William's jaw tightened when Arel reached out for a plate. "What are you doing? You can't stomach food."

Arel snatched up a pastry and quickly dropped it on his plate. "It's time for a change."

William felt his eye twitch. Arel was trying his best to appear peaceful and composed. Yet he held his dessert plate away from his body with a shaky hand and eyed his bakery item with the caution that one exercised around a stick of dynamite. "Arel, listen to me. Just because you're getting married that doesn't mean you have to do things that you don't want to do."

Arel ignored his advice and guided the pastry towards his face. After a hard swallow, he shoved part of the Napoleon into his mouth.

After he bit off a sizable portion, he started to chew deliberately, but his eyes took on a look of discomfort that bordered on dread. Yet, he seemed determined to complete what he'd started.

William, along with Annabel and Carey, watched and waited for Arel to swallow. Carey's hand, clinging to a half-eaten pastry was stalled in mid-air. Annabel's free hand covered her mouth as if she needed to hide her uneasiness.

Still unable to make his food go down, Arel grabbed the teapot and poured out some of its contents into a cup. When he took a hurried sip, it seemed to overpower whatever control he had on his body. Grabbing a linen napkin, he jumped up and ran for the kitchen.

Annabel jumped up too. "Poor dear, he's trying so hard to be what Claire wants him to be," she said as she followed him out of the room.

William remained where he was. The sound of Arel gagging elicited something in him. That something always made him angry. It was a need to protect Arel from himself. But why? Why did he have to act like he was Arel's guardian?

Carey smiled over at him. "He feels the same way about you."

"Is that why he's here? He wants to keep me on this earth like he did before?"

"No, quite the opposite. But it's hard, William. The bond that you two share runs deep. Yet, in the end, he'll force himself to let go of you. He wants you to be happy no matter what."

"Like he forced himself to eat that pastry?"

"Yes, he still doesn't know how to allow those he loves to make their own decisions. But he's determined to change no matter the pain to himself."

William knew the feeling. When Arel was a young man and determined to kill himself, William couldn't allow that to happen. He thought he knew better. His decision to stop Arel from taking that action started events they were both still dealing with. "And what about you, Carey? How does an angel fit into this tangled web we humans weave for ourselves?"

Carey brushed a few crumbs off his shirt. "I don't let confusion or doubts sway me. I remain focused on the positive, expansive side of creation, no matter what."

"And what would you say to someone who can't see beyond their doubts?"

146

Carey leaned in. "One trick that I've seen people use is to put off any decisions when they're in that state. In fact, Arel's first thought about your situation was to find a way to distract you, to give you time to find a better solution."

"What changed his mind?"

"He admires you, William, even looks up to you. He decided you know best."

William frowned at the thought. Life felt empty. Any wisdom he might have had in the past had slipped away, just like his passion. "He's wrong, again. But don't tell him I said that."

Carey returned a puzzled look. "Are you saying Arel should have tried his original plan?"

William shrugged. "I don't know. I'm betting that I would have been angry, even incensed at his interference."

"But—"

"But I'm sure his crazy antics would have been engaging too."

Carey looked away. "I don't think I should have had this conversation with you."

"Why?"

"Arel should have told you about his intentions, not me."

William clasped Carey's shoulder. "I won't let on that you said anything."

"Thanks, it might be better that way."

* * *

With Annabel next to him at the kitchen sink, Arel could feel his face redden with embarrassment. Annabel had been very kind. When he couldn't swallow the pastry and spit it out, she'd hovered close by, telling him to relax if possible, to let his body settle down slowly. When he turned to face her, she gave him a smile of concern. He tried to smile back. "I'm sorry about all this. I thought I could eat something, but I guess my body felt differently."

Annabel gestured him over to the kitchen table. "Sit down. Let yourself recover."

Arel took a seat and a few breaths. As he did, his embarrassment quickly gave way to emotions that were much deeper, but clearly making themselves known. He leaned forward and clasped his hands.

He needed to control a sensation that was coursing through his body. It was a terrible fear that his world was falling apart. He bowed his head, not wanting Annabel to see his face and the grief that was taking over. "What are we going to do, Annabel?"

Annabel leaned in too. "What are you talking about?"

Arel glanced up, hoping that Annabel still retained some of her former angelic wisdom. Instead, he saw a frightened woman staring back. "Nothing. Never mind."

"Arel, tell me what you're thinking!" Annabel demanded in a hushed, but insistent tone.

"I told you that I wouldn't let William leave this world, but I lied. After thinking about it, I know I can't keep enforcing my will over his. It's not right."

"Is that why you're here? To tell me you've given up on him?"

Arel felt his gut flare with outrage. "I'd do anything to change the way he feels, but I can't go on believing that I know what's best for him. If you were still an angel, you'd know that too."

"All that I know is that William has lost his way. You and your damnable world of soldier mice and battles have clouded his mind."

Arel sat back and closed his eyes. Annabel was right. Months before, he'd used his power to create his own fantastic world. It was an alternate reality where he'd hoped to escape his misguided life. He'd drawn William into that world. In the end, he'd resolved many of his own issues, but at the expense of William's sense of reality. "I pleaded with him, didn't I? I asked him not to involve himself, Annabel. But Will insisted on trying to help me. It's what we've been doing for a very long time. One of us has to stop."

"And you're deciding to bow out now? With William's life on the line?"

Arel felt another flare go off in his gut. It was a warning sign that he needed to get his emotions under control. But there was so much anger coming off of Annabel. She was holding him responsible for all of William's problems. He needed to put up his shields, to protect himself from her unrestrained temper, but the ex-angel had a point. Her desperate burden of pain shifted and was absorbed into the firestorm building in his gut. As he thought about what she'd said, his temperature escalated. He reached out for Annabel's hand. "I don't know what to do to fix any of it!"

Annabel pulled away, her brows heavily lined. "Arel, you're so hot! And your face—" Pushing back her chair, Annabel got up and ran from the room, calling out. "William, Carey! Come quick! Arel is turning purple!"

When Carey and William came running into the kitchen, Arel realized he'd let his inner core go beyond the limits of safety. Tendrils of fire had spread rapidly into every part of him. His body felt like it was in the midst of a great bonfire. But his spirit wasn't tethered to his body. It wasn't trapped by the fire. Instead, he felt it soaring upwards.

When he looked down from a much higher vantage point, he observed his body. It was slumped over, consumed with fever. Carey and William were on either side, trying to help. But in his spirit form, Arel felt like he could breathe again. And he wasn't alone. Michael was next to him. The angel's radiant, smooth countenance was comforting. They'd been working together for a long time, and he knew Michael's guiding hand could help him now. No matter how crazy he sometimes felt, Michael always found a way to set him straight.

"What must you think of us, Michael? With all our constant drama and pain?"

Michael smiled back. "I think you're trying to find balance, but time is moving very swiftly. You have to do your best not to let yourself fall back into guilt and regret. Their currents are treacherous and unyielding."

"But Annabel is right about my track record. And I don't want to repeat the past!"

"Then you have to let go of it. You can't let anything but the present moment exist if you want freedom for yourself."

"And William?"

Michael's smile broadened. "You might not think so, but he's learning the same thing."

Arel took another deep breath, inhaling Michael's message in the same way that he took in air. Michael's words were accompanied by blue, cooling waves of energy. They were so soothing that Arel relaxed completely. In the next moment, he felt himself slam back into his body. The idea of freedom for William and himself was still vibrating in his energy body. It was powerful and sustaining. He felt the strength to go beyond his mistakes. As soon as he made the decision, his physical form began to return to normal. A few moments later, he found himself smiling as he pushed William and Carey aside. His joyful expression came from his vision of a better future.

But William wasn't in a humorous mood. "You're still such a child, aren't you, Arel? You're always acting out when you can't get your way."

Arel's feelings were bruised by the statement. He turned and grabbed William's shirt with both hands. "It's not true. I'm smiling because I think we have a chance, Will. Both of us can find a solution to this mess we're in. I'm sure of it."

William sneered back. "Oh, please! You can't even see what a mistake you're making with Claire, much less solve anything."

"Why are you so critical of the woman I love?"

"Don't get me started on that subject, but I'll make a deal with you. Put off this marriage for a couple of months, and I'll put off leaving this earth for the same length of time."

Arel winced. "What's my marrying Claire got to do with anything?"

William removed Arel's hands from his clothing and stepped back. "I don't think she's the right woman for you. And I don't want you to marry someone that will make your life a living hell."

"I realized that you had objections, but I didn't know how strongly you felt about her."

William stuck out his hand. "So it's a deal? You'll give yourself some time, and so will I."

Arel hesitated. He loved Claire. He wanted to slip a ring on her finger and cement their bond in marriage as soon as possible. But William's life was at stake. What could he do but shake William's hand? Afterwards, he put his feelings in words. "It's a deal, Will, because I do trust you. But I want to tell you right now. I don't care how long it takes, I will marry Claire."

"Whatever," William said.

As Arel watched William leave the room, he felt Annabel's hand on his arm. When he looked at her, she smiled.

"Thank you for agreeing to William's proposal, Arel. And I'm sorry for being so hard on you."

Arel studied her face. The anger was gone, replaced by relief. "And I'm sorry that I've caused so much trouble since you took off your wings. Anyway, I'm sure you'll be happy to know that Carey and I are flying back to Chicago tomorrow."

Annabel's face brightened. "Have a good trip, and let's just hope the worst is over for both you and William."

Twenty-Two

AFTER THE GET-TOGETHER at Peggy's house and humiliating herself, Elise avoided seeing anyone. It was only when a couple of days had passed that she felt more at ease. She wasn't thinking about Arel as much as before. When she walked past his house, there were no rapid heartbeats or sweaty palms. A chance meeting with Michael at the mailbox made her wonder if her reactions had to do with Arel's absence. Michael told her that Arel had gone to London. Curious, she invited Michael in for a chat.

"How is the book coming?" he asked as he followed her into the living room.

She gestured towards the sofa. "Almost done. I'll go over it a time or two to make sure the story is consistent and free of any major flaws, but essentially, it's finished."

Michael sat down on the sofa. "I'm happy to hear that."

Elise began to remove books off of some built-in shelves. "I hope you don't mind if I do some packing while we talk."

"No, of course not. Would you like some help?"

Elise pointed to Freddie. The puppy was dragging in one of her tennis shoes. "I'm fine here, but could you retrieve my shoe? I must have forgotten to put it on a shelf after our walk."

Michael got up and crouched down. "Bring me the shoe, Freddie," he said in a quiet voice.

Elise was about to correct Michael's approach to doggie communication. Freddie never listened to anything she said once he had hold of one of her shoes. But when Freddie obediently trotted over to Michael, she was too surprised to utter any words. She couldn't believe it when Freddie even dropped the shoe in Michael's hand. "How did you do that?" she asked.

Michael came over and handed her the shoe. "Animals and I seem to understand each other."

"Is it a gift you were born with?"

Michael glanced upwards. "You might say that."

Elise picked at a chewed shoelace and frowned. "Can I ask you something about Arel? Peggy told me that he's unusual."

"In what way?"

"She says he's more reactive, physically. She thinks that's why he responded so negatively to my kiss on his cheek. Anyway, I'm hoping it's not just me."

"Perhaps you should check the matter out with him."

"Oh no, I wouldn't want to be around him if he's allergic to me."

"But the two of you dated for some time, and he was fine."

"That's true. So I can't understand what happened."

"Arel is returning home tonight. Why don't you stop over tomorrow morning and talk to him? I think you'll feel better if you come to some kind of understanding about what's going on."

Elise twisted the chewed shoelace. "Maybe you're right. It's hard thinking that I'm a danger to the opposite sex."

Michael smiled. "Come over around eleven. Carey will enjoy seeing you again too."

* * *

Arel sat on the sofa, glancing at Michael at regular intervals. "I can't believe you invited that woman over for a visit. I have way too much on my mind to spend time with a looney."

Carey walked in carrying a plate of treats. "I thought Elise might enjoy some of these oatmeal raisin cookies. I picked them up at the bakery when I took an early spin on my bike."

"Very thoughtful, Carey," Michael said.

Arel gave Carey a look of annoyance. "She doesn't need cookies. She needs a good psychiatrist."

Carey's face registered surprise. "I thought we talked about Elise, and you said you weren't going to make any more judgments about her."

"That was before I found out she was barging into my home again."

Michael edged forward. "Arel, Elise is upset. She thinks there's something wrong with her after what happened to your cheek."

Arel stiffened. He'd arrived home the night before, still going over his visit with William and hoping something good would come out of it. Now, low on energy and patience, he had to entertain his crazy neighbor. "Well, she's right. Her lips are dangerous."

Michael smiled. "I don't think so."

"I don't think so either," Carey said as he headed back towards the kitchen.

Arel crossed his arms. "So explain why my cheek blistered?"

Michael glanced out the front window, stood up and started for the foyer. "Elise is coming up the walk. Maybe you can discuss that question with her."

Arel jumped up and grabbed Michael's arm. All of his recent encounters with Elise had involved something that didn't feel right. The incident with the rug. Her kiss. Then her frenzied departure when she saw him at Peggy's. Elise was definitely unstable. "Do not leave me alone with that woman, Michael. Is that clear?"

"Yes, of course it is."

"Good, and when you let her in, make sure she sits on the sofa. I'll use your chair by the window."

Michael nodded. "I understand."

* * *

Arel positioned himself in Michael's chair, preparing himself for whatever was coming next. When he snatched a glance at Elise, her legs were crossed and she had a shaky foot going constantly. She barely looked at him, but when she did, her eyes were wide and anxious. He was sure it was just a matter of time before the woman did something irrational again. Presently, Michael and Carey were keeping her occupied with small talk.

Taking advantage of a momentary reprieve, Arel let his gaze wander to the window. Outside, a fresh layer of leaves blanketed the lawn. They'd probably blown over from a neighbor's oak tree. Perhaps Michael would volunteer to give the problem his attention later that day. The idea had barely crossed Arel's mind, when the sound of Elise clearing her throat made him glance back at her. Her blue eyes were focused and alert, on him. They were so attentive that he had the feeling that she could see right through him. He sat up immediately and made sure his shields were in place. It helped him feel more secure, but he couldn't stop Elise from asking him a question.

"Arel, I don't understand why my kiss hurt you, but it's really bothering me," she said in a quiet tone. "Can you think of any reason why something like that happened? Because it's never happened to the men I've kissed in the past."

Arel's mind was instantly side-tracked. He wondered how many men Elise had kissed before him. Two? Three? A dozen?

When he didn't comment, Elise continued her query. "I've known a lot of guys, Arel. So why didn't any of them have a problem? Maybe what happened isn't my fault. Have you ever noticed being overly sensitive when other women kissed you?"

Arel sat up, immediately offended by Elise's question. "First of all, I haven't kissed all that many women. Secondly, I've never had any problem when I did kiss someone."

Carey smiled. "Elise, in case you didn't know, Arel is kind of the reclusive type."

Elise looked down, studying her clasped hands. "I see. In that case, what happened must be some kind of fluke, maybe we have bad chemistry."

Arel sighed at the sound of Elise's disappointed lament. He knew he was contributing to her unease by being an ungracious host. She looked sad and troubled when she got to her feet. He stood up too. For some reason, he wanted to make amends for the way he was acting. Like Carey said, he'd been very judgmental ever since they'd broken off their relationship. And if Elise had interacted with a lot of men before they met, she couldn't have caustic lips. "I'm sorry I couldn't be more helpful," he said as he approached her. He held out his hand. "My body has been overly sensitive at times. So it's probably me that's the problem."

Elise put her hands behind her back. "Maybe we shouldn't touch if that's the case."

Arel laughed. "I'm okay, really. Besides, we have held hands before."

Elise smiled too, slowly bringing her hand forward. "I'll be moving soon. And it would be nice to part company knowing we can at least touch each other."

Arel took Elise's hand. "I wish you the best wherever you go."

Elise lifted her gaze enough to let their eyes meet for the briefest moment. When she pulled her hand away, she did it quickly. "I better go. I have more packing to do."

Arel didn't answer. He didn't know what to say or do as a feeling of familiarity lingered. It was so strong, he almost felt like an old friend was saying goodbye.

When Michael returned after showing Elise out, he smiled at Arel. "That went well, don't you think?"

"Yes, it did. In fact, I got the strangest feeling when she was leaving. It was almost like Elise is a kindred soul."

"Perhaps she reminds you of yourself."

Arel paused, remembering how he'd sensed an inner fire in Elise. When they shook hands, he felt that fire spark again. He recognized the feeling. "I think you're right. We're both people who are looking for someone to share our life. It took a long time for me, but I finally found Claire. I hope Elise finds someone soon too."

"Yes, she'd like that."

"I mean she's pretty enough, I suppose. Some men might even find her very attractive."

Michael smiled. "Yes, I agree."

"And she's smart too. Perhaps, since she's changed, she could be suitable dating material."

Carey came out of the kitchen and joined them. "Are you discussing Elise?"

Arel gave him the once-over, wondering if Carey was still hungry. "There's sandwich material in the refrigerator for lunch."

Carey smiled. "I'm fine. I finished off the extra cookies."

Arel crossed his arms and looked at Michael. "Shouldn't Carey take better care of his body?"

Michael crossed his arms too, looking more contemplative than usual. "Well, I suppose that's a good question, but look at you, Arel, you don't eat or drink at all. Yet, you're fine."

"That's true."

Carey patted Arel's back. "Technically, you're a little like us. Food is optional, but if we ingest something, and it contributes to a sense of well-being, the rules of health are a bit different than for most humans."

Arel shifted the conversation to his recent guest. "Speaking of normal humans, Elise looks like she's sufficiently fed. She's quite, how would I put it, she's very womanly."

"She's different than Claire," Carey added. "Claire isn't as, I don't know—"

Arel cut in. "Elise might have more curves, but Claire is perfect. There's not an extra ounce on her body. She's gorgeous."

Carey nodded. "But still, Elise has no reason to feel bad about her physical form. I think that both she and Claire are very well constructed."

"Well constructed?" Arel laughed. Most of the time Carey acted like any other young man, but at other times, his angelic side was evident. "That's one way of putting it. But I don't have time to discuss women. I have things I need to do."

He was about to return to his to-do list when his phone chirped. His eyes brightened when he saw who was texting him. "It's from Claire!"

Carey and Michael remained silent as Arel studied the long message he'd received. When he looked up, a surge of happiness took hold. "Guess what? Claire says that her dig has been temporarily put on hold. Something about the unstable politics in the region. She's going to take a plane out as soon as possible." His face lit up with a smile. "I can't believe my luck. She's going to be here within a couple of days! Isn't that the best news?"

* * *

Peggy was walking to her mailbox when she saw Elise leaving Arel's house. Her neighbor looked more relaxed. Perhaps her troubles with Arel were getting resolved. Peggy raised her hand and waved. "Hi, Elise! Can I talk to you for a moment?"

When Elise waved back and came over, Peggy gave her a welcoming smile. "Carol and I are meeting for coffee soon. Would you like to join us?"

Elise glanced back at her house. "I guess it would be okay to leave Freddie for a bit longer. We had a very big walk early this morning. When I left him, he was sleeping soundly."

Peggy grabbed the mail out of her box. "Little Sara is down for a nap too. And Kevin has the day off, so he's watching little Ariel."

Elise smiled. "So it'll just be the three of us."

"Yes. Do you want to come in and help me?"

"Sure, I'd love to," Elise said as they walked back to Peggy's house.

Once they were in the kitchen, Peggy handed Elise the teapot. "Would you put some water in this, and I'll put some cookies out."

Elise took the teapot to the sink and began to fill it. "I resisted some oatmeal raisin cookies when I visited Arel. They looked good, but I'm watching my diet."

Peggy beamed back with pride. "I made chocolate chip cookies last night. I'm told they're very tasty."

"They sound delicious. Maybe I could have one or two."

Peggy took the lid off the cookie jar and began putting cookies on a plate. "So, I don't want to pry, but I am curious. Did you and Arel work things out?"

Elise shrugged. "I think I'm in the clear. We shook hands, and he seemed fine."

"That's good news. You looked so upset the other night."

"I know. It was kind of freaky to think my kisses were toxic."

"Arel is always surprising me with something out of the ordinary."

Elise put the pot on the stove. "He seems a bit distracted. He didn't say much when I was at his house. Carey and Michael did most of the talking."

Peggy giggled. "He's totally preoccupied with his lady love, Claire. He's been alone for a long time. When we learned that he met someone, we were all happy about it." As soon as she made the statement Peggy realized how thoughtless she sounded. "Oh, my goodness, Elise, I'm sorry. You still have feelings for him."

Elise adjusted the flame on the stove burner. "It's okay. After seeing him today, it's clear that I'm barely on his radar. In a way, I'm glad. It makes me want to forget about him too."

"Who knows? You might have been spared?"

"Spared? How?"

Peggy took some plates out of the cupboard and started putting them out on the table. "Arel is wonderful in a lot of ways, but he is very, how should I put it, he's very—"

Elise laughed. "Are you trying to say that he's very particular about his stuff? A neat freak?"

"I'm afraid so. However, from what little I know, Claire isn't like that at all. When I talked to Annabel—"

"Is that Arel's friend's wife?"

158

"Yes, Annabel is William's wife. And she's as nice and sweet as they come. She said that Claire made a statement about being a terrible housekeeper. Not only that but when Annabel and Claire went out shopping, Claire made Annabel feel very uncomfortable." Peggy hesitated. "Oh heavens, I'm saying all the wrong things today."

"What do you mean?"

"First, I'm being insensitive about your feelings. Next, I'm telling tales about the woman Arel is going to marry."

Elise averted her eyes. "I hope things work out for him. After dating me, he deserves someone who'll appreciate him."

Peggy reached out for Elise's arm. "And so do you, Elise. You've done an amazing job in turning your life around."

"I have to give Carey and Michael most of the credit. They were like a couple of angels when they visited. They helped me to see myself and life so differently. The more I thought about what they said and observed how sincere they were, the more I wanted to change."

"I agree. They're something special."

"I'm going to miss them, but they both assured me that we'll always stay in touch. Normally, I wouldn't put much faith in such promises, but I believe them."

Twenty-Three

WILLIAM FROWNED AND tossed aside a book he'd been reading. Ever since Arel's visit he'd been trying to motivate himself. He had a certain amount of time to find his lost passion. Since science had once been extremely compelling, he poured over the latest scientific studies. If he could rekindle his love for mystery, perhaps he'd return to those remembered days when life was a bounty of riddles to be solved. If he could revive that interest, perhaps it would spread out to other areas of his life.

He also pursued new topics, especially ones that might help his connection to Annabel. He devoured books on relationships, family life and even the value of a hobby. He pushed himself in every way that might lead him back to a sense of excitement about life. And what had all his work done for him? He sat in his recliner in the downstairs living area feeling like a great lump of frustration.

Annabel seemed to exist in a different world than his. She quietly occupied herself without commenting on what he was doing. When he looked over at her, she sat on the sofa knitting. Her fingers moved in steady, repetitive motions as bright blue yarn was transformed into some kind of garment. She'd mentioned something about a sweater for Carol's little boy, Ariel.

Presently, her brows were smooth and relaxed. It made him wonder about her thoughts. He could have accessed them by tuning into her mind, but he didn't want to invade her privacy.

"Thank you, William," Annabel said without missing a stitch.

William jerked his recliner into an upright position. "Why are you thanking me?"

Annabel glanced up only briefly. "You're respecting my right to my own thoughts."

William's breath caught with a sudden realization. "But you think it's okay to eavesdrop on mine?"

Annabel held up her knitting and inspected it. "Yes, I do."

"I didn't know you still had that ability."

"I didn't know I still had it either. Then one day, when my worries got the best of me, I was able to check on you and know what you were thinking."

"Well, stop it immediately."

Annabel began knitting again. "No, I will not be kept in the dark when your life is at stake. If you start losing ground again, I want to know about it."

William sat back again letting the furrows in his brow deepen. Being married was one thing, but having Annabel privy to his private musings was unacceptable. "Fine, I can always use my shields."

Annabel stopped knitting again and gave him her full attention. "I wish you wouldn't. If I can't check on you, I'll think the worst. Then I'll worry constantly."

"Annabel, I hope you realize that you're still much too dependent on me. I might have a problem with a loss of passion, but you've got a problem too. You're making me the most important part of your life. And whether I stay on this earth or not, it will not solve your neediness. Instead of knitting, you should be finding a way to be your own person, with me or without me."

"Do you think it's that easy when you're always up to something upsetting? I want you to know that Arel isn't the only drama addict. Both of you constantly insist on being the stars in a never ending spectacle that involves life and death. I don't have a chance to relax, much less learn independence."

"I didn't ask you to fall in love with me. And I certainly didn't ask you to take off your wings."

Annabel tipped up her chin. "No, you didn't. I made that choice. I wanted to experience more than what I could experience as an angel. But why are you in this relationship, William? What made you sacrifice yourself to save me in the first place? Why did you drive that dagger into yourself instead of killing me?"

"You were an angel, Annabel, a beautiful, guiltless being. I couldn't allow the hatred I harbored to destroy a creature so pure."

"And now? Am I just an imperfect human like the rest?"

William saw the blaze in Annabel's eyes, but he didn't know how to answer her questions. He stared back mutely.

Annabel threw her knitting aside and got to her feet. "I take your silence as an indication that you haven't examined the deeper issues at hand."

161

"What do you mean?"

"I might be needy, but at least I'm not regretting my decisions. I'm living in the here and now, trying to find the best in the life I chose. But you can't do that. You're so busy looking for the glorious feelings you had on Arel's battlefield that you won't take the time to discover what glories might be available here, with me."

William picked up the book he'd been reading and held it aloft. "I won't take the time? I'm doing everything I can think of to change the state I'm in!"

"I know you think that's true, but what you're looking for isn't in a book. It's something hidden inside of you that's beyond your conscious fears."

"But I've gone beyond my fears!"

Annabel started for the stairs. "No, you haven't. You just think you have."

* * *

Annabel climbed the stairs to the upper level and went directly to the kitchen. It was her refuge, a place where she often sought comfort when she felt anxious. But anxiety over William's actions wasn't her only problem at this point in their relationship. Her own actions were a cause for concern.

She yanked open the refrigerator door with a disturbing thought. She was beginning to justify actions that she knew were wrong. Spying on William made her feel bad about herself. It compromised her values about honesty and being trustworthy. As she scanned the refrigerator shelves, she was mumbling to herself. "William doesn't know it, but I want my own life, too."

As soon as the words were out, she closed the refrigerator and thought about what she'd said. She wondered if her statement was true. Did she really want a life of her own? She often busied herself with sculpting and knitting, but did those activities help her to develop her sense of individuality?

When she was an angel, she cared about helping people, but she remained outside of their problems. At the end of an assignment, she knew who she was, and she was happy with herself. Presently, her energy was so mixed up with William's that she didn't think in terms of just who she was. She hardly had a thought that didn't involve what William was doing.

Sadly, her current approach wasn't helpful. Neither of them was happy with the other. And if she stepped back a little, she understood that William didn't need a spy in his life. He needed a woman who remained strong and able no matter what he was doing.

She opened the refrigerator again and took out some cheese and bread for a sandwich. She'd been so busy monitoring William that she'd forgotten to eat lunch. Her stomach growled in protest. As she began putting her lunch together, she felt better.

When she'd first taken off her wings, she wished that William ingested food. Over time, she found it rather nice to eat alone. It gave her time to learn more about her body and how that physical part responded to life. When she had a calm, relaxed meal, she felt happy and content.

The idea of food and being happy reminded her of the time she'd spent with Carol and Peggy. When she was in Chicago, the three of them often shared laughter and cozy, small talk over a simple serving of scones and tea. Of course, it wasn't only food that brought them together. When they went shopping or went for walks, everything felt so easy and simple. It contrasted sharply with the tension that often accompanied her time with William.

Remembering those happy occasions with her friends gave her an idea. What if she went to see them again? William was urging her to be more independent. Perhaps he was right. A week or two away from each other might be constructive. They'd have time to break the unhealthy patterns of communication they'd developed. And if she went to Chicago, she could stay with Arel.

She picked up her phone and called Carey instead. It was a relief to hear his voice when he answered the phone. He sounded so cheerful. After being subjected to William's serious grumblings, she welcomed Carey's easy-going tone. However, when she explained why she was calling, Carey told her about Arel's situation. Claire was on her way to Chicago.

As soon as Annabel heard Claire's name, she recoiled. "Maybe this is the wrong time for a visit," she said in a rush. She needed time to explore who she was and how to have faith in herself. There was no way that was going to happen around Claire.

Carey quickly came up with a solution. "There's a very nice motel not too far away. And if you stayed there, it would be easy to take a taxi wherever you wanted to go. I'd also be happy to borrow Arel's car if needed. What do you think?"

Annabel's breath caught. She'd never traveled very far without William by her side. On the other hand, she wanted to give him the space he needed. "I'm not sure."

"Oh, come on, Annabel. Where's your sense of adventure?"

Annabel tried to put on a brave face. After all, hadn't William told her to expand her horizons? "You're right, Carey. I'll check online for a ticket and get back to you very soon."

* * *

After Annabel went upstairs, William shut his eyes and tried to still his thoughts. Meditating could be a welcome practice, but no matter how hard he tried to relax, the total calm that he sought was beyond his reach. After weeks of feeling stuck in that mindset, he began to wonder if Annabel was right. She seemed convinced that he was living in denial, and that he refused to admit it.

The idea of denial was an interesting one. It was a coping mechanism. People used it when they didn't want to know something that was too painful to process. Before Michael showed up, Arel was a classic example of denial. William would not allow himself to go that route. His life had always been about exploration and ferreting out answers, not sitting back and remaining ignorant.

He opened his eyes and took a deep breath. He was in charge of his life. Painful or not, he was prepared to face anything he'd hidden away. But what was he hiding? He had to start looking for an answer, but where? He decided the clues might be physical in nature. A person's body was like a storehouse. Whatever was denied was stuffed away in its cells. If he was observant, perhaps the physical part of him would react and reveal something important.

It took a few minutes of calming the chatter in his mind before he pressed for information. Then he waited. Finally, in a quiet moment, he felt something. A slight tremor went through his limbs. A second followed.

The sensations weren't pleasant. They were warnings. Instead of heeding their counsel, he ignored them. In fact, he was pleased. He was sure he was on the right track. Again, he went back to his original question. What wanted to stay hidden? He repeated the words, each time with more determination.

But that hidden part of him was stubborn too. As he tried to force the issue, he met with massive resistance. His body felt extremely fatigued. His arms and legs became weights. When he tried to shift in his chair, his body felt too heavy to move. He wanted to sleep.

Next, rational explanations began to explain his weariness. He'd gone through hell in the recent past. Since he'd swallowed angelic blood, his world had been torn apart and completely rearranged. Then there were his interactions with Arel and Arel's constant dramas. William had nearly died on several occasions. With those experiences so fresh, didn't he deserve to rest, even drift for a while? Why did he have to stir the pot again?

His reply was delivered in a resolute voice. "No matter what, drifting through life is unacceptable. Whatever is going on, I want to know about it."

He placed a hand on his gut. It was an automatic gesture. In the past, everything that had ever frightened him seemed to reside there. And he wasn't disappointed this time. When he pressed harder, he got a reaction. Something deep in his bowels stirred, flooding his awareness with dread and a terrible foreboding.

He pulled his hand away quickly and took hold of the arms of the chair instead. Whatever he'd awakened was so powerful that his entire body trembled and shook. For long moments, he couldn't move. His body was letting him know that he'd disturbed something that he shouldn't. His heart seconded the motion. It pounded out another warning in his ears. "Stop what you're doing!"

It took all of his strength not to give in to the feelings. But the idea of being a victim to some buried fear was so unacceptable that he worked his fingers loose from the arms of the chair. He also managed to sit straighter and force his shoulders back. As he gathered up what felt like scattered parts of himself, he ordered his heart to slow down. On Arel's battlefield, he'd remained steadfast no matter what he faced. Surely he could navigate an experience from his past. "Whatever the hell this nightmare is, I want to wake up! I want to be free of it!"

Without another moment of hesitation, the demanding hands of his conscious mind went to work. They probed and prodded those dormant places that wanted to stay buried. And they weren't gentle. They became extensions of his need to dominate and subdue whatever life threw at him.

But William didn't understand what he was dealing with. His methods were too harsh. They went too deep, too soon. Flashes of his childhood weaved in and out. They were like brief, terrifying flares of pain that surfaced for only a moment and then dived back into the depths within. Luckily, he knew all about pain. It was something that he'd learned to endure and overcome. Perseverance was part of becoming a man, a strong, determined adult.

In spite of his breath heaving in and out and his body shaking uncontrollably, he kept going with fresh resolve. A man didn't quit. He had to discover what was causing the pain and deal with it, once and for all. That meant pushing even harder.

Through clenched teeth, he gave his body a direct order. It's tone had no room for disobedience. "I want to know what you're hiding! And I want to know now!"

His unbending demand was a terrible mistake. He'd never expected the enormity of what followed. Without pause, a treacherous, all-encompassing wave of despair hit him. It was the kind of despair that wiped out everything he thought he was in an instant. Self-determination was like some fragile bird that perished in a raging storm. Helplessness took its place.

He was on a battlefield again, but the battle was over and lost. Death was so heavy in the air that he could barely make his lungs work. His feet were leaden weights as he half-stumbled his way forward. The horrible death screams of a recent victim of treachery still replayed over and over. He knew that his own life was as good as finished too.

Something cold and ruthless was claiming victory and gobbling up everything in its path. As it caught up with him, its icy presence made his limbs stiff and useless. No matter how hard he struggled to go on, he couldn't break free. A terrible fear of what was going to happen to him and to everything he loved seized hold. It snatched away his breath and left him gasping. He hadn't just lost a battle, his world was headed towards total destruction.

166

The next thought was even more damning. He knew without a doubt that he was the one who was responsible. He'd been too weak to protect what was sacred. Now, everything he held close to his heart, everything that gave meaning to his life was being overrun by a force that only knew how to plunder and destroy.

As a shroud of death and darkness pinned him to the ground, he found himself pleading silently. That's when he saw a small glimmer of light hovering over him. It seemed to call to him, urging him to focus on its brightness. He tried to make his mouth work, to find his voice. "Raphael!"

The angel's name came out in barely a whisper, but it was enough. Raphael was instantly next to him, using his calming energy to help soothe William's grief. Within a few moments, William felt the first glimmers of hope seeping into the blackened landscape.

Slowly the darkness gave way to light. Slowly, his lungs began to breathe in and out without so much effort. When he finally opened his eyes, he was back in his recliner. Raphael was sitting on the sofa.

William blinked, trying to hold on to his normal surroundings as waves of hopelessness still clouded his mind. But when he connected with Raphael's eyes, they were so reassuring that he began to come back to himself. "How could there still be so much horror hidden away?"

Raphael remained very still. "You're dismantling your limitations, my friend. There are definitions within you that no longer serve purpose. You need more of yourself to handle the power you have."

William pushed the statement aside. "Somewhere long ago, I failed. That's all I know."

"William, believe me, you didn't fail. Sometimes the challenges in life are overwhelming at the time. It's only later that a person has the strength to deal with what they've experienced."

"No! I'd rather be dead than feel that kind of pain again!" William glanced around the room, trying to find something to cling to, something that would restore some sense of stability. A part of him was still running from the hell he'd just faced. His gaze lingered on the basket of wool and knitting supplies that sat next to the sofa. They offered a bit of comfort. Just thinking about his sweet Annabel, and how she patiently knit colorful garments that he refused to wear, quieted the shakiness that still had hold. For the first time, he realized how strong she was. Even though she constantly faced new fears, she never stopped trying to be there for him. He looked back at Raphael. "Annabel's life hasn't been easy since she fell in love with me. I've failed her too."

"You're much too hard on yourself."

William looked down at his hands. They were still clutching the arms of the recliner. "This blood thing has been a mistake, Raphael. Arel picked the wrong person when he gave it to me."

"William!"

Annabel's excited voice rang out, interrupting the moment and making William look up. Annabel was skipping down the stairs. As she hurried over to join them, she was smiling. Her smile broadened when she looked at Raphael.

"Good, you're here too, Raphael," she chirped.

Raphael nodded. "You're looking more enthusiastic than usual."

Annabel targeted the angel with sparkling, but adamant eyes. "I have a request. I want you to stay close to William when I leave."

William forced himself to sit up more attentively. "Leave? Where are you going? I thought you already went to the shops today."

Annabel walked over to where he sat and hugged him. "I'm getting a life, William, like you told me to do. In a few days, I'm taking myself to Chicago. Isn't that wonderful? You'll be free of my constant nagging. You can have the peace you need to think about your life. And I promise that I'm never going to invade your privacy again. No more meddling in your thoughts."

Twenty-Four

AREL COULDN'T HELP smiling as he got dressed. Was it Christmas already? No, it wasn't, but he knew the day would be better than Christmas. It was the day that Claire was arriving in Chicago. The woman who made his heart sing would soon be in his arms.

It hadn't been long since they'd last seen each other, but it felt like forever. Or maybe the forever feeling came from the longing and emptiness he'd known since he'd lost his first and only love before Claire, Justina. As he thought about how many things had changed since her passing, Michael knocked on his door.

"Good morning, Arel."

"Michael, I was just appreciating you. Come in."

Michael took a few steps forward and looked around. "So where is all this appreciation coming from?"

"Don't play dumb," Arel laughed. "You know that you made it possible for me to have a new life. And I'm so grateful." He went over to the angel and did something he never usually did. In a fit of happiness, he hugged Michael. "Thank you for helping me all this time!"

Michael patted his back. "You're welcome."

Arel pulled away and put a hand to his chest, trying to calm his fast-beating heart. "After I lost Justina, I didn't think I deserved another chance at love. I didn't think anyone would have me. But you never gave up on me."

Michael returned a puzzled look. "Why would I give up on you?"

"Because I've been a problem. I'm always making things difficult for myself and everyone around me."

"That's just a concept you were taught to believe as a child."

Arel sat down on his bed and clasped his hands together. "I guess you're right. My mother hated me from the time I was conceived."

"Yes, and your father wished you were dead, too. But whatever they thought, it didn't change the beautiful soul that resides in you."

169

"For a long time I lost touch with my soul. If you hadn't showed up in my life and kept encouraging and helping me all this time, I'd still be floundering."

"Even before I showed up in physical form, you never lost that spark of longing inside of you."

"If you say so, but I don't remember much of a spark, just the shame and guilt I felt."

Michael went over to Arel's dresser. He picked up a glass angel and held it up for inspection. "You would have tossed this in the trash if you truly lost that spark."

Arel had to swallow hard when he thought about the small crystal object that Michael was holding. "My poor grandmother, I miss her. She was a very kind lady who loved me. Before my father barred her from our house, she gave me that angel. She promised that he'd look out for me."

Michael set the angel back on the dresser and sighed. "I wish I could have helped you more, but—"

"But I think you did help me. Sometimes, after my father beat me, and I lay in my bed crying, I'd hold that little angel. It would help me to get to sleep and escape the pain."

"Very hard times indeed."

"But that's all behind me now."

"Yes, and this is a very special day."

Arel got up and went to the mirror, examining his facial hair for anything that wasn't in line with perfect grooming. "I hope I look alright. Claire is so beautiful. I don't want to be a disappointment."

"Is that why you've been so busy with the house? I don't think there's a corner or rug that you haven't cleaned or vacuumed."

"And you and Carey have helped too. Thank you for that."

"I just checked the lawn. You'll be happy to know that it's leaf free. The compost bin in the garden is full to overflowing."

Arel walked over to the spacious bedroom windows, noting how Michael had tidied the garden and readied it for winter. "I've probably gone overboard, but having spotless tile floors and a house that's at its best seemed important. When Claire gets here, I want her to see beautiful things everywhere she looks." He turned to Michael, hoping to steady a sudden bout of nervousness. "Do you think I've done a good job?"

"Arel, the house couldn't be more immaculate."

"Is that a good thing or not?"

"Beauty and order are part of who you are. Don't let your doubts erode your self-confidence or your belief in your good intentions. And please know that when I look at you, I see someone who always tries his best, a person who's caring and kind."

Arel returned a weak smile. "I hope that's enough for Claire."

* * *

When Arel saw Claire walking towards him in the greeting area of the airport, he was a little surprised. Then he remembered she was coming from an ambitious dig in a hot and humid country. Her rumpled clothes and mussed hair were a result of what she'd been through.

He straightened the lapels on his finely tailored, Italian suit. He'd overdressed and felt a flush of foolishness mar his expression of happiness. But as Claire got closer, nothing could stop the flood of delight that coursed through his body. He rushed forward the last few yards, closing the distance between them. "Welcome to Chicago, my love!"

Claire laughed. "Aren't you the dashing gentleman! Are you going to a wedding or some gala event after you get me home?"

Arel shook his head. "When we get home, all that I want to do is look at you."

Claire pushed a strand of hair out of her eyes. "First thing that I want is a shower."

"Of course," Arel said as he shifted a well-worn backpack off her shoulder. "If you'd like, I could run you a bath, and you could soak."

"No, that's not necessary. A quick shower will be fine. Besides, it can be a water saver."

Arel sucked in a breath. "Of course, I forgot about how conscientious you are."

Claire slipped her arm around his. "Yes, we only have one planet. It's important to do everything we can to respect it."

When they got to the parking garage, Arel was happy that Carey had washed the car. But then he thought about Claire's statement and made a mental note to avoid any unnecessary water expenditures in the future.

Claire inspected his Mustang with a critical eye. "Pretty vehicle but I bet it's a gas-guzzler."

"Actually, the salesman said it did very well for the size of its engine."

Claire patted Arel's arm as he started to put her bag in the trunk. "I can see that you're a bit self-indulgent when it comes to cars."

"Am I?" Arel stood up too quickly and bumped his head on the trunk lid. Rubbing the offended body part, he frowned. "I guess I didn't think in those terms when I bought it. Michael said a sporty model would be pleasurable to drive. He thinks I'm too serious at times, that I need to find more ways to enjoy myself."

"Maybe this Michael fellow needs to get serious. His advice sounds rather frivolous."

Arel hurried over to the passenger side and opened Claire's door. She gave him a quick smile and slipped into her seat. After closing her door and walking around to the driver's side, he felt a little disorientated. He'd never questioned Michael's guidance. But Claire did have a point. It made him wonder. Could an angel be negligent when it came to respecting the earth? It was a question he'd never thought to ask himself before.

* * *

Elise stood on a chair and handed Carey some china plates from the top shelf of one of the kitchen cupboards. "Thank you for helping, Carey."

Carey put the plates on the table and helped Elise down off the chair. "When you moved here, I think you were planning on staying for a while, weren't you?"

Elise smiled. "Yes, the people who own the house wanted to lease it out for three years. When I saw it, I liked it so much that I took a lot of stuff out of storage. Like this china set that belonged to a great aunt. I thought it would be nice to use if I entertained again."

"Are you going to put it all back in storage?"

"Yes, I guess so."

Carey began to put packing material between the plates. "By the way, I had a question about a different matter. You said you stayed at a motel before you moved in here. Would you recommend it?"

"Yes, it was nice. But why do you ask?"

"My friend, Annabel, is coming for a visit soon, and she needs a place to stay."

"The Annabel who lives in London?"

"Yes, that's right. It's kind of a spur of the moment idea."

"But isn't she a good friend of Arel's? Won't she want to stay with him?"

Carey hesitated. "Not with Claire being there."

"Oh, right. Peggy said something about Annabel not getting along with her."

Carey shrugged. "Maybe she wants to give Arel and Claire some privacy. I know that Michael and I try to stay to ourselves. Of course, Arel and Claire are using the lower level, which is perfect for privacy. It's like having their own apartment."

Elise went to the counter and removed a bakery bag from the bread keeper. "I think it's time for a break. What do you think, Carey?"

"I don't know. Arel is concerned about my eating habits."

Elise took some raspberry crème donuts out of the bag and put them on a serving dish. "Really? Maybe Arel needs to lighten up a bit. You look very fit to me."

Carey smiled. "I feel great."

"Then sit down and have a pastry with me. And while we're eating, you can tell me more about your friend—"

"Annabel? She's very nice. But I think she's trying to be more independent. That's why she's taking this trip."

"Did she come from a sheltered background?"

"I suppose that's true. Now, she's married to William. He's kind of her opposite, an independent man of the world. Annabel wants to be more of a match. She's trying to learn more about being on her own."

"Good for her," Elise said as she took a bite of her donut. A bit of raspberry filling dripped onto the plate. Elise scooped it up with her finger and gave Carey an attentive glance. "You know, Carey, your friend could stay with me."

"I'm sure she wouldn't want to impose."

"Don't be silly. I have a guest room that's perfect. When a writer friend was going to visit me, I bought a bed, linens, the whole deal, wanting to make her comfortable. Unfortunately, something came up, and she canceled. Now, I'm moving. It seems a shame to have gone to all that trouble for nothing."

"Still, it's very nice of you to want Annabel to stay here."

Elise washed down a bite of pastry with some tea and dabbed her mouth with a paper napkin. "I have my Freddie, but—"

"What is it? You look a little sad."

Elise gripped her cup. "Do I still seem needy to you, Carey? Because I know the books say that all we really need is ourselves."

Carey swallowed the remainder of his donut and smiled. "You seem okay to me."

"But I still get lonely. Maybe that's why I'd like your friend to stay with me. It would be nice to have someone around to talk to for a change." Elise sipped her tea, and her eyes flashed brighter. "I also like to dabble in the kitchen. If your friend stays here, I'll get out my old recipes and make something delicious. When it's just me, I don't bother very often."

"Something delicious? That's sounds great. I bet Annabel would love to stay here. I'll ask her about it when I talk to her."

"Are you sure?" Elise paused and studied Carey more closely. "Maybe you think I'm still too much of a downer."

Carey reached for a second donut. "Elise, you're not a downer. You're a lot of fun. And remember, if you need a dinner buddy to try out one of those recipes, I'm always available."

Twenty-Five

ANNABEL SAT IN Arel's Mustang, watching the scenery whiz by. Carey had picked her up at the airport, and they were headed back to his friend's house where she'd be staying. She hoped that Elise was as nice as Carey said. Arel's description had been quite the opposite. "Carey, are you sure that staying with Elise is my best option? Arel said she was, you know, rather harsh."

Carey kept his eyes on the road. "If you're the least bit uncomfortable, you can stay at a motel."

Annabel sat back in her seat, remembering when she'd been an angel. People could change, sometimes very quickly. William was a shining example. He'd become a very loving man in a very short amount of time. Or maybe he'd just allowed his true spirit to finally come through. She took a quick breath and looked at Carey. "Since Elise has been nice enough to extend the invitation, the least I can do is thank her."

"Good, I think when you meet her, you'll feel okay about being her guest."

Annabel laughed. "I'm surprised about how quickly everything fell into place once I decided to take this trip. In just a few days, I boarded a plane. Now, here I am."

"But it's not that new an adventure, you've been here before."

Annabel winced. "Yes, I know."

The last time Annabel had been in Chicago, William was with her, and they'd stayed with Arel. There were a lot of ups and downs. This time she was avoiding Arel. She needed time away from him, too. She gave Carey a quick glance. "What did you tell Arel when you asked to borrow the car? You didn't let on that I was here, did you?"

Carey grinned and returned a quick look of satisfaction. "I told him the truth."

Annabel's eyes flared with disappointment. "Oh, Carey, how could you? You know that I don't want to see him, especially with Claire around. At least not yet."

Carey continued to smile. "You didn't let me finish. I told him that I needed to pick up a friend who's staying with Elise. Elise's car is in for repairs so it was the perfect explanation."

"Oh, so Arel doesn't—"

"Please don't worry, Annabel. Arel has his hands full. He's not thinking about anything or anybody with Claire around."

Annabel shivered. "I don't want to be unkind, but one shopping trip with that woman nearly finished me off."

"Well, Elise isn't at all like Claire. She was a bit severe at first, but she's really made big strides recently."

"Peggy told me the same thing. She also said that Elise talks a lot about you and Michael and how helpful you've been."

"I'm happy we could be there for her."

"You're an angel, it's what you do."

Carey gave her a quick wink. "Yes, but there have been rewards that go beyond the angelic part. Elise found a fantastic bakery. Their chocolate cake is amazing. She also loves to cook. She's making something special for your dinner tonight."

Annabel felt her mood lift a little. "That's a relief. Remember when I stayed with Arel? He forgot to shop for food, and I got pretty hungry."

"You don't have to worry about being hungry around Elise. And here's the best part, I'm invited to dinner tonight."

* * *

Elise was inspecting the table settings and startled when she heard the doorbell ring. Her guest had arrived. It had been a long time since she'd entertained. But that hadn't curbed her enthusiasm or her preparations. She'd been so excited about Annabel's visit that she had been up half the night getting ready. The sheets on the guest bed were already clean, but she washed them again to make sure they were fresh. She also gave Freddie a bath, vacuumed and bought flowers for both the guest bedroom and for the dining room table.

It took a bit a digging, but she finally found her recipe box. It contained all the yummy dishes her grandmother used to make. She finally decided on lasagna because she could delay putting it in the oven if Annabel's plane was late. But Carey's text message let her know that all was on schedule.

She looked at the clock as she hurried to answer the door. The pasta dish would be coming out of the oven in thirty minutes. That gave Annabel time to get settled before she ate. With so many details on her mind, she forgot to grab Freddie. He took advantage of her mistake by running outside as soon as she opened the door. When he saw their visitors, he became a frenzied ball of white fur, jumping up on Annabel repeatedly.

"Who's this?" Annabel asked as she picked him up.

Elise smiled. "His name is Freddie, and I'm Elise," she said gesturing Annabel and Carey inside. "Please come in."

Later, after they dined on the lasagna and Freddie fell asleep in his dog bed, the three of them sat at the table chatting and finishing dessert. Elise had baked a homemade apple pie. She was pleased to see that Annabel seemed to enjoy her cooking. Of course, Carey looked extremely pleased too. "I'm so happy you accepted my invitation to stay here," she said to Annabel.

Annabel sat up straighter. "I'm grateful to be here. Your hospitality is so welcoming. I was a little anxious about leaving William and London, but now I feel better."

Carey stood up. "Would you like some help with cleaning up, Elise?"

"No, thank you. I'll put most of the dishes in the dishwasher and soak the rest."

"Then I better be getting back home. Arel is probably wondering where I am. Even though he's preoccupied with Claire, he's still very aware when I come in late."

Annabel reached out for his hand. "Thank you for all you've done, and for not letting Arel know that I'm here."

Elise frowned. "Arel doesn't know you're visiting?"

Annabel blushed. "No, my trip was a spur of the moment affair, and I don't want to disturb Arel while—"

Elise could see that Annabel was troubled by something. She wanted to help. "I'll do whatever you want, Annabel. If you'd rather not let Arel know you're here, we'll find a way to be sneaky."

Annabel returned a curious smile. "Sneaky?"

"Yes, if we go out in the car, you can keep your head down. In fact, I have a blond wig and big, sun glasses you could borrow if we take a walk."

Carey gave Annabel a knowing look. "Elise is a wonderful writer with a great imagination. She can think up lots of ways to keep you from being discovered."

Annabel's eyes sparkled with a playful glint. "It sounds like I'm going to learn a lot from you, Elise."

Elise glanced up at Carey. "And you can be our helper, letting us know about Arel's comings and goings. That way we'll have less of a chance of being spotted."

Carey started for the door. When he looked back, his face had a mischievous look too. "Annabel and Elise, I feel an adventure coming on."

* * *

At bedtime, Annabel shut the door to the guest room and paused. She liked the room's cozy decor. It was very different from her own home. William's tastes were more sophisticated than Elise's. There were no delicate, lace curtains on their windows. But William was willing to compromise. He was agreeable when she added feminine touches to those areas of their home where she spent more time, like her studio.

Now, in a new environment, she walked over to the bed and examined the linens. The colors of the quilt and pillow shams were inviting. With a patchwork design of pale greens, soft browns and rosy florals, they made her think of a quiet garden. When she folded back the coverlet, the sheets were a pretty rose color, and they were extra soft to the touch.

There wasn't a lot of furniture in the room, but there was a dresser that sported a vase full of white daisies and pink carnations. There was also a sitting chair and a side table. A nicely framed print of hollyhocks at the seaside hung over the bed. All in all, Annabel felt very comfortable when she settled into the pillow-top mattress. She drifted off to sleep thinking about little Freddie and how affectionate the puppy was.

* * *

As morning light filled the bedroom, Annabel awoke to the smell of coffee and something baking in the oven. She inhaled deeply and smiled. It reminded her of the pastry shop back home. Then she remembered William and how he wasn't next to her in bed. A bout of loneliness ruined the pleasant feeling she'd had the moment before.

She hoped that William was okay. When he saw her off at the airport, he was encouraging about her trip. However, no matter how hard he tried to hide his feelings, she sensed that he was more troubled than ever. That's when she had to remind herself that he had lived a very successful life and knew how to take care of himself.

A scratching sound at Annabel's door brought her back from her thoughts. A series of barks followed. She quickly got up and put on her robe and slippers. When she opened the door, Freddie greeted her like he had the night before. He bounced up and down with enthusiasm. His bright, black eyes emphasized his puppy smile.

"Freddie?" Elise called out from somewhere in the house. "Freddie, where are you? Don't bother our guest!"

Annabel picked up the puppy and stepped out into the hall. "It's okay, Elise. I was awake." She met Elise in the living room. She was about to hand her the puppy, but stopped when she saw Elise's hands. They were covered in flour. There was also a smudge of flour on Elise's cheek.

Elise smiled. "Sorry, I'm in the middle of a project."

Like Freddie, Elise was animated. When she headed back to the kitchen, her steps were hurried and purposeful. Annabel followed, intrigued by the energy in the house. There wasn't the usual quiet that she experienced at home. It felt like things were happening. Life had a feeling of excitement. "What kind of project?" she asked.

Elise gave her a backwards glance. "I know that in England scones are often served, so I was trying my hand at making some. But I'm not sure about the recipe I found online. I hope the batch I put in the oven comes out alright."

Annabel ran her hand over Freddie's soft head and smiled. "I can barely make toast, so I'm afraid I won't be much help."

Elise gave her a surprised look. "Don't you like to cook or bake?"

"I don't know how. No one has ever taught me."

Elise smiled. "My gram loved being in the kitchen. She helped me make my first cake."

"Did you spend much time with her?"

179

"Some, but she died when I was in my early teens." Elise paused and sniffed the air. Her eyes flared with panic as she rushed to the stove and grabbed a potholder. "Oh goodness, I think I left the scones in too long," she said as she retrieved a cookie sheet from the oven. She frowned as she stared at the overly brown pastries.

Annabel walked over to inspect them too. "I'm sure they're fine."

"Maybe, but I wanted your first morning to be extra special," Elise said as she put the cookie sheet on a cooling rack. She went to the sink and washed her hands. "Anyway, I have an idea. Let me take you to breakfast. There's a place that's supposed to serve every kind of pancake."

Annabel put Freddie down and approached the pastries again. She touched one gingerly and smiled. "Would it be okay if we ate these? I really don't feel like going out just yet."

Elise dried her hands and looked at Annabel. Her eyes had the same appraising qualities that she'd used on the scones. "You miss your guy, don't you?"

Annabel took a deep breath. "I've never been this far away from William before."

"When I dated Arel, he sometimes talked about the two of you. I think he envied your wonderful relationship. Of course, now he has Claire, so I'm happy for him." Elise smiled. "And I know I shouldn't be, but I'm a little jealous."

Annabel blinked back. Her former angel senses sometimes resurfaced and helped her to tune into other people. She could feel Elise's regret. "I'm sorry."

Elise shrugged. "What's done is done. Besides, as Carey pointed out, I'm a writer. I'll just write a new script for my life."

"You're going to find the right person. I can feel it in here," Annabel said tapping her chest.

Elise returned to her chores. "Thanks."

"Is there anything I can do to help?"

Elise put a second cookie sheet of pastries in the oven. "Please, get some coffee or I can make you tea. Then sit down and talk to me about this wonderful William of yours while I clean up. I'm always interested in what makes a relationship work."

Annabel went to the counter and took a cup off the mug tree. "I'd rather hear about your ideas on relationship. It's what you write about. How did you get started?"

Elise began putting bowls and utensils in the sink. "I guess I was a dreamer. In real life, the guys I settled for weren't very nice, so I began to invent stories about men and women who did find that perfect love."

Annabel took her coffee to the table and sat down. "But is there such a thing?"

"No, I don't believe there is, but I'm beginning to think there are people who can work things out and be happy more of the time than not. Take Michael or Carey. Those two guys never stress. They look for the best in everyone. Wouldn't it be great to find a guy like that to marry?"

Annabel thought about the two angels and smiled to herself. "I don't think they represent the norm."

"I know, but if I meet someone half as nice and considerate, I think I could be happy."

"You mean like Arel?"

Elise blushed. "Arel might be a bit obsessive when it comes to certain matters, but he's very sweet."

"So you could put up with his faults?"

"It wasn't his faults that kept our relationship from working. It was more me. I couldn't trust myself to love someone again. But hostility wasn't an answer either. Finally, I guess I got sick of being angry all the time."

"So what did you do?"

"I don't know exactly what happened, but I began to notice that people wanted to help. My neighbors, Peggy and her husband, Tim, were very nice, even after I was very rude. Then Carey and Michael came along. We'd talk about my novel and my characters. They challenged stuff that I believed. Then Michael suggested that I get Freddie. It's funny, but I thought I was incapable of love, but who can resist Freddie? All and all, I decided I wanted something better. So here I am, not knowing what's next, but whatever it is, I think that I can handle it."

"I wish I felt like you."

"What do you mean?"

"You seem so strong, Elise, but I don't feel that way. When you talk about handling whatever comes next, it scares me."

Elise pulled out a chair and sat down. "Believe me, I know how that is. But after being on my own for a long time, I realized that I'd always been strong inside. I just did what a lot of women do, I convinced myself otherwise."

"Is that the lie? We tell ourselves we're weak, and then we believe it?"

Elise's brows narrowed in thought. "Yes, I think that is what we do. In fact, I think I'll use that idea as the basis for my next book." She reached out and patted Annabel's hand. "Thanks, Annabel, you've got me thinking about writing a book from a new angle."

"I'm glad I could help."

Elise jumped up and got some plates out of the cupboard. "Let's eat and then we can go for a nice stroll around the neighborhood."

Annabel hesitated. "Maybe I should stay here in case—"

Elise laughed. "In case Arel is out and about? It's okay. I found my wig and my oversize, dark glasses. I also have this fake fur coat that will make you look a couple of sizes bigger. Even if Arel did see you, he'd never recognize you. Besides, he thinks I have a guest, so he won't pay us any attention."

"I don't know—"

"Annabel, what's wrong? You look so worried."

Annabel sucked in her breath. Why was she so afraid to see Arel or Claire? It didn't make sense, but she didn't know how to change the way she felt. She was reverting back to the time when she'd first taken off her wings. Once she was a human being, everything frightened her. "I know I must look silly to you, but—"

When Elise replied, her voice was soft. "No, you don't look silly. And I don't know you very well, but I can tell that you're too hard on yourself. Take it from someone who knows."

Annabel bit her lip, trying to keep her emotions from flaring up. "What if I stay this way forever?"

"No, I don't think so. You're too smart for that to happen."

Annabel blinked back in surprise. "How would you know that? Like you said, we just met."

"Maybe I see a little of myself in you. I used to be terrified of life and fitting in."

"Really? That's hard to believe."

"Believe it, because it's true," Elise said as she got up. She went to the oven and checked on the scones. "Great! This batch is just right. Look at that golden color."

Annabel got up to take a look. "I bet they're yummy."

Elise targeted Annabel with piercing, blue eyes. "It just takes practice. If the first batch isn't right, try again. If you'd like, I'd love to teach you to make them, now that I know what I'm doing."

Annabel stepped back. "I'd like that. And I'd also like to take that walk with you and Freddie."

As soon as Freddie heard his name and the word 'walk', he raised his head and abandoned his chew toy. He came running over to Elise. He let out insistent, little yaps as he did circles around her.

Elise leaned in to Annabel and lowered her voice to a whisper. "I forgot to tell you about watching what you say. Freddie has very good hearing, especially when it comes to that word, w-a-l-k." She spelled out the word and laughed. "It's one of his favorite activities."

Twenty-Six

WILLIAM PUT HIS phone on the side table, still feeling a bit confused about his conversation with Annabel. She seemed to be having a wonderful visit. She had nothing but praise for Elise. In Annabel's eyes, the woman was nothing short of a saint.

Elise's kindness came in unexpected ways. She was teaching Annabel to cook and bake. She also encouraged Annabel to keep a journal. On a lighter note, Elise helped Annabel to take on a secret identity to use when they went for walks. William smiled when he thought of the picture Annabel had sent him. She wore a blond wig and the biggest sunglasses William had ever seen. Her makeup was totally different. A deep, passionate red replaced her normally pink lips. She also wore rouge and dangly earrings. Annabel had been transformed into a new and intriguing temptress. William hardly recognized her, but he was glad that she was happy.

"Well, Raphael, it seems Annabel is doing very well. Maybe she just needed to get away from me."

"She needs time to find out how to be more of herself, that's all," Raphael replied.

The angel had been staying close after Annabel made him promise to watch over William. He sat on the downstairs sofa, paging through one of William's science magazines.

William frowned. "She was much too worried about me, especially when she asked you not to leave."

Raphael continued to study an article attentively. When he seemed satisfied with whatever he'd read, he put the magazine aside. "Would you like me to go?"

William felt his gut tighten. He wanted to answer in the affirmative, but his body had different ideas. If he thought about being on his own, his muscles seized up and his anxiety level rocketed. "I feel like I've lost control over my body."

184

"Do you remember a conversation that you had with Arel? It was during his first visit here. When you were dealing with your emotional mood swings, he said that you needed to connect with that boy inside of you, that young child who loved nature, who cherished the earth."

William's muscles tightened even more. "I remember. And I'll tell you what I told Arel. This world has no room for children. To live on this planet, you have to be tough. You can't care about the things a child loves. Look at Annabel. She's a prime example of what happens when you bring someone naïve into the world. She's constantly in a panic."

"Annabel sounds like she's fine."

"She's staying in a secure environment, with someone who's treating her very well."

"You're talking about Elise."

"Right, from what I know, Elise is another example of someone who knew abuse. It took Michael and Carey's assistance to help her get past her bitterness. Now, who knows how long she'll be able to maintain her new attitude."

"William, after all that you've been through recently, you've still triumphed. Why are you still so adamant about this topic?"

William held his gut, trying to resist the pain that was stirring there. "I remember what it was like to be a child. I'll never allow myself to feel like that again. So drop it."

Raphael nodded and ran a hand over the magazine he'd been reading. "So tell me, what have you heard from Arel?"

William sat back and relaxed a little. "Nothing. He's a man caught up in something that is crushing the life out of him. But he doesn't have a clue."

"Then the two of you have something in common."

William's angry protest was immediate and short-lived. Before he could tell Raphael how different he was from Arel, an all-consuming pain shot through his gut. He didn't know how long it lasted. He only knew that the punishing torment had encapsulated the cruelty and fierceness of everything he was fighting so hard to forget. After it passed, he sat immobilized and gasping.

Raphael called out to him from far away. "William, let it go!"

It was an impossible request. How could he let go of something that came and went of its own accord?

185

Raphael called to him again, still sounding very far away. "You're holding on to the pain, William! Let go!"

"No!" When William voiced his protest, the pain sliced through him a second time. He was at its mercy, helpless to save himself. He feared that his life would be snatched away at any moment! When he finally opened his eyes, Raphael was shaking him. He stared back with little hope. Deep down, he knew he was doomed.

Twenty-Seven

ROLPHE'S HANDS WERE braced on the frame of the kitchen window. A storm was closing in fast on Paris. Gloomy, grey clouds blanketed the city. The threatening weather matched the heavy feeling that had settled in Rolphe's bones. Arel and William were in trouble. He was sure of it.

William was especially worrisome. His energy was that of a warrior again, waging a fierce battle, this time with himself. Rolphe wanted to talk to him, but he couldn't go against William's wishes. The man had shut himself off with shields that said, "Stay away."

After days of reviewing the situation and finding no resolution, Rolphe knew he needed angelic advice. Carey came to mind. Rolphe felt more at ease talking to him than Michael.

Michael was kind and compassionate, but Rolphe had glimpsed Michael's true magnificent nature on several occasions. It was so awe inspiring that Rolphe found it intimidating. On the other hand, Carey kept his grandness hidden. He seemed to enjoy playing the role of a young man who dressed in torn jeans and tennis shoes with holes in the toe.

Still, when Rolphe turned away from the kitchen window and saw Carey sitting on his couch, he jumped back with surprise. He'd barely thought about asking for Carey's help, and the angel was instantly in his living room.

Carey smiled. "I'm sorry to startle you, but I heard you calling."

"It's always a great honor to speak with you," Rolphe said as he bowed his head. His background and beliefs demanded that he give the Creator's messenger his special due.

"Please, come and sit down, Rolphe," Carey said in an easy-going tone.

Rolphe obeyed at once, but he came forward slowly, reverently. Michael and Carey had always encouraged him to be relaxed around them, but he could never manage it. When he spoke, his voice

187

sounded weak and husky. "I'm worried about William. Please, tell me how to help him."

"I'm sorry, Rolphe, but I don't think that William is ready to deal with his problems."

Rolphe's eyes lit up with a beautiful memory. "I've seen him in visions while I was painting. His heart and soul shine so brightly."

"Good, keep your focus on that image."

"It's difficult to do that. Sometimes, when I tap into his current state, a sense of impending doom grabs hold. What if he slips out of this world?"

"Every person has free will, and it's important to respect their decisions."

"Are you saying that I shouldn't try to change his mind?"

"Perhaps you aren't giving yourself enough credit. By remaining resolute in your belief in William, you can be a steadying force without William even knowing it."

Rolphe settled into the couch with a scowl. "All that I've been able to do for either William or Arel is to pray for their safety."

"You don't seem convinced that your prayers have value."

Rolphe let out a gasp of despair. "I prayed for my wife and children when they got sick. And what good did it do? Perhaps the Creator thinks my petitions are inferior."

"Prayer can be a tricky business. Unfortunately, fearful prayers often have little faith behind them. But when you focus on Divine love and trust that there is a Divine plan for each person, it's much more effective."

"I wish I knew that when my family was suffering. My prayers were frantic and filled with dread."

"Rolphe, even if your prayers were aligned with their best interests, sometimes people come into physical form and live very brief lives. In those cases, their souls decide when it's time to leave the world."

"But my children didn't want to die!"

"They were born into very difficult times, violent times. Many people left the earth. Those who stayed were strong enough to keep going and searching for something better, people like you."

Rolphe's furrowed brows eased a little. He remembered how dark the world had been when he was a young man. If his sons had lived, they would have faced the draft and serving in the army too. He glanced up at Carey. "My boys were very sensitive. They didn't like hurting others. At least they weren't forced to kill anyone. Perhaps, that's something good to consider, but—"

"Is something else troubling you, Rolphe?"

"When you and Arel first helped me to let go of the terrible person I'd become, I began to have faith in who I really am. Now, I don't feel as sure about anything."

"What's making you doubt yourself?"

"I miss having a family. I have Myra in my life, but I thought I had a connection to Arel and William, too. But I'm fooling myself. When I'm around them, they tolerate my presence, nothing more."

"I thought Arel stayed in touch."

Rolphe laughed. "I think he feels a sense of duty to check on me. Maybe he's afraid I'll revert back to the ogre he once fought and hated."

"Did you enjoy his last visit?"

"When he came to Paris and Myra arranged for him to meet Claire, I hoped to convince him that all I want for him is his happiness, and that he think of me as a friend. I really tried my best, but I don't think he noticed my efforts."

"But he said he recently called you for advice."

"He gets frustrated. When he lived here, he used to come into the studio and complain, but he didn't seem interested in my views."

"Rolphe, please try not to let other people's actions steer you away from your joy. You've felt it many times when you were by yourself, painting your beautiful pictures."

"Thank you, but sometimes a human being needs more than their own company. They need others to validate their place on the earth. I'm sure that opinion is a weakness, but I haven't been able to get beyond it yet."

Rolphe pushed himself off the couch and walked back to the kitchen window. Sheets of rain had begun to pelt the panes of glass. Thunder rolled across the city as Rolphe heaved out a sigh. "Here I am asking about how to help William, but maybe I'm deluding myself. Maybe I need prayers more than he does."

Twenty-Eight

ANNABEL CAME OUT of her bedroom smiling. After a long soak in the tub, her body felt relaxed. She was also curious. As she was dressing, she heard music. When she opened her door, a lively dance tune filled the hallway. Annabel and William sometimes listened to a classical piece, but the volume was never as loud as the music that saturated the airways in Elise's home.

When Annabel walked into the living room, she discovered the reason for the music. Elise was dancing around the room with Freddie in her arms. She looked very happy.

Annabel watched from the sidelines until the song came to an end. Then she clapped enthusiastically. "Great job, Elise. You're a wonderful dancer."

"Thanks," Elise said as she grabbed a doggie biscuit off the counter. She put Freddie and the biscuit in the puppy's bed. "How was your bath?"

Annabel sighed contentedly. "The hot water was soothing, and the Hibiscus bath salts have a wonderful fragrance."

"Good, I was hoping you'd enjoy them as much as I do."

"I enjoyed watching you dance. You look like you have fun."

"How about you? Is dancing something you enjoy?"

Annabel took a step back. "I've never tried."

"You're kidding."

Annabel paused. What could she say? Since she'd been with William, he'd never mentioned dancing.

Elise came over with an apologetic face. "Oh, I'm so sorry. I didn't mean to make you feel bad. I'm just surprised. Did you grow up in a fundamental religion that didn't allow such things?"

Annabel stared down at the rug and shook her head.

It was Elise's turn to blush. "Forgive me. I think I keep saying the wrong thing."

Annabel studied her hands. They were clasping each other. "It's okay. Sometimes I feel so out of place, not knowing the basics that everyone should know."

"When it came to dancing, I had to teach myself. But I haven't danced like this in a long time. Then this morning, with you here, I turned on the music."

"It was nice." Annabel paused and took a breath. "You know, I had to teach myself to knit. It was challenging. My first projects were—"

Elise waited, but finally asked a question. "Your projects were what?"

"I guess they were terrible. William actually looked frightened when he thought the scarf I made might be for him."

Elise crossed her arms. "I'll tell you what. You teach me to knit, and I'll teach you to dance."

"That's sweet, but you're just being nice."

"I hope so, but knitting could be fun. I never had the patience to learn before, but I think I could give it a try. Besides, I could make Freddie a sweater."

"It's not too hard once you get into a rhythm."

"Dancing can be the same way."

Annabel thought about the music and how it made her spirits lift. "But I might not be any good."

Elise smiled. "The great thing about dancing nowadays is that you can do whatever feels right."

Annabel's fingers tightened on themselves. "I guess I could try."

"We'll go slowly, and after a bit your body will start to move naturally."

"Does everyone's body know how to dance?"

Elise went over to the coffee table and grabbed her phone. "Let me show you some videos of babies. You'll see how easy it can be."

"Babies can dance?"

"Yes, you bet they can, and so can you."

Elise was so adamant and sure of what she was saying that Annabel gave in, especially after seeing a nine-month-old baby swaying to music. By the end of the lesson that Elise conducted, Annabel forgot about trying so hard, and her body surprised her. It automatically started to move to the rhythm of a song. Elise applauded her and said she'd be dancing a jig before she knew it. Annabel didn't know what a jig was, but she liked the way Elise laughed and made the idea sound like fun.

Later, before bedtime, Annabel had lots to write in the journal that Elise gave her. The first point was underlined. "Elise is very patient!"

Elise was also funny. When Annabel found it impossible to relax, Elise showed her that it was okay to act silly and not worry about how she looked. To prove her point, Elise did something called the Chicken Dance. They both laughed after that.

Annabel's final journal entry contained three words. "Dancing is fun!"

* * *

Arel woke up, rubbed the sleep from his eyes and looked over at Claire's side of the bed. As usual, it was empty. He glanced at the clock. It was only six-thirty in the morning, and he'd already had his first disappointment of the day.

He threw back the covers, put on a robe, and took care to make himself presentable. He was still sleepy as he went in search of Claire. He found her in the lower-level, living space. She was sitting in a corner of the sofa. She looked beautiful in spite of the fact that her hair was uncombed. There was also a large coffee stain on her sleeper top. When she was unpacking her suitcase, he'd noticed that most of her belongings were in need of repair or cleaning. He'd asked if he could wash some of her clothes, but Claire dismissed his offer and his concern.

When he walked into the living area, she looked up briefly, gave him a little wave and went back to studying her laptop. He was tempted to be offended by Claire's lack of enthusiasm, but he stopped himself. After a number of talks with Michael, he was aware of how easy it was to lose oneself in a relationship. But when he thought of how much Claire meant to him, it was easy to go down that slippery slope.

In this case, he decided that retreating was his best option. He turned and went back to his bedroom. Perhaps if he meditated, he'd find the serenity he needed to see the situation with more clarity. Once he sat down and started to relax, he knew he'd made the right decision.

It was too early to be getting upset. Before he faced the day, he definitely needed some quiet time.

With continued practice, he'd become much better at meditating. It only took a few calming breaths for his muscles to relax. As the tension in his body eased, his mind was quick to follow. He smiled as his thoughts began to still.

As he gave himself over to that quiet state, he soon felt better about his relationship with Claire. Their different lifestyles didn't have to be a problem. In time, they could work together and also figure out ways to give each other space. Besides, while Claire did what she wanted to do, he'd have time to attend to his own affairs and projects.

He'd barely begun to cultivate a tranquil, soothing attitude when he felt a tap on his shoulder. When he glanced up, Claire stood in front to him.

"Arel? I wasn't trying to be rude when you came in to see me," she said in a matter-of-fact tone. "I'm very busy and have lots of things that need my attention."

Arel was still feeling so peaceful that he smiled back. "I'm sorry that I disturbed you. I just thought that maybe you'd like breakfast. I'll be happy to make you—"

"Stop it, please. I don't need you constantly trying to take care of me. If I'm hungry, I'll eat. I'm very self-sufficient."

He took a deep breath and frowned. As his meditative calm slipped away, he tried to remain thoughtful. But what could he say that wouldn't offend Claire in some way? Since she'd arrived, she took issue with most of his statements. Their conversations were often one-sided with Claire needing to educate him on countless issues. Perhaps, it was warranted. The points she made were valid. Still, he couldn't help but wonder about how differently they looked at life.

He reached out for her hand. "We were so happy in Paris. What's happened? Was all of this, you and me, a mistake?"

"What do you mean by that?"

"I thought we loved each other, but maybe I was fooling myself."

Claire laughed. "You are so sensitive. Just because we're not in bed all the time, and I tell you about my feelings, you come up with statements like that. Are you losing interest in me?"

"No, of course not." He studied Claire's eyes, how intense and determined they were. "I love you, but I don't know how to make you happy."

Claire gestured for him to stand up. "Come with me. I want to show you something."

Arel did as he was told, but his body resisted leaving his chair. He felt heavy and tired again.

Claire noticed his reluctance and urged him on. "I don't have all day, my darling."

Arel forced himself to move more quickly. He wondered about what Claire wanted him to see. She seemed very interested in energy conservation. He hoped she'd paid attention to some of his efforts. Perhaps she'd noticed all the literature on solar energy that he'd been reading in the library area. There were numerous magazines and circulars on the subject.

Claire paused and crossed her arms when they got to the living room space. Instead of speaking, she shook her head and sighed.

Arel's curiosity got the best of him. "What is it?"

Claire gave him an indulgent scowl. "Look at this room and tell me what you see."

Arel hesitated. "What do you want me to see?"

"Please, don't be difficult. Just look around."

Arel let his gaze travel over the room. The area contained so much of what he'd collected and cherished. Whether it was a favorite painting, a bronze or a first edition book, each work of art was a small treasure. In the past, when his life was at its lowest, the physical objects proved that beauty and wisdom still existed in the world.

He turned to Claire, hoping to share his feelings. "When I look around me, I see things that inspire me."

Claire took his arm firmly in hers. "Would you say it's a comfortable room?"

"Yes, very comfortable."

Claire kissed his cheek and sighed. "My poor Arel, I know you don't have a clue, but I have to tell you that you're living in a dream world. Nothing here has anything to do with reality."

Arel felt her words hit with an unexpected force. "You're right. I don't understand what you're saying."

"Arel, I do love you, but I'm afraid for you."

"Why?"

Instead of answering, Claire pulled him closer and paused, as if she was too burdened to go on.

"Why are you afraid for me?" he asked.

Claire turned and stared back with a frown. "You're kind and caring, but you're also like a child in a handsome man's body. Maybe that's why we met. You need guidance. You need to leave the dream world behind."

"What dream world?"

Claire straightened and tossed back her hair. "When I look at this room I see a small, self-serving retreat. It's a place where you can hide from everything you don't want to face. But if you want to live up to your potential, you need to free yourself."

"Free myself?"

"Yes, you've blinded yourself with possessions and taking care of those possessions. But life isn't about all these useless trifles. Sell it all! Leave this world of illusion behind. Once you do that, you can connect with the real world. That's where you can do some good for others."

Arel felt his jaws lock. His mind was just as incapable of processing what Claire had said. When he blinked back with vacant eyes, she seemed to understand and squeezed his hand again.

"I know it's a lot to take in all at once, but don't worry, I'm here. I'll help you to take charge of your life and exchange dreams for what's real."

* * *

Arel excused himself after his talk with Claire. If what she'd said was true, his values were foolish and immature. It was a terrible plight to ponder. In fact, his thoughts were so overwhelming that he couldn't face them head on. He went for a run instead. Once he was outside, the fresh air helped to revive his foggy mind, and jogging freed his body.

Running had been an outlet he'd used in the past. When there were issues he didn't feel strong enough to face, he ran harder. The exercise, like meditation, helped. It didn't solve anything, but it did allow him a brief respite. For a short amount of time, he was able to keep his focus on the simple joy that came from having a strong, healthy body. He wasn't ready to figure out how to digest Claire's assessment of his life.

After he'd gone a couple of miles, he couldn't put off the inevitable. He turned around and started back home. The closer he got, the more his fears surfaced. He'd always wanted to be responsible. Yet, hadn't William accused him of negligence on numerous occasions? And what about his lifestyle? Was it wrong to enjoy the beautiful things in life? Claire seemed to think so.

As he approached his street and saw his home only a short distance away, he went from running to walking. He told himself it was part of the cool-down process. As he started to pass Elise's house, he slowed even more. Her doors and windows were closed, but he could still hear music coming from the interior.

"Talk about self-absorbed," he muttered as he turned into her yard. "The woman needs to turn that noise down a notch."

He climbed the stairs. When he got to the door, he gave it a few sharp raps and waited. After another round of knocking and no response, he found himself boldly trying the knob. The action was totally out of character, but his manners had fallen victim to his desperate mood.

As soon as he opened the door, Freddie greeted him. He ignored the puppy's cordial tail wags and closed the door behind him. Freddie, the little escape artist, wouldn't get away on his watch. He was sure there'd be no escape for him either. Sooner or later, he'd have to face the fact that Claire seemed to think that he was a self-centered jerk.

He paused in Elise's foyer, letting himself take in the energy that filled the house. It had a casual feel, a sense of ease. It was very different than it had been when Arel had dated Elise. Maybe Carey and Michael's good vibes had been passed on to her.

He knew he should be happy for Elise, but when he heard the sound of cheerful voices and outbursts of laughter, he could only manage resentment. People were having a good time while his world was crumbling. It only took a little imagination to foresee his future. All the things that Claire affirmed as worthless would be dismantled and sold off. That kind of situation demanded a funeral dirge, not upbeat tunes and women giggling.

He stepped forward boldly. "Elise, I need to talk to you."

When he got no response, he started towards the kitchen. Elise and another woman came into view as he walked through the living room. He stopped abruptly when he realized who the second woman was. "Annabel!"

Annabel glanced back at him and froze. Her mouth hung open, but she seemed unable to say anything.

Elise stared at Arel too, then she hurried over to her entertainment center and turned off the music. "Arel! What are you doing here?"

Arel backed up a couple of steps. "I knocked, but no one answered."

Elise put on a friendly smile. "I didn't realize the music was so loud. Please, come in."

Annabel came forward hesitantly. She had her hands wrapped around herself. "It's good to see you, Arel."

Arel wasn't convinced by Annabel's greeting, but her shaky voice told him that he'd frightened her. Normally, he would have tried to make her feel better, but he was just as stressed as Annabel. "When did you get here? Why didn't you tell me you were coming?"

Annabel started to reply and stopped herself. She stared down at the fluffy, pink slippers she was wearing.

Arel recognized her footwear. The slippers were similar to the ones Elise sometimes wore when she took Freddie out in the morning.

Elise spoke up. "Would you like to sit down?"

Arel walked over to the sofa, sat down and clasped his hands. When his thoughts cleared a little, he looked at Annabel. She'd sat down on the other end of the sofa. "Have I done something to offend you?"

"No, it's not you. I should have let you know I was here, but—"

When Annabel hesitated, Elise pitched in. "I think Annabel is trying to say that she wanted to give you and your fiancé some space."

Annabel's face brightened. "Elise is right. I didn't want to spoil your time with . . . with—"

Arel scowled back. "Claire, her name is Claire."

Annabel blinked a few times as if she was distancing herself from the name. She finally smiled. "How is Claire?"

"She's fine."

"Is something wrong, Arel?" Elise asked. "You look upset."

Arel instantly resented her observation. Even if he was distressed, he was also angry that his mood was so transparent. He had to start behaving like the adult that Claire wanted him to be. "Claire's fine, and I'm fine, is that understood? In fact, we're more than fine. Claire is teaching me about doing something productive with my life."

Annabel studied her slippers again. "That's nice."

Arel got to his feet and threw his shoulders back. "Nice? The woman I'm engaged to is one of the most dedicated people on this planet! Hopefully, I'll be able to follow in her footsteps!"

Elise frowned. "Why are you shouting at us?"

"I'm sorry. I just get passionate about Claire." He turned to Annabel. "I hope you have a pleasant visit. If you want to see me, you know where I live."

Elise came over, almost reached out to him and then put her hands behind her back. "Arel, you're so flushed. Are you running a fever again?"

Arel did feel overly warm, but he couldn't be bothered by a fever, he kept having flashes of Claire's face. When she'd talked about his deficiencies, she looked at him with pity and disdain. Was he driving away the woman he loved? "No fever, I'm just being self-indulgent," he insisted.

"Self-indulgent? What do you mean?" Elise asked.

Arel knew exactly what Claire would want him to say. "Don't you understand? We're all wasting our lives, listening to loud music and laughing when we should be—" Before he could finish his sentence, he ran out of breath and mopped his forehead with his handkerchief. "Maybe you're right. I don't feel very well."

Annabel came over and took Arel's arm to steady him. As she held him in place, she looked at Elise. "Call Michael. Ask him to come over."

When Arel heard Michael's name, he jerked away. "Michael? He's always wasting time tending to roses! He should be out feeding the hungry."

Elise came forward with hands on hips. "Listen you, I don't know what your problem is but don't talk like that about Michael. He doesn't just take care of roses. If it weren't for him and Carey, I'd still be bitter and lost."

Annabel intervened. "Elise, don't upset yourself, please. When Arel is like this, he's not rational."

Arel glared back. The fever Elise mentioned was escalating. "I am rational. With Claire's help, I'm finally making sense."

Elise picked up Freddie and went to the door. "So glad to hear it, Arel. Now if you don't mind, Annabel and I would like to be left to a frivolous pursuit called lunch."

Elise watched Arel as he headed for home, then closed the door. When she turned back to Annabel, she realized that she was more upset than she'd been in weeks. "What is the matter with that man?"

Annabel sighed. "William warned me that this would happen. It's one of the reasons that I didn't want Arel to know I was here. I feel helpless to offer him any advice."

Elise cuddled Freddie, then put him down. As she watched the puppy hunt out a bit of biscuit, she frowned. "It's just that I've never seen this side of Arel. When we dated, he was so sweet."

"It's Claire. She can bring out the worst in a person."

Elise let out a huff of disapproval. "Not according to Arel. He just told us that she's one of the best things to come along since oxygen."

"He's been completely smitten since they met."

"All I know is that he was very rude."

"After I spent time with Claire, I was so depressed that I had to go to bed."

"Goodness, and I thought I was bad."

"Claire seems to have a knack for making you feel inadequate, especially if you suffer from any form of low self-esteem or self-doubt."

A tapping sound sent Freddie running for the door. Elise frowned and followed him. "Maybe Arel didn't make it home. I've never seen anyone who could look so feverish so quickly."

Annabel hurried to the door and picked up Freddie. "I hope he's okay."

Elise tried to appear as calm as possible, but her short discussion with Annabel made her stomach feel queasy. It felt even worse when she answered the door and saw Arel again. He started apologizing immediately.

"Elise and Annabel, I'm so sorry. By the time I got home, I realized how badly I'd behaved."

Elise opened the door a little wider. "Do you want to come in?"

Arel shook his head. "Thank you, but after my performance, I just had to try to make amends."

Annabel stepped forward. "Don't be too hard on yourself."

Arel gave her and Elise an awkward look of contrition. "I was completely out of line. I guess I was in a bit of a state after Claire pointed out my many deficiencies. Instead of being accountable, I took my problems out on you two."

Elise sighed. "And Michael too."

Arel nodded. "Yes, poor Michael. Like Claire said, I act like a child. But the good news is that I'm going to change."

"What do you mean?" Annabel asked.

Arel tried to straighten up, but his face remained drawn and anxious. "Claire is taking me under her wing. She said that she'll make a new man out of me."

"I kind of like the man you are," Elise said quietly.

Arel gave her a look of surprise. "That's kind of you, but I hope I haven't ruined your afternoon."

Before Elise could say anything, Arel had already turned and started down the stairs. Again, her stomach tightened, this time in a painful way. All her anger faded as she thought about Arel's fretful, apologetic face. "Annabel, I'm worried about him. Do you think he's going to be alright?"

Annabel hugged Freddie. "I don't know. When I talk to William, I'll ask him what he thinks about the situation."

Twenty-Nine

WILLIAM WALKED AROUND Annabel's studio and realized how much he missed her. He'd talked to her earlier, and she seemed to be getting along quite well. Her only concern was Arel. The man was obviously floundering. William tried to be sympathetic, but admitted that he didn't know how to help. What he didn't tell Annabel is that he didn't know how to help himself either.

Anxiety and dread continued to fester in his gut. It was a painful reminder that he was resisting what Raphael called his inner child. William found the concept annoying to say the least. Didn't Raphael recognize a simple fact? William had grown up. He was an adult who was in pain, and he couldn't shake it.

Annabel's room was a distraction. He smiled briefly as his gaze traveled over the cheerful, seafoam green walls and white cupboards. He would have chosen earth tones or neutral colors, but he had to admit Annabel's color scheme lifted his spirits. Her choice in wall art was a different story.

Recently, she'd purchased large, whimsical metal fish. Each of the three pieces boasted a bold, primary color. One was red. One was yellow, and one was blue. The oversized fish looked like they were swimming on the seafoam walls. But they weren't the only artwork that Annabel had delighted in. William had to take a couple of steps back when he looked at a lively unicorn with a rainbow-colored mane. With horn thrust forward, it looked like it was galloping straight towards him. He quickly shifted his attention to a three foot yellow sunflower and took a breath.

For William, the room was a sensory overload. Maybe that was the reason he decided to spend time there. It was a perfect place for him to practice focus, to strengthen his control over unwanted emotions. If he could maintain a composed attitude in Annabel's studio, he was definitely mastering some aspect of himself.

He also enjoyed looking at Annabel's works in progress. With her absence, he could take his time and contemplate what his wife was all about. Since she'd become a human, she was discovering her place in the world. Currently, her sculpting endeavors were varied. There was a mouse for Arel that made William smile. It was quite large, with a head that was off center. It had an overly long tail and its tiny feet looked too small to support it. Arel would surely faint dead away if he had to display it in his home.

Annabel was also working on another horse for him. She told him that it was going to be more realistic than the last. It was smaller than Arel's mouse. That was good. If he was forced to put it on one of his library shelves, it wouldn't be too prominent.

He picked up the small, clay figure and studied it, trying to see it as Annabel did. It did have four legs of sorts, but they were varied in thickness. The head had the general shape of a horse's head, but the ears were much too big.

"What was she thinking when she fashioned this?" he mused.

"She was thinking about you."

William turned and looked at Raphael. The tall, youthful angel was wearing jeans and a white sweater. His handsome features would make him the perfect sculptor's model.

"How can you say Annabel was thinking of me? I have nothing in common with this misshapen object."

Raphael walked over and glanced around Annabel's work table. "William, I'm surprised. With your abilities, I wouldn't think you'd be stuck on the outer form."

William blinked back, letting the angel's words sink in. "Go on."

"Look at the horse with your inner eye, the one that goes beyond the physical."

William almost did as he was told, but stopped himself in time. In his present condition, he had to be very careful. He didn't dare "go within." What if he activated another memory?

Instead, he allowed himself to simply hold the clay horse and tune into its energy. He immediately felt Annabel's sweet nature, her desire to enjoy life without cares or worries. Not to take things so seriously. He felt her desire to play . . . with him.

He immediately replaced the clay figure on the table. "I think I better get out of here before my senses have a meltdown."

Raphael followed him out into the hall. "Annabel still has so much of her angelic nature."

William turned. "In what way?"

202

"Humans don't think so, but our essence is about appreciating all the varied and delightful forms of creation. I guess in very simple terms, it's about having fun."

"Fun? Ever since I got angelic blood, I've been battling for my life and sanity."

"Believe me, William, angelic blood has nothing to do with destroying anyone. However, it does act as an agent of change. If you resist that change—"

"You die! That's what happens. Michael had to bring Arel back to life after his heart attack. And Arel had to storm heaven to get me back."

"I'm sorry that you feel that way."

"You're sorry? What good does that do when I'm headed towards my grave again?"

* * *

Peggy, Carol, Annabel and Elise sat at a sunny table, each sipping their beverage. The coffee house wasn't as busy as usual, and they'd found seating in a corner booth. Peggy enjoyed having some time away from home. Tim was watching little Sara while she got out with her friends. She smiled at Annabel. "I was happily surprised when you called and said you were visiting Chicago. Did you come on a sudden whim?"

Annabel smiled back. "Yes, I realized I needed a change. Happily, without much effort, everything fell into place."

Carol played with her napkin, folding it this way and that. "In the past, when I was going through some rough times, I would have flown off somewhere if it hadn't been for our little boy. Motherhood doesn't give you that option."

Annabel looked down. "I don't think I'll have to worry about children. William was sort of open to the idea for a while, but he's having his doubts."

Elise gave Annabel a sympathetic sigh. "Once I overheard Arel talking about me. He was sure I wasn't mother material. He was probably right."

Peggy frowned back. "Arel doesn't know what's right for another person. He barely knows how to keep his own life on track."

"That's for sure," Annabel said. "He stopped over at Elise's house, and he was very upset."

Elise joined in. "He told us that Claire is . . . how did he put it? Something about Claire making a new man out of him."

Annabel crossed her arms. "It's scary. He doesn't seem to know how to think on his own since he met her."

"What do you mean?" Peggy asked.

"From what Carey told me, he's thinking of getting rid of all his possessions, even selling his house," Annabel said. "Then he and Claire could go off to some foreign country and help the poor. And all that would be fine if Arel wanted that type of life, but he's only doing it for Claire."

Peggy let out a snort of disapproval. "I can't believe I'm hearing this. After all that we've gone through with him, trying to build up his self-confidence. Now, he's letting some woman dictate how he should live his life."

Carol put her napkin aside and clasped her hands. "I agree with Peggy. I'm very disappointed. After all his preaching about believing in ourselves, he sounds like he's doing the exact opposite."

Elise picked up some crumbs from the table and put them on her saucer. "I know I'm the outsider here. And I know I was terrible when I was dating Arel, but this Claire sounds worse than me, if that's possible."

Peggy smiled at her. "You were pretty bad, but at least you weren't trying to brainwash him."

"Looking back on what I did, I know I had big trust issues," Elise said. "It was hard for me to think somebody could be that nice. Now, I hate to see him look so lost."

Carol shook her head. "Can you see Arel in some third world country, trying to cope? He can barely handle Carey's sloppy eating habits."

Peggy slumped back. "Unfortunately, I can see him there. Arel would push himself until he dropped if he had to. It's the way he is."

Carol snatched up her napkin again. "You're right. He still doesn't seem to know how to give himself a break."

Elise sipped her tea. "Well, he's wrong if he thinks that self-sacrifice is the way to go. When I was younger, I thought I needed to take care of everyone but myself. And you saw how I ended up. I hated life."

Annabel reached out and patted Elise's hand. "I'm sorry, Elise. But look at you now. You inspire me. You've been so sweet and helpful."

"I've been lucky. Michael and Carey showed me a way to value myself again. And I guess once you like yourself, it's easy to be nice."

Annabel smiled. "You've made me realize that it's okay to laugh and have fun. After living with William and everything being so serious, I almost forgot those things."

Carol looked around the table expectantly. "Does anyone have any ideas about helping Arel?"

"We've tried to help before," Peggy said, "and where did it get us? Maybe Arel has to do what he has to do."

Carol's expression went sullen. "Just give up on him? Is that it?"

"I'm sorry, but I'm out of ideas," Peggy said.

Elise laughed. "The outlandish writer in me has a thought. I could storm his house and kidnap him!"

"And then what would you do once you had him?" Annabel asked. "He's a lot like William. Very stubborn."

"Not just stubborn," Peggy said, "once Arel gets an idea in his head, he's usually hell bent on holding on to that idea."

Elise sat back. "I see. So he'd probably start telling me how noble Claire is, and how shallow I am. Then I'd lose patience, and my mean streak might be resurrected very quickly."

Annabel gave Elise a pleading look. "Please, Elise, no more mean streaks, just keep doing what you're doing and let's keep having fun."

"I agree," Carol said. "As for Arel, let's just hope he comes to his senses."

Thirty

AREL HAD TRIED his best to understand how to proceed with his life. He thought about Claire's advice for hours on end. It didn't resolve anything. That's why he asked to meet Michael at the park. "Sorry, Michael, but I didn't want any interruptions while we're discussing some important matters."

"When you talk about interruptions, who do you have in mind?" Michael asked.

Arel fidgeted, picking at a bit of peeling paint on the bench seat. "That's not important. What's important is one's life and how a person is supposed to make choices. For instance, how does a person know when they're not living up to their potential?"

"Perhaps you could give me an example of what you're getting at."

"Okay, I didn't want to get personal, but if you insist—"

"Certainly, I have no problem with a personal question."

Arel avoided looking at Michael and scratched harder at the chipping paint. "Remember, you asked for it, so here goes. Claire said that you should be out in the world, doing more with your life. Instead, you're wasting time just helping me. What would you say to that?"

Michael smiled. "I'd say that Claire has every right to her opinion."

"But is she right?"

"If that's the way she feels, it's the right opinion for her."

"But how do you feel, Michael? Do you think you're being negligent?"

"No, I don't, but that doesn't make Claire wrong. It just means we each have an opinion. However, that said, let me make a comment. Our relationship isn't unique, Arel. Everyone in this world has a connection to the Divine part of themselves. And if they desire, they can strengthen that connection in a way that will be beneficial."

"Yes, but how many will ever get a chance at angelic blood?"

"How many would take that chance? Think about what you've gone through."

"I guess you're right. I even died at one point. So did William."

"Yours hasn't been an easy path."

Arel sat back. "So why do I feel so worthless when Claire is around?"

"That's a question only you can answer."

"So that's it. You won't give me any advice about how I'm feeling."

"Would it make any difference if I did?"

"No, I guess you've told me how you feel about me many times. But why hasn't it stuck? Why do I still get thrown off course like I do?"

"Perhaps you're still looking outside of yourself for answers."

Arel stopped rubbing the rough bench seat. "Michael, I just had a thought. Maybe Claire has some misguided ideas too."

"I'm listening."

"She's always talking about helping the unfortunate, but what if that's because she's not happy? Maybe she's trying to fix herself by fixing others."

"Whether that's true or not, she has a right to feel however she chooses to feel. Your responsibility is not to blame her if her choices conflict with your own."

"She says things that make me cringe. At the same time, I can't argue with her views. There are so many people in the world who are hurting."

"Yes, and if you feel in your heart that you'd like to help others in some way, I'd say to follow your heart and that path. But each person has to find the path that's right for them. Take Elise for instance."

"Elise? She writes romance stories. How's that helpful?"

"It's easy to point out people who are starving physically, but many of the women who read her books have very difficult lives too. They might live in a house and have food to eat, but that's not enough to sustain them. Many still feel very discouraged, even hopeless. Elise has been in their position, and she tries to address some of their needs. Her books don't provide a solution to people's problems, but they might provide some moments of relief, and maybe even the strength needed to face another day."

"I never thought of it that way."

"Now, let's consider a very different path, one where the person simply sits on their porch and admires their surroundings, the sun or the rain clouds, the birds or a mouse in the grass. What about that path? Some would say the person is lazy, but how is that person so very different than a contemplative monk? Aren't both of them honoring the Creator in their own way?"

"I guess that's true."

"Every person has a unique viewpoint. Everyone has the ability to contribute to the well-being of all. It might be something intangible like the joy a person feels about their life and the life around them. That joy can't be measured like the results that come from a more active lifestyle. But think about the effect a joyful person or a laughing, happy child can have on another. It can be an uplifting experience. The key is not to judge one person's path against another's."

Arel settled back and glanced at the barren trees that circled the park. When he felt a chill from a sharp gust of wind, he knew that winter was on the way. "Everything you've said makes perfect sense."

Michael laughed. "But—"

"But there's another side to all of this. Sometimes, when Claire and I are in bed, it's so wonderful to have her close. In those precious moments, I forget everything. I don't want those moments to ever end. That's why it feels impossible to say no to her."

Michael stood up and took in a deep breath of the brisk air. "I understand."

"So what am I going to do?"

"Give yourself some time. Don't try to figure it out all at once."

"That's not an option. Claire says I've wasted enough of my life, and I need to make some decisions, now."

Thirty-One

ELISE KNOCKED ON Annabel's door. "Annabel, can I talk to you in the living room? I know that it's getting late, but I have an idea."

"Be there in a minute," Annabel called out.

A few minutes later, when the two of them were seated on the sofa, Elise handed Annabel a cup of hot chocolate. Freddie was stretched out on the cushion between them. He was dozing soundly after a day of puppy crazies and long walks.

"So what is your idea?" Annabel asked.

Elise snickered and handed her a napkin. "You have a little mustache, sweetie."

"Mustache?" Annabel returned a look of surprise and dabbed at her upper lip.

"You got it," Elise said, still smiling.

Annabel laughed too. "You seem unusually happy. What's going on?"

"I want to have a party before you leave. We can invite our friends over to celebrate and enjoy lots of good food."

"What are we celebrating?"

"I don't know, but everything is changing very quickly. You're going back to London. I'm moving, and Claire and Arel are going to be traveling to who-knows-where. Before all that happens, we should get together and have some fun."

"Yes, I guess you're right. I saw a 'For Sale' sign in Arel's yard today."

Elise held her cup in both hands. "I haven't known all of you for very long, but I have fond memories of the time we've spent together."

"Me too, Elise. I never knew how much fun it could be to dress up in a wig or learn to dance. But I'm curious."

"About what?"

"Why are you inviting Claire and Arel to this party? Won't that be awkward for you?"

"I want to part with everyone on good terms."

Annabel gave Elise a playful look. "Are you also curious about Claire?"

"Maybe, she does seem rather interesting. And who knows, she might have some redeeming qualities."

Annabel took a big sip of her chocolate and grabbed for her napkin. "I guess you're right. Arel is a dear friend. I want to be okay with Claire, too."

"Well, I've been thinking a lot about her and what I've been told. If I picture her as one of my characters, it helps me to have a different perspective."

"Really? So describe how you see her as someone in one of your stories."

Elise paused for a moment, giving her imagination free rein. "The character named Claire is focused and filled with determination. She's the take charge type. She goes after what she wants and gets it."

"Does that include a man? I only ask since you write about romance."

"Of course, in my books, there's always a love interest."

"What about Arel? Would he make it into one of your novels?"

"Maybe, but he'd have to change. Claire needs someone as strong as she is. Plus, my readers don't want my male characters to be push-overs. They need a juicy partnership, where both the gal and guy bring something unexpected and challenging to the relationship."

"You're saying that Arel would have to stand up to Claire."

"That's right."

Annabel sighed. "The real Arel has no intention of doing that. From what I know, he's been alone for a long time. He wants someone to share his life. When he met Claire, he decided that she was the one."

"I'm kind of curious to see the two of them together. I hope they come to our little get-together. Sometimes a party brings out versions of a person that you don't expect."

Annabel let out a sudden gasp. "Goodness, I've never gone to a party."

"Never? Oh Annabel, that means we'll have to make it an extra-special celebration."

"I'll be happy to help with the food preparation."

"Thank you, I love having you in the kitchen. You're great company." Elise put her feet up on the coffee table and stared at her fuzzy slippers. "And Annabel?"

"Yes?"

"Wherever I go, wherever I end up, I hope we'll stay in touch. And remember, you'll always be welcome to visit me."

Annabel put her feet up too, looking pleased. "Thank you, and thank you for the matching slippers. I wonder if William will like them."

Elise sat back and let her thoughts drift. "Your fellow sounds like quite the man. Do you think he'd be able to stand up to Claire?"

Annabel swallowed wrong and started coughing. When she finally caught her breath, she gave Elise a mischievous look. "My William and Claire? I can only think of one scenario. War, with no holds barred."

"Hmm, I'm certainly not in favor of an all-out war, but some loud disagreements don't scare me."

"I've disagreed with William, but I always come away feeling bad. I don't like to fight."

"It's not about liking to fight necessarily. It's about both parties knowing it's safe to have their own ideas and if need be, to express them. It's about knowing that you love each other, even when you don't like each other. Anyway, that's how I think about disagreements."

"It's a shame that Arel didn't get to know the real you."

"Why?"

"Because you'd have been a good match for his stubbornness. I also think you'd have given him room to be himself. Not many people are like you, Elise. You're special."

"Thanks, and how about you and William? Are you two a good match?"

Annabel sat very still and took her time before answering. "I'm not sure."

"Do you know what I think?"

"What?"

"That the two of you are going to have a very long and happy marriage."

"Why do you say that?"

Elise ran her hand over Freddie's fur, calming some muscle twitches. "It just happens sometimes. My intuition kicks in, and things that I feel often turn out to be true."

Annabel smiled and stood up. "So when should we have this party?"

Elise stretched and stood up too. "I'd like to do what Peggy does and make it somewhat spontaneous. Why don't I call everyone in the morning? It'll be short notice, but maybe people can make it on Saturday night."

"That sounds wonderful."

* * *

Arel slipped his phone into his pocket and headed towards the living area. He'd given Elise a tentative "yes" regarding her party invitation. But he wanted to make sure that Claire was agreeable. When he walked into the room, she lowered her book.

"You look like something is on your mind," she said as she turned a page.

"My neighbor, Elise, is having a get-together tomorrow night. We're invited."

Claire shrugged. "Sure, why not? As long as we don't stay too long."

"You'll get a chance to meet some of my friends. You've been here for a bit, and I think they're eager to get to know you."

Claire paused and looked up. "I'm sorry that I haven't had the time to meet them sooner."

"It's fine. I think they're used to me being overly private."

"Arel?"

Arel stopped immediately and braced himself. When Claire used that tone and his name, she usually had something important she wanted to tell him. "Yes? What is it?"

"You know that has to change."

He glanced around. "What has to change?"

"Your ideas about personal space. When people go on digs or volunteer for projects in poverty-stricken areas, there isn't much privacy."

"But what about us? Don't we need time to ourselves? Don't you want us to get to know each other a little better?"

Claire patted the cushion next to her. "One of the best ways to get to know someone is to work with them in the field."

Arel smiled back. "Forget the field work, I'd like to start right now." He sat down and reached out for her hand. He studied her slender fingers and kissed her palm. Carefully, he cradled her hand close to his chest. "Everything about you is perfect, do you know that?"

Claire laughed. "Yes, as a matter of fact, I do. I can't tell you how many men have told me the same thing."

Arel replaced her hand on the cushion and sat up stiffly. "So I guess I remind you of a whole string of guys who annoyed you."

Claire waved his statement off. "Oh stop it. You're letting your feelings get bruised again. You need to toughen up a little, my darling. Besides, I'm not with any of those other men. I chose to be with you."

"That's true, but I don't think you've ever told me why."

"Maybe I feel that there's so much more to you than with most. I think you're someone who can achieve great things. Together, we'll make a wonderful team."

"That's not exactly romantic, is it?"

Claire gave him an impatient sigh. "I think you're letting your libido get mixed up with reality. When it comes to the business of day to day living, teamwork is much more important."

"When I mentioned romance, I was thinking about more than my libido, Claire. I love you."

"Love! What does that mean?"

"It means I'd do anything I could to make you happy."

Claire's eyes softened for a brief moment. "Poor Arel, you have such an attachment to the personal. And I appreciate that, but when I think of love, it goes beyond you and me. Love means being there for those who have no one. Do you understand?"

"I don't think so."

"It's okay. It takes time to learn what I'm trying to teach you."

"I feel like I should be in a classroom."

Claire laughed. "Don't start pouting, please. I don't find that to be an attractive trait in a man. Instead, do something constructive. Read about what it means to be a volunteer. Inform yourself about this planet and what needs doing."

Arel stood up and looked at his bride-to-be. "I don't know much about your world, do I?"

"No, but maybe that's just as well. When we begin working together, you'll start fresh. You won't have any bad habits that need correction."

"What bad habits could a volunteer have? I'd think they'd be very nice people."

"Oh, you'd be surprised at how hard it is to work with some people. They can be real nightmares. Happily, from what I've seen, you're very willing to learn, and you don't balk at taking orders."

Arel started for the hall. "With that in mind, I better get started on being informed." As he retreated to his bedroom, he thought about Claire's description of their future together. It almost sounded as if he was joining the army instead of getting married.

He rubbed his temples as he made his way to the bathroom. With a headache coming on, he needed to find an icepack he had in his vanity. If the headache got really bad, the cold would help to dull the pain. Unfortunately, he didn't have anything around to lessen his doubts and fears. With Claire at the helm, guiding his every step, he was headed for an alien world he'd never contemplated or wanted to contemplate.

Thirty-Two

ROLPHE FOUND THAT prayer filled his body with a lightness of spirit and added to the joy he felt when he painted. And his prayers flowed out so naturally. It was easy to envision William getting back on track with his life. William had proven who he was, a man of honor and courage. Before he engaged Arel in battle, he swore that he would not harm Arel or any of his soldiers. And in the end, he accomplished his goal. With angelic assistance, William thwarted Arel's attempt at playing the bad guy. He saved those who'd been caught up in Arel's twisted plans. In the aftermath of all that conflict, Rolphe was sure William would once again overcome any inner demons.

What Rolphe hadn't expected was an emotional upheaval in his own life. As he painted and prayed and thought about William's noble nature, his own nature and past looked anything but noble. He'd once been a soldier too. In fact, he'd spent years fighting on one battlefield after another. But never once had he known glory. No matter how many of the enemy he killed, he only felt more shame and loss of self.

He'd made peace with those memories since knowing Arel, Michael and Carey. Now, they began to haunt him again. And for some reason, he felt the need to talk to William about them.

* * *

William quickly made his way to the front entrance. With narrowed brows and frayed nerves, he was in no shape for visitors. Whatever he'd stirred up in his gut was getting more agitated by the day. His body refused to relax. He did his best to ignore the situation, but denial was becoming a losing battle.

At least Annabel wasn't around to witness the state he was in. Her decision to extend her stay in Chicago was a small respite. Otherwise she'd be hovering over him, letting him know how worried she was. Still, when they were talking on the phone, he felt compelled to tell her how much he loved her. He was saying goodbye to her when he heard someone pounding on his door. Whoever his visitor was, they sounded out their urgency in no uncertain terms.

As he was about to reach for the door knob, he noted that his hand hesitated. In fact, every muscle in his body was on alert. That's when he realized who his visitor was. His scowl deepened as he quickly undid the latch and swung open the door. His reward was a very tall, very large man who stood looking down at him. "Rolphe, what a surprise."

Rolphe took a step back and bowed his head. "Hello, William."

William hadn't seen Rolphe since he and Annabel accompanied Arel to Paris. He wasn't anxious to see him now. The man had been an ally in the past, and when he was around William, the man tried his best to demonstrate a penitent attitude. It was warranted. William had been at Rolphe's mercy on two occasions. Irrational or not, William's gut sent out warnings to stay vigilant. "What brings you to London?" he asked as he reluctantly showed his guest into the living room.

Instead of answering, Rolphe quickly took a seat on the sofa. As he settled into the confines of the couch, he checked out his surroundings with darting eyes. When they came to rest on William, they softened. "You and Annabel have a very nice home."

"Yes, I forgot that you've never been here before."

Rolphe stared down, clasping and unclasping his hands. "I'm sorry to show up like this, but I've been having visions that seem to be connected to you."

"Connected? How?"

Rolphe hedged. "I don't know. I'm sorry. Maybe 'connected' is the wrong word. I'm sorry."

William had to remind himself to be patient and restrain his tone of voice. Otherwise, Rolphe would continue apologizing and never get to the point. "Rolphe, take a breath and tell me about your vision."

Rolphe sucked in some air and glanced around the room again. "I'm sorry, I think I'm nervous."

"Your vision, Rolphe. Let's hear it."

"Yes, my vision. Remember when you faced Arel on the battlefield?" Rolphe paused and smiled. "You were so courageous."

"Thanks, but that's old news, Rolphe. Keep going."

"For me, it was different. I keep seeing myself. I'm standing on another field of battle. It's one of the many I remember from when I was a young soldier."

William didn't like the way Rolphe kept stealing glances at him. Rolphe's approach had gone from fervent to needy. "I don't know much about your personal history. You should probably talk to Arel about these matters."

Rolphe's body slumped forward, his face filled with weariness. "You're right. Arel does know a lot. But like you, he had no desire to acquaint himself with me. The first time he came to my apartment, it was after, you know, what I did to you. As soon as I saw his eyes, glowing with hatred, I couldn't look away. I thought he was an avenging angel who'd come for retribution. That's when my heart gave out." He clasped his hands tighter and offered a weak smile. "Arel was clearly disappointed when I keeled over. He wanted me to suffer like I made you suffer, not just check out."

For a moment, William slipped into the past. The memory that flashed through his mind made his breath catch. He was in Rolphe's clutches again. He was helpless to stop Rolphe from doing as he pleased. He wanted to kill William. "You were a monster who needed to be stopped."

Rolphe cringed. "Dying would have been a relief, except I was afraid of spending eternity in the fires of hell."

"Please, spare me and get to the point. You were talking about being a soldier."

Rolphe sat up and thrust his shoulders back. "In those days, I was nothing like you in battle. I cried the first time I faced an enemy. All I wanted to do was run back home."

William stared at Rolphe, a six-foot-five hulk, and found it hard to imagine the man bawling. "How old were you?"

Rolphe sighed. "Maybe twelve. I was big for my age, a head taller than most of the boys I knew."

"Twelve years old? You were a child."

"It was a very long time ago. I grew up in a tiny, backward village. So what did I know about the world? I helped my father work our small piece of land. When the military people came for us, they didn't ask much. They took the ones who looked like they could serve purpose. After some training, we were thrown into battle. The officers shouted orders, and we were supposed to obey. But—"

"But what?"

Rolphe peeked back, remorseful again. "I wasn't always a monster. Before they took us, I hid from my mother when she told me to kill a chicken. So when I faced the task of taking the life of another human being—"

"How did you cope?"

Rolphe threw his head back and roared with a laughter that was both bitter and woeful. "A child doesn't cope! He does what he's told. And later, if he survives, he goes back to his village and has nightmares."

"Rolphe, like you said, it was all a very long time ago. Why are you talking about all of this now?"

"I thought I put it all behind me. But sometimes, when I'm at my easel, I ask myself how I can paint beautiful scenes with angels after all I've done." He closed his eyes and sighed heavily. "So many died—"

"You were a boy. Let it go."

Rolphe jumped up, his face red with resentment and outrage. When he scowled at William, his eyes were dark pools of wrath and fury. "How can I let it go? It wasn't right! Don't you understand? They took everything that was good in me! You said it yourself. They made me a monster!"

William jerked to attention, momentarily alarmed by Rolphe's outburst. "Settle down, Rolphe," he ordered. "Yelling about it now isn't going to help."

After a long pause, Rolphe nodded and collapsed back into his seat. "Forgive me," he begged. "The last thing I want to do is add to your problems."

William huffed out his indignation. "My problems? What do you know about my problems?"

Rolphe began to rock back and forth slowly. "There's another vision that won't go away. In it, I see another young boy. He isn't thrown into battle, but he does face a terrible adversary who strips him of all that he loves." Rolphe stopped rocking and gave William a furtive glance. "I think the boy in my vision is you, William."

William glared back. "Again, my childhood is old news too, Rolphe. What good is it to rehash it?"

"I'm not trying to rehash it, but I did want your opinion. Do you think that child that we once were, the one who knew only goodness and love, is that child still inside of us?"

William got to his feet. "Look at us, Rolphe. We're grown men. End of story. So go back to Paris, and forget about your visions. Is that clear?"

Rolphe stood up obediently and quickly headed for the exit. When he reached the door, he turned to William. "Doesn't what I told you make you angry? Don't you want to find a way to get back what was taken from us?"

William stopped short and crossed his arms. "Do I want to be naïve and innocent again? Do I want to experience what happens when I'm weak and vulnerable? Is that what you're asking? What good would that do?"

"I don't know. I guess that's why I came here. I hoped if we talked, that maybe you could help me understand it all."

William grimaced when another bout of pain hit his gut. "Then you made a wasted trip."

Thirty-Three

ELISE STOOD NEXT to Annabel as they checked out their new dresses in the mirror. "What do you think, Annabel? I've gained some weight. Maybe I shouldn't have chosen something fitted. And what about this shade of red, is it too bright?"

Annabel took a long moment to study Elise's new frock. "I've been looking at some of your fashion magazines, and I think you'd be described as sexy."

Elise did a little pirouette and smiled. "I can live with 'sexy'."

Annabel turned to the mirror again. "What about mine? I like the teal color, but I think I should have chosen something more conservative."

Elise's eyes turned playful. "You're a beautiful woman, Annabel. The scalloped lace neckline plunges just enough to demonstrate that fact. But I have to say that if William were here, he'd ravish you on the spot."

"Poor William. Maybe I should have gone home tomorrow like I originally planned. He acts like he's fine, but I know he isn't."

"Did he seem disappointed when you suggested staying longer?"

"No, he said it was a good idea. A part of me agreed. I don't think I know how to help him."

Elise undid the side zipper on her dress and walked into her roomy closet. "William sounds like he needs more time to think."

"You're right. He's very independent. In fact, he was a bachelor for a long time before I came along."

"I see." Elise took off her dress, hung it up, and grabbed her jeans. After she slipped them on, she put on a baby-blue sweater and rejoined Annabel in the bedroom. "No wonder William and Arel are great friends. They both shared a love for the single life."

Annabel plopped down on the bed. "I don't think Arel liked being alone."

Elise took a seat in a bedroom chair. "After our break-up, he latched on to Claire like she was manna from heaven."

220

Annabel ran a hand over the lacy skirt of her dress. "He did jump into the relationship very quickly. He barely met Claire when he announced that he was in love."

"I write about love at first sight, but I don't really believe in it."

"Why not?"

"I'm not saying it can't happen. It's just unlikely that two people who don't know each other, think they're ready to devote themselves to a lifetime together."

Annabel gave Elise a thoughtful glance. "In Arel's case, I suppose he feels he can change enough to meet Claire's expectations."

"Arel is a nice guy, but from what I know, he's never pictured himself as the missionary type."

"No, but he is a very determined person when he decides on a course of action. If that means adapting to Clair's ideas, he'll try his best to comply."

Elise crossed her arms and snorted out her disgust. "Then they deserve each other."

"Why do you say that? I thought you cared about Arel and wanted his best."

"I do care, but if I let myself think about the choices that he's making, I might explode."

Annabel smiled. "You care that much?"

Elise sat back and picked some lint off her jeans. "I guess I do. I'll have to watch my temper when I meet Claire at the party tonight. As you already know, it's taken a bit of persistence on my part to tone down my emotions and make peace with myself. However, I don't know how far I can be pushed." She frowned at Annabel. "Promise me that if you see my eyes cross, you and Carey will escort me out of the room. I don't want to make a fool of myself."

Annabel's smile broadened. "I'll pass the word on to Carey."

* * *

Arel sat on the couch, looking at the clock, wondering about Elise's party and hoping the evening would go well. He was also nursing another headache. They were becoming increasingly frequent, but he tried to ignore that fact. Claire insisted that he needed to change his attitude and a tendency to indulge in his woes. Maybe she was right.

As for the party, they were ready to leave when Claire insisted on taking a call from a colleague.

They were thirty minutes late when she finally walked into the living room. Arel stared back, knowing he'd never seen anyone more stunning. With her dark hair pulled back to expose her lovely features, Claire exuded a flawless beauty. It was expressed elegantly in her arched brows, high-cheek bones and full lips. She was picture perfect as she gracefully came forward in her silky, grey dress. The new dress was Arel's idea. At first, Claire had objected to the shopping trip, but since she hadn't brought along anything suitable for a party, she gave in to his suggestion.

As he thought about the woman he'd soon marry, he wanted to feel his heart pounding at the sight of her, to know the thrill that he'd felt in Paris when they were first together. Maybe it was because beauty had always drawn him in. He could sit for hours admiring great art, wanting to immerse himself in something that fired his soul and made his heart soar.

Claire had different ideas about such intangible qualities. She seemed very aware of her gorgeous body and how it could affect others, but she was almost like a rich child who didn't appreciate luxury. She used her beauty when it suited her. Other times, she almost insisted that it had no place in the world.

So what did that say about him? Was his passion for Claire based solely on the physical? He hoped not. He certainly had the capacity to recognize and prize other ways that beauty was demonstrated. Years before, hadn't he'd treasured every moment he spent with the elderly woman who was dying in the hospital? Absolutely. He'd fallen in love with her inner beauty. Mrs. Hayes might have had an aged body, but her heart was a glowing, precious jewel of kindness and compassion.

But what about Claire's heart? At first, she'd acted as if she couldn't get enough of him. But that part of their relationship had withered very quickly once Claire came to Chicago. It was as if passion and desire had no place in her practical, efficient life. It was some separate part that she occasionally indulged and then forgot about. What she enjoyed most was getting on with the business end of things.

When he'd had a call from the realtor earlier that day, he was informed that the first buyers who saw the house were serious about making an offer. Claire lit up immediately, extremely pleased by the news. It meant they'd be free to do what she wanted. He thought about what she'd said to him. "Just think, Arel, from now on you're going to learn responsibility and how to live an unselfish life. Isn't that wonderful?"

She didn't seem to notice his reluctance. The fact that he was giving up his life style and even his beliefs for her was something she took for granted. Most of the time when they were together, he wondered if she really noticed his wants or desires at all.

When she came over to where he was sitting, he reached out, still hoping to bridge the gap that separated them. Taking her hand in his, he kissed it. "I know that you don't like me to comment on how lovely you are, but I can't help it."

She returned an indulgent smile. "That's very nice, but I've found that sentiment doesn't mean much if it isn't backed up by commitment to something more important."

He stood up and adjusted his tie. Claire seemed to think it necessary to always remind him of why his views were negligible. "But I am committed, to you."

"Yes, I know that," she replied.

He studied her face, noting her effort to smile. Her rather sharp tone made him step back. "Anyway, I'm happy that you're going to meet my friends at the party. I think you'll find them all very welcoming."

"But why should I get to know them when we're moving very soon? I'll never see them again."

"Never? But they mean a lot to me."

"Arel, I'm sure they do, but being dependent on others is unhealthy. Besides, there are nice people everywhere." Claire stifled a yawn. "Sorry, but I was up working very late last night. So please remember that I don't want to stay very long."

"Claire?"

"Yes?"

"Are you sure that you still want to marry me?"

"What a silly question. I don't understand why you always want to make a big deal out of everything, Arel."

"But marriage is a big deal, at least it is for me."

Claire took his arm, pulled him closer, and kissed his cheek. "Fine, I still want to marry you. Now, let's get this party over with. But remember, you can't expect me to automatically like your friends. I believe in honesty when I interact with others."

"Honesty? I don't think I understand what you mean."

Claire grabbed her coat and started for the door. "You have so much to learn, my darling. And by the way, if your lazy roommate, Carey, is there. I want to talk to him."

"Claire, I don't think of Carey as lazy. He's—"

Claire continued out the door. "He's like you, Arel, a person who's oblivious. Somebody has to wake him up and get him doing something useful."

* * *

Annabel was having a wonderful time. She'd been apprehensive about her first party, but when the guests began to arrive, she relaxed. Carey and Michael were her old friends, angels who reminded her that life was supposed to be a joyous affair. Peggy and Tim were examples of earth angels, humans who knew how to be kind and helpful. So were Carol and Kevin. And her newest friend, Elise, was an unexpected treasure. When interacting with Elise, life became an adventure to be explored and savored.

As everyone gathered around the lavish table of food in the dining room, Annabel could also feel a sense of accomplishment. She'd helped prepare all of the wonderful dishes, including cornmeal popovers. She'd managed to make them all by herself using a recipe that Elise gave her. When Elise tested one and told her how light and fluffy it was, Annabel knew she wanted to pursue the art of baking. Her decision was validated when she saw Tim and Kevin load up their plates with several each.

In the midst of laughter, happy conversations, and Freddie, the puppy, running around, vying for attention, Annabel's only concern was Claire and Arel. She kept waiting for the doorbell to ring and wondering if she'd find Claire upsetting again. Of course, when they'd had an outing together in London, they were alone. At least now, Annabel would have lots of friends around.

The occasion would've been perfect if William were there. As the days passed, the desire to be together was still as strong as ever. She had to keep telling herself that independence would make her a better partner, a more supportive partner. Because that's what she wanted to be. She wanted to let go of her fears and have the spunk that Elise demonstrated. And slowly, with Elise's encouragement, she was feeling more confident and self-reliant.

Just as she was smiling contentedly to herself, the doorbell rang. When she looked towards the foyer, Elise was inviting Claire and Arel into the house. Arel seemed to be introducing Claire to Elise. Claire was commenting.

Annabel looked away, knowing that her turn was coming. There was no way to avoid Claire in a small party gathering. Her smile wilted as she thought about what Claire would think of her now. Her first instinct was to rush to her bedroom and hide. It was prompted by an irrational feeling of guilt. Claire had made her views known when they last met. The woman had an agenda that included informing Annabel of her frivolity and self-indulgence. Surely, Claire would notice Annabel's new dress. She'd probably ask why Annabel was enjoying herself when she could be in service to the needy? A tap on her arm brought her out of her downward spiral.

"Annabel, are you okay?" Carey asked.

She looked up at him, happy that he'd come over to talk to her. She was standing in the middle of Elise's living room, but her mind was back in that little diner in London. "Why do I feel so small around that woman? Since becoming a human, most people have been so nice to me. But Claire—"

Carey hesitated. "I know that she makes you uncomfortable, but for now, I think we have bigger problems."

"What do you mean?"

"Look at Elise."

"Elise?" Annabel forced herself to forget her own worries long enough to snatch a glance at her friend. "I don't understand. Elise was so happy a few minutes ago. Why is she looking like that? I've never seen that face on her before."

"Remember how she instructed you to help her if she got upset?"

"Oh goodness, you're right."

"Perhaps we could go over and tell her that she needs to check on the pastries in the oven."

* * *

Elise stood on the back porch shivering, but she knew it was for her own good. After only a few words from Claire, her temper had flared up, a brush fire of anger and indignation. She had to take deep breaths of the crisp, cold air to calm herself. When she felt better, she turned to Annabel. Her co-host was shivering too. "Thank you for that quick intervention, but get back in the house where it's warm."

Annabel nodded. "I'll go get your coat."

Carey opened the back door for Annabel and then stepped up to the railing. "Your party is wonderful, Elise, and the food is the best. I'm sorry that you're upset."

Elise stared back at the thoughtful, young man. "I should know better than let anyone make me react like I did, but I'll be fine."

"Is there anything I can do?"

Elise shook her head. "Go inside. I'll join you shortly."

Carey turned to leave just as Michael stepped out of the house. He was carrying Elise's winter jacket and held it out so that she could put it on.

Elise felt warmer almost instantly. "Thank you. You're always the gentleman, Michael."

"Annabel was bringing you the coat, but I told her I wanted to talk to you," Michael said. "Is that alright?"

"Of course, I always welcome your wisdom. Just don't expect me to bounce back too quickly. Claire said some things that were very hurtful."

Michael stared up at the night sky. "I'm sorry to hear that."

Elise latched on to his arm. "I don't understand some people. Take Arel, how could he stand by and let that woman insult me like that."

"Do you want to tell me what she said?"

"Essentially, I'm a worthless hack."

"Is that how she said it?"

"No, but after Arel told Claire that I was a romance writer, she gave me a look that you give something disgusting, like gum on the street. Then she informed me that my passion for writing was frivolous, that my fantasies about romance led people astray and that the money I earned could be going to a much better cause."

"I see."

Elise hugged his arm a little tighter. "And do you want to know the worst part? I think she absolutely believes every word that comes out of her mouth."

"People believe a lot of things."

"Yes, but here's another scary fact. When I looked at those dark eyes of hers, I almost believed her too. Just thinking about her gives me a chill."

"Do you want to go back inside?"

Elise laughed. "Please, not yet, I'm still venting."

"About Claire?"

"No, I think I'm getting a handle on her, but Arel still makes me want to spit tacks."

"Spit tacks?"

"That's an old saying that my aunt used when she was angry. And Arel makes me furious. While Claire was spewing out her garbage, Arel wouldn't even look at me. He actually closed his eyes and rubbed his temples as if he was the one who was being judged worthless."

"Arel doesn't have much experience when it comes to relationships. In this case—"

"In this case, he's being totally manipulated." Elise released Michael's arm and grabbed hold of the railing. "I can't understand what's going through his head."

"But you told me that you also suffered through some difficult relationships."

"You're right. I guess I was once as bad off as Arel. I let men order me around for a long time. Thankfully, I finally wised up."

"And look at you now, Elise. Annabel says that you've been a wonderful friend. And as for your books, you give people ideas about relationships working out. You keep the idea of love alive with your stories."

"So you think I'm more than a useless hack who's pedaling dreams."

Michael smiled back, but before he could comment, the door swung open.

Elise turned and saw Carey leaning out. She'd never seen him look so alarmed. "Is something wrong?"

Carey nodded. "I think you better come in. Annabel is very upset with Claire."

Elise arrived in the living room just as Claire and Arel were headed towards the front door. Arel glanced back once, but then he continued trailing after his fiancé. Peggy, Carol, Tim and Kevin were all standing around Annabel, looking surprised but speechless. Even Freddie was acting strangely. He'd retreated to his doggie bed.

"What happened?" Elise asked as she hurried over to Annabel. "You're shaking. Maybe you should sit down."

Annabel's cheeks were a deep red and her pupils were wide and dark. She looked at Elise, but she didn't say anything.

Elise took her arm and guided her over to the sofa. The others followed and crowded around the couch. Carol sat down next to Annabel.

Peggy stepped closer. "Listen to me, Annabel. You should be happy with yourself. Somebody had to put this Claire person in her place. She was rude and obnoxious to say the least."

Carol put her hand on Annabel's. "Peggy is right. In fact, if you hadn't come to Carey's rescue, I was definitely going to speak up."

"What happened to Carey?" Elise felt a ping of anxiety as she glanced around and saw that her young friend was stationed away from the group. "Carey, what is Carol talking about? Did Claire say something inappropriate to you?"

When Carey shrugged, Kevin spoke up. "I don't think Claire wanted anybody to hear her when she took Carey aside. But of course, we all have big ears here."

Peggy agreed. "And it's a good thing too. When Annabel found out what was going on, she insisted that Claire come clean about what she'd said to Carey."

Annabel cleared her throat, but her voice was strained when she spoke. "Claire was awful. After she'd upset Elise, I didn't know what she'd do next. When she approached Carey, I stayed close enough to hear her tell him some horrible things. I think she's been waiting to talk to him about living in Arel's house. She made it sound like he was a free-loader, taking advantage of Arel's lenient attitude and contributing nothing to Arel or anyone else."

Elise stiffened with her own outrage. "You're right, Annabel. That is awful!"

In the months that she'd known Carey, Elise had found him to be sweet and thoughtful as anyone could be. To criticize him at all was a crime. To say the things that Claire said was totally unacceptable. She quickly went over to him, put her hands on her hips and eyed him with motherly concern. "Carey, don't believe a word that woman said. As far as I'm concerned, you're a blessing. Because of you and Michael, I've been able to change my life around. And if you ever need a place to live, you can stay with me. Is that clear?"

"Thank you, Elise, but please don't worry. I'm fine," Carey said.

"Are you sure?"

Carey smiled back. "Yes, I'm sure."

Elise felt her shoulders drop a couple of inches. Carey, like Michael, had a healthy sense of himself. On the other hand, when she went back to check on Annabel, Annabel still looked very shaky. "Sweetie, please, tell us what you're thinking."

Annabel shrugged. "I know Claire was out of line, but I've never been this angry before. When I heard what she was saying, I couldn't hold my feelings back. I started shouting, calling her callous and judgmental."

Elise laughed. "Annabel, I've never seen anyone who tries as hard as you do. Maybe it's time you gave yourself some leeway. You said things that needed to be said."

Carol smiled. "Elise is right. We all agree that you were great."

Annabel lifted her eyes a little. "So nobody thinks I did anything wrong?"

"Absolutely not," Peggy said in a firm tone.

Elise glanced around at her guests. They were all smiling back at Annabel. It was the perfect time to encourage the young woman to stand up and feel better about herself. "Listen, everyone, let's forget about rude people and enjoy ourselves. Annabel and I wanted to make this party special, and we did our best in the kitchen. There are meatball appetizers, crab puffs, deviled eggs, dips, cheeses, and lots of other yummy stuff to eat. Will everyone indulge us? Try out our buffet and let us know what you think about our culinary skills?"

Kevin looked at Carol, then back at Elise. "I know that Carol and I will do our part."

Tim hugged Peggy contentedly. "Count us in."

Elise looked at Carey. "How about you, Carey?"

Carey gave her a thumb's up. "You bet."

As everyone headed to the dining room, Elise saw Michael putting out some cabbage rolls that had been warming in the oven. She squeezed Annabel's hand. "Come on, let's join our friends and have a great time."

Annabel hesitated. "Are you sure? I was afraid I'd ruined everything."

"Just the opposite. I'm very proud of what you did."

"Why?" Annabel asked.

"Because you stood up for someone who's too nice to say anything when they're treated badly. You didn't let Claire get away with being a bully."

"Thank you."

"Plus, I bet it felt good to express yourself."

Annabel smiled shyly. "Yes, it felt very good."

Elise started to follow Annabel into the dining room and stopped short. Sometimes, she had intuitive flashes about other people. This one made her sad. Arel was in trouble. She was sure of it. "Annabel, is it crazy for me to be worried about Arel? I know he's an adult, and that he should be able to stand up to Claire, but—"

Annabel frowned. "I know how you feel. I wish I could help too, but he has very definite ideas about how he should conduct his life. So I guess we'll have to trust that he'll make better decisions in the future."

"The future?" Elise sighed. "If he marries Claire, I don't think he'll have a future."

* * *

As soon as Arel returned home from Elise's party, he excused himself and headed for the stairs to the lower level. Claire indicated that she was upset and wanted to talk, but he ignored her. It was the first time that he'd put her off. He had no choice. He was so nauseous that he was afraid he wouldn't make it to the bathroom.

As he was vomiting out copious amounts of bile, he hadn't counted on Claire banging on the door. Her voice was sharp and insistent, demanding that he let her in. Instead of answering her, his mind was focused on a question that repeated over and over. How had his life spun out of control?

230

His first thought was to talk to Michael. He needed the angel's advice to help him make sense of what was happening. But both of his angelic friends were next door, at Elise's house. In fact, all of his friends, with the exception of William and Rolphe, were at his neighbor's house. That's when the truth hit home. He was alone. All alone. Or was he?

Claire was on the other side of the door. The thought should have been comforting. Instead, he threw up again. When his stomach settled a little, he crawled over to a corner of the bathroom and propped himself up against the wall. "But I won't even have this wall for very long," he mumbled to himself.

Claire explained that they didn't need a house. They only needed a small apartment that would serve as a base of operations. That way they would be free to travel and volunteer wherever they were needed. Claire also explained that she wouldn't always be with him. She had other duties that involved working with her archaeology studies. When she could take time off, she'd join Arel, wherever he was.

Arel stifled a groan, afraid that Claire would hear him. He couldn't bear the chastisement that would follow. His life and freedom were slipping away, but he didn't know a way out. His relationship with Claire wasn't working, and he couldn't tell her how he felt.

A feeling of impending disaster closed in as he fell asleep. But letting himself doze off was a mistake too. He started dreaming immediately. Transported back in time, he found himself in the midst of a tragic affair from his past. He dreamed about the woman he'd loved, the woman who killed herself when she mistakenly thought he'd rejected her. The aftermath of guilt was unbearable.

When he woke himself up, he knew there was only one way out of his present situation. He'd have to go through with marrying Claire. No matter how that fact affected his life, it was better than the pain of guilt and regret.

With some effort, he managed to get to his feet. His stomach was only slightly better, and he still had a splitting headache, but that was becoming the norm. He wouldn't let his body's condition deter him from what he had to do. But before he sought out Claire, he had to make himself presentable. It didn't sound like a difficult task until he saw himself in the mirror.

"Bloody hell, I haven't looked this bad in a while." His face was drawn and haggard, and he had dark circles under pathetic eyes. They

231

belonged to one of those needy children Claire talked about. But if Claire loved him, she'd understand, wouldn't she?

He thought he heard her in their bedroom. But before he opened the door, he straightened up and tried to smile. Maybe he'd look more attractive if he demonstrated that most important "better attitude" she was always talking about. He said a quick prayer for help, swung open the door and stepped out into the bedroom.

He wasn't prepared to see an open suitcase on the bed. Before he had a chance to think, Claire came out of the closet with an armful of clothes.

"Claire? What's going on?" he asked as he closed the distance between them.

Claire walked around him, but for once she didn't have anything to say. Throwing her clothes into her suitcase, she traipsed back around him, going into the closet again.

"Claire, please, tell me why you're packing?"

She poked her head out and stared back with disgust. "Must I explain everything to you? Are you so incapable of understanding even the simplest of things?"

He sat down on the bed, thinking about how to answer and listening. From what he could tell, Claire was pulling clothes off of hangers. When she walked back into the room with another armful, he looked up at her. "I guess I am dense because I don't know what's happening."

Claire glared back. "I'm packing my clothes and leaving. Is that clear enough?"

"Where are you going?"

"Back to California. I'll stay with my parents for a while."

"Are they okay? Did I miss something while I was in the bathroom?"

Claire continued to stuff her clothes into her suitcase. "I'm just tired, Arel. You seem unable to stand up for anything. I don't think I've ever met someone as wishy-washy as you."

"What are you talking about? I've tried to support whatever you wanted."

"Exactly. You don't have a mind of your own. In fact, I think you're missing a very important part of your anatomy, a backbone."

"Is this about the party and what Annabel said to you?"

Claire went to the dresser and grabbed more of her belongings out of a drawer. "No, I'm not afraid of what other people say to me. They're just ignorant. They fight reason and moral obligation with outbursts of anger. But I can't marry someone who hides away in a bathroom as soon as a few harsh words are dished out."

He blinked back, trying to process the accusations that Claire was making about him. "Do you want to know what I think? You haven't given me a chance—"

Claire's laughter cut him off. "Please, I just explained that I've given you every chance to stand up for something. But you're like the kid who gets sent home from kindergarten because they're crybabies. Maybe you'll grow up some day, but I can't wait for that to happen."

He stood up to face her. "How can you judge me like this?"

Claire paused and stared back at him. "Arel, do you know why you always give in so easily?"

"Because I want you to be happy."

"No, that's not the reason."

"I know how I feel, Claire. And I'm trying to be there for you."

"Stop it, Arel, just stop it now! You're lying to me, and you're lying to yourself. But it's time to face the truth."

"What truth?"

"You live in a fantasy world. Look at this house. It's full of stuff that isolates you and makes you feel safe. When you saw me, I think you wanted to add me to your collection of beautiful objects. But when reality hits, you fold like you did tonight."

"That is so ridiculous."

Claire zipped up her suitcase, set it on the floor, and retrieved her backpack. "Maybe when I met you, I let myself dream a little too. I think I took a vacation from the real world. But that's not where I want to spend my life."

"I wasn't going to force you to want what I want. I'm willing to change. Doesn't that count in your book?"

"I've been through this before. People say they can change, but—"

"So you'd had other serious relationships?"

"Oh please, of course I have. Haven't you?"

"There was one, but it was a long time ago."

"And did you change for her?"

Arel thought about Justina. He'd loved her completely, but he thought he was cursed. How was he supposed to change that?

Claire snapped her fingers. "I asked you a question. Did you change for her?"

"No."

Claire threw the backpack over her shoulder. "I'm sorry, but this marriage idea was wrong from the start. I just let myself think you'd be different. Big mistake."

"So it's over? No more discussions? You just walk out the door?"

"Yes, but maybe you can hook up with that romance-writer neighbor of yours. The two of you would be perfect for each other."

"Elise and me? Why would you say something like that?"

Claire narrowed her eyes. "I saw how you looked at each other. You're like a couple of love-starved puppies who still haven't been weaned. Unfortunately, if you do get together, you'll end up sucking each other dry."

"That's so unfair, Claire."

Claire headed for the door, pulling her suitcase behind her. "Why is that unfair?"

Arel followed her. "Because you act like you always know everything. But I wasn't just hiding in the bathroom. I was sick. Why would you hold that against me?"

Claire headed for the stairs. "Keep making excuses, Arel. It's what you do best."

Thirty-Four

AFTER CLAIRE LEFT, Arel knew he couldn't think clearly. He went to bed instead of trying to process what had just happened. Once under the covers, exhaustion took over, and he let himself slip into a dreamless sleep. He didn't wake up until the next morning. Instead of lying in bed, he got up immediately and showered. It was a relief to have a body that almost felt normal again. When he looked in the mirror, he was also surprised to see that his color had returned and the dark circles under his eyes were barely visible.

Every time he thought about Claire, he felt numb. Perhaps he had to put the subject on hold for the moment. After he dressed, he went upstairs and found both Michael and Carey in the living room. Michael was in his chair by the window reading, and Carey was sitting on the sofa, paging through a biking magazine.

When Arel joined them, his first thought was to apologize. "I'm very sorry about last night, Carey. I should have stopped Claire when she said the things she said. Anyway, she's gone so you won't have to put up with her sharp tongue anymore."

Carey put his magazine on the end table. "I'm sorry, too. I know that things didn't work out for the two of you. But I'm okay. Besides, Annabel didn't have a problem defending me."

Arel sat down in a recliner. "She hasn't lost her fire, has she? William should have been there. But what happened after we left? Did we ruin the party?"

Michael closed his book. "Not at all, except for Elise. She seemed very concerned about you."

Arel looked away. "Elise, the love-starved puppy. I have to apologize to her too."

Michael's brows arched with surprise. "Did you say love-starved puppy?"

"Yes, that's what Claire called both of us. She thinks we're both needy, immature dreamers who deserve each other."

"Is that what you think?" Carey asked.

Arel shrugged. "I don't know, but I was impressed with Elise. When Claire attacked Elise's profession, Elise kept her temper in check. That was impressive. Claire doesn't think people can change, but Elise must be the exception."

"But she hasn't changed," Carey insisted. "She's come back to herself. That's all."

"Too bad she didn't come back to herself sooner. We could have had a much more enjoyable time together."

"Perhaps," Michael said.

"What's that mean?" Arel asked a little too loudly, suddenly irritated by the angel's short response.

Michael's eyes softened. "I was just speculating—"

"Speculating what, Michael? No, don't answer. I know how your mind works and what you're thinking. You're thinking that even if Elise were okay, I would have been the problem."

Michael opened his book again. "I'm sorry, but you know I don't think that."

Arel stopped and thought about the conversation they were having and moaned. "I can't believe it. I'm listening to myself, and I sound like Claire."

"What do you mean?" Carey asked.

"She found fault with everything I said. Now, I'm doing the same thing with Michael." Arel stared at the fabric on the arm of his chair. There was a new stain on it. Claire had spilled her coffee, but she'd made no attempt to blot it up.

Carey seemed to notice Arel's concern. "I want to apologize too, Arel. I've developed some messy habits, but from now on, I promise to be more thoughtful."

Arel opened his eyes and frowned. "Really? After all this time, you're going to try to be neat?" As soon as he asked the question, he stopped himself. "Oh no—"

Michael glanced up. "Are you alright. You've gone a bit pale."

Arel waved him off. "Pale? That's the least of my worries."

Carey's youthful face was attentive too. "What is it?"

Arel rubbed the soiled coffee stain. Claire had just left him and instead of thinking about the reason she'd left, he'd been wondering if he'd be able to get the coffee stain out. "I'm doing another 'Claire' thing. She was the type of person who only sees the glass half empty.

She only saw my shortcomings. And when she looked at the world, she only saw all the things that were wrong."

"How is that like you?" Carey asked.

"Don't you understand? I'm living with two angels, and I'm worried about crumbs on the floor."

Michael and Carey both laughed, but Arel found their merriment to be another irritant. "How can you be smiling when I've just told you how negative I can be?"

Carey leaned down and began picking up tiny pieces of oatmeal cookie off the carpet. "Dear friend, we're laughing because you're funny."

Michael stood up and came over to where Arel was sitting. "What Carey is saying is that you worry too much. When it comes to what's really important, your heart is always in the right place."

Arel lowered his gaze and exhaled heavily. "That's good to know."

"But?"

Arel's eyes flared when he looked up. "But when I mentioned Elise, you looked doubtful about my part in a relationship."

"Yes, that's right."

Arel stood up too, giving Michael a scathing look of annoyance. "Well, thank you. After all this time and all the ways I've tried to do better, I find out I'm still a loser."

Michael crossed his arms and assumed his more fatherly approach. "I was simply thinking that the best relationships are between two people who appreciate themselves and the other person. And even though you give others credit, you still have a hard time doing the same with yourself."

Arel hesitated, trying to make sure he understood what Michael was saying. "So my problem is that I don't have a problem?"

Carey started towards the kitchen with his hand full of crumbs. Halfway there he paused and glanced back at Arel. "It's really quite simple. Claire was very hard on you, and you accepted the way she treated you. That's not going to work if you want to be happy in a relationship."

"I tried to explain myself last night, but she wouldn't listen."

"Remember that it's not the words that you tell people," Michael said, "it's how you feel that comes across."

Elise sat at the breakfast table watching Annabel pour herself a second cup of coffee. Both of them had stayed up late, cleaning up after the party. "Annabel, maybe you should have slept in a little longer."

Annabel put her mug on the table and sat down. "You stayed up later than I did. Didn't I see your light on at three o'clock?"

Elise shrugged sheepishly. "I have to tell you something."

Annabel eyed her suspiciously. "What have you been up to?"

Elise reached into the pocket of her robe and held out a ring to Annabel. "Claire gave this to me last night. I was outside with Freddie before I went to bed, and a cab pulled up in Arel's driveway. The next thing I know, Claire is coming out of the house. When she saw me, she started waving, ordering me to come over. Well, what could I do? She was sounding off like a drill sergeant. I didn't want her waking up the neighborhood so I did as I was told."

Annabel's eyes widened. "Are you saying that Claire left Arel?"

"Yes, I think she did because she handed me this ring. She said something like, 'Arel is all yours now.' Then she turned and got into the cab. Anyway, she seemed so stiff and businesslike. Though I did notice her voice being a bit shaky. So I guess she's not completely made of stone."

"Don't you think you should return the ring?"

"Of course. I would have given it to Arel last night, but something told me that it wasn't a good time to be banging on his door."

Annabel examined the ring. "It's beautiful. I love the little vines on either side of the diamond."

"I know. I must have stared at it for an hour. That's why my light was on."

Annabel handed the ring back to Elise. "I think Arel wanted to get her a bigger diamond, but Claire wouldn't have it."

Elise put the ring on the table. "Whatever the size of the stone, Arel has exquisite taste."

"Elise, I don't want to get too personal, but I was wondering—"

"What is it?"

"Have you ever been engaged?"

Elise felt her chest cave a little. "No, I came close a couple of times, but I had the good sense to say 'no' on both occasions."

"I'd rather say 'no' to someone than get married and regret it."

"Definitely," Elise said as she stood up and put her cup in the sink. "Well, I better get dressed. Then I'll take the ring back to Arel."

"Do you want me to come with you?"

Elise paused on her way out of the kitchen. "No, but I think I better leave Freddie here. I don't want him messing up something of Arel's again."

As she continued on her way to her bedroom, the doorbell rang. "I'll get it," she called out to Annabel. She was expecting a package delivery when she opened the door. But instead of a delivery person, Arel stood waiting on the porch. He looked perfectly groomed and more handsome than ever. As soon as she saw him, she instantly forgot everything but her own appearance. She was in her old terry robe. As for her hair, she was sure it was a fright since she'd neglected to brush it when she got up.

Arel waited, looking embarrassed too.

Their mutual silence was broken when Annabel joined them, carrying Freddie. She seemed to be the only one who could speak. "Good morning, Arel. Won't you come in?"

Elise finally managed a few words as she turned and made a dash down the hall. "Excuse me while I get dressed."

After closing her bedroom door, she went straight to the mirror and let out a small cry of distress. "Oh goodness, it's worse than I thought! I'm a disaster."

Her blond hair was growing out, but it was at an awkward stage. Her natural waves were all headed in different directions. A curling iron would help, but she didn't have time for a curling iron. Instead, she tried to brush her unruly locks into submission. She followed up with a heavy dose of hair spray.

Throwing off her robe, she hurried to her closet. If she dressed in some attractive clothes maybe Arel wouldn't notice her hair. She started searching through her jeans only to remember that the ones that fit were in the clothes hamper. She'd have to wear an old pair that was too snug. Since she couldn't do anything to rectify the situation, she carried on bravely. It was a struggle, but she managed to get the jeans over her hips, promising herself not to indulge in any more late night ice cream. The zipper was a special challenge. By the time she succeeded getting it all the way up, her self-image was on a steady decline.

Fortunately, she had a thought that might save the day. She owned a bright pink, button down shirt that was extra-long. It would help to hide her extra pounds. Pleased with its cheery color, she smiled as she put it on. She hadn't counted on the fact that she'd washed it recently, and that the shirt's cotton fabric had shrunk a size. She could get the garment buttoned, but that was about all she could say that was positive.

She let out another gasp of alarm when she went back to the mirror. As she stood there observing the shape she was in, she knew she had to make a decision. She could worry about her appalling appearance, or she could remind herself of the facts.

"Face it, Elise, Arel has just broken up with a gorgeous woman whom he adored. The last thing he's going to do is pay attention to how you look."

As a final touch, she put on some makeup and then ventured out of her bedroom. She promised herself that she wouldn't worry about anything but Arel's needs and giving him back his ring.

* * *

As soon as Arel sat down in Elise's living room and looked at Annabel, he thought about Claire's unkind words to Carey. Annabel had been extremely upset with the situation. "I'm sorry that I wasn't more supportive last night. I wasn't in a very good space."

Annabel looked away apprehensively. "I don't like the way I handled it either."

"Don't say that. You did what you felt was necessary. But if possible, I hope you can forgive me for just standing there."

Annabel finally glanced at him and smiled. "Of course I forgive you. And I think that Freddie wants you to know that he forgives you too."

Arel smiled back while trying to avoid the puppy's advances and his doggie kisses. After a few minutes, it was obvious that it was a losing battle. When Arel stopped resisting, Freddie quickly made himself comfortable in Arel's lap.

Annabel looked pleased. "Sometimes, when I'm missing William, Freddie seems to understand. He comes over and cuddles up next to me. It always makes me feel better."

Arel started to stroke Freddie's fur and realized how soft it was. "I've been wanting to ask you about William? I've sent him a couple of texts, but he doesn't do much more than acknowledge them."

Annabel shrugged. "He's like you. He keeps his thoughts to himself most of the time."

"Perhaps it's our upbringing. Neither of us found our parents anxious to hear from us."

"Sorry to keep you waiting," Elise said as she walked into the living room.

Arel and Freddie both reacted at the same time. The puppy leapt to the floor and ran over to Elise. Arel jerked to his feet, but he remained stationary and observant. Elise's appearance had changed drastically. She'd gone from robe and slippers to a bright, engaging version of herself. The new look emphasized all of her womanly attributes.

Arel tried not to stare, but he couldn't help thinking how different Elise was compared to Claire. His former fiancé made all her clothes look a bit oversized. Elise was the opposite. Her jeans were filled to capacity, and her tight-fitting blouse had rosebud buttons that labored under a strain to do their duty. And while Claire often wore her hair back in a ponytail or bun, Elise's hair had a wild, untamed look, as if she was ready for an adventure in the outback.

He stammered out a few words. "Elise, I'm sorry for dropping in without calling—"

"Oh, don't think twice about it. And please, sit down," Elise said in a hurried tone.

Arel noticed her forced smile, and that her flushed cheeks almost matched her blouse. As she walked over to a chair to sit down, she held Freddie close, as if she wanted to use him as a shield. Unfortunately, as soon as she was seated, the puppy deserted her and ran back to Arel. Elise automatically grabbed a pillow, clutching it instead of the puppy.

Arel tugged at his collar, wondering again why Elise kept her house so warm. But he didn't want to appear rude. When Freddie jumped in his lap again, he began petting the puppy. "I think he likes me."

Elise nodded shyly. "I'm so glad that you came over. I was going to visit you later."

"Oh, did you need something?"

Elise exchanged a quick glance at Annabel. "I'm sorry, but I was outside last night when Claire left in a cab."

Arel hesitated. "I see. Then you probably figured out that we're no longer together."

Elise sprang to her feet. She was a blur of motion as she ran to the kitchen and back. A moment later she was holding something out to him. It was Claire's engagement ring.

He took the ring, then glanced up with questioning eyes.

Elise stepped back. "Claire insisted on giving it to me. I guess she forgot to return it before she left."

Arel remained silent, reliving the memory of Claire marching out of the house the night before. But there was no emotion behind the memory or their breakup.

"I'm so sorry about what happened," Elise continued. "I hope the party wasn't a contributing factor."

Annabel cleared her throat. "I'm sorry that I yelled at Claire. I should have been nicer to her."

Arel fingered the filigree decoration on the ring. When he'd bought it for Claire, he'd been so happy. "It's okay, Annabel, I'm the one at fault." He looked up at Elise. "And I'm sorry about the things that Claire said to you, Elise."

Elise sat down again. "Please, Arel, you weren't responsible for what happened. Claire is the one who caused all the unpleasantness." She paused. "Just like I was responsible for being so horrible when we were together."

Arel slipped the ring into his pocket. "That may be, but the bottom line is that I'm not ready for a relationship."

Elise picked up the pillow again and hugged it close. "That's understandable, but I wish you didn't feel that way. You'd make a wonderful catch in one of my stories."

Arel couldn't believe how much Elise had changed. When she looked at him, her blue eyes were soft, and her voice was caring. Claire didn't seem to possess those qualities. She remained the tough, no-nonsense professional. Her eyes were sharp and focused, always looking for problems. It was nice to have a conversation with someone who had a nicer approach.

But even though Elise was being kind, Arel still felt uncomfortable. The house was overly hot. He took out his handkerchief and patted down his brow. "Is there a reason for keeping the temperature in here so warm?"

Elise hesitated. "I keep it at seventy degrees, but I could turn it down if you want."

"Seventy degrees?" Arel returned a puzzled look. His house was kept at the same temperature. "No, that's not necessary, but you might want to have your thermostat checked."

"I will," Elise said. "On the bright side, at least you're sweating, not running a fever."

Arel pocketed his handkerchief. "No, I actually feel quite well physically. But that's enough about me. How is your move coming?"

Elise frowned. "Not as smoothly as I'd like. The problem is finding another place to live. Happily the owners of this house hadn't found new tenants so they let me extend my lease."

Annabel's eyes brightened. "Elise explained that she likes to live in different places and research those locations for her books. And since I'm staying for another week, I've agreed to go scouting with her. There are some towns within a hundred miles or so that she's interested in."

"I'm thinking of having my next story take place in a small town," Elise added.

Annabel gave Arel an expectant look. "Carey is coming with us. Why don't you come too?"

Elise hugged her pillow a little tighter. "Yes, why don't you? You've lived in the general area for some time. You could give us some suggestions and maybe point out things we'd miss otherwise."

Arel's hand abandoned Freddie's soft furry head, and he crossed his arms. "I'm really not that knowledgeable—"

"Oh come on, Arel," Annabel pleaded. "A day trip might be fun."

Arel hadn't taken many sight-seeing trips. And the idea of fun didn't compute very well. "Let me think about it." He looked down and saw that Freddie had fallen asleep and was dozing peacefully. He carefully lifted the small dog onto an adjoining cushion. "Your friend seems very content."

Elise smiled. "Freddie's life is simple. He loves everyone, and he expects everyone to love him."

Arel stood up to leave. "I'm happy one of us knows what he's doing. From what Claire said, I must be clueless."

As he started for the door, Annabel hurried over and took his hand.

"Would you please check on William? Maybe you could give him a call. Quiet or not, he talks to you."

Arel gave her an understanding smile. "Of course, I will. I'm sure he'll have plenty to say when I tell him that Claire walked out on me."

Thirty-Five

HOLDING HIS PHONE to his ear, Arel could imagine the person he was talking to perfectly. William was in his London residence with that serious look on his face. It conveyed a message, "I'm sorry that you've been an idiot again, Arel. But I only say things like that because I care about you. You're always letting yourself be hurt."

But in reality, William had stopped making such blatant statements. He wasn't just being quiet like Annabel explained. He was being too quiet. When Arel related the news about his breakup, William's tone was worn and his verbal response was short. He barely got out two words. "I see."

There was a long pause after William's reply. Arel finally broke it with an inquiry. "What's wrong, William? And don't tell me that there's nothing new going on. You know that I can feel your energy almost as keenly as I can feel my own. You're hiding from something."

When William remained silent, Arel didn't push for an answer. He knew William wouldn't appreciate being told that his fear was palpable. It was so raw and agonizing that Arel had to shield himself from its full intensity. Finally, he changed the subject, hoping to distract William from whatever was eating at him.

"You'll find this amusing. Claire told me that she thought Elise and I would be perfect together."

William barely rallied. "Why is that funny? Annabel said that Elise has been very nice, that Carey and Michael worked a miracle."

Arel laughed. "You wouldn't approve if you saw her. She dresses in garments that are the opposite of restrained, and her hair is—"

"What difference does it make, Arel? You thought Claire was perfect, but that didn't mean anything. In the end, your perfect woman turned out to be almost as bad as your father."

It was Arel's turn to be silent. William wouldn't discuss his own situation, but he finally voiced his opinion about Arel's recent relationship. Unfortunately, Arel knew that William's observation was

245

correct. For the first time since Claire left, his anger almost surfaced. "I don't want to talk about it—"

"You can't ignore what you let Claire do. She abused you, admit it."

Arel leaned back against the wall, clutching the phone and thinking about how hard he'd tried to be what people wanted. As a boy, his goal was to measure up to his brother. But he was so young, and his best wasn't good enough. His father rewarded his efforts by beating him and calling him useless. But he'd dealt with that abuse. At least he thought he had. So why would he have let Claire verbally beat him? The thought made him angry at himself for being so stupid, for being the idiot that William often called him.

He put the phone to his ear again. "I have to go. I'll call you later."

"I'm here if you need to talk," William said.

Arel ended the call as quickly as possible. He wasn't ready to process his relationship with Claire, not yet. For now, he needed to find something else to occupy his time. He grabbed his phone again and called Elise. "If you still want me, I'll come with you on your house hunting trip tomorrow."

Elise's answer was immediate. "Of course I still want you . . . to come, that is."

Before he could begin analyzing her forceful statement, he put it aside. He wanted to forget everything for a while.

* * *

William put his phone in his pocket. He didn't have the energy to think about Arel's problems. Instead, he went back to what he'd been doing. He was taking a kind of inventory of his home. He was going through each room, noting the furniture, the colors of the walls and fabrics, and the accessories. He paused in the guest bedroom, glancing over at some display shelves. A beautiful piece of satsuma pottery caught his eye. The vase had a vibrant floral design. The use of red, green, blue and gold colors was exquisite. The vase was a testament to the artist's ability to uplift the spirit with their handiwork.

In the not too distant past, each piece of art that he discovered in some auction house or gallery was classified as a small treasure. He delighted in bringing it home and finding a place for it, a place where he could admire its pleasing uniqueness. Recently, he didn't feel compelled to seek out any more of those treasures. He barely thought about art at all.

It was the same with his scientific studies. He'd spent years of his life in the lab, delving into matter and how it worked. When a mystery presented itself, he was full of curiosity and would work tirelessly to find an answer. But not even the mystery of angelic blood could peak his interest now.

At first, he attributed his apathy to what he'd been through with Arel. Perhaps he was addicted to the thrill of high drama as Annabel suggested. He also pondered his relationship with Annabel. He wondered if it was taking over his life. Then he'd contemplated the idea of leaving the world. That had some appeal, but also brought up more questions.

He'd had one near death experience, and it was wonderful, all brightness and light. But things were very different then. He'd been at peace with himself when he'd died that time. When he faced eternity, he still had questions and quests to spur him on. Now, all he had was a gnawing feeling deep down. It was a terrible foreboding that something horrible was going to gobble him up. If it did, what kind of afterlife would be waiting this time?

The thought of being a victim of something unknown made him angry, so angry that he wanted to smash every beautiful vase that he owned. But then he had to laugh at himself. To think such thoughts wasn't original. At a very low point in his life, Arel had acted out his anger and gone on a destructive rampage.

"Lord help me if I'm turning into another Arel."

He loved Arel as a brother, but the man wasn't a good role model. Arel made the same mistake over and over.

"Talk about a victim," William sighed. But as soon as he said the word, his muscles tensed. He stood in the doorway, fighting a sudden flash of impending disaster. His mind and body seemed to join forces at such times, making it hard for him to stay in control of himself.

The spell of doom was broken by the phone sounding. William didn't recognize the ring tone and didn't take the call. A couple of moments later, he got a voicemail. When he checked it out, he was surprised to hear from Rolphe's girlfriend, Myra. From what he knew about her, she was someone who was easy-going and usually had a smile in place. He didn't expect her voice to have a desperate, pleading tone.

"William, please, you have to help Rolphe. I've been taking care of his cat, Dantella, but he hasn't come back for her. He won't answer the door when I visit, and I'm afraid he's ill again. Can you call him and find out what's going on?"

William rubbed his brow with irritation. The last thing he wanted to do was to talk to Rolphe again. He walked into the living room. Raphael was sitting on the couch in a meditative posture with his eyes closed. He opened them as soon as William approached him.

"Problem?" Raphael asked.

"It's Rolphe. Myra thinks something is wrong with him."

"You said Rolphe was upset when he visited here."

William sat down and crossed his arms. "So what? Being upset is the norm when a person is sporting angelic blood."

"As we've discussed, that isn't what was intended. When Arel begged Michael to pass on his blood, he wanted—"

"I know all about what Arel wanted. But that's not what I wanted. Before Arel got his revenge and passed the stuff on to me, I had a life that suited my needs and desires. Maybe I was ignorant when it came to your world, but my world was ordered and dependable. Ever since I was a young man, I did exactly as I pleased."

"That was when you thought of yourself as a vampire, right? You enjoyed a heightened sense of power after Rolphe gave you his blood."

"That's right. But Rolphe didn't give me his blood out of the kindness of his heart. I had to beg him for a taste of the stuff. Afterwards, he left me to die. He didn't think I would survive. But I fought with everything I had to stay alive."

"Did you feel like Rolphe's blood connected the two of you?"

"No, we had nothing to do with each other."

"And now that he's changed, how do you feel about him?"

"Rolphe is someone I'd rather not associate with."

Raphael's eyes softened. "That's your right, William. You can do whatever you want."

"What I want is to be left alone! But dammit, I never get a chance to figure out my own problems. First, I had to deal with Arel going haywire. Now, Rolphe is supposedly in some kind of trouble."

"What does that have to do with you?"

"According to Myra, I'm supposed to help him."

"From my vantage point, assisting others because of obligation has limited value. On the other hand, love is a potent motivator."

"Love? For Rolphe? If he died this minute, I'd celebrate." He glanced over at Raphael, feeling more relaxed as soon as he voiced his opinion. "What do you think? Is there a possibility that he might move on?"

Raphael shrugged. "Like you said, he's in trouble. Of course, you were in trouble when you met Rolphe for the first time those many years ago."

"What are you talking about? I had it all when it came to the normal world. Women flocked to my side. Men respected me and gave me a wide berth. Ask Arel about the person that I was. Nobody dared cross me."

"I agree, but life was getting dull and boring. When you met Rolphe, you felt his power and were drawn to it."

"Was it wrong to want something more in life than parties, women and getting drunk?"

"But why go off with Rolphe? You didn't know him, and it was easy to see that he was dangerous."

William sat back and sighed heavily. "Rolphe was a scary beast of a man, and I usually had a good degree of common sense, but not that night. Scary or not, he fascinated me. When his eyes locked on to me, they glowed. He was like some animal who knows they're so much stronger than you. I wanted, no, I needed to learn where such power came from."

"But you knew powerful men in society—"

"You mean the privileged class, people like my father? Their titles gave them a pretense of power, but they were nothing compared to a man like Rolphe. His power radiated out from some inner strength. When he walked into the pub, the faint of heart scurried for cover." William let out a bitter laugh. "Even after Rolphe had Arel's blood coursing through his veins, it didn't stop him. He remained as formidable as they come. I couldn't battle Arel's tremendous abilities, but Rolphe gave him a hell of a run. No matter what Arel did, no matter how much pain he inflicted, Rolphe wouldn't give in."

"You respect Rolphe, even now."

William's fingers slowly closed into a fist. "The bastard nearly killed me, but you're right, I do respect his staying power."

"What about your staying power, William? You haven't talked about it recently, but I know your fears are growing."

William's muscles tensed even more. He'd been racking his brain, trying to understand why he was scared all the time. Recently, after Rolphe's visit, he was even more upset. But why? What did Rolphe have to do with his fears? Why did he still detest the man to the point of wanting him dead? He stared back at Raphael, letting a hint of a smile replace his frown. "I think my fears are starting to make sense."

"What do you mean?"

"When Arel threw me out of heaven, I was afraid of his extraordinary abilities. Then Rolphe came into the picture again. After he had me for lunch, I lost it. I thought I'd recovered, but I was wrong. That's why I was so nervous when he was here."

"Can I help?"

"No, this is between Rolphe and myself. I need to go to Paris and talk to him. I'm not going to let him die without clearing up a few things."

Thirty-Six

AFTER HIS DISCUSSION with Raphael, William caught the first available train to Paris. He was eager to see Rolphe. The more he thought about the intimidating man, the more convinced he was that Rolphe was the source of all his recent woes. Somehow, Rolphe had activated a sense of helplessness. That was probably why William had had a vision of being a helpless child being pursued by something evil. In reality, that evil thing was Rolphe.

Just the thought of finding an answer immediately lessened the tension in William's body. He even felt somewhat hopeful. When Raphael asked if he should accompany William, William decided to make the trip alone. He wanted to prove that he had the ability to handle whatever came his way, and that included facing Rolphe. As the train to Paris sped towards its destination, he also felt his confidence returning. He sat up straighter and faced his future with more certainty.

But a sense of fearlessness wasn't new to him. Before he'd been reunited with Arel in New York, he was well acquainted with being the bold master of his life. He'd basked in the glorious feeling that he wasn't like other humans. Even though he lived in the same world as all the rest, he never allowed that world to diminish his sense of self.

Angelic blood was the agent that put an end to his self-determined attitude. It put him through an ordeal that was so all consuming that it almost destroyed his ability to cope. He went from being in control to welcoming the release that death would bring.

In the end, he picked up the pieces of his life and tried to find a positive outcome. He no longer had the gift that Rolphe had given him, but he convinced himself that he had something better. When he and Arel were battling Rolphe, he tried to tell himself that he'd been given a new gift. Surely angelic blood would top whatever Rolphe had bestowed. That's where he went wrong. Later, when he visited Rolphe, he paid for his mistake and nearly died a most horrible death.

Currently, he was still paying for that mistake. After Rolphe's attack, he lost faith in himself. What he hadn't realized was that the damage he'd sustained was much more extensive than he thought. He believed he'd gotten over the worst of his fear. In truth, he'd deluded himself. It was there all along, just below the surface, growing in strength.

William was even starting to understand why he couldn't outrun his fears. In the new lower level of his London home, there was a painting hanging on his wall. It portrayed him astride an angelic horse, victorious in some alternate world that Arel created. But what worked there didn't work on planet earth. Raphael hyped the idea of love, but a human being needed much more than intangible virtues to successfully navigate the real world.

Annabel was a perfect example. When she took off her wings and tried to live like a normal person, she didn't know how to survive. She was totally helpless and frightened. At times, when William's fears grabbed hold, he was almost as scared as Annabel.

That's why he was anxious to visit Rolphe. Rolphe was the one person who seemed capable of straddling the real and the immaterial. Hopefully, he'd have the answers that William needed to reclaim his freedom.

* * *

William gave Rolphe's door another good pounding, waited, and then reached in his pocket. Since Rolphe wasn't answering, he'd have to let himself into the apartment. Rolphe had given him a spare key and said that he was always welcome. Still, he didn't like the idea of intruding on someone's privacy even if that someone was Rolphe.

He made sure to announce his presence once he was inside the foyer. There was no response. As he walked through to the living room, everything was just as he remembered, a model for neatness and good taste. Obviously, Rolphe was adhering to Arel's rules for order and a need for beauty. As he searched through the rooms, he called out again. "Rolphe? It's William. Are you here?"

Finally, he got a reply.

"William, is that you?"

At first, he didn't recognize the voice. It sounded too frail to belong to Rolphe. But he thought it came from one of the bedrooms. When he looked in the one that belonged to Rolphe, he wondered who was lying in Rolphe's bed. Then the occupant smiled.

"William, why are you here?"

"Rolphe?"

"Yes?"

William hesitated, not knowing what to say.

Rolphe gestured for him to come closer. "Tell me how you're doing. I've been worried about you."

William still couldn't reply. It had only been a few days since he'd last seen Rolphe, but the man had transformed in that small space of time. A thought came to mind. Rolphe might have shape-shifting abilities. But whatever the explanation, Rolphe's strong body was gone, replaced by one that looked wasted and gaunt. His dark eyes were still intense, but they seemed out of place in a face that was sunken and devoid of any color.

Rolphe looked away and straightened his blanket a little. "Sorry, I know I'm not looking my best—"

William came closer but stopped a couple of feet from the bed.

Rolphe continued to study his bedclothes. "It's alright. I'm not contagious, just unwell."

"You seemed fine when you visited me."

Rolphe started to laugh and ended up coughing. "I shouldn't have gone to London. It was wrong of me to think that you and I might—" Rolphe kept his eyes averted. "Never mind."

William scowled back. His intention in coming to Paris was to get answers. Even if Arel wasn't a role model, he realized that Rolphe was someone he'd admired.

Rolphe sighed. "I remember the first time I saw you. You were sitting in that drinking house, staring at me. For some reason, I thought you were special. I was disappointed, even angry, when you approached me."

"Why?"

"Because when I took a closer look at you, I knew you were like me. And that made me want to destroy you."

"How was I like you?"

"You'd already let the world ruin you just like I let it ruin me."

"Don't talk in riddles."

"I tried to explain myself when I saw you last."

"Let's not discuss your military service again. Just tell me why you gave me your blood?"

"Yes, what a surprise. I hadn't expected to ever pass on the damnable stuff. But weak as you were, you were still tenacious. I foolishly gave in to a dying man's wish."

"Is that it? I was just another person—"

"Yes, you were a cocky fool who didn't have the good sense to value your life."

"I saw something in you—"

"Then you were more ignorant than I thought."

William's face hardened with disappointment. "I can't believe I came here thinking you might have something to offer me now."

"But I do have something you want!" Rolphe insisted in a raspy voice.

"Like what?" William demanded.

Rolphe's head jerked up so fast that William jumped back. His heart pounded out a warning. He needed to leave at once, but he couldn't make his body move. Rolphe's eyes had already immobilized him. They'd become two powerful lasers, boring into him, robbing him of his strength, leaving him cold and shaking.

"Come here, boy!" Rolphe ordered.

William's physical vehicle trembled more violently, too weak to resist what was happening. No matter how hard he tried to regain control, he staggered over to the bed. He ended up so close to Rolphe that he felt the hateful man's hot, heavy breath warming the space between them.

Rolphe grabbed hold of William's arm. His bony fingers clamped down hard, and William almost cried out. He had flashes of being a helpless child again, a little boy in the hands of his father. Hatred and rage filled his bones, but he still couldn't move or look away.

Rolphe's heartless eyes held him in place, becoming cold, merciless instruments, cutting through William's weakened defenses.

"Do you think you can come here, wanting something?" Rolphe bellowed out.

Rolphe's voice thundered around William. It became a stormy vehicle that plucked William out of the moment and sent him hurling into the past. The thick walls that protected his sense of identity crumbled completely. There was nothing to stop his return to the most painful day in his childhood. When he looked around him, he wasn't in Rolphe's bedroom anymore.

* * *

William stood in a beautiful section of his father's estate. A flourishing stand of woods bordered rolling hills. But none of the beauty around him could stop his small child's body from shaking. Tears were streaming down his face as he looked up at the man who wanted to destroy everything that he loved.

The man was a hunter who sat astride a massive brute of a horse, one that was strong enough to carry the man's excessive weight over fences and hedges. Perched high in his saddle, this man thought himself above the rest of the world. His steely-blue eyes surveyed everything from a predator's viewpoint. He took great pleasure in tracking down the animals and birds that young William tried to protect.

And that day had been a successful one from a hunter's point of view. Young William had heard the hounds as they closed in on their prey. His young heart and mind were still replaying the horrific screams of a favorite fox. It had just been torn to shreds by his father's hounds. Now, he pleaded for mercy on behalf of the ones that remained. "Please, sir, don't hunt my foxes!"

His father's response was mocking and cruel. "Your foxes?" his father roared back. "Everything on this land belongs to me! And I'll do as I please, hunting down every last one of those animals you're always visiting. I promise you, I'll have my hounds tear them limb from limb. And as for you, you'll stop your sniveling. I won't have a whiner for a son!"

It was the most devastating moment of William's young life. His father's words were branding irons, searing his body and his heart. But as he tried to remain upright and withstand the pain, he realized his father wasn't finished with him.

His father dismounted and strode over to where he stood. The man's face contorted into a vicious smile as he spoke. "It's time for you to grow up. Do you understand me?"

William started to step back, but his father's big, meaty hand snatched him up before he could retreat. He struggled in his father's clutches, but the man was as strong as one of his prize bulls. He held William in place with ease, practically lifting him off his feet.

His father's sneer widened. "I asked you a question, William, my boy. And you better come up with the right answer, or I'll burn these woods to the ground. No living creature will escape my wrath."

William suddenly understood what his father wanted. But he also knew that if he gave in, the price would be damning. The woodlands would be safe, but everything he was, everything that defined him would be burnt to the ground. His soul would be torn apart as surely as his foxes were torn apart by the dogs. But what choice did he have? In the end, his father would have his way, and no matter what William did, he was just a child, a child who was dangling in his father's clutches.

Instead of continuing to fight his father, he suddenly went still. His world went quiet. All that he could hear was the sound of a door slamming shut, a door that he'd never open again, a door that housed all the pain that came from being a weakling, a little boy who had no power in his life.

When the sound of the world returned, his father was laughing as he mounted his horse. His hunting cronies were laughing too. They all stared down at William with a look of triumph. One of them was patting his father's shoulder, congratulating him with a contented statement. "It's time to set the young pup straight. It's time for him to act like your son."

As the vision faded, William came back to Rolphe's bedroom. Rolphe had released him, but he felt too weak to move away. All he could do was target Rolphe with his wrath and anger. If he'd had the strength, he might have killed Rolphe for what the man had done. It would have been justifiable. Rolphe had made him relive something unbearable.

"I'm sorry, William," Rolphe whispered. "But you have to understand why you were drawn to me. Ever since you were a boy, you needed something to best your father, something stronger and more powerful than he was. You thought I was that something. But your father was nothing, just like I was nothing. When a person loses the ability to feel, he becomes a shell, an empty vessel that feeds off of others."

William managed to stand up straighter. "How did you know about my father or what happened when I was a child?"

Rolphe sank back, looking wasted again. "I see it all now. Once I opened the door to my past, it's as if the pain of the world was waiting to show itself to me. All the pain you're in. Arel's pain. My own."

William's voice was raspy and thin. "I never asked you to feel anything."

Rolphe returned a look of kindness. "Go back to London, William. Forget about your vision if you want. But remember that child who's still inside of you. He's the answer, not me."

William turned and left the room, wanting to return home as Rolphe suggested. But he only managed to get as far as Rolphe's second bedroom. After what he'd just gone through, his body was failing. He collapsed on the bed and fell asleep immediately.

* * *

When William woke up, his body was sluggish, as if he'd been slumbering for a month. His mind wasn't working properly either. He was having difficulty thinking clearly. He glanced around and finally remembered that he was in Rolphe's spare bedroom.

But William wasn't alone. A young man was sitting on a chair in the corner. He looked like a younger version of William. This younger version had visited him before. "Not you again," William moaned.

Young Will smiled. "You keep pushing me away, but you know it's not going to happen. It's like trying to dam up the blood in your body. The only thing you're doing is hurting yourself."

"Go, now!"

"No."

William stared back, watching his visitor fade in and out. "Oh hell, I'm still dreaming." He tried to wake himself up, but nothing worked. Even more aggravating was the fact that he couldn't get rid of his visitor. "What do you want?" he demanded.

"You pushed me out of your life, or at least you thought you did. But you made a mistake. You need me."

"Why? So I can get my heart ripped to shreds again?"

"I won't let go, William. Is that clear? You might not like it, but you can't dispose of the part of you that houses your spirit."

"I see. That damnable angelic blood that has hold of me has an agenda."

257

"You created this situation long before you got Rolphe's blood or angelic blood. So forget all that. You have a choice again, just like you had a choice that day you believed your father had the power to destroy you."

William recoiled as the memory of his father's face loomed over him again, targeting him with greedy eyes. They were the same eyes that targeted a bird in flight just before his father's shotgun blew the bird out of the sky. William swallowed the hard lump in his throat. "Let's not go there."

"I'm not the one who won't let it go!" Young Will yelled.

"Are you saying I'm holding on to it? It's not like that. The damn memory won't let me go, just like you won't let me go!"

"Why should I? I was just a little boy, but you chose father over me! You left me! And you never even looked back! You became just like him! Totally cold and calculating!"

"I did what I did to survive! Don't you get that? That man owned me!"

Young Will glared back at him. "No, you gave yourself away! You gave me away! Why didn't you fight for me like you fought for the foxes!"

"Fight? For what? You're nothing! In a world of men who only know how to take whatever they want, you don't count!"

Young Will's blue eyes narrowed with disgust. "So that's it. You're a coward, William, a coward who sold himself, first to Father, then to Rolphe. No wonder you have nightmares!"

The words were missiles that hit William with such a burning force that a sudden rage took over. The young man had gone too far with his insults, and William refused to tolerate his presence for another second.

Forcing himself into a standing position, William stumbled over to where his dream visitor was sitting. The young man's blue eyes were still so bright, so trusting that life could be good and beautiful. But William knew what a fool Young Will was. As a cold chill took hold of his body, he pointed at him with a stiff, trembling finger. His voice was heated, not only with anger, but with a wrath that wanted to tear the younger man apart, just as the hounds had torn apart the fox.

"Let's get something straight!" William hissed. "My father could have killed everything I loved! If I sold myself, then I did it to save something that couldn't save itself!" He tried to shout out the words, but his voice had no volume in the dreamscape. It barely punctuated the silence.

As Young Will faded and darkness descended on the room, the young man delivered one more message. "You're forgetting something crucial with that kind of reasoning. You've always insisted that you were a free man, William. Yet, even as an adult, you've acted as if you were Rolphe's and Father's victim."

Thirty-Seven

IT WAS A BREEZY, cold day as Elise walked back home. She'd just dropped off Freddie at Peggy's house. Her friend had generously volunteered to watch the puppy while Elise went away for the day. As she passed by Arel's house, he came out to join her. She paused as he came down the porch steps and walked over to her.

Ever since Arel had called her the day before, she'd thought about the first few words he'd said to her. "If you still want me—"

She couldn't get the phrase out of her mind. When she asked herself why, the answer was simple. She hoped they could start over. She knew that didn't include dating. She wasn't Arel's type. And even if she was, Arel made it clear that he wasn't ready for another relationship. Still, there was something very special about him. He was a little like Carey and Michael, very considerate and kind. She'd settle for friendship.

As they walked the short distance to her house, she wanted to get to know him better. "So, are you ready for an adventure?" she asked. "Annabel and Carey seem excited about the trip. They're even making sandwiches to take along."

Arel smiled. "That's a good idea. Carey's appetite doubles as soon as he even thinks about a trip in a car."

"He's such a sweet guy. We started talking one day when I was getting my mail. After that, he and Michael volunteered to help me with my novel. I didn't think they'd be up for the job, but they surprised me. They seem to know a lot about human nature."

Arel scowled back. "Yes, they surprise me too."

Elise hesitated when they got to her yard. "How about you, Arel? Do you spend much time contemplating what makes people tick?"

Arel shrugged. "Do you?"

"Of course, a writer has to know how people are going to interact in different circumstances. My real problem was that I never figured out what I'm about. Well, that's not completely true. I knew enough to stop letting men take advantage of me. But I got stuck in a rut over time. That's when we met."

Arel eased over her statement. "Yes, but that's behind you now, and you have a house to find."

Elise hurried up the porch stairs. "Yes, in fact I rented an SUV for the day so we won't be crowded. But before we leave, I better check on Annabel and Carey. Hopefully, they're ready with their picnic basket of goodies."

* * *

Arel rode in the passenger seat of Elise's rental car. Annabel and Carey were in the back seat. Arel was reminded of his trip to New York and his reunion with William. So much had happened since that trip. It seemed to belong to another lifetime. Now, Arel's only goal was to relax, to learn to enjoy the moment like Michael suggested.

The group he was with seemed to have a similar goal in mind. Elise, Annabel and Carey were all animated and chatty as they discussed the town they were going to visit. Their happy banter agreed with Arel. He'd closed his eyes a few minutes into the conversation and allowed his mind to drift aimlessly. It was what he needed. After the disaster with Claire, thinking was prohibited.

Riding along with friends who were enjoying themselves, Arel was surprised. Life felt so simple, so easy. Of course, one of those friends was also an angel. But Carey wasn't letting his angelic origins interfere with his sense of entertainment and fun. He contributed more than his share of stories and even jokes that made the others laugh.

The cheerful atmosphere made Arel realize what a strain he'd been under since Claire came into his life. Claire's attitude was centered around life being serious. The idea of a joke was almost offensive to her stern outlook. Upon reflection, Arel had to admit that he too had been overly serious most of his life.

Even now, he wasn't taking part in any of the camaraderie around him. He wanted to be just as happy as the next person, but he didn't know how. Had he lost his sense of humor or was it possible that he'd never had one?

The only person who laughed when he was growing up was his brother. Aldwin wasn't the typical English gentleman. Although he acted within the rules and regulations required by his station, behind the scenes, he could be funny.

One of Arel's first happy memories took place when he was quite young and Aldwin tickled him. When his brother made him laugh, Arel started to apologize. That's when Aldwin tickled him again, and Arel gave in to simply being happy. But for most of Arel's life, there never seemed to be a reason to laugh so spontaneously. He used to joke around with William in their early, university days, but there was a mocking quality to their amusement. And recently, when they talked, neither seemed able to achieve any genuine sense of levity.

That was one of the reasons for Arel keeping their conversations short. He'd been having a tough time in the relationship department, and William was going through a very rough patch too. But William made it clear that he wanted no interference. Arel knew it was probably a sound decision. Arel's track record wasn't a good one. He didn't want to end up making things worse again. Fortunately, Raphael would be there for William. Arel hoped that was enough.

He was jostled back to the moment when Elise hit a bump in the road. It wasn't a big bump, just one that gave everyone a little shaking up and made them laugh again. Instead of joining in, Arel peeked over at Elise. There was a big smile on her face as she said she was sorry in a teasing tone. When she glanced back, he found himself smiling too. More importantly, he felt his shoulders relax. He even stretched out his legs and started listening to one of Carey's funny stories.

As the day continued in a stress-free fashion, Arel was particularly happy to see Annabel enjoying herself. She deserved a break after the rough time she'd had coping with both his own and William's problems. Now, with Elise's encouragement, Annabel indulged her excitement over the most ordinary of things. She gazed wide-eyed at changing landscapes. When they stopped and checked out a couple of gift shops, she'd excitedly scoured the store shelves for nick-knacks.

Annabel's curious spirit of adventure soon infected the group, including Arel. He was a bit taken back when he purchased something he normally wouldn't notice. It was a small ballerina statue that he saw Elise admiring. It only cost a few dollars in a second hand store, and it certainly wasn't a collectible, but it made Elise smile when she looked at it. Later, Arel asked Carey to give the statue to Elise. He didn't want to get involved again. After being with Claire, he needed a very long break from relationships.

But he did enjoy the day and the time he spent with the group. That evening, when the SUV pulled into Elise's driveway, he got out of the car feeling lighter than normal. Elise hadn't found a place to live, but he'd actually lost himself to the spirit of the group for a good part of the day. As he walked back home, his body felt content, and his mind wasn't buzzing with its usual concerns.

Thirty-Eight

AREL WOKE UP and almost smiled. He took a deep breath without any effort. He'd had a particularly sound sleep without any nightmares. Unfortunately, when he stretched and his hand came to rest on the space next to him, he remembered Claire. The cold sheets brought on a twinge of sadness, but the gloom didn't last. He didn't feel the loss he was sure he was supposed to feel. After all, he'd been madly in love with Claire. He'd been willing to go to almost any lengths to fulfill her wants. So why didn't he suffer more now that their wedding was off? Was William right about the abuse aspect? That might account for his feeling of freedom.

He sat up and grabbed his phone off of the night stand. It was his habit to check the time and weather. He rubbed the sleep from his eyes when he saw that he'd missed a number of calls. William had tried to contact him, but he never heard his phone. When he'd been in the car with Elise, Annabel, and Carey, he'd shut off the ringer as a courtesy. He'd forgotten to turn it back on.

When he checked William's voice message, any sense of ease was instantly replaced by concern. William's tone sounded way too grim, even for William.

"Arel, I'm calling from Rolphe's. I might be wrong, but I think he's on his way out. I think that you should come to Paris too."

The message was so unexpected that Arel hesitated. He couldn't imagine why William would visit Rolphe. As for Rolphe, the man seemed fine when they spoke last. Of course, weeks had passed since their last conversation.

Arel got to his feet, put on a robe and looked upwards, wondering about Michael's whereabouts. Why hadn't the angel informed him of Rolphe's situation? As a twinge of annoyance made him frown, he already knew the answer. Michael maintained an attitude of non-interference. That attitude meant Arel had to be accountable. If he'd wanted, he could have checked on Rolphe himself.

He went back to the night stand and picked up his phone. After he put in a call to William's number, he waited and braced himself for bad news. But now, William wasn't picking up. Arel tried to tune into William's thoughts, but all he got was a jumble of disconnected images. He couldn't access any helpful information.

* * *

William sat in Rolphe's bedroom, listening to Rolphe's labored breaths. He was also appreciating the fact that Arel had arrived from Chicago. William would be free to return home very soon.

He'd never had a chance to talk to Rolphe after the dream he'd had. Rolphe had lapsed into a deep sleep state, and his breathing was becoming more difficult by the hour. With Rolphe looking and sounding like he could die at any time, William decided not to leave him.

Arel's arrival was a relief. But at the moment, Arel was in the living room talking on his phone. He'd called Peggy in Chicago to explain his sudden departure to Paris. William used the time to consider his own condition. He felt better physically. His emotions were a different matter. He couldn't forget the person who'd haunted his dream. Young Will had been so cocky and sure of himself. Every time William thought about the young man's accusations, his anger flared. Happily, he could put Paris, Rolphe and Young Will behind him very soon.

He stood up and checked his watch. He might be able to make the next train back to London if he hurried. He gave Rolphe a final glance. It was time to say goodbye to Arel and be on his way. As he was about to leave the room, Arel came walking in. William nodded to him. "Rolphe's all yours, Arel. Good luck."

Arel stood for a long moment, staring at the bed where Rolphe was sleeping. When he looked at William, his scowl deepened. "Something is very wrong here," he said.

William wanted to know what Arel meant, but he didn't get a chance to ask. Arel was already headed out the door. William tried to be patient for a little longer and kept his voice calm and civil as he went after Arel. "Arel, what's going on with you? You've been acting weird ever since you got here?"

Arel didn't bother to answer. He walked briskly towards the living room, leaving William behind in the hall. William sighed knowingly. Arel had a very tough job ahead of him. Being around Rolphe was depressing, and the man's energy was draining. Arel was probably unhappy about being forced to contend with the situation.

William walked into the living room, feeling sympathetic to Arel's plight. He was surprised when he glanced around the room and found that Arel wasn't there. "Stop playing games, Arel. Where are you?"

William was somewhat accustomed to Arel's unusual comings and goings, but this felt different. When he quickly searched the rest of the apartment and didn't find Arel, his uneasiness increased. Surely, if Arel had decided to leave, he would have informed William. And what was Arel talking about when he said something was very wrong?

The question sent a shiver through William's body. Soon, he was shaking with cold. He remembered that he'd left his jacket in Rolphe's bedroom. He went back to retrieve it. When he got to the doorway, he let out a gasp of surprise. Arel was standing next to Rolphe's bed. "What the hell, Arel! Why didn't you answer me?"

Arel smiled back. "Hello, Will."

"Didn't you hear me calling you?"

Arel hesitated. "I just let myself into Rolphe's apartment a minute ago. How could I hear you?"

William realized how exhausted he felt. "Listen, I'm tired, and I have to leave."

"You do look a bit worn."

"I'll call you when I get home," William said as he turned to go.

A groan came from Rolphe's bed. "William!" Rolphe cried out. "Please, stop! I don't want to be alone!"

William turned and gave him a dismissive wave. "Arel is here now. He'll stay with you."

Rolphe tried to lift his head. "Arel? Here? Where?"

William frowned and pointed to Arel. "He's standing two feet away from you."

Rolphe's eyes flitted right and left and came to rest on William again. "No, there's only you and me."

William leaned against the bedroom door jamb and rubbed his temples. Nothing made any sense. He glowered at Arel. "What have you done this time? Why can't Rolphe see you?"

Arel shrugged and smiled back.

266

It was the kind of mindless smile that made William's skin crawl. "Whatever, I'm leaving," he announced as he backed away. "You deal with Rolphe."

He was passing by the living room again when he noticed something else that was strange. There was a large bouquet of yellow roses sitting on the piano. The flowers hadn't been there a few minutes ago. After a moment of confusion, he decided to let the matter go.

"I'm tired that's all," he said as he checked his watch again. "What the—" His mind stalled when he realized the second hand on his watch was going backwards. In fact, according to the time piece, he'd lost a whole day. "Dammit, this is an expensive watch, and I just had the battery replaced." He'd definitely have to revisit his jeweler.

As he was walking to the outer door, Arel called out to him.

"William, why are you leaving? Rolphe needs you."

"You're here now. You can take care of him."

Arel tilted his head, looking confused. "But how could I be here, William? I'm just arriving from Chicago. I'm still at the airport."

William started to reply just before Arel disappeared again. "Damn you, Arel, you're always doing something crazy, but I've had it."

William grabbed the door knob and tried to turn it, but it was stuck. When he tried to turn it more forcefully, the knob broke off in his hand. Something that trivial shouldn't have made his heart start pounding, but he was terrified as he stared at the broken knob. Something told him that he might not be able to ever leave Rolphe's apartment. He gasped out his fears. "I could be trapped here forever."

They were irrational thoughts, but he couldn't shake the feeling that something had him in its clutches again. He tried to calm himself by breathing, but his chest felt so constricted that it wouldn't expand. He could barely get any air. Panic started to take hold, and he began to pace. That's when he heard laughter.

Young Will appeared where Arel had been standing. "You can't run away, William," the young man insisted. "We're going to figure this out whether you like it or not."

William staggered back against the wall. "Oh hell, I think I'm still dreaming. Or maybe I've done something crazy like Arel."

For weeks, he'd been contemplating what it would be like to leave the world. Now, he realized that his wish might have come true. With his growing, but uncontrolled powers, he might have copied one of Arel's tricks and created his own alternate reality. But how and when could he have slipped away from the normal world?

Young Will's smile broadened. "Or maybe you're losing your mind. Wouldn't that be something? The one thing you prize so highly could be slipping away from you. If that happens, there'll be just you and me again."

Thirty-Nine

AREL STOOD IN Rolphe's guest bedroom, rubbing his eyes. They burned from too much worry and too little sleep. He'd arrived in Paris after a tiring flight from Chicago, but he couldn't think about himself or his bodily woes. William was in trouble, and Arel didn't know how to help him. No matter what he tried, he couldn't wake William up. Arel glanced at Rolphe. "What happened to him?"

Rolphe stepped forward. "I don't know. I've tried to wake him up, too."

"William called me, telling me that you were the one who was in bad shape."

"I was sick for a couple of days, but I'm better now. I thought that William had returned to London. I didn't know he was still here until I felt well enough to be up and about. I tried, but I couldn't wake him up either. When I called your home, Michael said you were on your way to Paris."

Arel went over to a dresser by the window and picked up William's phone. He checked the text messages and the calls that William had made. "His phone records indicate that he did call me and that he also left messages. But how could that be if he was sleeping the whole time?"

"I don't know, but I have heard of cases like this when I was young and traveling with some gypsies. There were stories—"

"Please, Rolphe, don't ever talk about such things around Will. He's still trying to adjust to angelic blood. To think he's having episodes akin to a gypsy would put him over the edge."

"I'm sorry." Rolphe backed away. "Maybe this is my fault."

"Your fault?" Arel felt his blood go instantly hot. "Did you do something to William, because if you did—"

"A couple of weeks ago, I sensed that William was having difficulties. I wanted to help him, so I started praying."

Arel was still dealing with his attack of instant rage and couldn't hold back a response. "You and your damnable prayers! Why can't you just paint your pictures and forget about everything else?"

"But I never meant any harm. I swear!" Rolphe stumbled over to a chair. "But while I was praying, I kept getting flashes of William's childhood and what happened to him. Then I started thinking about my own youth too. That's when I visited William in London—"

"Why would you visit him?"

"Because I knew he'd taken the wrong path, just like I did. I wanted him to stop giving away his power to ideas that are worthless. But he didn't seem to understand what I was saying. He was angry and almost threw me out. After I came home, I felt very bad about it all and got sick."

Arel walked over to where Rolphe was sitting. "Anything else? I want to know everything."

"For some reason, William came here to visit me. I think he still believed that I had something to offer, maybe an answer. I told him that he'd made a terrible mistake by wanting my blood those many years ago. I pointed out that he was just looking for a way to defeat his worthless father. I told him that what I gave him was worthless too."

"William believed your blood enabled him to have the life he wanted."

"Yes, but he was wrong."

"You can't know that! If a person believes that something is right for them, and you destroy their belief and call them a fool, you destroy their foundation. You leave them with nothing."

"Do you think that's what I did to William?"

"Look at him, Rolphe! He's checked out! Now, you better help me get him back. And you can start by telling me everything you know about those gypsy stories."

"It was a long time ago."

"Don't give me excuses, Rolphe."

Rolphe bowed his head. "I'll do my best."

"I want more than your best, but before you start telling me your tales, I better get Michael and Raphael in on this. It's the kind of thing that seems to come with their blood."

"I don't understand."

"I know you revere angels, but their world and ours don't mesh very well. And trying to incorporate their lofty ideals and values can be challenging to say the least."

"Why would you say that? They've helped me to turn my life around."

Arel thought about how Elise had said the same thing. But seeing William lying so still on the bed, hardly breathing, he had to wonder about angelic wisdom. "Yes, maybe they have helped you, but look at William. His mind has flown the coop. And do you know why?"

Rolphe shook his head.

"Because of your prayers and meddling advice about what you think is worthless!"

* * *

Arel narrowed his brows as he studied Michael and Raphael. The angels were sitting side-by-side on a sofa in Rolphe's living room. Rolphe was off to himself in a corner chair.

Arel was familiar with Michael who appeared older and more seasoned when it came to the world. Arel hadn't been around Raphael very much. The angel had a youthful appearance, but his eyes told a different story. If Arel had allowed himself to stare at them for very long, he was sure he'd find himself witnessing creation at its very beginning.

Both angels looked much more mature than Carey, but Arel knew that Carey only pretended to be young and reckless. He let out a huff of disapproval. "Poor William, when I got him mixed up with angelic blood, I should have been horse-whipped."

Michael sighed. "Arel, I'm sorry that you find us so threatening."

"Of course, I find you threatening. You two sit there all sweet and innocent, but think about the three of us, the recipients of your so-called heavenly gift! Rolphe's a menace at best. Most of the time, I'm half out of my mind, and William, according to Rolphe, is trapped in some convoluted, dream world."

"Is there something we can do to help?" Michael asked.

"Yes, you can shed some light on the subject. What are we dealing with?"

Michael sat back. "It's a little complicated. William is experiencing alternate worlds that are similar to this one."

Arel began to pace. "But they're still dreams in a sense."

"Yes, but they appear real and solid to William. The difference is that the rules of the normal world don't apply. For instance, linear time isn't a part of those worlds. Unexpected inconsistencies are common. People can be in two places at one time, or they can simply disappear and reappear in a different location."

Arel paused, trying to understand what Michael was saying. When he'd been involved with lucid dreaming, he'd experienced many of the conditions that Michael described. But William had never studied those lucid states. "You're saying that William doesn't know how to respond in those worlds."

Raphael spoke up. "There's more to it than that. William's fear has escalated. He feels like he's lost all control. He feels trapped."

"Why can't we wake him up?"

Raphael hesitated. "In a sense, he is lost. Before this happened, he couldn't accept or integrate that aspect of himself that he viewed as his child self. That part frightened him because he thought it held all of his pain."

A loud moan came from the corner where Rolphe was sitting. "So this *is* my fault. I should never have shared that vision with him."

Arel walked over to Rolphe. "What vision are you talking about now?"

Rolphe avoided Arel's eyes. "Are you sure you want to hear this?"

Arel glared back. "Tell me!"

Rolphe swallowed hard. "William was just a small boy, and he was begging his father to stop hunting his little fox friends. I could feel his precious heart breaking. Then his father did something even more terrible."

Arel was instantly sorry that he'd asked for details. As Rolphe talked about his vision, Arel didn't just hear the words, he became a bystander to events that chilled him to the bone. First, there were the screams of a pitiful animal. It was being torn apart by hounds while it was still breathing. Then Arel saw little William. He was just a young, frightened boy who was going mad with grief, a helpless witness to a monstrous event. And then there was William's father who stood there laughing and enjoying his son's torment.

272

As Arel came back to himself, he struggled to remain in control. "That bastard of a father! He wanted a son who was as cold and heartless as he was."

Arel's fury went into overdrive. If he could have resurrected the dead, he'd have brought back William's father only to murder him on the spot. When he calmed himself a little, he targeted Rolphe. "Why, Rolphe? Why would you do such a thing?"

Rolphe rocked back and forth, but remained mute. With head bowed and shoulders thrust forward, he seemed to be caving in on himself.

Arel wanted to hate Rolphe, but his inner sight was operating in spite of his emotional outrage. When he tuned into Rolphe, he saw the child that Rolphe had once been. That boy had been given a body that was too big for his age. That child didn't have an ounce of malice in his bones. Yet he'd been forced to be a soldier. As he was taught to kill and maim, that child gave up on himself, just like William had given up.

Arel stumbled back to a chair, overwhelmed by it all. Why did life have to be so painful? Why had his father beaten him? Why had William's heart been ravaged when he was just a child? Why had Rolphe suffered all that he'd suffered?

As he sat there pondering the countless cruelties, he felt someone tap his knee. When he looked up, Rolphe was kneeling in front of him. He'd never seen eyes that were so filled with sorrow as Rolphe's when he spoke.

"You and William are as precious to me as my boys were when they were alive on this earth. Yet, I've harmed William again, in a most grievous and unforgivable way. I don't deserve to live. If it would help, strike me down on the spot."

How could Arel respond to such a statement? How could he judge the man in front of him when he'd made so many unforgivable mistakes himself? Still, he didn't know how to get beyond his critical thoughts about the man.

When he looked up, Michael was staring back at him. The angel's summer-blue eyes were clear and untroubled. Arel knew that Michael never entertained any of the darkness that people experienced. Silently, he begged Michael for his help. As usual, his request was granted. Michael's light became a comforting oasis. It was a place where Arel could disengage from the heaviness of matter, if only for a few moments.

As he surrendered to Michael's caring gaze, Arel felt some of his strength return. He also felt the courage to do whatever he needed to do. When he looked at Rolphe, his words flowed out without effort. "Get up, Rolphe. You still have work to do. You're going to help me get William back."

Forty

ANNABEL LAY IN her bed, thinking about the vivid dream she'd just had. William had come to her, telling her how much he loved her. He also said that he was going to be away for a while, on a retreat of sorts. She was to stay in Chicago for the time being. When he'd accomplished what he had to do, he'd call her.

But Annabel's senses told her that the dream was more than just a normal one. When William had held her close and kissed her, she felt his deep, enduring affection. It was such a beautiful expression of the love they shared that it almost scared her. William wasn't usually willing to allow something so intimate. He could be somewhat guarded, even around her.

She turned on her light and looked at the clock. It was three in the morning, but she knew she couldn't go back to sleep. She threw off the covers and put on her robe and slippers. She thought about how much she wanted to share with William. She wanted to let him know that she was coming back to herself, to that strong spirit that she'd been as an angel.

She left her room and padded down the hallway, trying to be as quiet as possible. She was surprised to see a light on in the kitchen. Elise was sitting at the table. Freddie was in his bed, but he noticed her, lifted his head in greeting, then went back to sleep.

Elise smiled when she saw Annabel. "Looks like neither of us can sleep. Would you like a cup of chamomile tea?"

"No, thank you," Annabel said as she sat down.

Elise stared back with half-closed eyes. "I woke up an hour ago, and I've been awake since."

"Is there something troubling you?"

Elise cradled her tea cup. "It's strange, but I dreamed about Arel."

"I just dreamed about William, but you know that Arel and William are in Paris. It seems that their friend, Rolphe, took ill."

Elise nodded. "Yes, Carey told me about it when I was out with Freddie last night."

Annabel hesitated. "I'm sorry, I should have said something sooner. I've been a bit distracted."

"What's wrong?"

"It's just that when Arel and William get together, they can—" Annabel took a deep breath, hoping to dispel the worrisome feelings that kept swirling around in her mind.

"What are you trying to say, Annabel?"

"It's nothing. Sometimes I worry too much about them getting carried away."

Elise leaned in with expectant eyes. "I'm sorry, but my curiosity is getting the better of me. Can you tell me a little more?"

Annabel knew she had to word her answer carefully. After all, Elise wasn't privy to the idea of angelic blood or Arel and William's inability to handle the stuff properly. "I suppose I could say that both of them seem more accident prone when they're together."

Elise let out a small gasp of concern. "Oh my, there was an accident in my dream about Arel. He was out searching for something or someone. It was very dark, and he lost his footing. I woke up just as he was about to go over a cliff."

Annabel's heart did an anxious leap. She had to quickly remind herself that Elise was only describing a dream. "Nightmares can be upsetting, but let's not think the worst."

"Of course you're right. Arel's in Paris, the lucky duck! I don't think there are any dangerous cliffs around."

Annabel pushed back from the table and got to her feet. Her worries were escalating, and she didn't want to upset Elise. "I think I better go back to bed."

Elise stood up too. "Annabel, do you know how wonderful it's been having you here? I love that we can have these little chats."

Annabel bit her lip and went over to give Elise a hug. "Thank you. I enjoy spending time with you too. But I can get sidetracked, especially when it comes to Arel and William."

Elise laughed. "From what I can tell, they're both a handful."

Annabel smiled as she started back to bed. "Yes, a 'handful' is putting it mildly."

Later, as she lay under her warm covers and thought about visiting Elise, she realized what a comfort it was to have her as a friend. They were forming a bond that made Annabel's fears seem more manageable. Even so, she decided it would be a good idea to talk to Carey in the morning. She wanted his take on Elise's nightmare.

* * *

It was still early and Carey was in the kitchen when Annabel knocked on the back door. When he invited her in, he noted her frown lines and an expression that told him that she was bracing herself for the worst. After she was seated at the table, he knew she could use a distraction. "Can I get you anything? I made some hot cocoa."

Annabel's eyes flitted over to the stove. "Thank you, something hot might help to get rid of this chill that's taken hold."

Carey poured some of the contents of a saucepan into a mug. He handed it to Annabel. "You're worrying about William."

"Not just William, Arel too. If Elise's dream is at all accurate, he could be in serious danger."

Carey poured a second cup of the cocoa and sat down too. "Arel and adventure seem to go together."

Annabel's body trembled involuntarily. "Adventure? Oh please, Carcy, he's out-of-control most of the time."

"Do you really believe that? Do you question Michael's decision to give him angelic blood?"

Annabel's frown deepened. "I didn't when I had my wings, but from a human standpoint, I get confused. Last night, I told Elise that Arel and William are accident prone when they're together. But in truth, Arel's the one who's dangerous. Whenever he's around William, William ends up getting hurt."

"So you think Arel is to blame for all of William's troubles?"

Annabel clamped a shaky hand on the handle of her mug and guided it to her lips. After she took a sip, she trembled again, but she didn't answer.

Carey reached out and put his hand over hers. "You're cold. Are you feeling okay?"

Annabel smiled back. "You're playing your human role very convincingly, Carey. But you know I don't feel very good."

"While I'm playing this role, as you put it, I'm trying to maintain the human parameters of perception. That way, I allow people to reveal what they want to reveal."

277

"Well, stop it! I'm here to talk to the angel part of you, Carey. I want to know what's going on with Arel and William."

"And what about you? Has it ever helped you to know their affairs when you're not a part of what they're doing?"

Annabel's face turned into a full blown pout of annoyance. "You know it hasn't helped! It's made my life as a human pure misery!"

Carey sat back. "I'm sorry. I'm not trying to upset you, but—"

Annabel crossed her arms. "Oh yes you are!"

"Annabel, remember when we first worked together. Remember when you and I accompanied Arel on that trip to New York. Arel was so angry at William. Arel had spent so many years hating the thought that he was a vampire and that William was responsible. As an angel, you knew that his anger wasn't the answer. You knew that he had an opportunity to find peace in his life. We both wanted that for him."

Annabel bit her lip, trying to hold back the tears that began to stream down her cheeks. "It was all so clear from that point of view. Now, I'm like Arel. I get so angry sometimes."

Carey smiled and pulled out a handkerchief from his pocket. He handed it to Annabel.

Annabel took it and swiped at her face. "I didn't know you carried one of these."

"It was something that Michael learned from Arel. It's come in handy with Elise a couple of times. But crying can be a good release for the body."

Annabel laughed. "I've done a lot of 'releasing' since I took off my wings. You'd think I'd be more balanced by now."

"You've only been a human for a very short amount of time. You're doing very well considering the challenges you've had."

Annabel laughed again, but this time there was a touch of sullenness in her tone. "Why didn't I stay William's angel, at least for a little longer? I could have helped him so much more if I wasn't a bundle of fear and worry."

"Tell that to Raphael."

Annabel ran a finger over the rim of her mug. "Poor Raphael, I bet he hardly gets to voice any advice with William nowadays. My beautiful husband is so caught up in his drama."

"That's right, but William does think about you, Annabel. He loves you in a way that wouldn't be possible if you still had your wings."

"And I love him."

"That's true, and he feels that love. You know he does."

Annabel sneezed, grabbed the handkerchief and blew her nose. "I have this strange feeling in my body. It's not very pleasant."

Carey eyed her carefully. "I think you're getting a cold."

Annabel blinked back with questioning eyes. "You mean I'm getting sick? I've never been sick before. What should I do?"

"I doubt that my advice would be of much help."

"Why is that?"

"Getting sick can be a sign that you're not being very good to yourself. The body suffers. But to reverse that, a person has to let go of the negativity they've been holding."

Annabel pursed her lips. "You're saying that I have to stop worrying. But how do you expect me to do that when I can feel something bad is about to happen to either Arel or William?"

"Like I said, my advice isn't helpful if you feel that you can't change what you're doing."

* * *

Peggy stood at Elise's kitchen stove, warming up the soup she'd brought over. When Elise joined her, she gave her a hopeful glance. "How is Annabel feeling? She sounded so miserable when I talked to her on the phone this morning. That's when I thought about my mom's chicken soup. It seemed to help when I was a child."

"That was very kind of you," Elise said as she got a bowl out of the cupboard. "I think Annabel needs all the help she can get. She seems almost panicked by her symptoms. You'd think she'd never been sick before."

Peggy ladled a portion of the soup into the bowl. "My little Sara is the same way. When she gets a sniffle, she lets us all know she's not feeling well. I guess some people are more sensitive than others."

"I've had so many migraines that I think I've learned to suffer quietly. It doesn't do any good to make a fuss."

"Tell me about it," Peggy laughed. "Sometimes I feel like an old warhorse when it comes to life in general."

"As one old warhorse to another, I'm hoping to have more fun from now on. When I look back on my life, I don't feel like any good

279

came out of what I considered the bad parts. I hung on to my resentment, and in the end, I'm the one who suffered, not the people I was angry at."

Peggy laughed. "I think that's called wisdom. Unfortunately, it takes a while to see things from that vantage point. Take me, for instance. I'm a first class worrier like Annabel. I've tried to change, and I've made a bit of headway, but I can still get upset. Last night, I had this terrible dream about Arel. Afterwards, I could have let it go, but it's hard not to be alarmed. Some of my bad dreams were valid. Arel actually was in trouble."

Elise tugged anxiously at the heart necklace she was wearing. "I had the same kind of dream last night. Arel fell off a cliff."

Peggy put the bowl of soup on the table. "In my dream, Arel slipped down a flight of stairs."

"Maybe our similar dreams are a coincidence. Like you said, Annabel is a worrier too. She didn't dream about Arel. She dreamed about William and how loving he was."

"Maybe, but I tried to call Arel this morning, and he didn't answer. I got his voice mail."

"What do you usually do in these situations?"

Peggy picked up the soup and headed out of the kitchen. "Most of the time I have to wait and see if I have another dream."

Elise followed her. "I guess I'll do the same. We can compare notes tomorrow."

Peggy looked back and smiled. "Thanks, I feel better knowing I'm not alone in my strange dream escapades."

Forty-One

WILLIAM OFTEN SAT in Rolphe's living room, hoping to understand his situation. He'd started keeping notes of the time, but that didn't help. Sometimes the hands of the clock barely moved a minute even though he'd counted to a thousand. Other times, hours were lost in a blink of an eye. He was definitely dreaming. Waking up was another matter. He hadn't figured that one out. He'd even been desperate enough to try leaping off the balcony of Rolphe's apartment. A fright like that usually awoke the sleeper, but not in his case. He ended up falling into bed instead of landing on the sidewalk.

He'd been forced to wonder if his mind had derailed. Was he schizophrenic? Was he living in a delusional world because he couldn't handle reality? When he asked himself for answers, he'd wake up in a slightly different version of a dream.

There was only one time when he escaped Rolphe's apartment. He'd been thinking about Annabel and suddenly found himself at her bedside. As she slumbered, she was like the angel he remembered, so beautiful in every detail. When they were last together, he hadn't appreciated her as much as he could have. He regretted that fact.

During his dream visit, there were moments that felt so solid and real. Thankfully, he did have a chance to tell her that he loved her. But as he watched her sleep, he began to wonder why he hadn't been able to make a life with his ex-angel. Why had he felt so indifferent about their life together? Pondering his doubts was a mistake. After a few minutes of indulging in them, he was back in Rolphe's apartment. He hadn't been able to leave it since.

He was also finding it more difficult to have a conversation with anyone in the dream state. Rolphe had disappeared from his bed, and Arel was rarely around. There was only one person who appeared on command. The younger version of William was always available.

At first, William's anger had dominated the time they had together. But his outbursts didn't change anything. Young Will simply stared back, refusing to give in to the facts that William threw at him.

As the dream state continued, William knew he had to try a different approach.

All of his efforts had to be aimed at getting out of the dream. Since Young Will seemed much more in control in the situation, William seated himself on a sofa and summoned him again. "Okay, let's talk."

Young Will appeared immediately on the opposite sofa. His arms were stationed across his chest. "I'm glad you decided to come to your senses."

William crossed his arms too. "Don't start, I only want one thing from you. Tell me how to get out of this dream?"

"And I want to know why you're so stubborn about remaining in your fears."

"Is it my fear that's keeping me here?"

"You did what you had to as a child. But you grew up, and you became a man. Admit it, you had choices once you were on your own."

"I didn't see a reason to change. Having power makes life a lot easier. Besides, I found something I enjoyed. As a scientist of sorts, I studied and learned how to make sense of life."

"I know," Young Will said. "I was the part of you who was passionate about everything that you studied."

William glared back, but he didn't comment.

Young Will laughed. "My goodness, you can look so annoyed."

"I have reason to be annoyed. What you're saying makes me feel like I don't even know who I am."

"I'll let you in on a little secret. You might have thought you disposed of me, but I've been there anyway. You just refused to acknowledge me."

"What are you talking about?"

"When Arel showed up in your life, I was the part of you that saved him. Later, I helped you to make room for Annabel."

"And because I've cared about those two, I've suffered. I even died at one point!"

"Pain or no pain, they're the best parts of your life, William."

William looked away. "What good does it do to have them in my life if I can't cope anymore?"

"You can't cope because you've come face to face with some memories, which is fine, but let them go. Memories can help you to see where you went off the rails, but don't keep holding on to them."

"I'm not! I'm trying to let go of all of that horror."

"No, you're letting it run your life!" Young Will paused and sighed. "Look, as a child, you couldn't be some superhero. So what? It wasn't your time. Instead, you managed to stay alive and get stronger. Later, you saved Arel from taking his life. Now, the two of you are continuing to reclaim more of yourselves." Young Will laughed. "It felt pretty good to sit on that big horse when you were in Arel's world. When the battle started, you became that superhero you wanted to be. Of course, I was there too, whether you think so or not. We made a good team."

"What do you mean you were there?"

"Do you think your rational, scientific side saved those creatures that Arel turned into soldiers?" Young Will smiled again. "You're always going on about Arel not having a clue, but I think you might be worse. At least he's tried to integrate Michael's blood. All that rational mind of yours has done is look for ways to be like your father."

"I'm nothing like him!"

"I disagree!" Young Will stood up, suddenly red-faced and angry. "You're exactly like him when you can't acknowledge me. I'm the part of you that believes in more than hard facts. I'm the part that wouldn't hurt any of those creatures or Arel when we stepped onto that battlefield. I'm the part that has room for mystery that goes beyond science."

William put his head back on the sofa and closed his eyes. There were more accusations being thrown at him that needed time and energy to examine. But he felt suddenly sleepy and worn. "I can't just change everything I think I am."

Young Will stepped closer and snapped his fingers in William's face. "Don't give up on me now. This is important!"

William looked up with resentful eyes. "No matter what you say, I'm not a boy anymore—"

Young Will shook his head. "You're fixated on semantics. The 'inner child' is just a term people use. It's associated with childhood, but there's nothing childish about that part of yourself. It's who you are. It's who you'll always be."

"All that I know is that whoever I was, got trampled. That me was ground into the dirt, and I couldn't do a damn thing to help myself."

"Yes, but that's the challenge. Father made you believe you'd lost something, but it was a lie. Now your job is to prove him wrong."

William let out a bitter laugh. "Maybe that's why Arel is so gifted when it comes to demonstrating amazing abilities. He's never lost touch with that child part of himself."

"That's true, but he needs more balance, more maturity so that he can handle those abilities appropriately. But you have maturity, William. What you need is to trust in the mystery of life again. Ease up on the need for power and control. Let go and take another chance on life being beautiful again."

William rubbed his forehead. So much of his life had been built around being an adult who made life yield to his wants and desires. "Too tired to think anymore," he moaned as he closed his eyes and drifted off to sleep.

* * *

Arel glanced over at the cot that Rolphe had set up in the guest bedroom. It was a few feet away from where William lay sleeping. "Hang on, Will, we're trying, but it might take some time."

But William didn't have time. His vital signs were weakening. He was hardly breathing, and his pulse was so slow Arel could barely feel it. In a matter of hours, William's heart could stop beating.

According to Rolphe, William's energy essence was in a place that some gypsies called the Land of the Lost. It was an otherworldly plane of experience, a bit like a dream state, only much more focused.

People with very powerful minds were ideal when it came to maintaining these deep dreaming states. However, if they unknowingly accessed this plane of infinite possibilities, they could lose themselves in it. Once they did, their minds often gave their surroundings all their attention. If that happened, they ran the possibility of never finding their way back to reality.

Michael added his own take on William's personal situation. "Rolphe said that William had a very adverse reaction when he recalled a traumatic event in his childhood. Up until that point, he'd found a way to deal with that memory. He refused to let it surface. Now, in

William's mind, that child self has become a separate entity, one that William doesn't know how to integrate. As a result, he isn't only lost in a dream state, he's lost when it comes to living with himself."

Arel scowled at Rolphe. He had to control his tendency to point blame when he thought about the helpless, wounded child that William had witnessed in that memory. Yet, Rolphe wasn't accountable for William's reaction. It was a hard lesson for Arel to learn and live by, but he knew that each person was responsible for their life. To think otherwise was to take away that person's power. He turned his attention to Michael. "So how do you think I should proceed? My first attempt to find William didn't go very well."

In truth, Arel's first try almost ended in disaster. Finding William wasn't like the lucid dreaming he was familiar with. It wasn't like astral traveling either. Even when he set his intention to find William's energy signature, he failed miserably. He ended up in a very dark place. At one point, he felt like he was plunging downward into a black void. He'd almost been trapped there. Luckily, when he called for help, Michael was able to guide him back to a waking state.

"Let me go with you this time," Rolphe begged. "I'll never be able to live with myself if you both get lost."

Arel sat down on the cot. "Forget it. I don't want to worry about you too."

Rolphe's heavy brows narrowed. "But Arel, I've been in the land of the lost before. When I was with the gypsies, I once searched there for my boys."

"And did you find them?"

Rolphe shook his head. "No, I almost didn't make it back, but my teacher, Chessa, came after me."

"Wonderful, now you want to get lost again and take me with you."

"I knew enough to bypass the dark void you encountered. Some think of it as a place that contains all of your fears."

"I wish you could have shared that information before I went exploring."

"My journey took place a long time ago. I forgot most of what happened. But when I heard what you experienced, it all started to come back."

Arel looked at Michael. The angel was standing by the window, quietly gazing out at the dark skies. "Michael, if Rolphe accompanied me, do you think he might be helpful?"

Michael glanced back. "You both have skills that the other lacks. Together, you'd have a better chance of locating William."

Arel scanned Rolphe from head to toe. From what he could tell, the man was sincere and coming from a devoted intention. "Very well, Rolphe. However, I'm counting on you to be on your best behavior."

Rolphe stepped back. "Am I allowed to pray?"

Arel's patience was threadbare, but he tried to be understanding. "Fine, if you have to, but do it quietly. Is that clear?"

Rolphe nodded. "I'll say the prayers in my head. You won't even know I'm praying."

Michael came over to where Arel was sitting. "I'll try to help too, but if William has his shields up, I'll have to respect them."

"Yes, I know."

"And remember, Arel, even if you find William, you have to be careful not to let your emotions get out of hand. If you sympathize with William's pain, you could be drawn into his world. And you could lose your way back."

Arel glared at Rolphe again. "Did you hear what Michael just said, Rolphe? That means you have to stop thinking about William and I as your children. You can't give in to your fears."

Rolphe took in a deep breath and stood up straighter. "I understand."

* * *

The guest bedroom was dimly lit as Arel lay on his cot and prepared for his journey into the unknown. Rolphe laid on the floor a couple of feet away. Both of them were listening to Michael. Both of them had to clear their mind of any thoughts except one. They were to give themselves over completely to the guidance of a higher part of themselves.

It felt like only minutes passed before Arel achieved his aim. He knew he'd fallen asleep. In his misty surroundings, he noticed that Rolphe stood close by. Rolphe's lips were moving, but he wasn't praying aloud. "Are you ready, Rolphe?" he asked.

Arel hadn't expected Rolphe to disappear almost instantly. Fortunately, he was prepared for such a situation. He'd set an intention to follow Rolphe and soon found himself suspended in space next to him. As they both tried to adapt to their new circumstances, Arel kept thinking of William and how important it was to help him. His intention seemed to trigger another shift.

Everything began to spin. Arel and Rolphe were drawn into a funnel of sorts. As it picked up speed, Arel felt like he was in a scene from the Wizard of Oz. He tried, but he couldn't focus his eyes because everything was going round and round. It was ridiculous, but he felt like he was going to vomit in spite of the fact that he was in an energy body. As the speed accelerated even more, another irritating element was added to the mix. Rolphe's prayers were no longer silent petitions. Arel was trying his best to fight off an acute case of nausea, and Rolphe's fervent petitions were stuck inside of his head. Their clarity and magnified volume made it impossible for him to concentrate.

By the time he was able to shut out the prayers, the spinning had stopped. Arel had to take a few moments to push back his motion sickness before he could proceed. When he felt slightly better, his surroundings went from misty to solid, and a room came into view, Rolphe's living room.

Arel looked up at Rolphe and noticed that his fellow traveler was smiling. "I don't understand why you're happy. All that crazy spinning, and we only traveled a few feet."

Rolphe's smile broadened. "No, my dear friend, we're very close to William's dream body. I can feel his presence."

Arel blinked back, then looked around. The room was similar to Rolphe's actual living room, but there were definite differences. The piano was a different model and the wall clock was missing its hands. "Oh, I see. William believes he's still in your apartment."

Rolphe nodded. "Let's look around, but I think we should be quiet. We don't want to scare him. He could move to another dream version of reality if we're not careful."

Arel was about to agree when William came walking in from the hall. It was such a pleasant surprise that Arel forgot all about being soft-spoken. "William! It's so good to see you!" he said as he rushed over to where William was standing.

William crossed his arms and stepped back. "Great, it's you two again."

Arel laughed. "What do you mean? We just got here."

William frowned. "I am getting so tired of this."

Rolphe remained where he was standing and cleared his throat. "Arel, can I speak to you?"

Arel noticed that Rolphe's face had a sort of pleading look. It was the kind of a look a child gave to a parent when the child had an urgent request. Arel walked over and leaned in. "What is it?"

Rolphe put his finger to his lips. When he spoke, his voice was barely a whisper. "William thinks we're part of the dream he's been having."

Arel lowered his voice too. "How do you know that?"

"From what I was told, people who did return from this realm related long conversations they'd had. They said they talked to alternate versions of the people they knew in real life."

Arel glanced at William. The man was staring back, but he looked very annoyed. "How can we convince him that we're from the real world?"

Rolphe shrugged. "When Chessa found me, I had a problem too. I felt so lost that I thought she was just a vision. Even when she convinced me of the truth, I still didn't want to return to my life. I longed to find my family again."

"Hey, you two!" William yelled. "If you're going to pop in like this, I'd think you'd have the good manners not to ignore me."

Arel turned around at once and smiled. "Sorry, Will, but you have to believe me. We're here to help."

William walked over to the sofa and collapsed onto the cushions. "That's a laugh. You're not even here. You're figments of my imagination."

Arel hesitated. The problem he faced was very clear. He didn't have an argument that could counter William's conclusion. When he glanced at Rolphe, the man looked clueless too. Arel decided to give the truth a try. "William, you're right. None of this is real, not in the way you think of reality. What you see around you is part of your dream."

"Yes, I know that," William said forcefully.

Arel approached the sofa. "Here's what you don't know. Rolphe and I are different than what you've been experiencing. We're here to take you back to your body so that you can wake up."

William closed his eyes. "Sure, like I haven't heard that one before."

Arel hurriedly sat down next to William. "Please, try to stay with us, Will. We don't want to lose you again."

But Arel's plea came too late. William had already disappeared. A moment later, the room disappeared. Arel and Rolphe were standing in the mist again.

"We better go back," Rolphe advised. "We need to practice returning to our reality, or we could lose ourselves too."

* * *

William woke up in the guest bed again and glanced around. Arel and Rolphe had appeared briefly. Now they were gone, but something about their visit felt different. Arel was nervous and definitely stressed out. He'd been a confident know-it-all during his former visits. Rolphe had also changed. Unlike the Rolphe who'd forced William to relive his childhood, this version had reverted back to a gentler, very respectful person.

As William thought about the Rolphe who liked to pray, he noticed something strange about the apartment. Normally, when William was alone, the place was stone silent. Now, if he listened attentively, the silence was broken by a faint sound. In a flash of insight, he knew that Rolphe had left something behind after his recent visit. William wasn't sure what that something was, but he was determined to find out.

When he walked back into the living room, it hit him. It was an energy trail that was made up of sounds. When William closed his eyes, the sounds started to piece together. With a bit of concentration, they made sense.

William smiled. "I won't get my hopes up, but I think Rolphe's left behind a trail of prayers."

For the first time, hope eased William's feeling that he was stuck in some private hell forever. But he had to act quickly, before his chance at freedom was lost. He'd just shut his eyes to concentrate on the energy trail when a voice called out his name.

William sighed and opened his eyes again. Young Will stood a few feet away. "Please, I don't have time for you. I might only have one chance to find my way back."

Young Will smiled. "Before you go, I want to let you know that I believe in you."

"Thanks, but I don't think the feeling is mutual."

"It doesn't matter. Just trust me a little, and we'll work things out."

William held his midsection, hoping Young Will was right. He was ready to move on. But trust, that was a different matter. "I'll try."

Young Will nodded. "That's all I need. And for goodness sake, lighten up!"

His demand hung in the air and grew in volume. Soon, it joined the sounds that William had heard earlier and became part of Rolphe's prayers. The combination transformed into a deep, powerful resonance. The sound wasn't only audible, its vibration made the furniture shake.

William tried to steady himself against a wall, but the wall was shaking too. An explanation came to mind. The vibration was breaking up the dream state he was in. Perhaps he was returning to his normal reality.

It was a hopeful thought until powerful tremors took hold of the apartment. They were so violent that William was thrown to the floor. He closed his eyes, wondering if this was going to be the end of him. In his mind's eye, he saw Young Will again.

"Hold on to Annabel! She loves us!" Young Will called out.

It was enough to shift William's attention to the woman he'd taken as his wife. He could see Annabel in her true form, a form that was so full of light. She wasn't afraid or worried. She looked back at him with sparkling, angelic eyes. She loved him without any judgment attached.

As William held on to Annabel's love, the room came back into focus. It was still shaking violently, so violently that it shook William's bones. His teeth chattered. But then something else happened. Something broke open, something deep inside of William's chest.

For a moment he thought he was having a heart attack and almost panicked. But the feeling that followed wasn't painful. It flooded his body with a sense of ease. It lit up his mind, driving out the darkness and replacing it with a deep sense of knowing, of remembering.

William had once felt Annabel's kind of love when he was very young. He was outside, and he'd managed to wander away from his nanny. As he began to explore the world, he didn't label anything. Everything was his, be it tree or bird or rabbit, everything his eyes could see belonged to him. And he belonged to everything around him. He didn't think in terms of separation. In fact, he didn't think at all. He simply enjoyed the experience of being in a glorious, expansive world.

It was only as he got older that he was taught that he was something called a boy. And he was supposed to understand that there were other creatures that were there to serve him. Some were called hounds, some were called cows and others were called foxes.

It took a long time for him to grasp the idea that he had a role that wasn't like that of a tree or a deer. Instead he was supposed to be a great man someday, like his father. And William was told that great men used the world around them as they saw fit. It didn't matter if the ancient tree by the edge of the woods sometimes spoke to William. If his father wanted to cut it down, the tree had no say. It was just something that stood in the way of his father's view when he stared out his desk window.

As the memory died away, William suddenly understood how everything in his life was defined down to the last detail. No wonder he wasn't able to feel his passion. Passion couldn't be defined. Neither could a zest for life. And Annabel, his beautiful Annabel, wasn't a bundle of worries. She was like the birdsong in the meadow, a beautiful gift that he'd been given. As he thought about being with her again, the floor opened, and he began falling so fast that everything was a blur.

He finally slammed into something dense and solid. He blinked open his eyes and took a much needed breath. He was back in Rolphe's guest bedroom. But he wasn't alone. Arel, Rolphe and Michael were there too. They were talking together in the far corner of the room.

Slowly, with great effort, William was able to push himself up into a sitting position. He hoped against hope that he might truly be awake. His body felt very weak. He had to brace himself to keep from falling over. When he ran a hand over his face, it was rough and unshaven.

That was a good thing. In the dream, he was always clean shaven. "Arel?" he whispered in a hoarse voice.

Arel turned and froze, studying William as if he were some rare treasure washed up on a beach. Finally, he seemed able to speak. "William, thank goodness! You've come back to us!" As Arel shouted out his happiness, his golden eyes turned bright and a wide smile spread across his face. In the next moment, he was in motion, rushing over to William's bedside.

William reached out to him. "I hope you're right."

Arel grabbed William's hand and squeezed it with added vigor. "I am right! Believe me!"

William winced in pain. "Take it easy. I don't feel my best." He swallowed hard and took a deep, wheezy breath as he tried to hold on to Arel's glowing eyes. "Arel, you don't know what I've been through. Maybe I'm losing my mind."

Michael came over and put a hand on William's shoulder. "With Arel and Rolphe around, I'm sure they won't let your mind wander too far away."

Arel laughed. "That's right. We're learning new tracking skills."

Rolphe kept his distance, nodding with a smile.

William felt too tired to acknowledge any of them. Instead, a desire was surfacing. He rubbed his chest and turned his attention to Arel. "I want to see Annabel. Is she back in London yet?"

Arel sighed. "No, she's still in Chicago. She's got a terrible cold, and she's unable to travel. But you could come back with me. You could surprise her. I'm sure that would lift her spirits."

William nodded. "Yes, maybe we could recuperate together."

Forty-Two

ANNABEL DIDN'T WANT to be a terrible houseguest, but how could she help it. Her physical condition was a cause for alarm. As she suffered from an unaccustomed assault on her body, she indulged in frequent crying spells and bouts of self-pity. But Elise was a very understanding caregiver. During the time that Annabel had been in bed, Elise was always there for her. Now as she watched the enthusiastic woman coming in with a tea tray, Annabel wiped a tear off her cheek. "What must you think of me, Elise? I wish I wasn't acting like this, but I guess I'm scared."

Elise put the tray on the dresser and smiled back. "It's hard to believe that you've never had a cold before. You're very fortunate."

"Maybe, but everything hurts!"

Elise handed Annabel a cup of tea and sat down on the side of the bed. "Do you think the party and that scene with Claire brought this on?" She straightened Annabel's covers. "It's strange. You seemed to be okay when we went house hunting."

Annabel put the tea on the side table. "I don't know what I did to deserve this."

Elise's brows arched with surprise. "My dear Annabel, being sick isn't a punishment."

"It feels like it. It feels like my body hates me."

"I know it feels like that, but from what I understand, bodies get sick when we worry too much or get very upset."

"So what do I do to fix mine?"

"Bodies have a way of fixing themselves. But if you keep crying, it could take longer."

"How did you learn about all that?"

"I've been pretty rough on my own body," Elise said. She reached down and picked up Freddie. When she set him on the bed, the puppy immediately climbed into Annabel's lap.

"What did you do to your body?" Annabel asked.

"One time, when I got very angry, I kicked my trash can so hard that I hurt my toe. My body wasn't to blame. My bad mood was responsible for my pain."

Annabel began to pet Freddie. "I think I've been angry with William. He says that he loves me, but I wonder about what that really means. I don't think I matter to him in the way that I want."

"I understand. I've been with enough guys to know that if you value what they want more than what you want for yourself, it does hurt."

Annabel felt her compassionate side surfacing. She'd been with William for a very short time compared to all the years Elise had spent with ungrateful men. "You've been through a lot."

Elise laughed. "That's life. We all go through tough times. I'm just happy that I'm seeing a bit of daylight. With Michael and Carey's help, I realized that there are lots of good men out there. Kevin and Tim are great, and so is Arel. And even if you don't think so at the moment, I believe William is a very good man."

Annabel swallowed back her sadness. "You're right. William is a wonderful man. And I love him so much."

"It's nice to hear that," a male voice said from the doorway.

When Annabel looked up, William was standing a few feet away. It was such a surprise that she could barely contain the thrill that surged through her body. Freddie was excited too. He jumped up and ran to the edge of the bed. His little tail was wagging back and forth, like a metronome gone haywire.

Annabel threw back the covers, forgetting that she was sick. With unbounded energy, she ran over to where William was standing and threw her arms around his neck. "William, I've missed you so much!"

* * *

After William's arrival, Elise hastily gathered up Freddie and started for the door. As she was about to step into the hall, she couldn't help herself. She glanced back at Annabel. William had her in his arms, holding her close as Annabel hugged him back. All signs of distress were gone. Annabel was smiling and blissful. When she spoke, her voice had transformed. After days of miserable groans, the woman sounded happy again.

Elise closed the bedroom door and walked down the hall. She retrieved a tissue from her jean pocket and swiped at her teary eyes. Happy endings always made her cry.

"Are you okay?" Arel asked.

Elise let out a gasp. She hadn't expected to see Arel sitting in the living room. But she quickly recovered when she realized Arel's part in the happy ending. "Thank you for bringing William to Chicago. Annabel really needed to see him. She's been so sad these last couple of days."

Arel stood up and smiled. "I hope it's okay that we let ourselves in. William wanted to surprise Annabel. And from what I heard, I think he succeeded."

Elise tried, but she couldn't stop a fresh round of tears. They flowed freely down her cheeks. "I'm sorry, but I get so emotional when things work out the way they're supposed to."

Arel frowned, stepped forward and produced a monogrammed handkerchief to replace her soggy tissue. "Is that what you think, that things are supposed to work out?"

Elise quickly snatched the cloth out of his hand and gave him Freddie to hold. After more tears and sniffles, she wiped her cheeks. "Of course I do. I'm not one of those writers who can end a story badly."

"I suppose many people would feel you're too optimistic."

Elise laughed as she walked to the kitchen. "My books aren't for everyone. But I do try to make sure my characters deal with real situations. And if they figure out a way to be happy, what's the problem?"

"From what Michael's said, you've been very successful with your books."

Elise grabbed a mug off the counter. "Would you like something to drink?"

Arel shook his head. "No, thank you."

Elise poured some coffee into her cup. "I'm lucky to do something that I love and get paid for it. Realistic or not, my readers can't get enough of what I write."

"Romance sells."

Elise gazed dreamily into space. "He's quite handsome, isn't he?"

Arel glanced around. "Who?"

"William, of course. I only got a peek at him, but he'd make a good character for one of my books. He exudes charm and something else."

Arel crossed his arms. "What's that?"

Elise stared at her cup, thinking about how lucky Annabel was. Her new friend had found a man who clearly loved her. William's pale blue eyes lit up with so much happiness when Annabel ran over to him. Elise wondered if a man would ever look at her that way.

Arel cleared his throat. "Excuse me, but you were saying something about—"

"About William, yes," Elise sighed. "He has what some would call animal magnetism. In my books, I describe it as that confident, masculine presence that people notice. It's a quality that women find very appealing. It can affect them in very noticeable ways." She paused and studied Arel's questioning eyes, but she wouldn't let herself think about what those eyes could do to her. If she was ever the focus of Arel's fluid, golden orbs, she'd become one of those looney school girls who went around swooning. She looked away and cleared her throat. "You have it, too, Arel," she said in a matter-of-fact tone.

Arel blinked back as if she'd announced that he had green hair. "I do?"

Elise's mind wandered for a brief instant. When she remembered the first time Arel had asked her out, her body trembled with anticipation. It was definitely one of those "moth to the flame" situations. "Oh yes, the first time I saw you, I—" She stopped herself in time. "I'm sorry, sometimes I ramble on."

Arel's face turned red, and he quickly shifted his attention to Freddie. He stroked the puppy's head in a distracted sort of way. When he looked at Elise again, he returned a forced smile. "Anyway, Freddie looks well. I think he's grown since I saw him last."

Elise was happy to change the topic. "Yes, the little scamp doesn't feel feather-light anymore. Unfortunately, he still chews on things he shouldn't. He found Annabel's slipper yesterday. I'll have to buy her a new pair."

Arel handed Freddie back to Elise. "Oh well, he does seem to have a nice temperament in spite of his flaws. That counts for something."

Elise laughed. "Of course, no matter what, I can't stay mad at him for long."

Arel turned and started for the door. "I better be going. I have things to catch up on at home."

Elise followed him as he walked to the foyer. "I wonder if . . . if you—"

"Yes?" Arel turned around so quickly they nearly collided. "Do you need something?"

When Arel asked the question, his eyes went brighter than Elise had ever seen them. They were so bright and compelling that she was tempted to tell Arel exactly what she needed. She needed for him to forget about the past with her and with Claire. She needed him to come to his senses and see that he had the perfect woman standing in front of him. Well, maybe not a perfect woman, but certainly a willing-to-try-again woman. After a hasty breath, she managed a more reasonable request. "I have to run to the store. Annabel's almost out of cold medicine. If I leave Freddie here, he'll be scratching on her door. And I don't think that Annabel or William would want that. Could I leave him with you for a few minutes?"

Arel's expectant face went instantly flat as his frown slipped into place again. "Oh, yes, Freddie . . . I see. No problem."

"If you close all your bedroom doors, I think your shoes will be safe. And I'll only be gone for thirty minutes. And don't worry, he doesn't have any accidents now."

"Do you think I could take him for a walk? After sitting on a plane, I could use the exercise."

Elise smiled. "He'd love a walk. I haven't been out with him as much since Annabel's been sick. I'll get his leash."

* * *

Arel had never taken a dog for a walk before. He'd never had much to do with any animals for that matter. Growing up, his father's hounds were kept in the kennels. He didn't mind. Once his brother was killed, animals weren't on his radar. His mind was centered on staying out of his father's reaches and staying alive. Recently, mice were the exception. He'd had some incredible experiences with the tiny, intelligent creatures.

Now, Arel had another animal in his care, little Freddie. As they made their way down the street, the puppy didn't seem to mind the weather. As a cold wind ripped through Arel's body and forced him to zip up his jacket, the puppy seemed oblivious. Freddie was all about forward motion and pulled on the leash with all his strength.

Arel worried that Freddie might hurt himself and decided the only answer was to step up his own pace. Before he knew it, he was jogging. Freddie seemed thrilled by Arel's decision. He matched Arel's speed and became a little blur of fur.

After a block, Freddie suddenly slowed down, found a patch of grass and relieved himself. Afterwards, his agenda changed from running to exploration. As Freddie's nose sniffed out every bush and tree in the area, he reminded Arel of a stockbroker studying the morning paper's business section.

Arel's mind began to wander too. He'd dated two women recently. They were very different. While Claire contemplated a campaign to eradicate hunger in some third world country, Elise was worried about her houseguest. Peggy told him that Elise spent many an hour with Annabel, trying to distract her and help her to feel better.

Arel wondered how Annabel would fare in Claire's care. When he'd been ill, Claire saw it as a weakness. He doubted that she'd have much sympathy for Annabel's bout with a cold. No matter, he hoped that Claire was doing well. She hadn't taken his calls or bothered to respond to his texts. The more he thought about their relationship, the more he believed that Claire did what she thought was best. At the same time, he wondered why her heart was so closed when it came to any real intimacy. Why was she so judgmental about everyone who didn't conform to her strict code of conduct?

On the other hand, Elise seemed to have room for various opinions. If only she'd have been receptive when they were dating, perhaps they could have had more of a future.

Arel was brought back to the moment by Freddie. The puppy tugged on his leash again, ready to move on to a new section of real estate that needed sniffing.

Arel scowled as his thoughts moved on too. He couldn't believe how animated Elise became when she talked about William. "I think your owner is very impressed with him, Freddie. Did you notice how rosy her cheeks got when she talked about his animal magnetism? Of course, she did say I possessed the same quality, but her tone was about as enthusiastic as warm milk."

Arel stooped over and ran a hand over Freddie's quivering, inquisitive body. "We better head back, Freddie. Elise said she'd only be gone for a few minutes."

Freddie responded happily to Arel's shared confidences and affection. The puppy turned around and tried to lick Arel's face.

Arel jerked to his feet and smiled. "I don't think so, my small friend."

As they approached Elise's house, her car was pulling into her driveway. Arel waved to her as she got out. Freddie's greeting was more enthusiastic. He whined and struggled on his leash again.

Elise hurried over, clutching her coat against the gusting wind. "This cold snap is brutal," she gasped.

Arel handed her Freddie's leash. "Would you like to come into the house for a few minutes? I could fix you a hot cup of tea."

Elise's eyes sparkled with surprise, and she turned suddenly shy. "That would be nice."

Arel tried not to think about how sweet Elise's voice could be. He also tried to dismiss the instant heat he felt. Unzipping his jacket, he smiled back. "Yes, if you come in for a while, you'd give Annabel and William a few more minutes of privacy."

Elise blushed as she picked up Freddie. "Yes, Annabel and William, I'm sure they're catching up."

Forty-Three

ROLPHE WALKED THROUGH his apartment and paused outside the guest bedroom. With William and Arel gone, the place felt empty. It was a feeling he knew all too well. After he lost his family, it swallowed him up, heart and soul. He was a ghost who walked through life. As a vampire he became a monster who killed without remorse. Nothing mattered to him. Eventually, the killing stopped, and he purchased the blood that sustained his physical form. But he didn't stop killing because he'd reformed. He just got tired.

Now, he was tired again. His steps were labored as he wandered into his studio. When he looked at the painting on the easel, one of Gabriel, he wanted to weep. He grabbed a sheet and covered the portrait. Without inspiration, he had no desire to paint. All he wanted to do was to go back to his bed again. As he started for the studio door, his eyes drifted to one of his other paintings.

Arel and William stared out at him from a large canvas. He'd portrayed them as he often saw them in his mind's eye. There was a glow around them, a golden aura that infused the picture with a feeling of heavenly beings. But in the real world William looked like he'd just been through purgatory. When he left Rolphe's apartment, his glow had been replaced by a grim pallor.

Rolphe remembered Arel's explanation. Rolphe had been ignorant and meddled in William's life. "And I almost destroyed him with that meddling," he groaned to himself.

Rolphe turned to the door again, but his breath caught. Michael stood in the doorway, smiling.

"I thought I'd ask how you're doing," Michael said. "I know you've been through a lot with Arel and William's recent visit."

Rolphe squinted back. Most of the time, he was able to relax a little in the angel's presence, but not this time. Rolphe's inner vision was wide open. It enabled him to see Michael's glorious nature. Waves of brilliant, golden-blue light radiated from Michael's person. It contrasted sharply with how Rolphe viewed himself. He didn't feel worthy of Michael's light or his love.

When Michael's love penetrated Rolphe's chest and stirred within his heart, he had to stagger back. It felt like a great fire burned inside of him. Rolphe knew that Michael was there to help him, to bring a loving presence into his dark world, but he couldn't allow that to happen. He didn't deserve to be blessed in such a way.

As soon as he made that decision, his chest exploded in pain. It was so great that Rolphe fell to his knees, begging the Creator to take him once and for all. He needed to leave the earth and put an end to all the misery he'd felt in his long life.

* * *

Arel shut the front door and smiled. He and Elise had spent a pleasant hour in the kitchen. Elise drank tea and chatted while Freddie slept in a make-shift bed that Arel had put together. He'd borrowed a large basket that Michael used when gathering flowers from the garden and lined it with a soft blanket. He also added some bits of carrot, one of Freddie's favorite treats. Freddie wolfed down the treats and then decided on a nap.

Elise seemed pleased with Arel's ingenuity. She'd confided that when she took Freddie to someone's house, the puppy was constantly exploring. It was a relief for her to see him so content. The visit was also filled with small talk. They chatted about Elise's writing, her move and other mutual interests.

After Elise left, Arel closed the front door feeling satisfied that Elise could appreciate something he did. He was still smiling when he went back into the kitchen to tidy up. He was surprised to see Carey standing by the back door. "Well, Carey, after all my complaining, I'm sure you're thrilled to see things are headed in the right direction. William is with Annabel, and Elise seems like she's doing well."

Carey continued to stare out at the back garden. "Have you forgotten about Rolphe?"

Arel put Elise's tea cup in the sink. "Rolphe? Why would I think about him? He's fine."

Carey turned around and sighed. "Are you sure about that?"

301

Arel hesitated. Carey's youthful face was normally cheerful, as if the angel had a smile hidden just below the surface. Now, his smile was missing. "I didn't think I had to. He keeps himself busy with painting."

Carey pulled out a chair and sat down. "I know you've had very strong opinions about Rolphe. But he did try his best to make amends. Have you ever forgiven him?"

Arel put down his dish cloth. "Forgiveness is tough. Maybe I still harbor some resentment when I think about what he did to William." He sat down too and drummed his fingers on the table. "And now that he's been interfering again—"

"Do you blame him for William's current condition?"

"Why shouldn't I? William got a call from Myra, and he went to Paris to see if Rolphe was sick. After five minutes with the man, William went into a tail spin. I didn't know if we'd even get William back."

"Are you sure that William went to Paris out of concern for Rolphe?"

"What are you getting at?" Arel asked.

"Perhaps you could think in terms of Rolphe's welfare too."

Instead of responding, Arel studied the table mat. There was a single crumb sitting on the linen fabric. It was from the cookie that Elise had eaten. He picked it up and carried it to the sink. "I don't want to think about Rolphe. Is that a crime?"

Carey stood up and started out of the room. "No, it's not a crime," he said quietly.

Arel followed Carey into the living room and targeted him with an irritated scowl. "I'm sorry if my feelings aren't in line with yours, but from my vantage point, Rolphe is still a menace."

Carey's gray-blue eyes shifted in Arel's direction. "Isn't he entitled to a life, too?"

"All I know is that he was an ogre who fed on William twice and nearly killed him both times."

"Fair enough, but do you really think he meant to harm William recently?"

"Does it matter? Whatever Rolphe's intention, William almost died again."

"He played a role, a very difficult role."

"What do you mean?"

Carey's gaze met Arel's and softened. "You've talked about angels and how we approach life differently, and you're right. We can only do so much. For instance, Raphael tried to talk to William about the issues he was facing, but William wouldn't listen. Rolphe's approach was much harsher. Perhaps it was a negative method in your estimation, but it goaded William into facing a scary part of himself. Now, he has a much better chance of integrating that part."

Arel frowned back. "So you're saying that Rolphe did William a service?"

"I'm not recommending his approach, but Rolphe does care about William. He did his best with what he had to work with. In his visions, he understood William's early life and his trauma. Rolphe experienced something similar as a boy. And after all he's been through, he also knows about true power. To wield it properly, a person needs a proper foundation. They have to integrate all aspects of themselves to be truly free and happy."

Arel sat down in his recliner, clenching his fists and trying to find a way out of his bias. "I guess I've been so busy trying to protect William that I haven't been looking at the big picture."

"We both know that William has been stuck for quite some time. He's even talked about checking out."

Arel sighed. "From everything I know, William has been very afraid of being vulnerable again."

"Yes, and Rolphe knew that William believed that control was the answer."

Arel thought about Claire and how she needed everyone to conform to her ideas. He also thought about the crumb he'd removed from Elise's place mat. He was guilty too. "It's called the human condition, Carey."

"Perhaps, but Rolphe could feel William's desire to be free. In fact, he was willing to have both William and you despise him if he could expose the lie William had bought into. What Rolphe didn't know is that even a lie can help a person hold on to life."

Arel rubbed his temples. Carey was making a good case in Rolphe's favor. "When I was young and suicidal, William tried the same thing with me. As a result, I was forced to live, but I hated him for what he did."

Carey smiled knowingly. "But you did survive, and you finally asked for our help."

Arel looked up and sighed. "It was quite the surprise when Michael appeared at my door. Then you came along."

"Believe it or not, people and angels are all working together. We all have gifts to offer, but at times, one gift works better than another. Rolphe used the only gift he thought he had. He shared the vision of William's childhood. But he never meant for William to get lost."

Arel looked away, still trying to assimilate Carey's take on Rolphe when his phone rang. He glanced at the phone, then at Carey. "Can you believe it? It's Rolphe's girlfriend, Myra."

A couple of minutes later, Arel pocketed the phone and shared Myra's message. "Rolphe's girlfriend sounds very upset. Today Rolphe asked Myra to keep his cat, Dantella, permanently. Then he hung up on her."

"So what do you think you should do?"

Arel stood up. "What can I do? I suppose I better pay Rolphe a quick astral visit."

Carey stood up too. "Do you want me to come along?"

"No, stay here in case Annabel or William need something. I'm sure I can handle Rolphe. He probably just wants some attention. He's always going on about missing his boys."

* * *

Arel sat in his downstairs bedroom and contemplated visiting Rolphe again. Even though Myra told him that she was very worried about his old nemesis, Arel felt no bond to Rolphe. No matter what Carey said, a long and complicated past still haunted Arel. And it all started with Rolphe.

In his youth, William had acquired Rolphe's blood. He thought the blood would give him the power he needed to control his world. William then forced that blood on Arel, using it to keep Arel on the earth. Of course, the blood didn't really make them vampires. It contained a virus that triggered certain effects that mimicked a vampire-like condition. The virus also extended both their lives. For Arel, that wasn't a good thing. He'd fought his condition every waking moment. The passing years felt like an eternity of misery. It was only Michael's blood that brought his suffering to an end.

But maybe Carey was right. According to the angel, Rolphe was a transformed man who deserved more than Arel's condemnation. It was a point that was backed up by Rolphe's actions. After William was lost, Rolphe had done his best to rectify his mistake and get William back.

Thinking about Rolphe's rescue efforts, Arel let out a heavy breath. It was filled with obligation, but little consideration or kindness. He needed to lighten his mood. The next breaths were used more constructively. They were slow and steady as he prepared himself for an astral trip to Paris.

As he lowered his shoulders and thought about how happy Annabel and William were, his body responded and began to calm down. With more breathing, he was able to clear his head of thoughts. He drifted into a pleasing, neutral state where he simply sat and observed. Within a few minutes, his etheric form slipped out of his body.

Being free of his physical vessel, Arel enjoyed a sense of lightness and ease. So little effort was required when he was in his astral body. In that realm, it was all about one's attention and focus. Combined, they became a powerful force that propelled a person wherever they intended. It felt effortless to travel to Rolphe's apartment.

Arel soon found himself standing in Rolphe's living room, but he knew something was wrong. He tried to turn around to get his bearings and couldn't move. Everything felt claustrophobic, as if some great weight was pressing in on him from all sides. When he shifted his vision and allowed it to operate more fully, he could see the heavy, dark energy that surrounded him. Then he thought of Rolphe and his anger took over. His eyes filled with fresh resentment. He'd come on an errand of mercy and been slammed with more of Rolphe's unwanted negativity.

"So Carey, I listened to you and this is my reward! Thanks a lot," he grumbled.

Carey's response was immediate. Arel could hear the angel laughing. He paused again, tempted to let Carey's levity feed his anger. Then he smiled too. Carey was trying to help him understand how to help himself. He needed to relax and stop fighting the situation.

Arel was reliving the past. He still associated astral travel and Rolphe's apartment with a hostile enemy. As soon as he thought of Rolphe's prayers and how the man had helped William, Arel felt better. He was even able to move again. The apartment was still infused with a heavy vibration, but unless he bought into it, it couldn't harm him or keep him trapped.

It was a pleasing thought to feel free again. "Maybe I am becoming more like your kind, Carey."

As he started towards Rolphe's bedroom, he waded through the muddy energy without a problem. He called out to Rolphe as he went forward. With Rolphe's psychic gifts, he knew Rolphe should be able to hear him. When he reached Rolphe's bedroom, the door was open, and he looked in. He wasn't prepared for the heat and flames that greeted him. He jumped back into the hall, thankful that his astral reflexes were better than his physical ones.

His first thought was to contact the fire department. A moment of panic followed when he remembered that he probably couldn't interact with physical matter. He'd only managed such a feat one time on a very special occasion. So what could he do to help?

A strong masculine voice called out to him. "It's not a physical fire," Michael said.

Arel glanced to his side and saw the angel standing close. "Thank goodness you're here! What's happening?"

"Look more closely at the flames. They're contained in the room. Notice that none of the furniture is burning."

Arel stepped forward a little. Michael was right, the flames stopped at the open doorway, and even though the flames were everywhere, the fire wasn't consuming anything. He had a moment of relief until his gaze settled on two boys who were standing next to the bedside.

Just as he was about to panic, Michael explained more of what was happening.

"Arel, it's alright. The boys aren't physical either. The children you see are Rolphe's boys, and they're trying to help him,"

Arel stared at the bed and realized that it was occupied by Rolphe. That's when he finally understood what was going on. "Great, Rolphe has created this inferno, hasn't he?"

Before Michael could answer, one of the boys appeared at the doorway. He was very young, maybe six or seven years old, but his stance was erect and fierce when he addressed Arel.

"Why are you here?" the boy asked. "Don't you know how hurtful you've been?"

The child's voice was angry, but there was also a deep sadness in it. The child was letting Arel know that he'd added to Rolphe's extreme condition in a very significant way.

Arel tried to appease the boy. "I'm sorry—"

"You're not sorry!" the boy screamed back.

Arel wasn't prepared for the energy behind the boy's statement. It struck him with a terrible force, a missile of blame delivered to his core. The blow was so unexpected that he decided to retreat. The trip back to his physical body was almost immediate. When he opened his eyes, he wasn't alone. The boy from Rolphe's apartment had followed him back and was hovering in front of him.

Arel had never come up against many ghosts, and even though this one appeared as a child, that didn't make him less frightening. The boy's glowing eyes were only inches away. They conveyed both fearlessness and a commanding presence.

"What do you want from me?" Arel asked in a hoarse whisper.

"We need to talk," the boy said.

Arel automatically threw up his shields, not enjoying the idea that he was communing with one of the long-deceased children that Rolphe often talked about.

The boy eyed him with amusement. "Don't worry. I'm not here to hurt you, only to give you fair warning."

Arel tried to calm himself, but he was confused about what the child wanted. "What kind of warning are you talking about?"

"All your judgments about my father come from your ignorance. If you don't free yourself from such limited thoughts, their harshness and condemnation will destroy your chance at finding what you desire most."

Arel thought about his relationship with Claire and how much he'd wanted it to work. He'd thought Claire wanted the same thing. When they were alone in Paris, he'd felt her need for love. Sometimes, when she was in his arms, he felt a shudder go through her body. It was as if she was letting go of a great, invisible wall that she'd built around herself.

Arel knew about that kind of wall. As a child growing up, he'd suffered grievous hurts that others doled out. His need for safety and protection became greater than his need for affection. Loneliness gnawed at him year after year, but he'd been too afraid to take a chance on people again with the exception of Justina.

307

A barrier remained in Arel's life until Michael showed up. Gradually, as Arel began to trust the angel, he began to take a chance on letting others come back into his life. But in Claire's case, he could only guess that she wasn't ready for that kind of trust. For some reason, she couldn't give their togetherness a place to blossom in her heart.

"You're right," the child said in a soft voice. "Most humans take that wall to their grave."

"That's not what I want," Arel replied insistently.

The child's young face was suddenly sad again. "Don't be too sure about that." As his wispy form faded, his voice lingered in the room for a few moments. "If only you could have seen the goodness in my father instead of his past sins, things could have been different for both of you."

The visit left Arel swimming in the heaviness again, but this time it wasn't Rolphe's energy, it was his own. He could only conclude that the child was right about his feelings. Michael and Carey had helped him with open hearts. Those angelic hearts were devoid of judgment. But he still wasn't ready to extend that kind of help to Rolphe. He still had too much resentment weighing him down.

Forty-Four

WILLIAM WOKE UP in a twin size bed, in a strange bedroom. But it didn't matter where he was or how small the bed was, Annabel was next to him. They'd both been exhausted when they were reunited. Annabel was battling a bad cold, and William was still worn out after his scary, sleep adventures. They had fallen asleep in each other's arms.

William felt better as he came awake and glanced at the clock. He'd been napping for a couple of hours. Annabel was still sleeping soundly. Her disheveled, auburn hair and reddened nose were signs that she wasn't at her best, but William only saw his beautiful ex-angel. He smiled. No matter how she appeared, Annabel would always be the person he'd love forever.

After he got up and dressed, he quietly let himself out of the room. He'd barely started down the hall when he was met by a white, fluffy dog. As the puppy bounced up and down on William's leg, a petite woman came hurrying over.

"Come back here, you little rascal," Elise whispered as she scooped up the puppy. When she glanced at William, she apologized. "Sorry, I had him in my office, but as soon as I opened the door, he slipped out." She smiled. "By the way, I'm Elise."

William paused and put out his hand. "I'm William."

Elise's face lit up as she shifted the puppy to one arm and shook his hand. "Hi, William, Annabel has told me so many good things about you."

"Thank you for taking care of her."

"Poor thing, she's been very unhappy ever since she got sick. But I think she'll recuperate now that you're here."

"Let's hope so."

Elise motioned for William to follow her. "Let's talk in the kitchen so we don't wake up Annabel."

As William followed Elise through the living room, he noted that everything was tidy but not overly so. A few dog toys littered the floor and a slipper was half-hidden under a chair.

Elise saw him checking out his surroundings and smiled again. "Having a puppy has definitely added a lived-in look to the house. But I've enjoyed the company. Anyway, can I get you anything? Coffee or tea?"

"No, perhaps I better go over to Arel's while Annabel is sleeping."

"I'm sure he'd like that. Annabel said that you two are best friends."

William bulked a bit at the thought. His relationship with Arel hadn't always gone smoothly to say the least. "Yes, we've survived our ups and downs."

Elise's eyes dimmed a little. "I'm sure that Arel told you about our history. When we were dating, Arel was wonderful. I was the one who wasn't ready to be with someone. Hopefully, he's becoming a friend."

William sized up the woman in front of him. Elise's real feelings were easy to read. She was definitely still pining over her relationship with Arel. "Sometimes, Elise, things work out for the best. Maybe being a friend is better in the long run."

Elise kissed the top of Freddie's fluffy head and sighed. "I suppose you're right. Friendship sometimes survives where a relationship falters."

"I'm just saying that Arel wouldn't be an easy fit for any woman, not unless she was wearing a halo."

Elise laughed. "Peggy said something like that to me. Of course, after living with myself, I've learned a lot about difficult people. They're sort of like kids. You either love them just because, or they'll drive you crazy."

William crossed his arms and frowned back. "You sound like you've made peace with yourself."

Elise walked over to the counter and retrieved a doggie treat from a jar. After she put the biscuit on Freddie's bed, she put the puppy down next to it. "According to Michael, making peace with one's faults is best if you want to be happy."

* * *

William reflected on Elise's statement as he returned to Arel's house, but he didn't have time to form any opinion. He barely stepped into Arel's foyer when he saw Carey. After a brief greeting, William stood back and addressed the angel. "So, Carey, it must have been rather intense when Claire came and went so abruptly."

Carey paused, letting his grey-blue eyes wander for a moment. When he spoke, his tone was more serious than usual. "Yes, Claire is a very intense woman."

"And how do you think Arel is doing with her hasty departure?"

"He hasn't had much time to think about it. When he found out about your situation, he put all his energy into helping you."

"Right." William knew he hadn't taken the time to properly thank Arel for his efforts. "I have to ask myself why I dismiss his actions so quickly."

"From what I've observed in humans, appreciation begins with the self."

"I've always appreciated who I am."

Carey's expression eased. "Of course. Now, if you'll excuse me, I have some chores I need to take care of."

William watched Carey disappear into the garage, but he didn't feel that the angel was wholly forthcoming. Still, maybe it was better not to question Carey's motives. Angels thought about life in a totally different way than human beings.

After William checked the upper level for signs of Arel, he went down the stairs to the lower apartment. As soon as he entered the space, he stopped short and glanced around. A human's defense mechanism was a built-in part of the physical. When a person visited a lion's cage, something always warned them not to stand too close. In this case, being around Arel could be a cause for caution. The man's energy could be intense, especially when William was still recuperating and not at his best. William started searching the rooms. "Arel? Where are you?"

After a moment, Arel answered. "I'm in the living area, Will."

William was surprised when he saw Arel. Arel didn't look like a lion at all. With his head back on the sofa, the man looked battle-weary, as if he'd returned home after a long campaign. "Arel, are you okay?"

Arel sat up more attentively. "I'll survive. I always do. How about you?"

"I'm better than I was when you found me."

"How's Annabel?"

"She's still sleeping at Elise's. After she gets some rest, I think she'll be better too."

"While you're here, you and Annabel can use the upstairs master bedroom. I'll stay in these lower quarters."

William walked over to the library area and sat down. His wing back chair was located close to some built in shelves that held Arel's collection of rare and first edition books. He'd have to check them out more closely later. For now, he continued to scan Arel's energy. The power he'd sensed was there, but this lion was almost lethargic. "You were fine when we arrived in Chicago. Did something happen since I last saw you?"

Arel avoided letting their eyes connect. "Rolphe happened."

"Rolphe," William sighed out the name. "What's he up to now?"

"I'm not sure. I paid him an astral visit and didn't get very far. His bedroom looked like a depiction of hell."

"Hell? What are you talking about?"

Arel's gaze flared in William's direction for a split second. "Nothing, I'm just babbling away like I always do. What's important is that you're safe, and that you're with Annabel again."

"Don't try to change the subject."

Arel stood up and smiled. "Sorry, but I have to talk to Carey. In the meantime, make yourself at home."

Before William had a chance to question Arel further, Arel was out of the room and on his way to the stairs.

* * *

Arel avoided William's questions and quickly left the room. As he slowly climbed the stairs to the upper level, his body felt heavy, like he was back in Rolphe's apartment. His thoughts were dull too. After returning to the physical and having a conversation with Rolphe's son, he'd begun to think about Rolphe again. Rolphe wasn't just sick. He was in the middle of some hellish experience.

Arel knew he should be doing something to help, but his mind and body felt like they were stuck in limbo. He let himself into the garage, hoping to get an angelic perspective on the situation.

He walked over to where Carey was working on his motorcycle. It was an ancient machine, but with Carey's attention and ongoing maintenance, it ran fairly well. Its dependability was a different matter. Arel scowled with concern. "Carey, don't you think it's time to get rid of that antique? I'll buy you something reliable instead?"

Carey flashed a quick smile and went back to checking his tires. "I like Betsy."

"Betsy? You named your bike? Isn't that taking it a little too far, even for an angel? I know Michael talks to his roses, but really, that pile of metal isn't alive."

"It's a great bike."

Arel wandered over to the workbench and sighed. "Why do I waste my breath?"

"You sound tired. Does it have something to do with your visit to Rolphe's?"

Arel leaned wearily against the bench. "I tried to check on him. I didn't get very far. His children's spirits sent me packing."

Carey stood up, grabbed an oily cloth and wiped his hands. "I see."

"Please don't say, 'I see.' That's Michael's line, and I find it very irritating."

"Why's that?"

Arel opened one of the wall cabinets and retrieved a clean rag. He handed it to Carey. "The truth is that I'm in trouble. I just witnessed a horrible scene in my astral visit to Paris. Like you warned, something is very wrong with Rolphe."

Carey wiped his hands again and handed the cloth back to Arel. "Go on."

Arel threw the cloth on the workbench. "It's hard to admit, but I have no feelings about Rolphe's welfare. It's as if I'm made of stone."

Carey went back to his bike and crouched down again. "Maybe you should talk to Michael."

Arel crossed his arms as a surge of anger began to thaw out his numbness. Angels could be both irritating and evasive. He didn't have the time or energy to deal with either character trait. "Just stop your tinkering and help me understand myself."

"Really?" Carey stood up and faced Arel.

Arel backed up. Even boyish-looking angels like Carey could be intimidating, especially if a person wasn't prepared to face something painful.

Carey smiled. "Let's start with something easy. Tell me the first word that comes to mind when you think about Rolphe."

Arel let a word slip out. "Monster."

"Really?"

"First off, Rolphe is physically scary. Secondly, a guy who's supposed to be reformed doesn't start a bonfire in his room. Even if it's not a physical fire, it was certainly intense. From what my senses told me, Rolphe is angry, very angry."

"Did it feel as intense as your father's anger?"

"My father? What's he got to do with Rolphe's situation?"

"You thought of him as a monster too."

Arel returned to the work bench and hung some tools back on a pegboard. "I did, but that's all in the past. I've learned to put my childhood behind me."

"Are you sure about that? Have you truly put your father's world behind you?" Carey asked.

Arel swiveled round to reply and found himself face to face with the angel. But Carey's face had morphed into one that was lined with age and resentment. His blue-grey eyes were darkened with sudden rage. He looked exactly like Arel's father.

Arel shrank back in terror until he realized what had happened. As soon as he did, he immediately broke free of Carey's mesmerizing eyes and things returned to normal. Still, he had to put a hand to his heart to try to calm himself. "Why did you do that?" he demanded.

Carey turned and walked back to his bike. "Sorry, I was trying to help you remember the person who first taught you how to conjure up a monster. It was a gift your father gave you."

"Gift? You call what my father did to me a gift?"

"It's a somewhat accurate term. When a child is growing up and old enough to start to reason things out, they try to understand how to function in the world around them. They observe their parents and teachers and how these adults react to each situation. Be it positive or negative, it's up to the child to accept the patterns of behavior they've witnessed. That's why two children in the same family sometimes adopt different viewpoints and opinions about life."

"I never thought I had a choice."

"I know, but you did change your beliefs about life when your brother died."

"Yes, the night before, I went to bed happy. My brother was home from university, and I was looking forward to spending time with him the next day."

"Exactly. As a young child you understood some of the tough realities of life, but you still believed that life could be good. However, when you found out that your brother was dead, you learned to construct a new world, one that was ruled by monsters and fear. Your father showed you how."

"I don't understand what you're trying to tell me."

"Actually, I'm the one who doesn't understand. When it comes to the world of fear and monsters, angels are aware of such concepts, but they don't actively participate in that kind of world. Our minds aren't made for that kind of thing."

"Are you saying that our minds are what make us different?"

"Absolutely. A human's mind is capable of being totally fixated on what's going on outside of themselves."

"And what about an angel's mind?"

"My thoughts never stray in that way. I simply know who I am as part of the Divine. But people can learn to define themselves in very limiting ways, especially after some traumatic event. And trauma can affect people of every age. When your brother was killed, it was a blow that changed your father's life, too."

Arel's fists tightened. His father was a stern, but reasonable man before the death of his favorite child. "My father became a raging maniac."

"It was a terrible day for him, one that shifted his focus drastically. Up until that time, his hopes and dreams were centered around his firstborn son. When that son was killed, he felt he was left with nothing but grief. And you became a symbol for the emptiness in his life."

"He tried to beat me to death."

"Yes, and in his rage, he kept beating you until your focus was aligned with his. In the end, you accepted and believed in his world of pain and fear so completely that you lost touch with who you were."

Arel went over to the bike and fingered one of the handlebars. "If Michael hadn't helped me, I'd probably still live in that hopeless world."

Carey smiled. "Michael couldn't have helped you if you hadn't wanted to change. So give yourself some credit."

"Strange, but all this talk about my father makes me think of Claire. I didn't measure up in my father's eyes. When Claire left, I think she felt the same way. Maybe I am deficient and just don't know it."

"Claire judges others to see if they fit into her idea of what reality should be. But that doesn't mean her beliefs are absolute. Remember that humans and angels are all made from the same Divine energy. And in the Creator's eyes, everyone is perfect."

"I wish I felt perfect once in a while."

Carey put a hand on Arel's shoulder and shook it gently. "If your heart is happy, take it as a clue that you're on the right track."

Arel pulled away and started for the garage door. "A happy heart? With Rolphe going ballistic? Give me a break." As he was letting himself out, the doorbell in the foyer chimed. "Maybe that's Annabel. She's probably looking for William."

Carey's smile broadened. "Annabel's had a most informative visit with Elise, but I think she's very glad to have William here too."

"Hopefully, the two of them can relax and begin to enjoy each other."

* * *

Arel left the garage, ready to greet Annabel, but William was already at the front door. He wasn't welcoming in Annabel. He was talking to Arel's neighbor, Elise.

"What's wrong?" William asked with concern. "Is Annabel okay?"

"Annabel is still sleeping, but my Freddie ran away!"

Arel grabbed his gut and had to brace himself. It was the second time that day that he'd been overcome with someone else's energy. In Elise's case, she was projecting a stormy ocean wave of panic.

Elise stepped into the foyer, gasping out her news. "I planned to give Freddie a bath after he got muddy. As usual, I took off his collar and tags! When I opened the door for a delivery, he got away from me. He usually doesn't run off, but he saw a cat going by. Now, even if someone finds him, they won't know how to contact me."

William reached out to Elise. "We'll do our best to help. But for the moment, try to stay calm. Tell me where you last saw the puppy."

As Elise confided in William, Arel tried to settle his stomach. He also shifted his focus and went into search mode. Perhaps he could locate the puppy's energy signature. He soon learned that tracking a puppy was much easier than tracking someone in a dream reality. As soon as he closed his eyes, he was rewarded with a vision of Freddie. Unfortunately, Arel's dodgy stomach was aggravated by a frightening awareness. "Oh hell," Arel moaned to himself. "Freddie's running towards an intersection."

The puppy's energy was a little like Elise's. He was very confused. He wasn't thinking about consequences when he ran out into the street without looking. The sound of horns and cars screeching were so loud that Arel covered his ears. Luckily, Freddie made it to the other side of the street, but the dog was badly shaken.

Arel was as panicked as Elise after what he'd seen. He wanted to help, but how? First of all, he tried to identify the intersection he'd just seen. It was familiar, but he'd been so busy watching Freddie and the busy traffic, he didn't pay attention to buildings or landmarks.

He closed his eyes and concentrated again. He was just starting to remember more details when his mind was hijacked by another vision. This one was so overpowering that it blotted out all his thoughts about a lost puppy. He was suddenly face to face with Rolphe.

Arel stared at a man who was filled with rage and a searing fire that crackled and hissed in Arel's ears. The vision was enough to totally thaw out Arel's numbness. Rolphe was in some kind of crisis. Arel knew he had to act swiftly, but he was having trouble thinking. It was only after he heard William calling out his name that he was able to open his eyes and stare back. "What? What is it?"

"Arel, what are you doing? Didn't you hear Elise?" William asked.

"Sorry, I must have spaced for a moment."

Elise balked at his explanation. She came over and grabbed his arm. "Arel, please, you have to help me find Freddie."

Arel avoided looking at her. The situation with Rolphe was escalating. "I'm sorry, Elise, but I can't."

Elise stepped back and glared at him with dark, imploring eyes. "Freddie means everything to me! Don't you understand?"

"Again, I'm really sorry," Arel said as he turned and started for the stairs to the lower level. "I have to go. William will help you."

Forty-Five

ROLPHE WAS IN the grip of a violent, unshakable wrath, and it was escalating. It started with Michael's visit. The angel's light was so brilliant that Rolphe's own flawed nature became even more damning. That fact hit his heart first. The vessel in his chest exploded in misery and torment. After that, he continued to slip deeper into the darkness he'd thought he'd escaped once and for all.

Rolphe's descent was fueled by Arel's constant scrutiny and condemnation. The man clearly saw Rolphe as an inferior part of creation, something to be abhorred simply because it existed. When Rolphe first repented his sins and his former life, he had fought Arel's judgment. He'd seen it as a challenge, something he could change once he demonstrated his sincerity.

Rolphe had been totally earnest in his desire to be a good man. He longed to walk the earth knowing he belonged. The beautiful visions he had during that time encouraged him. He began to paint what he saw, and as he painted, his mind soared in the heavens.

He also found comfort in a heavenly gift he'd been given. He could talk to angels about his problems. What a privilege and blessing that was. Michael and Carey were so kind and compassionate. They gave him hope. He began to think he had purpose in the world and that his future was bright.

But Arel didn't acknowledge the changes Rolphe had made. Not for a single moment did the man forget what Rolphe had once been, a blight on humanity. Still, Rolphe didn't give up. As a soldier, he'd been taught not to accept defeat. That meant giving Arel time to change his mind. But after the recent, frightening events involving William, Rolphe began to see the wisdom of Arel's unwavering attitude.

Rolphe had always imagined that if his sons had lived, he would have been their most devoted advocate. He would have been a wise, loving parent, a person who helped his boys to navigate the treacherous waters of life successfully.

But recent facts revealed the truth. When Rolphe was given a chance to help William, a man who could have been his son, what happened? Was he a source of guidance and wisdom? No, he was just the opposite. He'd exposed all of William's vulnerabilities and sent him into a downward spiral. In the end, William had almost been lost forever. And Rolphe was to blame.

Just thinking about William's terror-stricken face, Rolphe's breath labored under the burden of what he'd done. His guilt was enough to send him plummeting towards despair. He caught himself just before he'd gone too far.

Despair was the cruelest of places. Rolphe should know. Some of his visits had lasted for years. Despair tore a man apart, piece by piece until a person was nothing but bits of flesh scattered over the hot coals of blame and remorse. Just remembering what he'd been through, both frightened and infuriated him. He didn't have the courage to go there again. He couldn't endure the merciless ways of that dark, unforgiving fortress of destruction. Yet Arel discounted all of Rolphe's previous suffering as if it was nothing.

"The man is like that fortress of pain. He has no compassion or understanding."

But what could Rolphe do if Arel was right? That's when a great surge of anger shot through his bones. It was so powerful that it ignited all the horrors he'd experienced in his life. His innocent childhood had been snatched up and destroyed by soldiers. His beloved family was snuffed out by a ravaging disease. And then, after he was given angelic blood and done his best to open his heart, his very existence was tossed aside as contemptible.

That last fact was also the last step that threw Rolphe into a living hell. His anger escalated so fast that it became a volatile energy that filled every cell in his body. It took over his mind and turned his thoughts into firestorms of rage.

His rage became so all-consuming that it projected itself outwardly. The projection didn't quite make it to the material world. But on the astral plane that surrounded Rolphe, everything was on fire, and he was its source. It was as if his bones, bowels, and flesh were saturated with some combustible substance and a match had ignited what he thought of as his essence.

Arel sat in his bedroom, trying not to think about Elise and her puppy. He needed to make another trip to Paris via astral travel. He'd have to be wise about what he did when he got there. In the past, he'd frequently let his emotions guide his actions. He didn't want to make the same mistake this time. On the other hand, the situation with Rolphe was tricky. Rolphe seemed to have slipped into some emotional hell. He could be dangerous.

It wasn't a comforting thought. Arel had to steel himself for the worst. "Dammit, Rolphe, why do you have to always be so—"

He didn't know how to finish his complaint. In truth, if he considered Rolphe's actions, the way the man tried to always be helpful, he had to admit that Rolphe wasn't always the monster Arel had claimed him to be. "Not until now, that is."

Rolphe's dead children seemed to think that Arel was at fault. Was it true? With his dismissive attitude, had he driven Rolphe into some emotional downfall?

Arel squared his shoulders, fortified by Michael's advice. The angel had repeatedly said that each person was responsible for themselves. Even so, Arel also knew that he'd been on the receiving end of a lot of help from others. Maybe it was payback time.

After a couple of calming breaths, he closed his eyes and tried to clear his mind. He had to check on Rolphe and figure out what to do when he knew more about the problem.

After he felt a release from his body, he let himself float upwards and hover in mid-air. The next step was simple. He thought about Rolphe and getting the man back on track. Without meaning to, he also thought about Freddie. He hoped the puppy got home safely.

As usual with an out-of-body experience, there was always a moment of disorientation and a feeling of rapid movement. But when everything slowed down, he knew something wasn't right.

Arel took one look around and knew that he wasn't in Paris. In fact, he was still close to his neighborhood. He stood on a street corner that he recognized. When he checked for more details, he saw a small, white dog. It was wandering down the sidewalk, starting and stopping as if it was searching for something.

"Freddie!" Arel called out to the puppy, forgetting that he was in his astral body. "Freddie, come here!"

* * *

William sat in the passenger seat of Elise's car, gripping the center console for support. His job was to watch for Elise's puppy as they cruised the neighborhood. It was a task he wished he didn't have. Being lost was the last thing he wanted to think about. Like the puppy named Freddie, he'd recently been floundering in the unknown too. Now, all his fears were resurfacing. What if he fell asleep later that day and couldn't wake up again? What if no one could find him this time? His questions were cut short by Elise's shout.

"Who said that?" Elise cried as she swerved the car and quickly tried to straighten it out. "What's going on?"

Elise's sudden outburst and being thrown against his side window made William's hand tighten its grip. "Elise, what's wrong?"

Elise gave him the briefest glance. "I just heard a voice in my head!"

"Who's voice?"

"That's not the point. I've never had that happen before. It's scary."

William returned a weak smile. After all his crazy experiences, hearing a voice wasn't out of the ordinary. "Please, calm down. It's no big deal."

Elise glanced at him again. "What do you mean? I'm serious, this voice was very loud and very insistent."

"Look, there are lots of things that scare people. The trick is to stay as composed as possible."

"Oh no! I heard it again! It sounded like Arel's voice!"

William relaxed a little. "Of course, I should have known."

"Known what?"

"Arel has some abilities that are unusual."

"Are you talking about psychic abilities? Because I've read a few books about gifted people."

William moaned quietly. "Yes, Arel is gifted if you want to call it that. Anyway, telepathy is one of those gifts. What's he telling you?"

"He said that I'm going the wrong way."

"Then it's simple. Turn around."

Elise pulled over to the curb, grabbed a tissue, and dabbed her eyes.

William waited for her to say something and finally frowned back. "What is it now?"

"The second time Arel spoke, his voice was stern. It reminded me of an old boyfriend who used to shout at me, and all these feelings came up."

"But I thought you told me that you were happy with the life you're living now."

"Maybe I'm kidding myself. Michael and Carey said that I'd be a great mom, but I can't even take care of a puppy. Now, hearing Arel yell at me—"

"Elise, take it from someone who knows. You can't worry about Arel yelling or getting upset. It's what he does. I'm sure it's not personal. As for your puppy getting lost, it's what puppies do. Almost every pet owner goes through something similar."

Elise blinked back and sniffled. "Really?"

"Yes, so stop worrying and let's find your Freddie."

"How?"

"First of all, send Arel a message. Tell him to keep a civil tongue in his head. And secondly, tell him to keep the directions coming."

"But how would he know how to give me directions?"

"Never mind that. For now, take my word for it. Arel can be full of surprises. Hopefully, this is a good one."

* * *

Arel amazed himself. He'd managed to get Freddie's attention. The puppy wasn't only listening to him, he was taking directions. Arel was able to steer the dog away from the busy thoroughfare and onto a side street that was quiet. Of course, Freddie deserved some credit too. The puppy could see Arel when Arel appeared in his astral form. The puppy even tried to jump up on Arel's person. That didn't work, but Arel used his voice to praise the dog. It wasn't as rewarding to Freddie as physical contact, but when he called to the puppy, Freddie listened and trailed after him.

Arel's second task was to contact Elise. It would have been easier to connect with William, but William had his shields up. Arel was impressed with how competent Willian was getting at shutting him out.

One problem with communicating with Elise was her state of mind. It was a jumble of thoughts with a million worries coursing through. He tried to get a word in, so to speak, but she paid no attention. Finally, he resorted to another approach. He projected as powerfully as possible, linking his mind to hers. Next, he yelled out a message. The result was unexpected. Elise heard him and nearly drove off the road.

Arel didn't want to endanger her life, but every time he tried a softer approach, she ignored him. He had to shout out his message a second time. "You're going the wrong way!"

Unfortunately, Freddie's ability to tune into Arel's astral voice was excellent. He was startled every time Arel shouted. Arel tried his best to calm the puppy, but the little run-away wasn't appeased. In a state of panic, he took off running again. Arel panicked too and called after him. "Freddie, no, come back!"

His pleas were useless. Freddie was tearing up the walk, putting distance between himself and Arel. Arel's fears escalated. Even if he caught up with Freddie, he had no way to control the puppy. Astral travel wasn't helpful when you couldn't interact with the physical. Now, a small dog was going to get run over if he didn't intercede. He yelled out his frustration, filling the etheric airways with his appeal. "Please, I need some help!"

Forty-Six

ROLPHE LAY IN his bed and stared out through bloodshot eyes. He was coming to his senses after making a terrible mistake. As his brain toiled under the burden of heat and destruction, one thought was crystal clear. He shouldn't have allowed his anger and resentment to get the upper hand. He should have been grateful for what he had. Instead, he'd been a fool and given in to pettiness.

The price for his blunder was steep. His violent emotions had affected his body. He lay weak and helpless as a terrible fever ravaged his tissues and made his trillions of cells cry out for mercy. Arel's repeated warnings came to mind. If a person carried angelic blood in their veins, they shouldn't misuse that gift.

Rolphe had respected Arel's warnings for a long time. It was only recently, in a moment of weakness and self-pity that he'd given into a volatile resentment. He'd pushed away Michael's help and allowed his anger to overrule the beliefs that he lived by. He'd taken all the energy he had to create something beautiful and used it to fuel a firestorm of negativity.

But why? He had so much to love about his life. His sweetheart, Myra, wasn't just another beautiful woman. She was truly an extraordinary person whose generous heart had taken him in. Even when he disappointed her, she was patient, understanding and forgiving.

When he thought about his artwork, tears stung his dry, burning eyes. Gallery owners and his patrons had described his talent as "God-given" and incredible. He took paint, a substance that came out of tiny tubes, and created wondrous worlds of awesome beauty. Angels appeared on his canvases. They smiled back at him with glorious, beatific faces.

The list of his blessings was long. He had a little cat friend, Dantela, that was sweet and devoted. He had a beautiful home in a beautiful city. He didn't have to worry about money or buying whatever he liked. The world was his to enjoy.

Instead of reveling in his bounty, he'd thrown everything away in a rash need to vent. Like Arel, he'd also taken judgment into his hands. He'd judged Arel. He'd judged William. And he'd judged himself. He'd slammed his gavel of ignorance down hard, declaring all of them as guilty of misconduct.

But in truth, after burning in the flames of his self-condemnation, he knew he had no right to censure anyone. He didn't have enough wisdom. Life was too complex. The bigger picture was beyond his ability to understand it all.

Yet, he had to smile. Sometimes, when he was painting, he could "feel" the bigger picture. There were occasions when he caught a glimpse of the Creator's plan and how perfect it was. Those were the best of times when his heart would open wide, and his spirit would break free of boundaries. If he allowed himself to soar in the bliss of the divine, he'd hear the music of the spheres.

Recalling those times helped him to feel better. The fires receded a little. His lungs expanded, and he breathed easier. He realized that he didn't want to be angry at anyone. He wanted to be back in the fold again, in that place where angels existed.

His change of heart worked. First, his boys, who had appeared earlier, seemed pleased and encouraged him to have faith. He also saw Michael's magnificent person fade in and out a number of times. The angel made it clear that Rolphe wasn't alone.

Rolphe took comfort from his children and from Michael's visitations and the angel's soothing energy. It helped to stabilize his body. He began to relax and listen. He longed to hear heaven's music again. But this time he only heard a call for help. Arel's voice filled the etheric airways. He was asking for assistance.

Arel's plea affected Rolphe in a way that surprised him. He suddenly had the strength to sit up. After he heard Arel's request a second time, his emotions shifted from chastising himself to being a person who cared about others. It filled him with purpose. And that purpose at the moment was to respond to Arel's need. Maybe it was the father in him who was called into action. That protective side would have walked through fire to save his boys when they were alive. Now, he quickly slipped out of his body to help Arel.

* * *

Arel's frustration levels were topping the charts. Freddie was quickly putting distance between them. Arel had tried approaching the puppy and speaking softly, but nothing worked. Freddie took one look at Arel's wispy form and ran faster than ever.

After trying different approaches to the problem and getting nowhere, Arel paused. He was hoping to come up with a new plan when a sharp chill passed through his astral body. The unpleasant sensation came without warning and activated an old memory. During his first experience with astral traveling, he'd nearly died. Since that time he'd learned a lot about how to manage his travels, but that didn't mean he couldn't be spooked. When another chill hit, his body went on instant alert.

"Arel, please don't get upset. It's only me," a deep, booming voice announced.

Arel jerked around with relief. He recognized the voice. "Rolphe? What are you doing here? I thought you were sick."

Rolphe smiled back. "I heard you shouting, and I thought I better find out if you were in trouble."

Arel felt a pang of embarrassment. Rolphe's compassionate attitude was noteworthy in comparison to his own. He wished he'd been more helpful with Rolphe's situation. "I was going to visit you, but something went wrong. I ended up here instead."

Rolphe chuckled and pointed at Arel's chest. "Your heart took you where you were needed most."

"I'm afraid for my neighbor's lost dog."

"Elise's dog?"

"Yes, it's still a puppy, and it's going to get itself killed if I—" Arel paused in mid-sentence when Rolphe suddenly disappeared. "Rolphe? Where did you go?"

Arel scanned the area and realized he was alone again. "Maybe Rolphe isn't as helpful as I thought," he grumbled.

But he didn't have time to think about Rolphe. Freddie's situation came first. The puppy was already nearing the top of the street and would soon be back at the busy intersection. "Freddie, no! If you die, what's going to happen to Elise?"

As he anxiously tracked Freddie's progress, he observed something very strange. Freddie suddenly skidded to a stop, froze for a moment, then turned tail. In the next instant, he made a mad dash back towards Arel.

Arel smiled when he realized what or more correctly who had scared the puppy. "Rolphe, I'm sorry for misjudging you again. You really do have your moments!"

Rolphe hadn't just disappeared. He'd tapped into Arel's thoughts and understood the problem. He'd quickly taken action. He reappeared directly in front of Freddie, waved his ghostly hands, and startled the puppy enough to make him reverse course.

As Freddie raced towards him, Arel had to get Elise's attention again. But instead of yelling at her, he'd send her an image of where he was standing. He was at a corner, under intersecting street signs. Since she was familiar with the neighborhood, she'd know his location once she saw the street names.

Freddie arrived as he flashed out the image a second time. Again, the puppy tried to jump up on Arel and failed. After that the puppy crept under a bush with exhaustion. The little dog was panting hard and clearly ready for his adventure to end.

Five minutes later, Elise's car pulled up to the curb. Arel didn't have a chance to celebrate or even smile. Whatever was governing his movements set his astral body in motion. He felt himself speeding towards his next appointment.

* * *

Elise had never experienced anything like the strange communications that she was getting from Arel. With William's encouragement, she felt more at ease with the process, but having someone's voice in her head was unnerving.

She gave William a quick glance when the latest message came in. "I just got this very strong flash. I saw a street sign. It's not too far away. I should be there in a few minutes."

William continued clasping the console and bracing his other hand on the side door. "You seem to be very good at picking up Arel's messages. Not everyone is as receptive."

"I guess that's a good thing, right? I'm not some feeble-minded stooge who's easy to control, am I?"

"I'm sure that's not the case."

Elise noted William's rigid posture. "I'm sorry if my driving frightened you when I got that first message. Are you alright?"

"I'm still tired from my trip, that's all."

"And worried about Annabel? I think she'll get better very quickly with you here. She's an amazing person. She can be so innocent about the world one minute and so wise and brilliant the next. We've had a lot of fun since she arrived."

William pulled a hand back from the side door and sat up a straighter. "Annabel's spoken very highly of you, too."

"William?"

"Yes?"

"About Arel, it's strange, but with his messages and communications, I feel like I'm getting to know him a little better."

"What do you mean?"

"I could feel his concern for Freddie. I think he was very intent on helping."

William let out a mocking laugh. "I'm sorry, Elise. It's just that I've been on the receiving end of Arel's 'helpfulness' and his panic. I suppose he means well, but let's just remember that old saying about the road to hell being paved with good intentions."

Elise didn't have time to question William's response. She pulled up to the curb and turned off the engine. "We're here. Hopefully, Freddie's close too."

Elise jumped out of the car and immediately called out Freddie's name. As she looked at her surroundings, a small ball of white fur shot out from some nearby bushes. Elise felt her heart do a leap of triumph as she stooped down to greet Freddie. When she had him safely in her grasp, she realized she'd been almost afraid to breathe when she thought he was lost forever.

As she kissed Freddie's fuzzy head, she was mentally sending out prayers of gratitude. She hoped that Arel knew how much he'd done for her. There was an added bonus. Once she got used to hearing Arel's voice in her head, she liked having him so close. Now that he was gone, she missed him.

William tapped her shoulder. "Elise, do you want me to hold Freddie while you drive back home?"

Elise handed over the puppy and watched as Freddie made himself comfortable in William's arms. She gave William a weak smile and a fitful sigh. "You have a way with animals. Freddie likes you."

"Did I miss something, Elise? You found your puppy, but you don't look too happy."

"It's just that it was kind of nice to work with Arel like that."

"You said he shouted at you."

"Yes, but now I realize it was because he cared so much. Michael and Carey were right when they sang his praises. Arel is a very passionate man."

"I would have thought you knew that about him. The two of you did date for a couple of months."

Elise blinked back and finally shrugged. "I don't think he ever showed that side to me. He was nice and very kind, but looking back, I realize that he never expressed any real passion." Elise paused as her brows narrowed with sudden apprehension. "Do you think it's because I'm not attractive?"

William began to pet Freddie, but he avoided her question.

Elise pressed on. She needed to know if there was something about her physically that might have prevented Arel from wanting her. "William, please, you're a man, and you know me a little. So talk to me. I know I'm not a Claire, but do you think a man like Arel could find me desirable?"

This time, she didn't have to wait for her question to get a response. When William shifted his gaze and looked back at her, his pale blue eyes were intense and penetrating. His focus was so one-pointed that Elise found herself blushing. Still, William seemed to be the type of person who could be trusted to come up with an honest answer.

Finally, William looked away and cleared his throat. "All that I can say is that you would have made a very good match for him. But like I told you before, Arel can also drive a person crazy. So maybe you should forget about him and get on with your life."

"But I don't want to forget about him. I want to know why he acted the way he did. I know I wasn't the nicest, but when we first started dating, I wasn't that bad. In the beginning, I think I was waiting for Arel to give me a reason to care about the relationship. Instead, it's almost like he wanted me to be bitter. It gave him an excuse to push me aside."

Forty-Seven

AREL'S ASTRAL FORM traveled so quickly from a street in Chicago to Paris that he let out a gasp on arrival. He was still celebrating Freddie's safe return when he glanced around Rolphe's bedroom. It wasn't on fire anymore. The boys were gone, and so was Rolphe. "Dammit, what if he's dead, and his ghost was helping me find Freddie?"

"I'm sorry that I'm a cause for concern," Rolphe said as he came in from the hall.

Arel swiveled around with irritation. "Will you ever stop sneaking up on me?"

Rolphe braced a hand on the door jamb, but he didn't reply.

"There I go again, getting mad when I came here to help. I'm the one who should be apologizing."

Rolphe turned and slowly made his way down the hall. "Let's talk in the studio. I've spent too much time in my bedroom recently."

Arel followed Rolphe, wondering how the tall, muscular man looked as well as he did after being so sick. He could only guess that Rolphe's recuperative abilities were excellent. "The last time I was here, your bedroom looked like a scene out of Dante's Inferno. What happened?"

Rolphe walked over to his easel and sat down heavily. "I came to my senses. You kept telling me not to let my emotions get out of control. I should have listened."

Arel sighed. "So many times, I should have listened to myself."

"Are you still angry with me, Arel? If you are, I understand. In fact, I'll understand if you ban me from your life entirely."

Arel thought about the time he'd first spent with Rolphe. While Rolphe recuperated from a heart attack, Arel hadn't been easy to appease. Still, Rolphe tried his best to show his appreciation. At one point, Arel realized that Rolphe was sincere. "Rolphe, I once told you that I'd try to be your friend. I guess I haven't lived up to that statement."

330

Rolphe inspected one of his brushes but didn't respond.

Arel wandered over to a chair and sat down. "What the hell, Rolphe. I should be so much further along than I am."

"You've recently gone through a very painful experience. Your relationship with Claire stirred up the past."

"What are you talking about?"

"I'm sorry that I introduced you to her. I should have been more careful." Rolphe replaced the brush and looked away. "That's another thing you're always telling me, that I don't think enough about the consequences of my actions."

"You introduced me to Claire, but how were you to know that things wouldn't work out?"

"When William warned me, I should have probed deeper into who Claire was and what she thought."

Arel let out a scoffing laugh. "Don't worry about that one, Rolphe. I wouldn't have listened to you any more than I listened to William. When I was with Claire, I only saw what I wanted to see until—"

"What happened?"

"Oh please, Rolphe. It's obvious that you're able to tune into my mind."

"Yes, sometimes, when your shields are down. But I try not to pry."

"But you do pry, don't you?"

Rolphe glanced up and frowned. "Sometimes, but it's not because of curiosity. When the people I care about are having problems, I get these bad feelings." Rolphe clasped his hands in his lap. "It's difficult because I want to help, but most of the time, I can't."

Arel leaned back in his chair. He'd almost forgotten that he was in his astral body. Everything felt so real. He and Rolphe were talking as if he was there in the flesh. Yet, not many people saw Arel in his astral body. "You're very gifted, Rolphe, and I suspect that you've always had psychic abilities."

Rolphe shrugged. "Yes, whether I wanted them or not."

"What did you mean when you said that my relationship with Claire stirred up the past?"

Rolphe looked away again. "I spoke out of turn. Forget what I said."

Arel stood up and walked over to Rolphe's easel. "No, I will not forget it. If you have something to say, say it."

Rolphe shook his head. "Please, I need to take a vow of silence around you and William. Look what happened when I spoke my mind about William's childhood."

"I'm not William. He's had a problem with that subject for a very long time. I'm ready to get on with my life. If I have a problem too, I want to deal with it. So tell me what you're thinking."

Rolphe groaned. "Is that an order?"

Arel noted Rolphe's face and posture. His humility was evident, but he had his shields up. That meant he was denying Arel access to his thoughts. "What's going on with you?"

"I've been fooling myself, playing at being a father, like helping you with that puppy. But it's wrong. I have to stay out of your life, out of William's life. If you want to know something, talk to the blessed one, Michael."

"Michael? He's not going to give me a straight answer! He'll do what he always does. He'll turn every question I have back on me."

Rolphe returned a quick smile. "He believes in you. He knows you already have the answers."

Arel wandered back to his chair and sat down again. "I wish that was true. When I think about Claire, I don't understand what I did wrong. I tried to be what she wanted, and she seemed to almost hate me for it."

"What attracted you to her beside the fact that she's beautiful?"

Arel sighed. "Claire isn't just beautiful, she's her own person. She doesn't back down when it comes to her beliefs."

"But what if a person's beliefs are very different from your own? Will a relationship still work?"

"I hoped so. I tried my best to adopt Claire's view of the world."

"But why would you do that? What's wrong with how you see things?"

"Oh, please, you know my track record. I'm self-centered and small minded."

"No, you're wrong," Rolphe said in a loud, insistent voice. He stood up and walked over to where Arel sat, glaring down at him. "When I lusted after William's blood, you nearly killed yourself trying to stop me. But you also had mercy on me after my heart attack. So please, once and for all, stop putting yourself down."

Arel shrank back. Rolphe's energy suddenly went from soft and submissive to fervent and determined. Fortunately, Arel could tell Rolphe's passion was centered around a concern for Arel's well-being. "Fine, I have my moments, but when it comes to a relationship, maybe I'm not cut out for one."

Rolphe scratched his head and finally sighed. "I'm sorry, but perhaps you're not."

"So you see me as hopeless?"

"My opinion is of no consequence, but like I just told you, I think the key to your feelings is in the past."

Arel searched his memories and thought about Justina and how her death nearly destroyed him. "You're referring to the woman I first loved so long ago."

Rolphe's green eyes became dark and hard. "Oh no, you'll have to look deeper and much further into the past than that."

"Just tell me what you see," Arel insisted. "Whether or not I pursue a relationship in the future, I have to know what's standing in my way."

Rolphe hesitated again, but finally nodded. "If you think it's best then—"

Arel stood up. "Yes! Show me what I'm missing!"

* * *

Rolphe gave into Arel's orders. By allowing a much more powerful aspect of himself to take over, he was able to let Arel access a glimpse of his vision. He realized his mistake almost immediately. Arel was in too volatile a mood to delve into such appalling events. If he pursued the vision, Rolphe was afraid that Arel could get lost just as William had.

Rolphe tried to correct his error by holding on to Arel's astral body. But the harder he tried to keep Arel from witnessing something harmful, the more Arel fought him. After a short struggle, Arel's abilities suddenly intensified in such a powerful way that Arel's astral body was gone in a flash.

Rolphe was left standing alone in his studio. He was sick with dread and could hardly breathe. As he stumbled back to his chair by his easel, he was sure that Arel was headed towards his doom. The feeling was so overwhelming that Rolphe almost faltered too.

After his recent bout with his negative emotions and nearly destroying himself, he knew better than give into his bleak thoughts. Instead, he began to pray. "Oh Lord of all creation, protect my friend! Help him to find his way back to his true self. Surround him with your loving presence and keep him safe."

As Rolphe prayed, his faith was sorely tested. Were his prayers of any use when free will was involved? If a human being didn't allow themselves to be helped, the angels had no power to intervene.

Instead of giving up, Rolphe prayed even more fervently. "Please, dearest One, rally all the forces that might be there for Arel. Please find a way where there is no way. Please bring Arel back to this world unharmed."

* * *

Arel's demand that Rolphe share his vision filled the space and seemed to affect Rolphe deeply. The giant of a man straightened his shoulders, drawing himself up to his full height. When he looked at Arel, his eyes became dark, black orbs. Once they locked onto Arel, they bore into him, going deeper and deeper. That's when Arel had a terrible thought. After their previous battles, Rolphe wanted the upper hand again. A flood of distrust and fear followed. No matter what it took, Arel had to break their connection and regain control. That meant throwing everything he had into the fray.

Arel was still fighting Rolphe when the scene suddenly shifted. He wasn't in Rolphe's studio anymore. He'd escaped Rolphe's bondage only to plunge into darkness and something that reminded him of the deep end of a pool. He fought his descent, but his flailing arms and legs were useless. When he calmed down a little, he took stock of where he was. A fluid enclosure, soft and undulating, surrounded him.

Whatever he was floating in had a caustic element. It burned his skin and seared every part of his body. But he couldn't allow himself to focus on the pain. Somehow, he had to shift his attention. "Think! Try to remember what you saw before this started!"

Rolphe had talked about something buried deep in Arel's past. When he got a brief preview of Rolphe's vision, he'd sensed that he was seeing a very tiny version of himself. It didn't make sense at the time, but now it did. Before Arel was born, while he was still in his mother's womb, he wasn't wanted. His mother already abhorred the fact that she had given him life. Now, he was reliving that experience. He was remembering what it was like to exist in a place that seemed determined to rob him of life.

The thought was backed up by the waves of hate and loathing that battered him mercilessly. The torment was worse than the caustic burns. Yet he was helpless. He might have escaped Rolphe's clutches, but he couldn't fight his mother's rage.

Tossed about by terrifying contractions, he had another thought. He wasn't a fetus this time. He was revisiting his past as a miniature version of his adult self. That meant he was even more helpless than the unborn child he'd once been. In his present body, his lungs were starving, wanting oxygen. Astral body or no, he was going to drown. His mother's wish would finally be realized.

He resisted as long as he could, but his need for air won out. He had an urge to breathe that wouldn't be denied. Fluid immediately filled his lungs. Agonizing pain in his chest followed. In the midst of his misery, he glimpsed the face of a woman, the woman who wanted him dead, his mother's face.

Was his mother correct? Was it a mistake to think he had a right to live? Michael was always trying to tell him that he was a part of the Divine, but being in his mother's womb, experiencing what she felt was devastating and primal. He didn't know how to fight her malice. It was like the fluid in his lungs. It wanted to obliterate his existence.

As he was blacking out, he heard a muffled voice. "Drop your shields, Arel! You have to drop your shields!" He tried to hold on to the voice, but everything was fading. He began to drift away, entering the unknown. Darkness beckoned as he faced his death.

* * *

William stepped into Arel's foyer and barely shut the door when he heard Michael's shout. He stiffened with alarm. Angels didn't yell. When Michael shouted again, William ran to the stairs that led to the lower level. He went down them so fast that he nearly tripped. "Michael! Where are you?"

As he raced towards the sound of the angel's voice, he realized what Michael was saying. He was ordering Arel to lower his shields. That could mean only one thing. Arel was in trouble, and Michael couldn't help. When William got to Arel's bedroom, he came to an abrupt halt. As soon as he saw Arel stretched out on the floor and Michael kneeling over him, he was tempted to think the worst.

Michael looked up with troubled eyes. "I'm sorry, William, but I couldn't get through to him in time."

William pushed Michael out of the way and knelt down. "His lips are blue!" He grabbed for Arel's wrist. There was no pulse. "Michael, do something! He's dying!"

Michael shook his head. "He's not dying. He's dead."

William took a moment to digest the information. "How can that be? A half hour ago he was helping Elise find her puppy. Did he have a heart attack? We have to do CPR!"

"He's already moving towards the other side, William. If he doesn't want to come back this time—"

"Why wouldn't he want to come back? He's free of Claire, and Elise is crazy about him. He has everything to live for."

"Something happened when he visited Rolphe."

William felt a sudden burst of outrage. "Rolphe? Again?"

Michael held up a hand. "Please don't jump to conclusions. Arel insisted that Rolphe—"

"Conclusions? Arel went to see Rolphe, right?"

"Yes."

"And now Arel is dead, correct?"

Michael nodded. "Yes."

"Those are facts! But we're wasting time. I have to go after Arel before he snaps that damn silver cord."

Michael hesitated. "What do you mean?"

"You know exactly what I mean. Arel tossed me out of the afterlife. It's time that I return the favor."

"Arel had very special powers at his command."

"Dammit, are you saying I'm not as gifted as he is? And if the answer is 'yes,' then you'll have to help me. Boost my powers, Michael! Please, I don't want any excuses. Help me!"

* * *

William hadn't expected Michael to be so quick to respond. He could only guess that the angel was as anxious to get Arel back as he was. William's part was easy in one way, difficult in another. He was accustomed to directing his own actions. In this case, he had to totally surrender to Michael's powerful energy.

Thankfully, he soon lost himself to a feeling of ease. Even his fears about Arel's fate dissolved for a few minutes as he was transported out of his body. Once he was in his astral form, Michael's energy enhanced William's tracking abilities. He was able to focus on Arel's energy trail. Wherever Arel had gone, William was determined to follow.

His journey through other dimensions ended up in a dismal park setting. The skies were stormy, the trees were barren and the flowers in the beds were all dying. He had a moment of dread when he thought he might get trapped in the bleak place.

He didn't allow himself to dwell on his fears. He scanned for Arel, but the man was nowhere to be seen. It didn't make sense. William felt Arel's energy. He had to be very close. "Arel! Arel, where are you?"

"Stop shouting that horrible name!"

The reply made William swivel around. His gaze settled on a bench located a few yards away. It was occupied by someone very small. "Arel? Is that you?"

"I told you to stop saying that name!" The voice that cried out was higher-pitched, but very insistent.

William quickly approached the bench and pulled back. A little boy was sitting there. He was pale and small, with lots of dark curls and a rigid posture. When the boy glanced up, William recognized the boy's golden eyes. "Arel, is it you?"

The young boy bulked. "I hate my name."

William wondered if he'd traveled back in time. Then he remembered that time had no meaning in some alternate realities. He moved closer. "Why don't you like your name? What's wrong with it?"

The child pulled in on himself, clasping his hands tightly in his lap. "Mother said my name belongs to the devil. That's why she gave it to me. She said I'm a curse."

William sat down on the bench. "Your mother is wrong."

The child flinched and returned a disapproving scowl. "How would you know? Have you met my mother?"

"No, but I'm your friend."

"You're not my friend. I don't know you."

William couldn't believe it. Arel's child self was just as obstinate as the adult Arel. "How old are you?"

"I'm five. In the summer, I'll be six, old enough for my brother to take me riding." The boy paused and let out a great sigh. "Unless father doesn't let him. Father says I'm too excitable, and I scare the animals. But I don't mean to."

"I'm sure you don't."

The child looked up with wide, hopeful eyes. "You believe me?"

"Yes, of course I do."

"Nobody believes me except for my brother and my angel friend. But my brother is always away at school, and I'm the only one who sees my angel. My nurse says that my angel isn't real."

William crossed his arms. "Your nurse is a ninny."

The child laughed. "That's funny, but don't let her hear you, or she'll use her willow switch on your legs. And that really hurts."

"Thank you. I appreciate your concern."

The child let out another big sigh. "I don't like it when people get in trouble."

William put out his hand. "Let me introduce myself. My name is William, and when you grow up, we'll be the best of friends."

The child took William's hand and gave it a quick shake. Then he sat back and stared straight ahead. "That's very nice, William, but I don't think I'll grow up."

"Why wouldn't you grow up?"

The child leaned in and lowered his voice. "Mother wants me dead. She's already tried to kill me once."

"She what? She tried to kill you? When?"

The boy looked away and began to rub the arm of the bench.

"Arel, please, when did she try to kill you?"

"When . . . when I was in her . . . her stomach. But I didn't die, and she was very angry about that."

"I'm sorry. That was a terrible thing to do."

"Mother hates me, but I wish she wouldn't." The child looked away and rubbed the bench again. "My mother is beautiful. Father seems very proud of her and buys her pretty necklaces. But I don't think she'll ever like me. That's why I have to go away."

"Where are you going?"

"I heard mother praying. When I walked past her bedroom, her voice was very loud. She told God she was sorry, but she hoped I'd get sick and die. Then the house wouldn't be cursed anymore."

"Don't think about such things."

"My angel says that too. I wish he was real. Then I'd have a friend."

"Arel, listen to me. I've met angels, too. They are real, and you have to listen to the one that visits you."

The little boy's eyes widened in surprise. "You've met angels?"

"Yes, but it's very important that you forget all this silliness about curses. You're a very fine boy, and you're going to grow up to be a very fine man. Can you remember that?"

"I suppose."

"I want you to promise me that you'll remember our talk, and that I care about you."

"Thank you. My brother cares about me too. I want to grow up. I really do, then I can be like him."

"Promise me, Arel, promise me that you won't die, that you'll find a way to grow up no matter what your mother thinks."

"I could try."

"No, that's not good enough. You have to promise."

The child's brows narrowed in contemplation. After several moments, he finally responded. "Very well, I promise."

William let out a breath that he'd been holding. "Good, I'm glad that's settled."

The child smiled up at him. "Thank you, sir."

As William smiled back, he noticed that the chill in the air was gone. He glanced around and discovered that the park had changed drastically. The trees were leafed out in rich, vibrant, green foliage. Roses of every color were blooming along the garden path, and birdsong filled the air.

When he turned back to the child, the boy was gone. After a moment of concern, William contented himself with the promise he'd coaxed out of the little boy. Hopefully, that promise would have an effect on the boy's future life. William was still giving the concept some thought when he heard someone behind him. He looked around and saw the adult Arel standing a few feet away. The man was smiling. "Arel, it's great to see you!"

"William, are you going to do what you came here for?" Arel asked.

William leapt out of his seat. "I was looking for you, but the most amazing thing happened. I talked to your child self!"

"Yes, that's fine, but you came here to kick me out of this place. If you do, then you can be pleased with yourself and even the score."

William scowled. He'd come on a mission of mercy, and Arel seemed to be taking the whole matter of his death too casually. "I wanted to keep you from crossing over because I care about you."

Arel stepped closer and put an arm around William's shoulder. "I know. You're being that best friend that you promised you'd be. But now it's time for us to go back."

"Good idea—" William didn't get to finish his sentence. He was still commenting when Arel gave him a hard shove forward. His thrashing arms did nothing to stop him from falling. The descent was so swift and disorientating that he shut his eyes. Everything was spinning. He stopped fighting the sensation when he heard Arel's laughter.

"Relax, Will, I've got this," Arel chuckled.

William wanted to object to Arel's cavalier attitude, but he was overwhelmed by the feeling that he wasn't just falling, he was falling asleep. He knew that Arel had something to do with his shifting mindset. It didn't matter. In the next instant, he drifted off into a deep slumber.

* * *

Michael was positioned close to Arel, watching Arel's chest rise and fall. When Carey joined them, Michael smiled. "William was determined to bring Arel back, and he succeeded."

Carey knelt down next to William. "From what I can tell, William is dozing peacefully."

"I called to him a couple of times, but he seems to be in a very deep state of sleep."

"How about Arel?"

Before Michael answered, Arel let out a soft moan and opened his eyes. After blinking a couple of times, he reached up and touched Michael's arm. "Michael, is it you? Am I back?"

Michael nodded. "Yes, you're back."

"William? What about William?"

"He's back too."

Arel tightened his grip on Michael's arm. "Help me up, please."

Michael hesitated. "Maybe you should take a moment to—"

Arel heaved himself into a sitting position and rubbed his eyes. "I'm fine."

"Arel, you might want to take it easy," Michael cautioned. "Your body has been through—"

"Michael, my body has your blood, remember?" Arel looked around and saw Carey helping William to stand up. "What happened to William? I thought you said that he was okay. Why does he look like he's in a stupor?"

Michael took Arel's arm and got him to his feet too. "I think you had something to do with his condition."

Arel paused and smiled. "Oh yes, you're right. He looked so panicked coming back into his body. I had to do something to help him relax. He's not as tough as I am."

Michael laughed. "William is very strong, but he's still recuperating from being lost in the dream state."

"Thank goodness we're both back to the land of the living, and we can forget about all that."

Michael crossed his arms. "Yes, that's true, but Arel, you just had quite the experience too. Do you want to talk about any of it?"

Arel's eyes flared. "No, I don't."

Forty-Eight

WILLIAM WOKE UP appreciating the comfort of the bed where he lay. He felt better physically. He wasn't so tired. He felt so contented that he didn't want to open his eyes. He was tempted to remain where he was and simply appreciate the moment. It was only a flashback of almost losing Arel that made him panic. Was Arel safely back on the earth plane?

It took some effort, but William forced his drowsy eyes to open. When he did, he saw Annabel. She was standing by the bed. "Where am I? Where's Arel?"

"My goodness, you've been asleep for hours, William," Annabel said with a smile. "You must have needed a good nap."

William quickly sat up and rubbed his eyes. "Yes, I guess so, but about Arel, is he okay?"

"He's in the living room. He's reading."

William stared back, trying to get his bearings. Arel had just returned from the dead. How could he be in the living room reading? "Are you kidding?"

"Arel was very sweet when I got here. He asked about how I was feeling, then he explained that you were worn out and suggested that I should let you sleep." Annabel's smile turned playful. "I couldn't help myself. I had to check on you. I'm so happy that you came to Chicago."

William let himself fall back against his pillows. He studied Annabel and sighed. "You look like you're feeling better."

"I am. In fact, according to Elise, I'm over the worst of my cold."

William reached out for her hand. "I missed you."

Annabel's face brightened even more. "I missed you, too, but at least Elise was there."

"I met Elise and talked to her. She seems very nice."

"She's been more than nice since I got sick. I'm afraid I was rather difficult, but she never let it faze her."

"It's too bad that her relationship with Arel didn't work out. He could use a person who doesn't get fazed."

"Yes, that's true," Annabel laughed. "Anyway, I better get back to Elise's and get my things together. Arel said we can use this bedroom. He's sleeping downstairs while we're here."

"Do you need me to come too?"

"No, rest for a bit. I'm sure that Elise will want to give me a hand."

William pulled her close and kissed her lips before he let her go. "See you soon."

After Annabel was gone, William thought about the past couple of months. It hadn't been an easy time for either of them. Happily, something had recently changed. When he'd looked into Annabel's beautiful, emerald eyes, he knew that the love that had brought them together was still there. He began to smile as he let himself imagine ways to rekindle their mutual passion.

Unfortunately, his reveries were interrupted when he thought about Arel again. William had been relieved with the way things turned out when they were on the other side. After his conversation with the younger version of Arel, the adult Arel wasn't just cheerful. He acted as if he was ready to start over and enjoy life.

But William knew from experience that the heavenly version of Arel and the earth-bound Arel could be very different. That being the case, Arel might not take the time to integrate the knowledge he'd gleaned. Instead, his old habit of avoiding his emotions might be allowed to have free rein. William felt exhausted again just thinking about that scenario.

* * *

After seeing Annabel to the door, Arel walked back into the living room and sat down on the sofa. He glanced at Michael. "She seems happy."

Michael continued to stare out the front window. "Yes, she does."

Arel grabbed his book and was about to go back to reading, but he could feel Michael's energy. The angel generated a feeling that was normally even and serene, but that wasn't the case now. "Michael, talk to me. What's going through that angelic mind of yours?"

Michael hesitated. When he finally stared back at Arel, his clear, blue eyes were laced with an uneasy glimmer. "Another close call, my friend, that's what's going on."

Arel threw his book aside and sucked in some air. He didn't want to think about "close calls" or all the unsettled feelings in his gut. He wanted to forget everything for a while. He wanted life to feel normal for a change. "Michael, look at me. I'm fine. There was a problem during my astral trip, but—"

"Arel, you almost checked out permanently. And once again, I couldn't help because your shields were up."

"I'm sorry if I upset you—"

"It's not that. I respect your decisions, but I'm trying to understand what you want."

"I'm here, aren't I?"

"Yes, but if William hadn't gone after you—"

"But I didn't plan on checking out. Things got out of hand. As for my shields, I was trying to protect myself from Rolphe. Everything escalated so quickly that I forgot about letting you help."

"Yes, but you seem very removed from what you experienced."

Arel tightened his jaw, reaching for something to hold on to that helped him navigate the latest episode of craziness. "I've been through so much in the past couple of years. Maybe I'm starting to take it all in stride."

A voice answered from the foyer. William stood there with his arms crossed. "Oh, give us a break, Arel. You don't take things in your stride. You trample problems like some wild horse when is sees a rattlesnake. Afterwards, you check on what's left and trample the problem again just for good measure."

Arel smiled back. William had arrived in Chicago that day, and he'd already played the hero. He was a good friend. "And you're the knight on a mission. You like to rush in and save people."

William trudged over to a recliner and sat down. "I found you dead. What else was I supposed to do?"

Arel stared at the sofa arm and shrugged. "Good point, but it was an accident."

"Michael said you were in your astral form, trying to help Rolphe."

"That's one problem I didn't have to trample. By the time I got to his apartment, Rolphe had already cured himself."

"And you let him attack you?"

Michael interrupted. "From my perspective, I don't believe Rolphe attacked anyone."

Arel picked at the linen nap of the sofa fabric. His head felt spacey when he thought about Rolphe. He didn't have the energy to figure out the man's motives. "If you say so, I only know that I wanted answers to what happened with Claire. Rolphe seemed to know something, so I asked him for information. That's when he started staring at me, and I couldn't break the connection."

William frowned back. "He did the same thing with me, and you know how I ended up."

Arel focused his attention on Michael. "So how do you explain what happened, Michael? Is Rolphe reverting to some former, evil self?"

Michael stared out the window again. Chicago was in the grip of an early cold spell. The tree in the front yard had lost its leaves, but it was host to a half dozen black birds. When he replied, his voice was quiet and thoughtful. "Rolphe has power too, like both of you. But that's not the problem here. Even though he's tried to prove himself, I don't think either of you have made your peace with the past."

"It's hard to forget the past when it includes someone trying to murder you," William complained.

"Will's right," Arel sighed. "Rolphe professes to be a changed man, but when I was with him, he seemed ill at ease, even a little scary."

"What do you mean?" William asked.

"Like I said, I couldn't break the hold he had on me."

Michael turned around and smiled. "I think he was holding on to you, but not to control you. After what happened to William, I think Rolphe was trying to keep you from losing yourself in his vision."

William leaned forward. "What was his vision, Arel?"

Arel stilled his hand on the sofa arm. "I don't want to discuss it."

"Arel, you nearly died. I think you need to talk about what happened."

"Look Will, you already know the story about my mother. She hated me. So there's nothing new to talk about."

William leaned forward. "I never knew she tried to get rid of you before you were born, did you?"

345

"There was gossip among the servants when I was a boy, but I think my father intervened on my behalf. Maybe he wanted another son like Aldwin, someone fair and perfect. Then he got me."

William's brows narrowed with concern. "Arel, there was never anything wrong with you. I thought you finally knew that."

Arel stood up. He was suddenly too tired to argue with William. "Tell that to Elise or Claire. Neither of them thought I was good enough. So maybe my mother got it right." He started out of the room. "Anyway, I'm going to get some rest. I think 'dying' is catching up with me."

The doorbell rang as Arel walked through the foyer. He glanced back at William. "Maybe it's Annabel."

Arel opened the door and was surprised to see Elise. Then he remembered Freddie. "Hi Elise, is everything okay with your puppy?"

Elise frowned. "Yes, Freddie is fine. Thank you for your help."

Arel nodded. "You're welcome."

William joined them. "Does Annabel need something?"

Elise shook her head. "Annabel is fine. She's packing. But I wanted to talk to Arel."

William stepped forward. "Oh, then maybe I'll go over to your house and—"

Elise held up her hand. "No, please stay, William. I want you here too."

Arel sighed. "This might not be a good time, Elise. I'm not at my best."

Elise's frown deepened. "Sorry, but I have to speak my piece, then I'll go."

Arel reluctantly backed up and gestured for Elise to come in. "Let's talk in the living room."

* * *

When Elise decided that she needed to talk to Arel, it felt like the right thing to do. But when she stood on Arel's porch, she had to calm her nervous stomach. The matter she'd come to discuss could be embarrassing.

When she broke up with Arel, she'd blamed herself for everything that had gone wrong. But after talking to William, she began to see their involvement in a different light. She'd come to the conclusion that Arel had played a significant part in the problems they'd had. Before they parted company permanently, she wanted to be clear about both their roles in their failed relationship.

She almost lost her resolve to tackle the subject when Arel answered the door. His face looked tired and stressed, and his skin was very pale. Even so, he asked about Freddie. When Elise explained her need to talk to him, Arel hesitated, but finally gave in.

Once Arel stepped aside and welcomed her into the living room, Elise saw Michael. Her wise advisor was leaving the room. "Michael, please come back. If Carey is around, I'd like him here too."

Arel gave her a confused look. "I thought you wanted to talk to me. Why do you want them here?"

Elise cleared her throat, put her shoulders back and stood up straighter. "I want everyone to hear what I have to say. If I'm out of line, I'm counting on your friends to let me know it."

Carey walked in from the foyer, waved to Elise and took a seat.

With the room quiet and with everyone staring at her with expectant eyes, Elise blushed. What if she was wrong and accused Arel of something that wasn't true? She didn't want to add to his stress. The man had never looked so worn. Still, she pressed on. "Arel, ever since we broke up, I've been apologizing to you. And my apology was called for. I did behave poorly to say the least. However, I don't think I was the only one at fault."

Arel's gaze instantly sparked a little. "What do you mean? I'm sure that I always treated you with respect and kindness."

Elise met his questioning eyes. "I know you did. But did you ever think to treat me like someone you were interested in as a partner? Looking back on our time together, I realize that you never considered me as someone to love passionately and with all your heart. But that's how I looked at you. I know you have your shortcomings, but for me, you were everything I've always wanted. And now, I realize that deep down, you never intended for our relationship to succeed."

Arel stared at her with the look of a child being accused of something they knew nothing about. "Elise, I'm at a loss, but I'm sorry if I've hurt you or misled you. I truly am."

Elise bit her lip. Arel's voice was strained when he spoke. And the worst part was that she believed what he said. He didn't seem to understand a word she'd told him. It was an unexpected blow. That's when she knew she'd been counting on a totally different response.

After her admission of love and her accusations, she felt foolish and exposed. She'd done nothing to change the situation. She only made it worse. There was only one thing left to do. She had to let go of Arel once and for all.

She held out a hand to him. "Goodbye, Arel, and good luck with your life. I wish you the best."

Arel gave her a weak smile and shook her hand.

She quickly pulled away, turned and briskly walked to the front door. Once outside, she hurried down the stairs and started running. But she didn't go back to her house. She continued down the street, trying to wipe away her tears. Once she was safely on her way, they flowed freely, coming from a place of heartache that she'd never experienced before.

* * *

Arel's eyes were vacant as he stared at the front door. He knew he should feel something about what had just happened, but he couldn't access any significant feelings. The numbness started after the breakup with Claire. Later, he found it impossible to care about Rolphe's condition. Now, Elise had just poured her heart out, and he still couldn't rouse himself from his apathy. He turned to look at William, then Carey, and finally Michael. "What just happened?"

William crossed his arms and directed his attention to the carpet as if he needed to study it. Carey stared back, but he didn't answer. Michael was the only one to react. He stood up, came over to Arel and put a hand on Arel's shoulder. "Elise just said goodbye, dear friend. That's what happened."

Arel rubbed his brow, trying to make sense of what Elise told him. "Did she say something about me, something about how I was everything she wanted?"

William stood up and started out of the room. "Forget it, Arel. Forget the whole idea of love. I don't think you're ready to take on a relationship."

Arel followed William into the foyer. "Of course I am. I was totally smitten with Claire. We were going to be married."

348

William turned and laughed. "Oh please, you chose someone who was emotionally unavailable."

Arel stepped back and thought about Claire and how much he'd wanted her, how much he wanted someone who loved him. "She rejected me! What was I supposed to do?"

"Sure you think that, but in the end, when she walked out on you, did you go after her? Did you fight to stay in that relationship? I don't think so."

"I thought it was hopeless! She made it clear that I wasn't the person she wanted in her life? How could I deal with that attitude?"

William continued down the hall. "I don't know! I just brought you back from the dead. I'm too tired to try to figure out more of your problems."

"William, I'm grateful, but—"

William turned and huffed out a reply. "But what? Nothing is ever enough for you. Poor Elise, I feel for her. Trying to love a person like you is impossible. You could drive a saint crazy."

Arel glared back. "You think I'm impossible to live with? Is that what you're saying?"

William turned around again. "You won't let anyone in, Arel! Sure you go around helping puppies and saving people, but you're so walled off that you won't even trust an angel!"

"That's so untrue! If I hadn't trusted Michael, I'd still be hunting rats in an alley!"

"Fine, but you sure didn't trust him today! When it comes to simply being open to life, you're as unavailable as Claire."

"We'll just see about that!" Arel shouted as he returned to the living room. He went over to where Michael was standing by a recliner. "Do you agree with William, Michael? Am I like Claire?"

Before Michael could answer Arel's question, William came striding forward. He pushed Arel aside and asked Michael one of his own questions. "Michael, could you and Carey leave us alone for a while?"

Michael stepped back. "Of course."

After the two angels excused themselves, Arel crossed his arms. "Why did you ask them to leave? Were you afraid Michael would agree with me?"

"No! This has nothing to do with me being afraid."

"Then what's the problem?"

William's blue eyes hardened with resentment. "Don't you get it? Michael's an angel! All he can see is your soul! He can't see how screwed up you are as a human being!"

Arel narrowed his brows with resentment too. "I'm not the only one who's screwed up! You've been running away from yourself since you were a boy!"

"Maybe so, but at least I had enough guts to love somebody and get married!"

"Big deal! You've acted like you've regretted falling in love ever since!"

William sucked in a breath. "But I don't feel like that now. I know how lucky I am to have Annabel in my life. And from now on, I'm going to be there for her."

Arel paused and blinked back. He could always tell when William was revealing some truth about himself. "Really? What happened to change your mind?"

"When I was trapped in that horrible, dream world, I learned quite a bit about the part of myself that I'd rejected. I realized how much I'd given up in the process."

Arel smiled. "I've always known that part of you, Will. Even if you tried to bury it, it was still there. It's the part of you that cared about me."

William smiled too. "Yes, you're right."

Arel grabbed for his chest. "Did you just agree with me? I think that's the first time you've ever told me that I was right about something. You always tell me that I'm an idiot."

William shrugged. "Actually, when I talked to that little boy that you once were, I found him to be very bright and very courageous. He helped me to understand how strong we can be if we don't give up on ourselves."

Arel walked over to the couch and sat down. "I wish I felt courageous now. Instead, all that I feel is tired."

"Of course you feel tired. You died a few hours ago."

Arel slowly rubbed his hand over the arm of the sofa. "Do you want to know something?"

"What's that?"

"Elise has it all wrong. She thinks I was some kind of cold fish, but it's not true. When I was first with her, there were times when I wanted to take her in my arms. I wanted to tell her how beautiful she was. I wanted to make love to her. But I didn't think she wanted me. Eventually, I guess it was easier to think she had a problem than to face my own fears."

William slumped down in a recliner. "You two have a lot in common. You're both too hard on yourselves. It's too bad you can't just start over."

Arel jerked to attention. "Is that an option? Do you think Elise would give it another go?"

William sighed. "Didn't you see her face when she left? She's devastated over the thought of losing you."

Arel pressed down hard on the sofa arm, clutching at the upholstery. "Are you sure?"

When Arel asked the question, he felt like he couldn't get enough air. He had to fight to take another breath and gasped out his fears. "William, the truth is that I don't think I can face more rejection. After feeling how much my mother hated me, maybe I do need those walls you talked about."

William laid his head back on the sofa, ignoring the urgency in Arel's voice. "Elise isn't like your mother. So get your tired butt off that sofa and go after her."

Arel sucked in another breath. For a moment, he almost felt like he was drowning again. "I don't know. I'm so confused about life, about love."

William closed his eyes. "Please, if you can't trust yourself, trust me."

Arel heard the deep weariness in William's voice. It wasn't a weariness that came from lack of sleep. This weariness came from a lifetime of trying to hold on to life and find out its meaning. But William didn't just hold on to his own life, he held on to Arel's life too. He'd been there for Arel even when Arel was at his worst and taken his anger and rage out on William. In other words, William was the exact opposite of Arel's mother. Even though William had been brutally wounded as a child too, he kept fighting to keep Arel on the earth.

Then there was Michael. Michael had tried every way he knew to help Arel believe in himself. Carey gave it his best shot too. All in all, Arel had been given proof after proof that he was cared about and wanted. Yet, he'd still managed to ignore what was so plain to see.

As he allowed the truth to filter through, he felt like he could finally breathe again. As soon as his strength began to return, he forced himself off the sofa. He went over to where William was sitting and put his hand on William's shoulder. "I do trust you, Will, more than anyone. Thank you for always believing in me."

William opened his eyes a little and stared back. "Elise believes in you, too."

William's statement, so matter-of-fact, shifted something in Arel's chest. It was a strange sensation. As the feeling intensified, it was almost like ice melting in spring. Warmth began to drive out the numbness.

William glanced up again. "Remember when we came back from that battle on your alternate world? I told you that I saw someone in your future."

"Yes, what about it?"

"That someone was Elise. I'm sure of it."

"Why didn't you tell me sooner?"

"I didn't know. I only met Elise today."

Arel paused and let himself remember his encounters with his pretty neighbor. But it wasn't the Elise who was angry or bitter. It was the Elise who loved to laugh and dance. It was the Elise who could change into a fairy, a magical creature with short, spiky hair who sprinted across his lawn in a Minnie Mouse shirt. It was the Elise who got down on bloody knees, ordering angels around as she tried to save Arel's carpet. It was the Elise who had the courage to come over and confess her love for him. Now, she'd not only left his house, but possibly his life.

Arel started for the front door. "I've got to go after her, Will!"

William laughed. "Of course you do, you idiot."

Arel laughed too. He had been an idiot, but now he didn't care. The only thing that mattered was finding Elise. He flung open the door and charged out into the cold. Once he reached the street, he stopped. He looked up and down the sidewalk. "Oh hell, I don't think she went home, so which way did she go?"

He suddenly smiled. Thanks to Michael's blood, he had powers at his command. He could tune into Elise's whereabouts. He relaxed and let his mind clear. After that, it only took a few moments before he saw Elise in his mind's eye. She was sitting on a bench in a park located a couple of blocks away.

When he noted how sad she looked, he began to sprint down the walk. By the time he got to the park, he was out of breath, but that didn't stop him from rushing over to where Elise was sitting. He stood a few feet away, gasping and trying to think about what to say.

Elise didn't notice him. Her eyes were red, and she was sniffling. She seemed deep in thought as she stared at the tissue she was gripping.

"Elise, I'm so sorry," he whispered. He held out a hand and called to her again. "Elise?"

Elise startled and looked up with surprise. When she saw his hand, she stared at it for a long moment as if she had to figure out what to do next. Finally, she took hold of it and stood up.

Arel carefully pulled her into his arms and held her close. As he did, he realized how small she was, how he could lay his head on top of hers. As he rocked her gently, it felt so natural to be with her. The familiar feeling made his heart stir again. It wasn't a gentle stirring, but rather one that fought the boundaries of flesh and blood. The feeling was so consuming that he was flung into the ethers again. For an instant, he was that young boy in the garden, the one who talked to William. That boy had so much love in his heart. It was a love that he wanted to share in spite of his mother's hatred.

When Arel returned to himself and held Elise in his arms, he was determined to leave his fears behind. In a moment of abandon, he blurted out his feelings. "Elise, I think I might be in love with you."

His announcement had an immediate effect. Elise pulled away and stared up at him with teary eyes. But the more she looked at him, the more her gaze crystallized into one of concern.

"Oh my, Arel, for an instant I almost let myself think that you share my feelings."

Arel stepped back. "Is there a problem with that?"

"Yes, I don't believe you're yourself." Elise put her hand to his cheek. "You poor dear, you told me that you're not well. But I didn't listen. Now I realize you've come running after me when you should be in bed." Elise dug a hand in her pocket and pulled out her phone. "I'll call Michael and tell him to come pick you up."

"But Elise, I'm fine."

Elise shook her head as she made her call. "You're hot and probably running a fever. Maybe you have the same bug that Annabel has."

Arel paused and felt his forehead. Elise was right. He did seem to have an elevated temperature. But for him, it was almost normal. "Don't worry about it, Elise."

Elise stilled his protest by putting up a hand as she talked to Michael. When she finished her conversation, she pocketed her phone. Taking Arel's arm, she started walking towards the street. "Michael will meet us along the way. In the meantime, try to calm yourself, Arel. Conserve your energy."

Elise was so sincere and convincing that Arel did as he was told. A few minutes later, Michael pulled up to the curb in the Mustang. As soon as Elise saw Michael, she went into full-out nursing mode, giving Michael directions.

"Michael, take Arel home and make sure he rests. After overexerting himself trying to help me, he's probably coming down with the flu."

Arel didn't have a chance to say anything more. Elise helped him into the passenger seat of the car, waved goodbye and started walking back home on her own.

Arel frowned as Michael put the car in gear and started home too. "Elise thinks I'm ill. Maybe she's right."

Michael glanced over with a smile. "She's very concerned about your welfare."

"But Michael, when I was holding her, all that I felt was this wonderful, blissful warmth."

"Yes, I'm sure you did."

A short time later, the Mustang pulled into Arel's garage. As Arel got out of the car, the door to the house opened.

William stared out with curiosity. "Arel, what happened?"

Arel slammed the car door shut. "First I fall in love with someone who could care less if I was on my sick bed dying. Now, with Elise, it's the opposite. She'd probably call for an ambulance if I skinned a knee. I just can't win, William."

"Maybe Elise needs some time to sort things out."

"She is right about one thing. I'm exhausted. I need to go to bed and get some sleep."

Forty-Nine

ELISE SAT AT her kitchen table listening. With Annabel gone, the house was quiet. It was the perfect time to think about her recent experience. When Arel came after her and found her in the park, he talked about a change of heart. He'd mentioned the word, love. She was instantly thrilled. She wrote about those kinds of happy endings.

But standing next to him and realizing that Arel's face was flushed with fever, she'd come to her senses. Things that felt too good to be true were often too good to be true. That's when she started to put some facts together.

Earlier, when she visited Arel, he'd told her that it wasn't a good time. But did she listen? No, she'd been pushy and ignored his protest. Afterwards, she'd expressed her deepest feelings and left the house crying. "Arel is probably ill, but he forced himself to come after me just like he'd helped me find Freddie.

The more she thought about Arel's behavior, the more convinced she was that she was right. But being right didn't make her feel better. She was back where she'd started. She was in a one-sided relationship when she needed to be getting on with her life.

She stood up and went to the counter. There were still dishes in the sink from breakfast. She was about to tackle a skillet when the doorbell rang. The sound roused Freddie from his nap. The puppy was instantly up and running to the door. Elise wished she felt so enthusiastic. Instead, a kind of lethargy was taking over as she picked up Freddie and opened the door. When she saw her visitors, she tried to smile. "Annabel, William! Annabel, did you forget something?"

Annabel smiled and kissed Elise's cheek. "No, we slipped out while Arel was sleeping."

Elise pulled back as a shiver coursed through her body. The physical part of her seemed intent on reacting to Arel's name.

Annabel and William both gave her looks of concern.

355

"Is something wrong, Elise?" William asked.

Elise took some fortifying breaths and shook her head. "No, it's just been a demanding day."

Annabel took Elise's arm and ushered her into the living room. "Let's all sit down and chat."

Elise didn't protest. She was happy to have some company.

Once everyone was seated, William crossed his arms and frowned at Elise. "Does your look of confusion have something to do with Arel?"

Elise avoided William's eyes and turned her attention to Freddie. The puppy was lying on the cushion next to her as she petted him. "I'm worried about Arel. I think he might be ill. Is he running a fever again?"

"He's fine," Annabel insisted.

Elise stalled. "Fine? I don't think so. Did he tell you that he thinks he's in love with me?"

Annabel's face lit up a bit brighter. "Yes, he did. He said that you were pleased with the idea at first, but then—"

Elise caressed one of Freddie's ears. "I suppose I would be pleased if I didn't think he was delusional."

William sucked in an uneasy breath. "Let me assure you that Arel will always be slightly delusional. It's one of his many charms."

Elise paused and stared back. "I don't know what that means."

Annabel frowned at William and then back at Elise. "Elise, as your friend and Arel's friend, I'd like to warn you that a life with Arel might be challenging."

William looked heavenward. "That's an understatement."

Elise stiffened. "Define challenging, Annabel."

"His moods can shift dramatically—"

"His moods?" Elise asked. "When he said he loved me, was he just expressing a mood or was he physically sick?"

William put his hand on Annabel's arm. "We're getting off track, Annabel."

Annabel nudged William back. "Please, let me explain." When she looked at Elise, Annabel's eyes were intense, but she kept her voice steady and soft. "What I'm saying is that Arel tends to be a bit too enthusiastic at times."

"Like when he was in love with Claire?" Elise asked.

Annabel shook her head. "That wasn't exactly love. That was Arel trying to please someone. It's an old pattern that didn't work out. With you, I'm sure he'd be very different."

Elise felt her confusion mounting. "He wouldn't want to please me?"

Annabel laughed. "Of course, he would. But in a different way."

Elise rubbed her temples. "I'm sorry, but I think I'm more mixed up than ever."

William cleared his throat. "Maybe this will help. Arel can be difficult. He can be crazy. But the bottom line is that if he commits to you, he'll do everything in his power to be there for you."

"That's true," Annabel said as she sniffled. "Anyway, I hope we cleared a few things up. Arel seems to think you have the wrong idea about his feelings."

"I don't have a clue about his feelings, Annabel."

William stood up. "I'm sure you'll figure it out."

Elise picked up Freddie and held him close. "I doubt that, but thank you for the encouragement."

Annabel stood up too and took a tissue out of her pocket. "We better go. I still have this cold."

William put an arm around Annabel's shoulders. "I told you not to overdo."

Elise noted that Annabel's nose wasn't as red as it had been, but she was still a bit pale. "William is right, Annabel. But maybe with your cold, Arel should keep his distance. No matter what you think, he needs to take care of himself."

Annabel gave William a thoughtful look. "Perhaps, you're right. Both William and Arel have been through a lot recently."

As they all headed to the foyer, the doorbell rang again. Elise was surprised that she was getting so much company. She called out to her newest visitor. "Come in! The door's open!"

A moment later, Carey let himself in. As soon as he saw Annabel and William, he hesitated. "What are you two doing here?"

Annabel used the tissue to dab at her nose. "We were just chatting with Elise."

Carey smiled back. "Oh, that's nice."

* * *

Elise was sure something was wrong with Carey when he said he didn't want a donut. But no matter, his smile seemed genuine as he sat at the kitchen table. He agreed to a glass of tea, but he didn't have much to say. Elise started a conversation. "So Carey, what do you think about Arel telling me that he might love me? Could it be true?"

Carey paused and took a sip of tea before he answered. "Arel is great and so are you. You could be great together."

"Yes, but isn't his change of heart sort of sudden? I'm wondering if it has something to do with William's comment. He talked about Arel's delusional spells."

"I'm sure Arel is sincere."

"Yes, I'm sure he is, but Annabel mentioned his moods. Maybe Arel felt magnanimous in the moment and spoke without thinking."

"Elise, please, why don't you think he could love you?"

"Annabel also said something about Arel's need to please. When he was with Claire, he seemed so determined to do what she wanted. It was almost scary."

"He's a good man. Please believe that."

"I do."

Carey sipped his tea. "The thing is that Arel can be a worrier."

"Yes, I'm aware of that."

"Try not to buy into that part of his personality."

"Okay, but what's that got to do with Arel liking me?"

"Arel can get distracted. Please be patient if he starts to brood about something. The best thing you can do is remain very positive."

"Just how much brooding are you talking about?"

"Maybe brooding is the wrong word. He can be very introspective."

"Please, be more specific. At this point I'm beginning to think I fell for someone with both physical and emotional disorders."

Carey leaned in. "Do you think you could still love him in spite of his issues?"

"That's not the point. If Arel does have those kinds of problems, he might not be capable of having a relationship." Elise sat back and sighed. "Poor thing, I wish I knew what to do, but I'm just a writer. I'm not equipped to deal with the problems Arel seems to have."

Carey stood up. "Really, Arel can be quite capable. You need to believe in him."

"I do believe in him, but that isn't enough."

"What do you mean?"

Elise grabbed Carey's empty glass, stood up and walked over to the sink. "I know you have Arel's best in mind. So please, as his friend, get him the professional help he needs."

Carey laughed. "I think you have the wrong idea about Arel."

Elise glanced back. "Do I?"

"You've gone through so many changes since we met. Arel's been going through changes too. I think that both of you are ready to take the next step."

Elise noted the sparkle in Carey's blue eyes. It was enough to make her feel a little better about Arel. "You can be quite the matchmaker for someone so young, Carey."

Carey smiled. "Maybe Michael's wisdom is rubbing off on me."

As soon as Elise thought of Michael, she remembered all the times his quiet presence gave her the courage to trust herself. "He's been Arel's friend for a long time."

"Yes, he has."

"Maybe I should talk to him."

Carey retrieved his phone. "I'll give him a call and ask him to come over."

Elise crossed her arms. "Good. Maybe he can clear up a few things."

* * *

Arel opened his eyes, stretched and was pleased that he felt better. William was right. Dying could be very draining. Thankfully, it didn't take much more than a good nap for him to feel almost normal.

After he dressed, he went upstairs, paused in the foyer and smiled. If he listened attentively, he could hear the sound of Annabel and William talking in their bedroom. He was happy that William had finally come to his senses and knew how lucky he was to have Annabel. The thought was followed by one about Elise. He began to go over his recent encounter with her. As he did, Michael came walking through the foyer. After the tall angel gave Arel a brief greeting, he continued to the door.

"Where are you going?" Arel asked.

Michael smiled. "To Elise's. She wanted to talk to me."

359

"Elise? I was just thinking about how frustrating she is. Why did she have to call you and tell you I was ill? She's always so dramatic."

"She said she was worried about you. Is that a bad thing?"

"I think she overreacts."

"Arel, you told her you might be in love with her. I don't think she expected you to say something like that."

Arel waved to Michael. "Come into the living room. I need to talk to you."

"What is it?" Michael asked.

Arel sat down on the couch. "Look, I surprised myself when I was with Elise. It started when I talked to William. The next thing I know, I was running after Elise."

"Why?"

"I suddenly felt some strange connection to her. I had a flash of insight about some of her caring qualities. Next thing I know, I'm standing there in the park, holding the blasted woman. And for some reason, I told her I loved her."

"Are you saying that you don't love her?"

"Who knows? When I had her in my arms, it felt like I didn't want to let her go. But love? What is love anyway?"

"But what if love was a possibility?"

Arel drummed his fingers on the arm of the sofa. "Her response wasn't encouraging. She essentially told me that I was ranting. And maybe she was right. Every time I'm around her, I'm either feverish or the room's too hot, or I feel very frustrated."

Michael smiled. "I see."

Arel stood up and glared back. "Don't start, Michael."

"What are you talking about?"

"You have an annoying habit of always keeping me in the dark. But that's going to stop here and now. If you know something that I don't, then tell me what you're thinking."

"Arel, it's better if you come to your own conclusions. But if you want something to consider—"

Arel clenched his fists. "Yes, help me out here."

"When you were holding Elise in the park, how did it differ from holding Claire when you were with her in Paris?"

Arel walked over to the window and stared out. As he let his mind relax, he remembered when he was first with Claire. "It's strange, but being in Paris felt dreamy. I'd had so many visions of love and what it was supposed to feel like. Thinking back, it was if Claire was part of that dream. When I held her, it was like I was trying to hold on to those visions."

"And with Elise?"

Arel laughed. "Elise isn't a dream by any stretch. She's the crazy person who locks herself out in the cold while she's wearing those little, short pajamas. She's the woman who wears tight blouses with rosebud buttons." He touched his cheek and stared at Michael. "She's a woman with the power to brand a person with only a kiss."

"Or maybe the person being kissed has the power to understand what that kiss was trying to convey. Maybe that person was frightened by Elise's love."

Arel bristled. "That person couldn't let himself think about Elise! That person was engaged!"

"True, but that person isn't engaged anymore," Michael said as he turned to leave again.

"Michael, where are you going? I thought we were having a conversation."

Michael paused at the front door. "Elise is waiting to talk to me."

"About me?"

"Perhaps."

Arel crossed his arms. "What are you going to say?"

"I'm not sure. What do you want me to say?"

Arel scowled back. "Tell Elise that I'm not sick, and that I am perfectly sound in mind and body. And tell her to stop thinking that I need her help."

Michael opened the door and paused. "Arel, maybe you can tell her yourself. She's coming up the walk."

"Elise?" Arel rushed to the window again. "Oh hell! I don't want to see her!"

Michael hesitated. "Why not?"

Arel's heart began to race. "Michael, maybe you're right. Maybe Elise does frighten me!"

"What do you want me to do?" Michael asked.

"I don't know!" Arel fell back from the window as an attack of panic hit. He staggered over to the sofa as he started feeling a need for all the oxygen he could get. What if he did love Elise? Would the relationship be suffocating? Would he lose his freedom like he had with Claire? Would some other untold dangers be in store for him?

361

Was that virtue called love really a terrible deception that always ended badly? As the questions kept coming, he kept sucking in more air, hoping against hope to somehow save himself.

He heard Elise's voice in the foyer, and Michael telling her something. In the next moment, when he glanced up, Elise was rushing over to him. He was overcome with embarrassment and a feeling of doom.

Elise grabbed his hand. "Arel, what's wrong?"

With his free hand, Arel tried to wave her off. He also tried to stop himself from breathing so fast. His body resisted his efforts and insisted on getting more oxygen. "Fine . . . I'm fine," he gasped between breaths. "I just . . . need some air."

Elise stared back with bright, blue eyes. "I think you're hyperventilating." She glanced up at Michael who'd come over too. "Michael, get a paper bag! And hurry!"

Arel fought for control. "I'm okay!" he panted. "Perfectly fine, just—" His words were cut short by a bout of lightheadedness.

Elise's grip on his hand tightened. "Don't try to talk. If you're having a panic attack, it's important to slow down your breathing."

Arel gasped. "Panic attack?"

Elise smiled reassuringly. "Yes, I've had lots of them. I can teach you how to control them, but for now, just relax a little."

Michael came hurrying over with a brown paper bag and handed it to Elise.

Elise quickly opened it and gave it to Arel. "Breathe into this, and you'll be right as rain before you know it."

Arel heard the kindness in her voice. As he followed her instructions and stared back at her, he also tuned into her heart. It had no intention of harming him. In fact, as he allowed himself a closer peek at the vessel, he was impressed with how much love he saw coming from it.

His own heart responded by slowing down and sending out its own message. Elise could be trusted. The thought helped to soothe his anxiety. His panic began to subside. Within a few minutes, he felt like he could breathe normally. He glanced over at Elise. She was sitting next to him, chatting away about what a quick learner he was. He managed a few words. "Thank you for helping me, Elise."

Elise was relieved. Arel looked himself again. She picked up the paper bag that he'd tossed aside and began to fold it back into its original shape. "You better keep this handy. If you feel any more attacks coming on, use it before the panic escalates. If you want, I'll send you some information that I found on the subject."

"Right." Arel paused and fingered the cushion between them. "By the way, why did you come over? Did you need something?"

Elise sighed. "I wanted to make sure you were okay. Carey told me that you were fine, but I wanted to check anyway. I also wanted to tell you that I got a confirmation call from a rental agency. As you know, I've been looking online at houses in different areas of the country, and I've decided on a place to live." She lowered her gaze. "So you'll have no more annoying visits from me. I'm sure that will be a relief."

Arel reached out for her hand. "It would be fine with me if you changed your mind."

"That's nice, but—"

Arel brought Elise's hand closer and studied it attentively. "Pink nail polish. I bet it matches those fuzzy slippers you like."

Elise laughed and was about to comment when she heard Arel's voice in her head. Its tone was almost demanding.

"Don't go, Elise! We're just starting to know each other!"

Elise immediately let out a little gasp of surprise. Even though she'd had the same experience once before, she wasn't used to someone speaking directly to her mind. "What did you say?"

Arel smiled back absently. "I commented on your nail polish."

"No, that's not what I'm talking about. You spoke to me telepathically, like you did when Freddie was lost."

Arel frowned. "I did?"

"Arel, you just told me not to leave."

Arel's frown deepened, and he looked away.

A moment later, Elise heard his voice in her mind again.

"How do you feel about my wanting you to stay? Is it okay with you?"

Elise didn't know how to respond. She'd never encountered anyone like Arel before. She thought about William's comments. He agreed that Arel could be delusional. William also mentioned something about Arel being difficult and even crazy at times.

Arel laughed knowingly. "Heed what he said. William's right."

Elise sat up straighter. "Oh my goodness, you're reading my thoughts too."

Arel sighed and answered her verbally. "Sorry, I didn't mean to invade your privacy, but it's important that you know more about me. I'm not like other people."

Elise almost got angry. Arel had taken liberties with his gifts. She stopped herself before her emotions took over. Arel wasn't just listening in on her thoughts, he was being very candid about himself. "You could have hidden your abilities from me, but I guess you're trying to be honest."

Arel sat back. "If you do stay, and we do get involved, I want you to know what you're getting yourself into."

Elise stared down and saw that Arel was still holding her hand. His touch was gentle, but surprisingly calming too. Even though he'd just recovered from a panic attack, his person radiated a strength she'd never encountered before. There were two exceptions. Michael exuded the same kind of powerful presence, and young Carey was as steady as they came. Feeling bold, she tried Arel's method of communication by sending out her thoughts on mental air waves.

"I want to stay. I want to find out more about you. And maybe you'll find out more about me."

Arel's face went bright with color. "I'm looking forward to it," he whispered. "But Elise, you have to stop worrying about me."

Elise gave him a sideways glance and smiled. "Sorry, you'll just have to put up with being fussed over. I can't ignore someone I care about."

Arel's golden eyes softened. "Or someone you might love?"

Fifty

PEGGY STOOD AT her kitchen counter. It was Saturday night, and Carol was standing next to her, helping her clear away some dishes. "Thank you for always being such a good friend, Carol."

Carol smiled. "And thank you for inviting us over for another spur of the moment pizza party."

"I love impromptu get-togethers."

"It's nice that Elise and Arel could make it too."

Peggy let out a wistful sigh. "I would have never believed it possible, would you?"

Carol put a dish in the dishwasher. "What are you talking about?"

"Elise and Arel have been together again for two months. And from what I can tell, they're definitely in love."

Carol laughed. "Last fall, when they broke up, we both thought the worst, but I'm happy that things turned out like they did."

Peggy scraped a dish and handed it to Carol. "Yes, after all my misgivings, Elise has become a good friend."

"I think Annabel's visit helped Elise feel like she fits in."

"Elise seemed to enjoy sharing her skills. Annabel went back home knowing how to cook and bake."

Carol closed the dishwasher. "And dance! Annabel said she puts on music and dances around her kitchen while she's making lunch."

"What does William think about that? He and Arel can be pretty stiff at times."

"It seems he gives Annabel some very confused looks, but he's happy that she's enjoying herself." Carol paused. "I think William is a bit like Kevin. Remember when I went through my own changes?"

Peggy shrugged. "Kevin probably doubted his ability to keep up with you."

"Yes, he was all wide-eyed and panicky when I started wearing sexy lingerie to bed. But that changed pretty fast once he got used to the new me."

"My brother can be a bit slow when it comes to something new, but once he adjusts—"

Carol blushed. "Believe me, he's definitely adjusted."

"I'm so relieved that things worked out with you two."

"You're not the only one. You're like a sister, Peggy, a wonderful sister. And I'd never want that to change."

"Isn't it great? Elise is starting to fit into our little family group too. Even the kids seem to love her now."

"My Ariel tries to call her Aunt Elise, but the best he can do is say something like Andy Lee."

"After dinner, little Sara insisted that Elise read to her. It's becoming a regular thing when Elise comes over."

Carol looked at the clock. "Speaking of the kids, I think it's Ariel's bedtime. I better check on him."

"Sara is probably ready too," Peggy said as she followed Carol out of the kitchen. She nearly ran into Carol when Carol stopped abruptly. "What's the matter?"

Carol held up a hand and pointed to the living room. "You need to get a picture of this," she whispered.

Peggy moved to Carol's side and smiled at the scene in the living room. Kevin and Tim were stretched out in chairs. Both were dozing. Freddie the puppy was napping on the sofa where Elise and Arel were sitting next to each other. Elise was cradling Sara in her arms, and Arel was holding Ariel. All four of them had fallen asleep too. Elise and Arel were leaned into one another and looked very comfortable. Peggy crossed her arms and let out a sigh of contentment. "It's the happy ending that Elise always talks about."

"Do you think that happy ending includes a wedding?" Carol asked.

"Of course, it does. Arel just has to pop the question." Peggy nudged Carol. "I'm not supposed to say anything, but Arel told Tim that he was going to propose this weekend."

Carol tried to hold back a mischievous grin. "I know. Kevin told me the same thing."

Fifty-One

WILLIAM SHIFTED HIS phone from one hand to the other. He tried to remind himself that patience was a virtue, but his hold on virtue was long gone. "Please Arel, stop whining!"

Arel's response was immediate. "I'm not whining! I'm trying not to have another panic attack! Elise says—"

"Elise, Elise, Elise! I'm tired of hearing what she says. Just get on with what you want to tell me!"

"Stop shouting! You never used to shout!"

"I never had to talk to you for hours on end!"

"Well, I'm sorry that I'm such a burden, William, but you are going to be my best man. I have to make sure you understand what that means."

"I'll tell you exactly what it means! It means that I'm going to give you a ring that you'll put on Elise's finger. You'll take her for your wife, and you'll be out of my hair for a few weeks!"

"William, am I being too hasty? Will I end up like you?"

"What's that supposed to mean?"

"I know that you said you and Annabel are doing well, but sometimes you still sound a little—"

"A little what?"

"Uncertain. Do you regret getting married?"

"Look, Arel, marriage is a big step, but I'm learning that a partnership can be very nice."

"Nice? I want more than nice if I'm going to commit to Elise."

"Fine, then back out of the relationship."

"But I like being with Elise."

"Liking her isn't enough if you're going to marry the woman."

"Don't call her 'the woman.' Elise is an amazing person. She's sweet and kind and very giving."

"If that's what you're looking for, get yourself a golden retriever. I'm sure it would be sweet and giving too. It'll even bring you the paper if you train it correctly."

Arel heaved out a heavy breath. "Stop being a comedian and listen to me. If anything happened to Elise, I'd be devastated. Do you think that means I'm in love?"

"I know you're in love. The problem is that you're doing what you always do."

"What's that?"

"You have to trust yourself, Arel."

"You of all people know that trust is my weak spot. I've made a lot of bad decisions. What if getting married is the worst decision of all?"

"Then I suppose you'll have to get divorced."

"That's not helping!"

"Look, we've been going round and round this trust issue for years. I've done my best to advise you, and you never listen. So once and for all, you're going to have to figure this out yourself."

Arel let out a groan. "Will?"

"Yes?"

"If you were Elise, would you marry me?"

"If I were Elise, I'd throw myself off a cliff. But from what I can tell, she has a lot more patience than I have."

Arel sighed. "She is very patient. On the other hand, there have been incidents."

"Incidents? What did Elise do?"

"Well, it's probably not important, but—"

"Just spit it out. She's not bossing you around like Claire, is she?"

"No, but when I was trying to get a stain out of her carpet, she insisted on taking over. She said that I was being too rough in my approach. She said I was going to ruin the carpet fibers. Can you imagine that? After all my experience with carpeting, she had the audacity to think she knew better."

William slumped back in his chair. "My goodness, maybe you should have her flogged for that kind of infraction."

"Well, I wouldn't go that far—"

"Arel, I was kidding! Nobody on this earth is perfect, but Elise seems willing to put up with most of your insanity. So stop knit picking and marry her."

"Really?"

"Yes! Now, I have to go. I'm taking Annabel to a pottery exhibition. I'm hoping she'll pick up a few hints on how to sculpt a vase she's making for me."

"Will, don't go!"

"Why, what's wrong now?"

"I can't get any air!" Arel started breathing heavily into the phone. Soon, he was gasping.

William rubbed his forehead, trying to ward off a headache. "Arel, do you have that paper bag that Elise told you to use if you get panicky."

"Yes," Arel gasped.

"Use it!"

* * *

Rolphe sat at his easel, happily working on a new landscape. When Arel told him that he'd had asked Elise to marry him, Rolphe decided to paint something very special as a wedding present. Arel said that Elise loved the splendor of Michael's garden the summer before. That gave Rolphe the idea of painting the most beautiful garden he could imagine.

He was just starting to add more color to some of the flowers when he was startled so badly that he jumped up from his seat. He stared at his unannounced visitor. "Arel, what are you doing here?"

"Sorry if I scared you," Arel apologized.

Rolphe nodded as he calmed himself. Arel was in his astral form, but his energy field felt more diminished than usual. "I just didn't expect to see you here. Is everything alright?"

Arel sighed as he wandered over to some of the canvases that lined the walls of the studio. "William has lost all patience with me. And Michael and Carey think they're helping, but they're angels. So I thought that maybe you could give me some advice."

Rolphe heeded the feeling that he needed to tread carefully. Months before, he'd interacted with Arel when Arel had appeared in his astral form. Their meeting hadn't gone well. Still, he wanted to help if he could. "Arel, I'll do my best."

Arel swiveled and flashed bright, etheric eyes at Rolphe. His gaze was intense and penetrating. When Rolphe felt a chill take hold, he

369

knew that Arel wasn't there for a friendly chat. He stumbled back a few steps in anticipation.

Arel seemed to take the gesture as an invitation to walk over to where Rolphe was standing. "Rolphe, just give me some straight answers, that's all that I ask. Do you understand?"

Rolphe nodded again.

Arel crossed his arms and scowled. "As you know, I've asked Elise to marry me. Was that a mistake?"

"I'm sorry, but I couldn't possibly advise you about such an important matter."

Arel's tone became more demanding. "Why not? You've been married. You said you loved your wife. You're the perfect person to talk to about getting married."

"What about your friends, Kevin and Tim. You told me that they're happy with their situation."

Arel waved his comment off. "They approve of Elise. They think she's very nice. They're biased."

"So what you're saying is that you're having doubts?"

"I don't know. William says I should trust myself, but it's hard when I'm making a lifetime commitment. After Claire—"

"Maybe you're worrying too much," Rolphe suggested.

"But what if it doesn't work out?"

Rolphe could see Arel's anxiety mounting. "When I got married, I hoped it would last forever. I'd found a person to love, and then we had two beautiful children. And I was fortunate to have a number of years living what I considered my dream. When I lost it all, I became bitter, and—"

"That's my point. So many things I've tried have ended badly."

"Arel, you didn't let me finish."

Arel's form flickered a bit too brightly and then steadied again. "Fine, go on."

"After my family was gone, I wasted so much time being angry. Now, I realize how foolish that was."

"You had a terrible loss. Why wouldn't you be devastated?"

"Because my anger and rage led me down the wrong path. Look where I ended up. Like you've often told me, I became a monster."

"What's your point, Rolphe?"

"Maybe if I'd remembered the gift I had and the happiness I experienced, I could have made better choices. I might have married again." Rolphe's chest tightened. "Recently, I had another bout of self-pity and look where it got me. I nearly destroyed my life."

Arel had started to pace, but he stopped and gave Rolphe a quick glance. "For years, I felt guilty about my first relationship. I never allowed myself to think about all the happiness that Justina and I had."

"Never?"

Arel shook his head. "No, I just tried to put it all behind me."

Rolphe stepped forward cautiously. "Then my advice is simple. Don't just make peace with the past, remember the gift that your time with this lady gave you."

"What gift? Justina killed herself!"

"Arel, please, I know many people only remember the pain they experienced in the past, but shouldn't we also be thankful for the happy times we had, the times when our hearts were filled with love?"

"I don't know. How would that change anything?"

"Did you have any problem loving this person, Justina?"

Arel let a weak smile replace his frown. "No, we were both young and innocent. When we met, neither of us held back our feelings. We adored each other."

"And when you let yourself remember those times, how do you feel?"

Arel paused. After a few moments, his gaze softened. "It's almost like I'm young again . . . like I'm in another world where only the joy of love exists."

Rolphe laughed. "That's the miracle that I discovered too."

Arel's eyes widened again. "Miracle?"

"What else would you call it? We never lose the happiness we once felt. It's like a treasure that we've hidden away. But if we give ourselves permission to look for it, it's there. The joy, the happiness is there."

Arel stared back for a long moment, as if he didn't know how to quite understand what Rolphe was saying. Without a word, Arel's astral body disappeared.

Rolphe went back to his easel and sat down. At first he was troubled. Had he given Arel the words of wisdom that the man had come for? He picked up his brush and sighed. It didn't matter. He only knew that what he'd told Arel resonated deep in his own heart.

A person could always find happiness in the past and bring it forward. When he remembered being back with his wife and children, just the thought of enjoying a meal together brought a smile to his face. The memory was enough to get him painting again.

As he dabbed a bit of crimson onto the canvas and allowed his good memories to join his present moment, his smile broadened. Past and present seemed to come together. Everything he'd experienced joined the moment and became a vast palette that he could choose from. He could decide how to create his life, just like he decided what colors to use on his paintings. It was a heady thought that he hoped he could remember. But for the time being, he knew his only job was to enjoy his vision of a glorious garden and bring it to life on his canvas.

* * *

Arel found Rolphe's advice to be so unexpected that he lost his astral connection. In an instant, he returned to his body with a strange excitement rippling through his bones. Rolphe, of all people, had come up with a new and positive approach to the past. It was such a different way of thinking that Arel was slightly dazed by its implications. As his mind began to clear, Michael knocked on his door and looked in.

Arel gave him a welcoming smile. "Good to see you, Michael. I need to bounce some ideas around. And I suspect that what I want to discuss is right up your alley."

"Is this about your recent excursion?" Michael asked as he sat down. "I can always tell when you're doing a bit of traveling."

"After my almost fatal trip to Rolphe's, I'm sure you're wary of my astral journeys."

"Yes, I can be concerned."

"My recent visit was a very positive one if I can believe what Rolphe told me. He has a different way of viewing the past. He advised me to only think about the positive parts. And when I remembered my love for Justina, he was right. Without the guilt, the experience felt beautiful and wondrous again."

Michael laughed. "So why are you frowning?"

"I always thought that the past was there to instruct us, to help us do a better job with the future. I guess that's why I've held on to remorse and my failings. I don't want to repeat my mistakes."

"In my world, there are no mistakes."

372

"How can you say that? What about me creating an alternate world and going to war with the Creator's views? I criticized the Divine plan. Surely that was a mistake."

"Or was it a way for you to learn more about how you defined the idea of good and evil? Remember what you learned?"

Arel let out a wistful sigh. "I realized that I was holding on to my father's hatred and letting it govern how I saw life."

"And?"

Arel sat up more attentively. "When I let go of the hatred and asked for your help, everything shifted and the battle was over."

"Maybe viewing the past and looking for the good parts is another way of doing the same thing. But if you keep holding on to your mistakes, it's like holding on to your father's anger. Life becomes a dark place."

Arel paused and stared back at his angelic mentor. Michael's bright, serene gaze was a place of calm and certainty. "When I've been in those dark places, you've been the light, Michael. Your presence has been so steady, like a beacon in every storm I've been through. So why do I ever forget to heed your wisdom?"

"It takes time to know yourself, my friend. After receiving my blood, so much discord and pain came to the surface. You had to face so much that you'd denied. And the events that followed came so quickly that you were overwhelmed. But you've done a remarkable job staying the course. I know you've almost given up a number of times, but in the end, you found the courage to keep going. If you can focus on that one fact alone, it will help you to see the light in yourself."

Fifty-Two

ELISE LOOKED AT Arel and smiled. He sat next to her physically, and yet he was so far away. She didn't mind. The man she was going to marry was often absorbed in some inner musings. It wasn't a fault. It was part of his nature. She leaned over and kissed his cheek. "What are you thinking about?" she asked.

Arel jerked a little and smiled back. "What did you say?"

Elise sighed. "I think I've fallen in love with a philosopher."

"Me, a philosopher? I don't think so."

"But you do spend a lot of time trying to understand life, don't you?"

Arel was holding Freddie, and he began to run his hand over the sleeping puppy's soft fur. "I was thinking about something that Rolphe told me today."

"He's your friend in Paris, right?"

Arel hesitated. "Yes, I suppose he is a friend. Anyway, he said that people need to remember the good parts of life, not the bad ones."

"That makes sense. When I held on to memories that fed my bitterness, I wasn't happy with myself or anyone else."

"And now?"

Elise giggled. "Look at me. I'm in love with the most gorgeous guy in the world."

Arel's golden eyes became animated, and he sat up a little straighter. "You really feel that way about me even though—"

"Even though you're always trying to make the world a perfect place?"

Arel hesitated. "I never thought of myself in that way. I thought I was merely obsessive."

"There might be some of that too, but I love that you care about everything. It's what makes you gorgeous inside too."

"It's strange that you'd say that. Claire claimed to be the one who cared about everything."

"Oh please, I associate caring with kindness and a good heart."

374

"In Claire's eyes, I was totally deficient in any quality that made me worthwhile."

"I don't want to hear any more about Claire's overbearing opinions."

Arel laughed. "But you should be happy that I was with her."

Elise crossed her arms. The idea of Arel and Claire together brought on a sudden bout of annoyance. "And why would I want to think of you with a beautiful woman like Claire."

Arel carefully shifted Freddie's dozing body to the cushion next to him, turned to Elise and put his arm around her shoulders. "My dearest Elise, after being with Claire, I recognize what true beauty is. And you're the perfect example of that quality. The longer we're together, the more I realize how fortunate I am."

Elise gave him a sideways glance. Then she began to finger the engagement ring on her finger. "Really? You've been very quiet ever since you asked me to marry you."

Arel pulled her closer. "Please try not to read too much into my 'insanity' as William calls it."

Elise put her head on his shoulder. "You can be as insane as you want as long as you truly love me. But sometimes, I wonder if—"

"Elise, sometimes I don't have a clue about what love is. I think I've shut it out of my life for so long I don't know how I'm supposed to feel, especially after Claire."

"I understand that. Why do you think I fought the idea of loving you? I was afraid of getting hurt again."

Arel stiffened. "Have I hurt you? If I have, I'm sorry."

"I'd accept your apology, but I'm not someone's victim anymore. And that feels very good, so does being in love with you. It's like I can see beneath the 'insanity' that you mentioned. In fact, we've all been slightly insane if you ask me."

"And what do you see beneath my insanity?"

Elise kissed his cheek again. "You're going to think this strange, but sometimes I see you as a little boy. Your hair is black and curly, and you have these big, amazing golden eyes. The vision is so clear that I feel like I'm a little girl who's sitting next to you. When we look at each other, you're like a friend that I've known forever."

Arel glanced at her and smiled. "I can see you clearly, too. What an adorable child you were."

"Are you reading my mind?"

"Maybe or perhaps I'm tapping into my own vision."

"Wouldn't that be interesting if we could both see the same thing?"

Arel's smile broadened into a grin. "I have a better idea. Let's forget about childhood. I'd like to appreciate who we are now."

Elise shrugged contentedly. "I agree. I'm happier than I've ever been before."

Arel remained very still. Only his eyes strayed and targeted Elise with a glowing intensity. After a brief pause, he stood up and reached out for her hand. "Elise, why stop at happiness?"

Elise took Arel's hand and let him pull her to her feet. "I don't understand."

"Really? I'm surprised."

"What are you getting at?"

Arel tightened his grip just a little before he spoke. "Elise, you're a romance writer. You should know all about that subject and what it leads to?"

"Romance?" Elise returned a look of confusion, but as she studied the way Arel was looking at her, everything became very clear. She felt a flush of excitement warm her cheeks. "I was beginning to think you didn't want me in that way."

Arel put his arms around her and pulled her close. "And I wanted to make sure you knew what you'd be getting into."

Elise blinked back and noticed how bright Arel's eyes had become. Supposedly, they were windows to a person's soul, and Arel's glowing windows seemed to be inviting her to explore their depths. She hesitated. What if she saw something she didn't want to see?

Arel pushed a strand of her hair back and smiled. "It's okay, I won't bite, I promise."

Arel's comment made her laugh. It also broke her spell of uncertainty. She immediately lifted her eyes to look into his. She didn't know what she'd see, but her immediate reaction was voiced in a hushed tone. "Oh, how amazing!"

Nothing had prepared Elise for the portals to Arel's soul. Their golden brilliance was dazzling. Like small twin stars, they filled her with a wonderful sense of well-being and joy. Staring back, she was mesmerized and almost lost herself in their boundless expanse. "Oh my, Arel, I don't think you have to worry about the definition of love. From what I'm seeing, it can't be defined."

She heard his laughter in her mind and drew back enough to examine his face. Even if his inner light was other-worldly, his mischievous grin was definitely earth bound.

Arel's telepathic voice drifted across her thoughts.

"You're lovely, Elise! And I've wanted you for so long."

His words were fluid and capable of going beyond the limits of her mind. Each syllable was like a small flame that coursed through every part of her. She felt a burning blush of desire take hold that matched his. "You said something about going beyond my idea of happiness. Just what do you have in mind?"

Arel's lips brushed her ear. "Let's just say I've heard about unknown places where ecstasy resides. But not everyone is ready for those places."

His warm breath, so close, made her throw her hands around his neck without further hesitation. "I'm ready!"

Arel stared down at her for a long moment as if he was still evaluating her sincerity. "Are you really sure that this is what you want, Elise? Because if it isn't—"

She pressed herself against him and sighed. "Arel, no matter how you see yourself or how you think about the idea of love, I know what I want."

"I see," Arel said as he nibbled her ear.

Elise pulled away enough to run a finger over his lips. "Good! Then I take it that we agree."

"Oh yes, we certainly do!"

Arel's adamant statement was followed by his laughter. It was expressed openly this time, and it filled the room. Without any sign of effort, he swept Elise up in his arms. At first, he kissed her softly, then with more passion.

As he swung her around in joyful abandon, Elise knew that they both burned with an inner fire. But it wasn't a fire that consumed the other. Instead, this fire wanted to find a common place to burn freely. Elise gave herself to the feeling. She wanted to go beyond her dreams, to that place that Arel spoke about, to that place of ecstasy.

Fifty-Three

WILLIAM FOLLOWED ANNABEL into their London foyer. After he brought in their luggage, he shut the door behind him. "I can't believe it. It's over."

Annabel hung up her coat and gave him a puzzled look. "What's over?"

"Arel's solitary trek through life. I didn't think he would ever find someone. When he put that ring on Elise's finger and said, 'I do' to her, I nearly collapsed with relief."

"It was nice that they waited until spring when they could have the wedding in Arel's back yard. The garden was so gorgeous, thanks to Michael."

"Are you kidding? Those months of waiting for them to tie the knot were the worst."

"I thought that once Arel made up his mind, he stopped complaining."

"That's true, but you know how unpredictable Arel can be. Every time I heard his ring tone, my heart sped up. I was sure he'd found some reason to back out."

Annabel took his hand and smiled. "You have been rather tense at times, but luckily we also managed to enjoy each other."

William pulled her close. "On the plane, all I could think about was coming home, forgetting everything and being with you."

"Really?"

"I think I'm finally getting into the idea that a normal life could have some wonderful advantages."

"I'm so glad that you've made peace with those inner demons that plagued you a few months ago."

"Yes, I feel like I'm able to appreciate more about myself and my life with you."

Annabel stared back with hopeful eyes. "And maybe you'll also have room for someone else."

"What do you mean? Does someone want to visit us?"

"Maybe."

"Who?"

"A very tiny someone."

William felt his legs go weak. He had to grab for the wall to steady himself. "Are you saying—"

Annabel's smile broadened. "I'm not sure, my dearest William, but it's a definite possibility that you're going to be a father."

To be continued in Book Six!

FORGOTTEN BLOOD

Note From The Author

Thank you for reading the fifth book, *Tainted Blood*, in THE VAMPIRE RECLAMATION PROJECT series. If you enjoyed it, please consider telling your friends or posting a short review. Word of mouth is an author's best friend and much appreciated.

For more information and the latest news about my books, please go to my website, SSBazinet.com. — S. S. Bazinet

Other Books by S. S. Bazinet

THE VAMPIRE RECLAMATION PROJECT
Book One: Michael's Blood
Book Two: Arel's Blood
Book Three: William's Blood
Book Four: Brother's Blood
Book Five: Tainted Blood

IN THE CARE OF WOLVES SERIES
Book One: My Brother's Keeper

THE MADONNA DIARIES
Dying Takes It Out Of You

SENTENCED TO HEAVEN
An Inmate's Tale from the Other Side
Book Two: A Vampire In Heaven

OPEN WIDE MY HEART
Book One: Traces Of Home

www.ingramcontent.com/pod-product-compliance
Lightning Source LLC
Chambersburg PA
CBHW031422240626
47154CB00001B/158